TOWN AT THE EDGE OF DARKNESS

THE EXCOMS THRILLERS NO. 2

THE ALEXANDRA POE THRILLERS
(with Robert Gregory Browne)
POE
TAKEDOWN

STANDALONES
THE PULL OF GRAVITY
NO RETURN
MINE

For Younger Readers

THE TROUBLE FAMILY CHRONICLES
HERE COMES MR. TROUBLE

TOWN AT THE EDGE OF DARKNESS

OF DARKNESS

THE EXCOMS THRILLERS NO. 2

BRETT BATTLES

ONE

June 2014

"HANG BACK, HANG back," Dalton Slater said.

Two of the young men who worked for him stepped in front of the trial participants to make sure the hunters held their ground while their boss checked the prey.

A head shot, just below the cheek. That didn't always guarantee a kill, but in this case, the bullet had done more than enough damage on the way out to seal the deal. A second shot had caught the prey in the chest, a little high to hit the heart, but the clients wouldn't know that.

Slater turned back to the others and smiled. "Great job, gentlemen. Two kill shots."

"Which of us was first?" asked one of the participants. He had been designated Mr. Grant for the weekend.

Slater shrugged. "You shot pretty much at the same time. So you were both first."

"Mine was the head shot," Mr. Van Buren said. Slater and the other organizers had gone for a president's theme on this, the inaugural gathering of the trials.

"Hold on," Mr. Grant said. "I'm pretty sure the head shot was mine."

They were both wrong, but instead of saying anything, Slater caught the eye of his daughter, Monica—using the name Miss Roosevelt this weekend—and gave her a subtle nod. She said, "Gentleman, the observer has declared a shared kill. The trials are over. It's time to join the other participants and celebrate the conclusion."

As had been the case since the start of the festivities three days before, Monica had them eating out of her hand. With the appropriate amount of grumbling, they nodded their assent and followed her back to the lodge.

As soon as they were out of earshot, Slater nodded at the prey and said to his boys, "Get it out of here and make sure everything is nice and pretty."

"Yes, sir."

SLATER RODE HIS ATV back to the lodge and entered the large kitchen. A few of the others he'd recruited into the organization—a trio of teen boys and two men in their twenties—were putting the finishing touches on the closing banquet.

Each took time to acknowledge Slater with a *hello, sir* or a *good afternoon, sir*.

"Afternoon, gentlemen," he replied as he crossed the room. In the back hallway, he stopped at the basement entrance, punched in the code, and opened the door.

His brother and their cousin were waiting for Slater in the central room below.

"They finally got the son of a bitch, huh?" his brother said. "Took 'em long enough."

"They didn't get him," Slater smirked. "Jerry did."

"What?" his cousin said.

"Did you want them to keep going all night? Because that's what would have happened. Those two idiots couldn't hit a tree if they were standing in the middle of the woods. Finally had Jerry hide out of sight and put the prey down with a double tap, head and chest."

"Damn, Dalton!" the cousin said. "What if they'd have figured it out? They could've demanded their money back. Think what would have happened if they spread *that* around? We'd be ruined just as we're starting!"

"We talked about this, remember?" Slater's brother said. "Dalt was just following procedure."

"Procedure you two came up with. I had no part of that, as I recall."

"Because you were too busy to meet with us, as *I* recall.

And a decision had to be made."

Slater said, "Relax. No reason for anyone to get worked up. It worked, okay? They're happy. They'll tell their friends about this, and pretty soon we're going to be turning people away."

"We'd better be," his cousin said.

"We will. I guarantee it."

NOT ONLY WAS Slater proven right, but business picked up so much that instead of quarterly events, they started holding the trials every other month, and then, in 2017, every month.

TWO

TASHA PATTERSON MOUTHED a silent *thank God* as the portal to the company's cloud storage servers appeared on the screen.

She was using the computer in the mobile office at the Scolareon solar farm construction site, north of Bradbury, at night when no one else would be around. Until that very moment, she'd been unsure if this particular machine was authorized to connect to that part of the system. If it hadn't been, she would have been forced to attempt the riskier route of using a computer at company headquarters back in Bradbury.

Getting into the cloud was only step one, however. She still needed to locate and access the hidden files. She glanced at the paper she'd set next to the keyboard, on which she'd written a list of drive locations she thought would be the most logical places to find the files.

They had to be there somewhere. The one she'd stumbled upon couldn't be the only document. Its discovery had prompted this insane mission to investigate further. The file was a simple transportation log and had looked innocent enough at first. But on closer examination, it matched none of the company's records.

Whoever controlled the document had apparently discovered their mistake, because when she tried to pull it up again the next day, it had disappeared. Thankfully she'd made a copy. She *always* made a copy.

Still unsure of what she'd found, she'd asked one of her

employees to look into the discrepancies. Two days later, before he reported back, she received his emailed resignation. An opportunity had come up with a company in Shanghai, he'd written, and he'd had to leave right away.

She tried contacting him but he never returned her call. She would have called the company he went to work for but he hadn't named it.

Though he had talked about wanting to work abroad someday, Tasha felt sure he would have told her first, in person. Over the next couple of days, her thoughts transitioned from confusion to wondering if his inquiries on her behalf had been met with a get-out-of-town-now ultimatum.

Maybe she was reading too many thriller novels.

Whatever the case, his abrupt departure made her reluctant to bring anyone else into her private investigation. The most she allowed herself were a few cryptic emails to her mentor and former employer Scott Davos in California. Until she had concrete evidence, she was keeping the bulk of her suspicions to herself.

She logged into the cloud, using the still active username and password of her China relocated ex-employee, and brought up the directory. She had whittled down her list to four possible areas where the files could be hidden. Back at her office, she hadn't dared probe any of the areas. Now she dove in, searching for anything that shouldn't be there. The first two areas proved to be dead ends, and she couldn't help thinking the files had been removed.

Or you've been wrong all this time, her subconscious suggested. *And you've been seeing shadows where there were none.*

God, she hoped that was true. She would love nothing more than to prove her suspicions were completely groundless, and that someone on the inside wasn't trying to skim product from the company.

As she accessed the third area, however, she came up against a firewall that shouldn't have been there.

One of Davos's many imprints on Tasha's life was the importance of "understanding everything," as in all parts of the businesses she worked for. Because of her adherence to this philosophy, she'd been continually promoted until—with the recommendation and blessing of Davos—she landed her current CFO position at Scolareon, Inc., in Bradbury, Washington. So, even though her area of expertise was finance, she had studied information technology on the job and knew as much about IT as many of those who worked in the field.

She searched the firewall for a weakness, and when she found one, slipped through the gap utilizing a trick she'd learned from a Davos coder. On the screen was a log of hundreds of files that should have been there. She opened a spreadsheet document, and immediately recognized strings of characters almost identical to the ones she'd written in her notebook at home. It contained information she'd scrounged up over the last few weeks that she thought might be connected.

Somewhere within this set of files must be the proof she'd been looking for. She would figure out who was involved and the monetary damage they'd done to Scolareon, and then present everything to the CEO and president, Kyle Scudder.

She scrolled through the list and was surprised to find a group of photographs. Could the embezzlers have possibly been stupid enough to take pictures of themselves? It would definitely be a nice shortcut.

She opened the first four images.

Her elation about possibly uncovering proof of her suspicions turned instantly to revulsion. Criminal activity *had* been going on, but it wasn't being committed by rogue employees stealing solar panels. What the pictures showed was so much worse and more repugnant than her imagination could have dreamt up.

For a horrified moment, she could do nothing but stare at the monitor. When she finally closed the files, she glanced over her shoulder, half expecting to find someone holding a gun to her head. But the trailer was still empty.

She plugged one of her jump drives into the computer and began copying everything onto it. There were a lot of files, but the trailer office had a decent satellite connection, and in a little over seven minutes, the task was completed. She inserted a second jump drive into another slot and started duplicating everything from the first drive onto it. With two sets of documents, she could keep one and send the other to Davos in case something happened to her or her drive.

The display said it would take four minutes.

She paced the trailer, glancing nervously out each window she passed. The moonless night offered little for her to see beyond the outline of the forest around the edge of the clearing. Each time she passed the computer, she checked the copy status bar.

Three minutes.

Two.

On—

A light on the desk phone blinked—no ring, just the glow for line one.

She took a few deep breaths to try to calm herself. It didn't work. The call could have been nothing more than someone wanting to leave a message, but she couldn't help thinking IT had registered the computer's activity.

"It's okay," she whispered. The construction site was nearly thirty minutes north of Bradbury. If the company sent someone to check, she'd be long gone by then.

The final seconds of the file-copy countdown seemed to last forever. When the status bar hit zero, a voice in her head screamed at her to get out of there, but she needed to do one last thing.

With shaking hands, she opened the browser in incognito mode, brought up Gmail, and created an email account. In another window, she found the contact information for Darren Gaines, the US attorney in charge of this part of the state, and copied his address onto the message. Sending him everything would take way too long, so she attached the first document she'd found and two of the jpegs, wrote THIS IS JUST A START as the subject title, and hit SEND.

She snatched the two thumb drives, stuffed them in her pocket, closed the browser, and put the computer back to sleep. After scanning the desk to make sure everything looked as it had when she arrived, she headed for the door.

The construction site was half a mile from the main dirt road, which was at least a mile from the highway. When she stepped outside, she expected to hear only a gentle wind blowing through the trees, maybe an owl at most. What she didn't expect was the drone of a car's engine. The vehicle wasn't close, but it did sound as if it was coming from the construction site access road.

It can't be someone from the company already, can it? How could they have gotten here so fast?

She had to get out of there. The problem was that the access road was the only way in and out, so if the other vehicle was on it, she was already as good as discovered.

Wait. When she'd taken the management tour of the site, she had noted a few old, overgrown roads leading into the woods from the access road. If she could find one of them before the incoming car saw her, she could hide and while it went on to the trailer, she could escape.

She jumped into her Prius and took off for the gate, leaving her lights off. She'd left the gate open when she arrived, so she raced through and onto the road. She figured the others, if they were indeed coming for her, already knew someone was out here. If they found an open gate, they might approach with caution, slowing and giving her even more time to get away.

Eyes glued to the road, she drove as fast as she dared through the darkness.

The flash of headlights ahead caused her gaze to jerk up. It had shone through a momentary perfect alignment of gaps between trees, confirming the other car was heading her way.

"Come on, come on, come on," she said, willing her escape route to show itself.

Despite her vigilance, the old road was so overgrown, she almost missed it. When she realized it was there, she whipped the wheel to the right and pressed the accelerator enough to help the vehicle up a small incline.

Just a bit farther, she thought. *Another thirty—*

The car lurched to the left.

Out of instinct, her foot shoved the brake pedal, bathing the trees behind her in red light. She yanked her foot away, returning the vehicle to darkness. Whatever had pulled the Prius to the side had also stopped it.

Breathing deeply, she killed the engine, and after making sure the dome light was off, opened the door and listened.

She could hear the other vehicle loud and clear now. Leaning outside, she looked back the way she'd come. Headlights, not a quick burst like before but a series of blinks between trees, were no more than fifty feet from the end of the old road.

Had the driver seen her brake lights?

Subconsciously, her hand slipped into her pocket and caressed the drives as if they were talismans that would turn her and her car invisible.

The lights moved closer and closer.

Tasha eased one foot out the door, ready to run if the other car turned toward her.

Another blink, and then the car drove past the old road without stopping or turning.

She let out her breath and listened to the engine move farther and farther away. When it became a distant rumble, she climbed out to search ahead for a place to turn around without having to reverse. She quickly discovered that wasn't an option.

The front left wheel had fallen into a channel that grew deeper and wider the farther ahead it went. If she were to continue in that direction, she'd become permanently stuck within a few feet.

Reversing was her only choice.

She knew it was possible to remove the bulbs in the reverse light, but figuring it out would take time she didn't have. Instead, she draped a blanket from her cargo area over the back of the car, tucking the top and sides in around the hatch before she closed it. The extra bulk made it hard for the lock to catch, but after a few tries she got the hatch closed.

Back behind the wheel, she muttered a prayer as she shifted into reverse, using her side mirror to back down the road because the blanket prevented her from seeing through the rear window. Much to her surprise, she made it unscathed and, by the looks of things, undetected.

As fast as she could safely go, she headed for the dirt road that would take her back to the highway. Her tuck job at the back hadn't been as perfect as she'd hoped, and the blanket flapped. But the glimpses of the road in her rearview mirror showed no lights heading her way.

When she felt there were enough trees between her and the construction site, she flipped on her headlights and pushed the pedal to the floor.

She was going to make it. She was going to get out of this. *With* the proof.

Those bastards, whoever they were, would go down. Hard.

As she came out of the final bend, she slammed on her brakes.

A sedan sat diagonally across the end of the access road. And not just any sedan—a Scolareon security vehicle, with two men in front.

There was a moment when neither Tasha nor the men did anything. She had no idea what they were thinking but knew she had a choice. It was possible security knew nothing about the crimes she'd uncovered, meaning they would help her. But what if they were well aware of the issue, or even involved? For now, she knew trusting anyone who worked for Scolareon would be a mistake.

Putting the Prius in reverse, she looked back.

"Dammit."

She'd forgotten about the blanket. She switched her gaze to the side mirror and raced backward as best she could. For the first fifty feet she did fine, but she made the mistake of glancing forward to check on the security car. When she returned her eyes to the mirror, she misjudged her position and swerved the car back toward the center of the road. But she overcorrected, and the car rocked as the passenger side drifted off the shoulder and swiped a tree.

She jerked the wheel, angling the Prius's back end toward the center of the road, but before she could straighten again, the front passenger fender smashed into the same trunk, stopping her.

Ahead, the security sedan was driving toward her.

Tasha didn't waste any time trying to see if she could get the car back on the road. She gunned it forward toward a wide spot between the trees, hoping there would be enough room to weave her way through.

Of course there wasn't, and the natural trail lasted no more than forty yards before a tree seemed to jump in front of her.

She slammed on the brakes, but the tree was too close and the Prius smashed into the trunk. The airbag ejected from the steering wheel, knocking her back against her seat, stunning her.

Get out!

Her hand pawed at the door, taking what seemed like forever to find the handle. When it did, she yanked the lever back and shoved the door open.

Her car's headlights were still on, bouncing off the trees. The pine she struck tilted away from her at an angle, not enough to fall but it wouldn't take much for it to do so.

Go! Go!

She stumbled out of the cab.

"Hey! Hey, you! Stay right there!"

The security car was parked at the spot where she'd left the road, and the officers who'd been in it were now outside, one standing near the front end pointing at her, the other already running in her direction.

She shot into the woods, having no destination in mind except anywhere but where she was. The guard shouted again but she didn't even try to understand him.

The highway, she thought. If she could get there, she could flag down another driver. Though it was at least a mile away, getting there was the only chance she had of evading capture.

She turned what she hoped was westward, and ran like she hadn't run since high school, leaping over bushes she saw and smashing through those she didn't. She hoped her course correction would throw off the guards, but when she glanced back, she spotted flashlight beams bobbing among the trees, heading her way.

The forest seemed to go on forever, and soon she lost all sense of how long she had been running. Ten minutes? Fifteen? However long, the highway had to be coming up soon.

After she cut through a slot between two trees, and raced down and up a narrow ravine, she heard something that nearly stopped her in her tracks. A rumble that sounded like an engine.

She raced toward the noise, and within a few seconds caught a glimpse of headlights ahead to the right.

Her moment of joy was tempered, however, by the cracking of a branch somewhere behind her, and the sound of running steps, closer than before. The Scolareon security guards must have heard the engine, too, and knew they would lose her if she reached the highway.

As the headlights sped past, a second set appeared. Judging by its speed, the car would also be gone before she reached the highway. She scanned left and right, hoping to spot other cars, but either the trees were blocking them or there were no others at the moment.

Her panic increased. If she reached the highway but found no vehicles to flag down, the men chasing her would still nab her.

Rig the game in your favor, Davos had preached over and over. *If you control the options, you control the ultimate outcome.*

But how could she control this outcome? She couldn't keep running all the way back to Bradbury.

Her hand brushed against her pants—catching on the jump drives in her pocket.

Not this outcome. The *ultimate* outcome.

Maybe she couldn't get away right now, but she could give herself a fighting chance later.

She looked around for a landmark she could remember, and after several seconds spotted a dead tree leaning at an angle against two live ones.

Near the highway. West of the access road. Leaning dead tree.

She could remember that. She repeated the location a few more times to commit it to memory as she pulled out one of the drives and angled toward the three trees. When she was positive she was out of sight of her pursuers, she paused just long enough to stuff the jump drive into a split in the wood, and then resumed running.

She saw another distant set of headlights, and knew this time she would reach the road in time. The only question was whether the car would arrive before the guards did. She channeled her remaining energy into an all-out sprint.

Almost there. Almost there. Almost—

Twenty feet shy of the forest's edge, hands latched onto her shoulders and pulled her back. Her feet flew out from under her and she fell, landing first on her hip and then flopping onto her back, her head bouncing off the ground like a basketball.

She lay on a bed of needles, dazed and gasping for air. Gray hovered at the edges of her vision, threatening to drag her into unconsciousness.

A foot jabbed her in the ribs. "Nice try, bitch."

Her brow creased as she tried to focus. The fuzzy form of a man looked down at her. Another couple of blinks and she could make out his face and security uniform. She didn't recognize him, but that didn't mean anything. She could have passed him a million times at the office and never really seen him.

He seemed to be talking into his hand, but her brain couldn't untangle what he was saying.

Another voice, this one altered, like coming out of a TV, and then the guard again. "Roger."

Was that his name? Or the name of the man he was talking to?

She tried to sit up, but the man shoved her back down.

"Better if you stay right there, Miss Patterson."

She closed her eyes, the fog in her head clearing at a glacial rate. She was aware enough, however, to realize he'd recognized her.

When she opened her eyes again, the guard who'd tackled her had become two men. She blinked, thinking one would vanish, and then realized the second man was not a clone of the first. This man she knew. Leonard Yates, Scolareon's head of security.

He knelt beside her, looking disappointed. "Well, well, Ms. Patterson. You are a long way from the office."

She pressed her lips together.

"Yeah, I wouldn't say anything, either." He grinned. "You're a tricky one, you know that? Coming all the way out here to get onto the network. That was…unexpected. You don't mind if I pat you down, do you?"

She kept her expression as blank as she could manage. But it was no easy task. Though he hadn't said it directly, he'd implied he knew why she was out here, which meant he was one of them.

"No objection?" he said. "Good."

He removed her shoes and pulled out the soles. He then moved his hands up her pant legs to her hips, tapping his palms over her pockets. All very professional, with no hint of inappropriate intentions. He moved on to her shoulders, the sleeves of her light jacket, and the jacket's pockets. That's where he paused.

"What do we have here?" He reached inside and pulled out the jump drive. "Oh, Ms. Patterson. I gotta tell you, this does not look good. If this has on it what I think it does, you're in some pretty deep shit."

Like she didn't know that already.

Get this over with and take me wherever you're going to take me, asshole. She knew they couldn't keep her locked up forever. When she was free again, she would return here and retrieve the backup drive.

She would have the last laugh.

Near the highway. West of the access road. Leaning dead tree.

She would not let herself forget.

"What were you planning on doing with this?" he said, holding the stick in front of her face.

Near the highway. West of the access road. Leaning dead tree.

"Give it to that lawyer you sent the email to?"

She halted halfway through her mantra, her eyes

widening. He *was* one of them.

Yates chuckled. "You didn't think we'd actually let your message get through, did you? No, I'm afraid Mr. Gaines will *not* be hearing from you."

It doesn't matter. When I get the backup drive, none of this will matter. Near the highway. West of the access road. Leaning dead tree.

Yates stood up and twirled the jump drive in his hand. "In fact, no one will be hearing from you ever again."

Near the highway. West of the access—

His boot slammed into her head.

"WATCH HER. I'LL get the car," Yates said. "If she comes to, give her another kick."

Yates hiked over to the dirt road. It would get him back to the access road and their patrol car a lot faster than tramping through the woods. Before he emerged from the trees, he pulled out his phone and called his brother.

"So?"

"It's done," Yates said. "We got her."

"So it was Patterson."

"Yep. And get this, she had a portable drive on her."

A pause. "Do you know what's on it?"

"Not yet. But I think we both can guess."

"And her condition?"

"Nothing a few aspirin and a Band-Aid or two wouldn't take care of. We'll get things cleaned up here. As soon as I get back to the office, I'll check the drive then destroy it."

"You're sure she hasn't tried to contact anyone other than that lawyer?"

"I'm sure." That was not completely true. Yates was sure she hadn't used Scolareon's network to contact anyone, but she could have used other means. Still, if she had, why did she come out here on her own? "I was thinking you might be able to use her for the upcoming session. She put up a hell of an effort trying to get away from us."

"Is that so? Not a bad idea. Have your boys bring her to the barn and I'll meet them there."

"Will do."

Yates hung up and dialed his office.

"Scolareon Security, how can I help you?"

"It's Yates. Put me through to Jennings."

"Yes, sir. One moment."

Jennings picked up a few seconds later. "Hey, boss. Any luck?"

"It was Patterson, all right. We got her."

"Great!"

"I'm going to have Murphy and Howell take her to the barn, so they won't be back on rotation for at least ninety minutes."

"I'll adjust coverage."

"Good. One other thing. Starting tomorrow morning, I want two people on duty at the solar farm at all times. Set up one of the temp gates on the access road and have one guy stationed there, and put the other inside the fence."

"On it."

THREE

Two Weeks Later

AS WAS HIS habit, the Administrator took a moment to check his notes and straighten his tie prior to activating the video call with his employer.

The wall in front of him was filled with monitors, each presenting a silent feed from different news outlets around the world. When he tapped ENTER on his keyboard, the center monitor switched from a visual of a news desk in Tokyo to a blue screen. Out of the speakers, the soft *dong* of the ringing line sounded twice, before the blue screen cut to a live image of committee member Monday.

"Good afternoon, sir," the Administrator said.

"Good afternoon." Monday looked at his watch. "You have ten minutes."

"Yes, sir."

The committee consisted of extremely wealthy individuals from around the world. There were supposed to be seven members, but they were down to five due to the unexpected murder of one member and the ouster of another for breaking committee rules.

Other than their wealth, the members shared one other quality. At some point in their lives, all had experienced devastating pain caused by the death or deaths of loved ones whose lives could have been saved if someone had had the guts to intervene. This idea of intervention was the reason the committee existed, its purpose. Their sole focus was to identify dire situations that could be made right if someone stepped in, and then do just that. The members themselves didn't perform the actual "saving," of course. They were the deciders of the missions, the funders, the judges of those who needed to be judged.

For the missions, the Administrator—who served as the committee's chief operations officer—had recently assembled a strike team. It was a mix of highly skilled agents from the worlds of espionage and personal security. They had completed one mission so far, admirably. The problem weighing on the Administrator's mind was that only one member of the team had committed to continue working with the committee, and that was due to the member's unique circumstances. If the man had not agreed to stay on, he would have been returned to prison. The others, who had no such stick hanging over them, had yet to decide.

The Administrator wanted to change that, hence the call to Monday, who, unbeknownst to his colleagues on the committee, was the founder and driving force behind their work.

"I would like your permission to hold a meeting this evening," the Administrator said.

"The purpose?"

"A new mission."

"Davos?"

"Yes, sir."

"So you *did* find something."

"It's more what we didn't find."

Scott Davos, a billionaire entrepreneur, was a friend of Monday's, and would have been a perfect candidate to fill one of the committee's openings if not for the fact he was missing that crucial personal-loss requirement. While he remained unaware of the committee, he did know Monday could discreetly look into sensitive matters in a way Davos lacked.

"And what didn't you find?" Monday asked.

"The woman, sir. Like Mr. Davos mentioned, there are emails and texts sent not only to Davos, but some of the woman's family and friends that attempted to make everything seem okay. What we have not found, though, is any physical evidence of her being where 'she' says she is. We have expanded the scope to places she might logically have gone, with still no luck."

"It could be she just wanted some time off the grid."

"A few days perhaps," the Administrator admitted. "But two weeks for someone in her position? Not very likely."

"What's your proposal?"

"I would like the committee to vote on activating the team."

"It's only been a few days since they finished the Nevada incident. Should we be rushing them back into action so soon?"

"They're professionals. This is what they do." Though that was true, the Administrator's real motivation was born out of concern that the more time between the first and second missions, the more likely the team members would decide to never take his calls again. The busier he kept them now, the better chance he had at convincing them to sign on permanently.

"The committee will wonder why this mission instead of the Lambert matter," Monday said.

The Lambert matter was supposed to be the next job on their list.

"Yes, sir. I will be happy to inform everyone that the Lambert case is no longer an issue."

This solicited a rare look of surprise from Monday. "Explain."

"I have it on good authority that early tomorrow morning, federal agents will arrive simultaneously at the Lambert ranch and at their distribution centers in Fairbanks and Anchorage with search and arrest warrants."

"And how did the feds get involved?"

"I really can't say, sir. What I do know is that their intervention comes at a fortuitous time, and that they are likely to take the Lamberts unaware. The terror and reprisals experienced by those who have run afoul of the family should cease immediately."

Federal involvement had, of course, been the Administrator's doing. The two men both knew it. Though looping in the government was not something they wanted to make a habit of, it had cleared the way for the Davos job to come front and center.

"Lucky us, I guess," Monday said. He leaned forward. "Send out the invitation, and make preparations to send the team in."

"Thank you, sir."

Four

ANANKE SLEPT RIGHT through her alarm, through the repeatedly ringing bell indicating someone was at her front gate, through the squawking of crows outside her bedroom window, and through the buzzing of her phone all eight times Shinji called her.

When her finally eyes parted, it was nearly noon.

Though she had returned from London the previous day, it wasn't jet lag that had kept her in bed. She seldom suffered from it, and she'd been in the UK for only a little over twenty-four hours, not nearly enough time to reset her internal clock.

No, what she'd just experienced was the first decent night's sleep since waking up the previous week aboard the *Karas Evonus*, where she learned she'd been "recruited" into an elite team of operatives, by a committee represented by a man known to her and the others only as the Administrator. Oh, and there was also the small matter that she and most of her new colleagues had all been excommunicated from their previous professions.

Since then, her life had been moving at a whirlwind pace. With the promise that their names would be cleared, she and the others had agreed to take on the job the Administrator presented them, and spent the next couple of days tracking down and rescuing a group of kidnapped school kids.

That alone would have justified sleeping in, but on the heels of the rescue, she'd received a call from Jonathan Quinn, a highly respected associate she'd worked with in the past, asking for her help on a personal matter. Hence the quick trip to London, on which she'd brought three of her new friends— Rosario, Liesel, and Dylan.

As with the kidnapped kids, Quinn's mission had been a success. At least, Ananke thought so. The targets had been neutralized, but there was some personal fallout between Quinn and his partner Nate that still needed to be sorted out. That was their business, though, not hers.

She'd arrived at her place in Boulder, Colorado, around 7:30 the previous evening, and by 7:45, she was asleep.

With a satisfied sigh, she rolled onto her back, thinking maybe she should spend the whole day right where she was. She could read a book, peruse the internet on her laptop, and if she became hungry, order food.

She frowned.

She would have to figure out a way of getting said food from her security gate to her bedroom without getting up. And then there was the issue of the bathroom, which she'd have to visit soon.

Dammit.

She *really* didn't want to get up.

She groaned, threw the covers back, and shuffled across the bedroom to the bathroom. As she entered, her phone buzzed back on her nightstand, but now that her bladder was so close to the toilet, the phone would have to wait.

After Ananke finished her business, she decided a shower would be a good idea. She was hesitant to do the math, but it had been more than twenty-four hours since her last one. She'd meant to wash off last night but her bed had been too inviting.

By the time she finished getting clean and returned to her bedroom, nearly forty minutes had passed since her phone last buzzed.

"Ugh. Really, Shinji?" she said. Shinji was Ananke's personal information specialist. He worked from the comforts of his apartment in the San Gabriel Valley, east of Los Angeles, coordinating whatever she needed. The call she'd heard before her shower was his *ninth* one. Four last night and five already today.

Double ugh.

Well, he'd waited this long. Might as well wait until she'd had some coffee.

In the kitchen, as the brown liquid filled her Emma Peel mug, she looked across the living room, out the large windows at the Rocky Mountains, and sighed in contentment. There really was nothing like being home.

Once Emma was filled, Ananke carried her across the living room, pulled open one of the sliders that opened onto the deck, and stepped outside.

A perfect day—temperature seventy-two, maybe seventy-three; sunshine and blue sky; and the glorious mountains reminding all who saw them who the real boss of the planet was. It didn't get much better than this.

As she took her first sip, her phone rattled in her pocket.

She kept her gaze on the mountains and took another sip, letting the call go to voice mail.

No matter how long she lived here, she never failed to be captivated by the beauty that surrounded her. It was like she was in a whole different world. Like she'd been given a special ticket to Earth's—

Her phone rang again.

"Are you kidding me?"

She put Emma down and pulled out the damn thing. Shinji again. She poked ACCEPT. "What? What, what, what, what? Why are you calling me so much?"

"Oh, my God. Are you all right? You are, right? You're all right? Please tell me you're all right."

"What do you mean, am I all right? Of course I'm all right. Why wouldn't I be all right?"

"B-b-because you didn't answer your phone."

"Maybe I was *sleeping*!"

"For more than sixteen hours?"

"Look, I was tired."

"You can't do that to me," he said. "I thought someone took you again!"

It was a fair point. When the Administrator's people had "extracted" her from a tricky situation—by drugging her and keeping her unconscious for nearly a week—Shinji had had no idea what had happened to her.

"I should have checked in," she admitted. "Sorry. I, um, haven't been getting much rest lately."

"It's…it's okay. Sorry I was so…whiny."

"No problem. I'm used to it."

"What does that—"

"Shinji, let's focus. What's so important you've tried calling a dozen times?"

"It hasn't been a dozen, it's been…never mind. The Administrator called and wanted me to tell you to expect a package."

"The Administrator? He called *you*?"

"He did."

"Why didn't he just call me directly?"

"I don't know. Maybe *he* knew you were sleeping."

Ananke glanced back at her house, her eyes narrowing. Had the Administrator bugged her place while she was away? She had systems in place to prevent that, but it would be worth doing an electronics sweep, just in case.

"When's this package supposed to come?" she asked.

"It should have been there first thing this morning."

"I didn't get anything."

"You mean, while you were sleeping?"

She grimaced, silently conceding the point. "Hold on."

She set the phone down next to Emma Peel, crossed through the house, and out again via the front door. Between there and the fence fronting her property lay a six meter-wide strip of grass, with a stone path cutting through it to the walk-in security gate. She scanned the lawn for the package, in case it had been tossed over the fence. Nothing but a few leaves and an errant pine cone. Farther to the left, another gate closed off the driveway that led to her garage, but she didn't see anything there, either.

She walked over and pulled the gate open. No note stuck on the other side, and nothing on the ground. Either Shinji had gotten the time wrong, or the Administrator needed to find a better delivery service.

34

As she stepped back into her yard and started to close her gate, she heard a car door open.

She looked back at the street and spotted two men who had exited a sedan half a block away. They crossed the road and started down the sidewalk toward her house.

Shinji hadn't been wrong after all.

They were a mismatched pair. The trailing man, dressed in a gray suit, was a head taller and half a person wider than the guy in front, and had the barely noticeable bulge of a weapon under his left arm. The smaller guy was more casually dressed, in jeans and a green, V-neck T-shirt. No visible bulges on this guy, but he was carrying a briefcase.

One of Ananke's biggest pet peeves was people coming to her house for business. This was her sanctuary, not her office. Not that she actually had an office. One of the few things she disliked even more was an armed man walking down her street. What would the neighbors think?

When the men were five meters away, the small guy smiled.

Ananke let them approach another few steps before she said, "That's far enough."

Both men stopped, and the small guy said, "I have a package for you."

"What is it?"

His eyes clouded. "Um, I don't know. No one ever tells me what I'm carrying."

"I mean, show it to me, idiot."

"Oh. Right." He started to open the briefcase, but when he almost dropped it, he turned to his companion. "I could use your help."

The big guy, who had been staring at Ananke, gave the small guy a sideways glance. Then, with what could only be described as bored reluctance, he took a step forward.

Small Guy said, "Arms out."

When the giant complied, Small Guy set the case on the big man's outstretched arms and popped it open. He extracted a nine-by-twelve manila envelope. Black and yellow striped tape ran along all four sides. He held it so Ananke could get a good look.

She gave it a beat before waving him forward. "Just you."

The courier brought the package over.

"Did you try ringing the bell?" she asked, nodding at the button next to her gate.

"Several times. I assumed it's broken."

"Yeah. It…is. Just give me the package."

He handed it to her, said, "Have a good day," and turned back to his partner.

Ananke watched them return to their vehicle. Once they drove off, she closed the gate.

On her way through the house, she grabbed a pair of scissors from the kitchen and returned to the deck. She tapped the speaker function on her phone and heard rapid tapping of computer keys and action music. "Are you playing video games?"

"Oh, hey," Shinji said. "No…I mean, well, yeah. Just killing time." The music cut off. "So, package or no package?"

"About to open it. I'll check in with you later."

"Wait. I'd kind of like to know what's inside, too."

"Was it sent to you?"

"Um, no."

"Good-bye, Shinji."

She hit DISCONNECT and sat back down on the patio chair.

As she took a drink from Emma Peel, she glanced at the envelope, half thinking she should ignore it. But after a few seconds, she set the mug down, slit one end of the envelope, and slid the contents onto her lap.

On top of the stack was a mobile phone. At least the Administrator hadn't forgotten her previous work phone had been lost during the last mission.

The papers consisted of printouts of three news articles, two photographs, and a receipt for an airline ticket with a notation reading BOARDING PASS ON PHONE. At the bottom of the stack was a second envelope, which contained a Texas driver's license with Ananke's picture, several credit cards, a Triple A card, and two insurance cards—one health, and the other for a 2015 Ford Mustang. Everything was under the same name: Shawn Ramey.

Ananke set the IDs aside and looked at the ticket. Apparently Ms. Ramey was due to fly out of Denver to Seattle, Washington, that very night.

Ananke wasn't sure she liked where this was going.

The articles were next. The first was a feature on a town in northeast Washington State, a place called Bradbury near the Columbia River. It had apparently undergone a renaissance over the past few years, transforming from a dying former logging village to a growing tech hub. Not that it rivaled Seattle or Silicon Valley or big-city places like them. Still, according to the article, nearly two dozen, mostly small firms had made Bradbury their home. The companies were all "looking for alternatives to the congestion-filled environments their competitors were mired in."

Sounded like a nice place to work. Like Boulder, only smaller.

The next article was about a revolutionary new solar panel that worked at near capacity even when not pointed directly at the sun. According to a spokesman, the product also worked at the same rate on cloudy days, making it an ideal device for locations where traditional solar panels were less effective. The device was still undergoing testing, but all indications were it would hit the market within the next couple of years. The company was called Scolareon and already produced a popular, efficient model, but "what's coming next," the spokesman said, "is going to revolutionize the business." Scolareon was located in—surprise, surprise—Bradbury, Washington. The head of the company was a man named Kyle Scudder.

Scudder + Solar = Scolar, then *eon* for the cool factor, she guessed.

The last article was from a business news site and dated nearly ten months earlier. It was a typical PR release, announcing Scolareon's hiring of a woman named Natasha Patterson as their new CFO. According to the article, Patterson joined Scolareon from Davos Home Fortress, one of billionaire Scott Davos's many ventures. Though Scolareon was nowhere near the industrial force of Davos's empire, Ananke figured the

CFO position would have been a step up. Patterson was clearly a woman with plans.

Ananke flipped the paper over, hoping there was something on the back that would let her know why the woman was important, but no such luck.

She turned her attention to the pictures. The first was the headshot of a man in a crisp black T-shirt, smiling at the camera. He was in his early forties at the most, and exuded a confidence that some probably found intimidating.

In the white border at the bottom of the picture was written KYLE SCUDDER.

Mr. Scolareon himself.

Okay. And?

The second photo also had a name at the bottom. NATASHA PATTERSON. The new CFO. Like Scudder's picture, it was one of those business headshots—high school yearbook, only in more expensive clothes and taken by considerably better photographers. Patterson was Caucasian, with long sandy brown hair tucked behind her ears. She appeared to be in her early to mid-thirties, and had that ambitious, I'll-get-it-done aura Ananke appreciated.

Ananke set the papers down and leaned back, thinking. The Administrator had told her, Rosario, Liesel, Dylan, and Ricky after they completed their mission that there would be more projects for which his organization would like to use the team. She hadn't realized the next one would come up so soon.

Did she really want to work for him again? She hadn't had much of a choice on the first job. Sure, she and the others had been promised the Administrator would do everything necessary to clear their name, whether they accepted that initial mission or not. But given the nature of what the Administrator had wanted her and the others to do—the aforementioned saving of the kids—she would have taken the assignment no matter what.

To accept this second assignment from the mysterious committee felt like she'd be moving down a path that would become harder to extract herself from the longer she stayed on it.

But would that be so bad? If all the jobs were about providing help where none was previously available, wouldn't that make them worth doing?

For years, she had this vision of herself, like Marley from Dickens's *A Christmas Carol*, wandering the afterlife, lugging a chain even longer and heavier than the one awaiting Scrooge. Until recently, she'd been an assassin by trade, and a good one to boot. Perhaps doing some good now and then would remove a few links from her post-life burden.

She picked up the new mobile and tapped the pre-entered number for the Administrator, still unsure what she would say.

"Ananke, I'm pleased to hear from you," the Administrator said.

"Sorry for not calling earlier. I was…"

"No explanation necessary. I had no expectations of a time. I assumed you'd call when you were ready. Did you look through the information I sent?"

"I did."

"Then I'm sure you've gathered we'd like to send you and your team to Bradbury."

"Yeah, I got that part. It's the why I don't know yet."

"Of course not. The why is that we think there's something suspicious going on there."

She snorted. "I didn't think you were sending us there on vacation. How about a detail or two?"

"Natasha Patterson is missing."

That hit Ananke harder than it probably should have. She'd liked what she read about the woman. "What happened?"

"I will be happy to elaborate, but only after you accept the job."

Naturally. "So, the missing woman, that's the something suspicious? Or is there something more?"

Silence.

She took a deep breath. "And I'm betting if there's indeed a problem that extends beyond just this woman being missing, and we don't do anything about it, people will get hurt."

"I don't know. But it seems likely."

She closed her eyes. Why, oh, why, couldn't she have had

a few more days hanging around her house before he reached out to her again?

Gritting her teeth, she said, "All right. I'm in. Tell me what's going on."

"Thank you," the Administrator said, sounding relieved. He told her about the mystery surrounding Patterson's disappearance more than two weeks earlier.

"The police don't have any leads?" she asked.

"The police are unaware of the situation."

"She's been gone two weeks and no one's called the police?"

"It's our understanding that most people are unaware there's anything wrong."

"Hold on. I have an article right here that says she's a bigwig at this Scolareon place. Someone's got to have noticed she's not coming in to the office."

"Late on the evening of April fifth, an email was sent to both Kyle Scudder and the Scolareon HR department, ostensibly from Natasha Patterson."

"*Ostensibly?*"

"In it, she says she needed to take an immediate leave of absence due to the unforeseen hospitalization of a family member on the East Coast. She apologized for the suddenness and promised to be in touch. She has since responded to several work emails, but when any personal questions are asked, her replies have been brief and vague. Calls made to her mobile phone go straight to voice mail. No one has talked to her."

"Then you aren't even sure she's missing. I mean, she could be telling the truth, couldn't she?"

"She could be, if we thought she was the one writing the emails."

"But you don't think that."

"We've been in touch with someone who knows her well. In fact, he's the one who brought the case to our attention."

"Couldn't he be wrong?"

"His name is Scott Davos."

"Scott Davos? *The* Scott Davos?"

"Correct. Davos has been a mentor to her."

"Just a mentor? Or more?"

"My understanding is just a mentor. About a month ago, she contacted him and hinted that there was a problem."

"At Scolareon?"

"That's not clear, but is a fair assumption. When he pushed her on it, she played it down, said it was probably nothing and not to worry. They have been in the habit of emailing at least every other day, if not every day. After this exchange, their correspondence carried on as usual until the night before she disappeared. When he emailed on the evening of the fourth, she replied within minutes that she would soon be sending him a present to mark the anniversary of the first time they worked together. Only that had happened in the fall, not in April. What this told him was that she was worried about someone reading her email, so he replied that he looked forward to receiving it, and said it had been a while since they'd had a chat and for her to call when she had a chance. She promised she would, even going so far as to say perhaps the following evening. When the night of the fifth came, however, she didn't call, nor did she respond to his email as quickly as she usually did. Her reply didn't arrive until the following day, only instead of the usual message, it was brief, businesslike, and nothing like the way she usually responded. He tried calling her but was sent to voice mail every time."

"That's it?"

"That's it."

"No mention of what she was worried about?"

"None."

"And the present she mentioned, I'm guessing it didn't show up."

"Not as of this morning."

"Okay, I get that's kind of troubling. But how did he make the leap to assuming she's missing?"

"After a few days, she stopped responding to any of his emails, so he phoned her work number and was told she was away on a family emergency. But Davos knows her family. Her only immediate relations are her brother and his wife and kids in Chicago. He had an associate contact the brother on some pretense having to do with Natasha's former employment, and it was clear that the brother had no knowledge of any family emergency."

"It could have been something else. Perhaps a friend who needed her help or a personal matter she didn't want to share."

"That's true. But Davos did as much as he could to locate her and found nothing. That's when he came to us."

"Excuse me if I'm missing something here, but you gave me the impression that your organization was secret. How would he even know to come to you?"

The Administrator hesitated. "I misspoke. He didn't come to us specifically. He came to his friend, who happens to be a member of the board. The board member was concerned enough to ask me to look into it. After a preliminary investigation, I concurred with Mr. Davos's assessment that Miss Patterson is missing, and the committee decided to activate our full involvement."

"Meaning me and the team."

"Correct."

FIVE

The Great State of Washington

A DELAY OUT of Seattle meant Ananke's flight to Spokane didn't land until nearly one a.m. Except for a cleaning crew and a few airport police officers, the place was deserted. Thankfully, the Mustang registered to her new alias was exactly where she'd been told she'd find it. She retrieved the key fob from under the rear bumper, climbed in, and got underway.

After her conversation with the Administrator, he had emailed her a link and an access code that she used to download additional information. It wasn't much. Natasha Patterson went by the name Tasha. She was thirty-four, never married, no kids. Other info included the woman's social security number, credit cards and bank account numbers, and her known habits and social media links.

A second file provided specifics about her brother, and the names and basic info on the three people in Bradbury with whom she was closest. Instructions from the Administrator stressed, however, that the brother should not be contacted unless absolutely necessary, and even then, only if the Administrator cleared it.

The drive from Spokane was mostly due north through a valley that cut through the Colville National Forest. Ananke guessed it was a beautiful route during the day, but with the moon yet to rise, she saw little beyond the halos of her headlights.

It took about an hour and a half to reach the Columbia River, and another twenty minutes before she arrived in

Bradbury. Though she was tired enough to justify heading straight for her hotel, her professional habits would not let that happen. To survive as long as she had in the secret world, especially doing what she had been doing for a living, didn't happen by luck. She had taken to heart the precautions instilled in her by the trio of operatives who'd served as her mentors. One of those precautions was, whenever possible, don't sleep someplace new until you have the lay of the land. So, even though it was the middle of the night, she wasn't going to feel settled until she took a drive around town.

There was no missing the charm of Bradbury. The brick buildings lining the central road—Main Street, of course—all appeared to be well over a century old. Most had been refurbished, but in keeping with their historic roots rather than being plastered over with ugly commercial facades. Instead of the old five-and-dimes and general stores and insurance offices the buildings had probably once housed, there were now trendy-looking cafés and coffee houses and shops, all clearly intending to appeal to the nouveau adults the area's tech boom attracted.

About the only businesses that looked like they'd been there longer than a few years were a doctor's office, a shoe store with a neon sign that must've been nearly as old as the building itself, and the office for the *Bradbury Evening Independent*, the local paper.

On the roads surrounding Main Street were the old homes that made up the heart of the original town. Along the highway just a few blocks north of downtown, however, things began to change. The first sign of the town's new direction was the Bury Business Park. It stretched off to the right, its buildings designed to pay homage to the historic downtown. Next came a housing tract that could easily have been found in Portland or Seattle or even parts of Los Angeles, the homes stylish and hip, in a mix of bright colors and subdued tones. None appeared to be smaller than eighteen hundred square feet, with several that must have been double that. These were the kinds of houses that would have been out of the average family's price range in a big city, but here they were likely affordable for most, if not

44

all, residents. Parked in the driveways were Mini Coopers and Priuses and the occasional German import. Ananke figured that here lived the coders and the developers and the management who were the breath of the burgeoning industry.

Another few minutes up the highway, at the edge of town, were two large hangar-like buildings, one on either side of the highway. At the entrances to both were identical signs indicating the buildings were home to Scolareon.

She continued north, passing more businesses and scattered homes. Then, right before the wilderness crowded the highway again, she came to a road running into the hills opposite the river. Attached to a curved rock wall at the intersection were illuminated metal letters that read GREEN HILLS ESTATES.

Down the road about twenty-five yards sat a guard hut and a gate. She could see the top of someone's head through the hut's window.

Home to Bradbury's elite? Some of them, she guessed. She'd love to take a drive through and look around, but that would require getting past the guard, and she didn't think he'd raise the gate just because she asked him to, especially at this time of night. There'd be opportunity later to look around, if a visit proved necessary.

She made a U-turn and started back toward her hotel near the heart of town. Almost immediately she spotted headlights coming toward her. This was the first car she'd seen since she began her recon of the area.

As the gap between them closed, she realized it was a police sedan. She checked her speedometer. She was driving at the limit, but eased back on the accelerator anyway. Even then, she was pretty sure the officer looked over at her as he drove by. When the squad car made a quick U-turn, she was sure he had.

The police car sped up until it was right behind her, and stayed there.

"Nothing to see here," Ananke whispered. "Feel free to pass me at any time."

The words were barely out of her mouth when the cop

car's rooftop lights started flashing.

Annoyed, Ananke flipped on her blinker and pulled to the side of the road, just shy of the entrance to the Scolareon complex.

While she waited, she retrieved her Shawn Ramey ID, the equally fake vehicle registration from the glove box, and rolled the window down.

In her rearview mirror, she could see the cop still in his car, face faintly lit by the screen of a laptop. Running Ananke's plates, no doubt.

All right, Mr. Administrator, you damn well had better have my ass covered.

Finally, the cop got out of his car. From his silhouette, she guessed he was almost six feet tall. He sauntered up to her window, leaned down, and looked in.

"Good morning, ma'am," the cop said.

Not a policeman. A police*woman*. The name tag on her uniform read M. HARRIS.

"Morning, Officer."

"Are you lost?" There was a definite you-must-be-lost-because-you-don't-belong-here tone to her voice.

"I'm sorry?"

"Haven't seen you before, so was wondering if maybe you took a wrong turn somewhere."

At another time, Ananke might have said, "Is it illegal for someone you don't know to be driving on the highway?" or "That's none of your business," or the old standby "Screw you." Instead, professional Ananke smiled demurely and said, "Actually, I *am* a little lost. I was looking for the Collins Inn and Suites."

Her response seemed to take Harris by surprise. "You mean the one here in Bradbury?"

Fighting hard to keep her voice innocent, Ananke said, "That's the one."

"Your driver's license and registration, please."

"Have I done something wrong?"

"License and registration."

Ananke handed them over, and Harris carried them back

to her car.

Ananke monitored the cop via her mirror as Harris sat in her driver's seat and worked her computer again. After a couple of minutes, she picked up a radio mic and spoke into it. This was followed by more computer time before Harris finally climbed out again and returned to the Mustang.

"Here you are, Ms. Ramey." The cop handed Ananke the documents. "Head back through town. Then turn right on Clearwater Drive. It's just past A&R Diner. Go a quarter of a mile. You'll see the Collins Inn. Can't miss it."

"Thank you."

Harris touched her cap, said, "You have a good night," and returned to her car.

If things had ended right there, Ananke might have been willing to brush off the encounter as an asshole graveyard-shift cop playing tough.

But they didn't.

When Ananke pulled onto the road, Harris did the same, following her a couple of car lengths back, all the way to the Collins Inn. There, Harris parked on the street and watched Ananke walk from the Mustang into the building.

Deputy M. Harris, you just made my list.

The clerk behind the desk was a college-aged guy who, at the sound of the door swishing open, looked up from a TV and quickly stood when he realized he had a customer.

"Good morning," he said, with a lot more cheer than Harris had managed. "How can I help you?"

"Checking in."

"Do you have a reservation?"

She gave him the pertinent information, and he gave her a pair of key cards to room 312.

Before she could walk away, he said, "We have a reservation linked to yours for a Caroline Cruz, arriving later this morning. We have her staying in the room next to yours."

"Great. Thank you."

"Those rooms have connecting doors. If you'd rather have something more private, I could arrange that."

"Nope. Connecting doors are fine. Thanks again."

Seven minutes later, Ananke was sound asleep.

ROSARIO ARRIVED AT Sea-Tac International Airport at 8:30 a.m., after spending a grand total of thirty-four hours in Mexico City. That had barely been enough time to get some decent food, a few hours of rest, and to make sure her absence over the last couple of weeks hadn't resulted in anyone raiding one of the stashes of equipment and valuables she'd hidden around the city.

When the Administrator had contacted her about another job, her inclination was to tell him not this time. Trust was not something that came easily to Rosario. The Administrator and the organization he represented had a long way to go to earn that from her. But when he told her Ananke was already on board, Rosario had reconsidered.

While she hadn't known Ananke any longer than she'd known the Administrator, she'd worked with Ananke on two missions already, and in that short time had developed considerable respect for the woman. If Ananke had said yes, then Rosario wanted to be at her side.

She made her way to the appropriate departure wing and headed to her gate.

"Well, hey now. Look who's here." Ricky Orbits waved at her from inside a bar along the walkway. "Come! Join me for a drink. We've got plenty of time." He patted the stool next to him.

The Administrator had warned her Ricky would be on this flight, and that since their cover identities weren't supposed to know each other, it would be best if they ignored each other.

Cursing under her breath, she scanned the area to make sure no one was paying them undue attention. Her internal threat radar remained silent, so she reluctantly walked into the bar. She did not sit.

"Whatever you're drinking, I'm buying," Ricky said, a half empty pint of beer in front of him.

"What are you doing?"

"Uh, what does it look like I'm doing? What are *you* doing?"

She narrowed her eyes and whispered, "We do not know each other."

He frowned. "Really? I wasn't told that."

"*I* was told." She turned to leave.

"Wait, you're already here. Just one drink. If anyone asks, we'll say I was trying to hit on you."

The thought of that sent a shiver up her spine, but walking away now might draw more attention than if she stayed for a bit. "Fine." She flagged down the bartender. "An orange juice, please."

"Orange juice?" Ricky said. "How about a shot of vodka in that?"

The bartender paused, looking at them.

"It is 8:45 a.m.," Rosario said.

"So?" Ricky asked.

She glanced at the bartender. "Orange juice. No vodka."

While the man went to get her drink, Ricky snickered. "Not a morning drinker, either, huh?"

She eyed his beer.

"Oh, this is an exception," he said defensively. "Did you know that the *Karas Evonus* is a *dry* ship? Can you believe that?"

Part of the deal allowing Ricky to be sprung from prison and be part of the team was that between missions, he was restricted to the ship—the *Karas Evonus*—that served as the team's floating headquarters.

"I do not care," she said.

"Ah, come on, Rosy. You can't be that heartless."

As he raised his beer to his lips, she said, "What is your problem? Why can you never call anyone by their proper name? It is annoying and rude. Everyone thinks this."

He started to snort, but caught himself before beer could spew out of his mouth and nose. With great difficulty, he swallowed, then said, "Not everyone."

"*Everyone*. You need to stop."

"Has anyone told you you're too serious?"

The bartender returned with the orange juice. Rosario drank it down without stopping. "From this point forward, I am

Caroline Cruz and you are Rudy Schmidt, and we do not know each other."

"Can you believe that name? Rudy Schmidt? Sounds like I should be serving bratwurst at Soldier Field."

Turning away, she said, "I am going to the gate now."

"Wait up. I'm almost done."

She kept walking.

UPON LANDING IN Spokane, Rosario proceeded to the Hertz rental counter and picked up the car that had been reserved for her, avoiding any further encounters with Ricky. He'd been seated at the back of the plane, far from her—*thank you, Mr. Administrator*—so she had walked as quickly as possible to make sure their paths didn't cross.

She did see him one more time before reaching Bradbury. A few miles north of Spokane, he raced by on a motorcycle, beeping as he passed.

At the Collins Inn, she picked up a key to room 314, and was told her colleague was staying in the room next door. The rooms turned out to have adjoining doors, so as soon as she finished freshening up, she opened the one on her side and knocked on the other.

A moment later, a deadbolt slipped free and the door swung open.

"You made it!" Ananke said, smiling.

After a hug, she motioned Rosario into her room.

"Any problems?" Ananke asked as they walked over to a sitting area where an opened laptop sat on a table.

"Other than Ricky? No."

Ananke paused mid-step. "Ricky?"

"We were on the same flight from Seattle."

"Please tell me he got thrown off mid-flight."

"If only we were so lucky."

Ananke snickered and Rosario joined in, and soon both were laughing loudly.

When they finally calmed down, Rosario relayed what had happened on the trip to Bradbury, ending with, "He passed me a long time ago so he should be here by now. Has he checked in yet?"

"Of course not." Ananke grabbed her phone and shot off a text.

"What about Dylan and Liesel?"

"Due in tomorrow." Ananke's phone buzzed. "Well, look at that. Ricky *is* here."

"Is he staying in this hotel?"

"Yeah, but I made it clear to the Administrator I didn't want him anywhere near us." She sent another message, and the response came back within seconds. "He's in room 201. Which is on the other side of the hotel."

"Good."

"Definitely."

"So," Rosario said, "do we wait for everyone to arrive, or...?"

"Absolutely not." Ananke woke up her computer. On the screen was a Google map of Bradbury, with several manually added markers scattered across it. Ananke pointed at one. "This is Natasha Patterson's home. It's in a development at the north end of town. I drove through the area last night. Big lawns, a nice car in every driveway, quiet."

"Sounds boring."

"No kidding."

"What is the status of her place at the moment?"

"As far as I know, no one's been inside since she disappeared." Ananke pointed at a pair of markers along the highway, a bit farther north. "These two buildings belong to Scolareon. Natasha worked in the east building, second floor. I have Shinji working on obtaining floor plans."

"I can help, if need be."

"Let him do it. Makes him feel useful." Ananke pointed at the marker farthest north. "Way up here is where Kyle Scudder lives. It's a gated community called Green Hills Estates."

"Any word on whether there is a boyfriend?"

"Nothing."

"Girlfriend?"

"Same answer. The Administrator told you about the Davos connection, right?"

"Yes."

"Good." Ananke motioned at the map. "The other markers are places she's mentioned to him. Cafes she's eaten at, the market she frequents, a bookstore. Not sure any of those are going to help us, though. What we really need to figure out is where she was the night she went missing."

"Do we know where her phone is?"

Ananke shook her head. "The Administrator told me that it hasn't shown up on any system since the evening of the fifth."

"I will double-check the records and get a final location. There was no mobile number in the brief I received. Do you have that?"

"I do." Ananke accessed the information on her phone and texted it to Rosario. "There is one other thing you can look into for me."

"Of course."

Ananke told her about the encounter she'd had with the cop the night before. "The name on her badge read M. Harris. I'd like you to see what you can find out about her."

"Easy enough." Rosario paused, still troubled by something she'd been thinking about since she left Mexico. "I am still confused about what our mission is here. I understand that a woman might be missing, but is this not something the police should handle?"

"Normally, yes. But because someone has been posing as her, at least with emails and texts, there's no reason for most people to think she's missing. Add in that the Administrator thinks there's something larger going on and here we are."

"Larger like what?"

"Apparently that's up to us to figure out."

WHAT ANANKE REALLY wanted to do was get a look inside the missing woman's house. There must be clues there to indicate if she was missing or simply on a trip. But that was a task best left until after dark. For now, Ananke would have to settle for establishing the cover story the Administrator had given her.

While Rosario set to work reviewing the phone records, Ananke drove back through the old part of town to a Victorian house off Main Street that had been converted into an office. She parked in the small lot beside the building and entered.

A teenage girl sat behind a desk in the center of the front room, engrossed in one of the thicker Harry Potter books. Ananke waited for the girl to look up, but the teen remained glued to the page.

Not wanting to wait for Hermione to pull Harry out of yet another mess, Ananke said, "Hello."

The girl looked up, startled. "Oh. Oh, uh…" She jammed an index card into the book to mark her page before saying, "Good, uh, afternoon. How may I help you?"

Using the slight Texas twang her cover identity required, Ananke said, "I'm looking for Antonia Mahoney."

"Of course." The girl popped up with an exuberance only a person her age could muster, and dashed into the hallway behind the desk. She was gone for no more than two seconds before she popped her head back around the corner. "Do you have an appointment?"

"She should be expecting me. Tell her it's Shawn Ramey."

"Shawn Ramey. Got it. I'll be right back."

Ananke occupied herself by looking around the small lobby, taking in first a large landscape painting of what she guessed was a local area, and then the long, expensive-looking sign with raised letters on the opposite wall that read:

MAHONEY REALTY
THE BRADBURY EXPERTS

That should have given the receptionist more than enough time to return, and yet Ananke remained alone.

On the desk was a bowl of packaged candies. She snapped up a mini peanut butter cup, unwrapped it, and popped it into her mouth.

Still no receptionist.

Ananke moved around the desk and peeked into the hall. Empty.

She grabbed a second chocolate and took her time eating it. When she finished, she checked the hall again.

Not a soul in sight.

Hmm.

Though she'd had no appointment, she'd been told the Realtor would be expecting Ms. Ramey at some point that morning. Given the size of the potential commissions Ananke's visit represented—however fake they were—Ananke had expected the agent to come rushing out at the mention of her name.

Enough of this BS. Ananke headed into the hallway.

The corridor opened into another room not far down, perhaps a parlor back in the day, or the dining room. It had been converted into a four-desk bullpen. A middle-aged, balding guy in a business suit occupied one of the desks, while the others were empty. Ananke felt safe in assuming he wasn't Antonia Mahoney.

A female voice drifted into the room from another hall to the right. Ananke followed it, past a couple of empty offices to the open doorway at the very end.

"That's more than fine," the voice was saying. "Of course, I understand. We'll just reschedule for next week."

Ananke stopped shy of the threshold and peered in. The receptionist stood fidgeting, her back to the door, in front of a desk that dominated the room. The girl was watching a fortysomething woman with perfectly coiffed hair talking on the phone. The woman also faced the other direction, looking out the window.

Ananke leaned against the doorframe. "Problem?"

The teen swiveled around, her eyes widening. "Oh, Miss Raintree. I'm sorry. It'll just be another minute."

The woman behind the desk—Antonia Mahoney, presumably—turned and looked from the receptionist to Ananke and back. "Mr. Drake, if you could hold for one moment." She put her hand over the phone and whispered, "Karina, what's going on?"

"Sorry, Mrs. Mahoney. This is, um, Shawn Raintree. She-she said you were expecting her?"

Mahoney's brow furrowed. "Raintree?"

"Ramey," Ananke corrected.

Instantly Mahoney's face brightened. "Ms. Ramey! Of course. I'm so sorry. I'm just finishing up." She gestured at the chairs in front of her desk. "Please. Have a seat."

"Thank you," Ananke said and took the chair on the left.

Karina looked unsure if she should leave or stay.

When Mahoney noticed this, she whispered, "See if she wants something to *drink*."

"Oh, right." Karina smiled at Ananke. "Would you like something to drink? We have water, and, um, Diet Coke, and, um—"

"Water is fine," Ananke said.

The girl hurried out and returned with the bottle as Mahoney wrapped up her phone conversation. Karina handed the bottle to Ananke, and once more seemed puzzled about her next move.

"You can go back to your desk," Mahoney said.

"Yes, ma'am."

As soon as the girl was out of the room, Mahoney put a hand at the side of her mouth and stage whispered to Ananke, "High school work-study program. Her first job. At least I don't have to pay her." The Realtor smiled and came around the desk, hand extended. "Antonia Mahoney. A pleasure to meet you."

Ananke stood and shook. "Shawn Ramey. I appreciate you taking the time to see me, Mrs. Mahoney."

Toni motioned back at Ananke's seat and retreated to her own chair. "It's my pleasure, and please call me Toni."

"Toni. Toni Mahoney?"

"Cute, isn't it?" Toni said without any irony at all.

Trying to sound convincing, Ananke said, "Sure."

Toni clicked open a file on her computer. "How was the trip here?"

"Fine. Beautiful country."

"I understand you drove in."

"That's right. Last night."

"The good news is that we're expanding our airport, and by late summer we'll have daily commuter flights to and from Spokane. Much better for businesses."

"That's good to hear."

Toni smiled. "We may look like a small town but we're larger than people think. Now let's see." She studied her screen. "I have the specifications of what your company is looking for. Unless those have changed…?"

"No, you have the latest." Ananke's cover was that of a tech executive looking for a new research facility. As far as Toni knew, Bradbury was only one of several potential locations on Ananke's list.

"In that case, there shouldn't be any problem finding exactly what you're looking for. I made a list of about a dozen properties that should suit your needs. Some already finished, and some ready for development."

"That's encouraging."

"Can I just say, you have come to the right place at the right time. Bradbury is truly special. Not only am I confident you'll find your perfect property, but I know you will soon realize you've found your perfect town for your employees as well. Honestly, we have so much to offer." She paused, a sparkle dancing across her eyes. "I hope you don't mind, but the chamber of commerce and I have set up a welcome party for tomorrow evening. A kind of meet-and-greet with some of the town's movers and shakers."

"What a great idea. That sounds wonderful." It did *not* sound wonderful, but it did sound useful.

"I'm glad you approve. The heads of several companies that have moved here in recent years will be there. Also the mayor and the chief of police." She leaned forward and, in what was apparently a signature move, stage whispered, "I think there's a good chance Kyle Scudder will come, too."

"The head of Scolareon?"

"One and the same."

"Fantastic." This time Ananke was not blowing smoke. "I look forward to finding out how he and the others feel about relocating here."

"I can tell you that right now. They all love Bradbury." Toni laughed. "I don't know what your schedule is, but if you're free right now, I could show you some of those properties."

"I am free, but I think that can wait. What I'd really appreciate is a tour of the town, something to help me get a feel of the place."

"What an excellent idea!"

Six

CONSCIOUSNESS RETURNED IN dribs and drabs, slowly stealing Tasha from the comforting arms of sleep. At least her head wasn't throbbing as badly as all the other times she'd woken since being caught in the woods. She'd had moments when she was sure her skull was on the verge of splitting.

Lying there, eyes still closed, she realized the intense vertigo that had greeted her every day for the last—week? Ten days? A month?—seemed to have subsided.

She didn't know. Those first several days had been a blur.

She winced as she rolled onto her back. Her rib cage was still bruised so that hadn't changed.

Slowly, she parted her eyelids. And realized something was different. Gone was the white plaster ceiling she'd been staring at. The ceiling now was bare concrete.

She looked to the side. Before, she'd been in a small room with a boarded-up window. This place was larger, containing oddly shaped items she couldn't quite make out with her cloudy mind from her prone position.

Tasha sat up and swung her legs off the bed. Not a real bed, she saw now. A canvas-covered cot propped up on a wooden frame.

Odd. Something hung in the air between her and the rest of the room. Glass? Maybe, but it had no frame, and wasn't just in front of her but continued above and to the sides. The only place it was absent from was on the floor. It was like she was in a giant, see-through box that was barely tall enough for her to stand in beside the cot, but plenty long enough for the portable bed. She guessed the roof topped out half a foot above her, at around six feet.

She touched the wall. Not glass. *Plexi*glas. Set into a groove that ran along the floor.

She sucked in a deep breath, and another, as panic bloomed in her chest.

Stop it. Get a hold of yourself.

Her situation had already been dire, so there was no sense in losing her head over a change of scenery. Besides, panic meant allowing someone else to control you. What she needed was to be the one in charge, to focus her energies on figuring out how to escape.

She pushed against the wall, hoping to tip the enclosure over, but her shove not only failed, it shot a crippling wave of pain across her rib cage. She leaned against the wall to keep from falling and wrapped an arm across her chest, her eyes squeezed shut as the spasms washed over her.

When they finally dissipated, she opened her eyes again and took a long look at the area beyond her transparent cell. Spaced evenly throughout the place were nearly a dozen other identical containers. They weren't on the ground at all. Each is set on its own platform, and under the few she could see, there were wheels. Most of the enclosures were empty, but three held other prisoners, all motionless on their cots.

Tasha banged on the wall. "Hey! Hey, wake up!"

None of the others even twitched.

She pounded and yelled a few more times, but either they were too far away to hear her, or the Plexiglas cells were soundproof.

A light change across the room drew her attention. A door along the far wall had opened, and through it walked two men, both wearing dark blue jumpsuits and Halloween masks. They headed straight to Tasha's cell and stopped beside it.

The one wearing an alien mask touched something out of sight below the lip of her platform, and then twisted up a goose-neck stand.

"Back on the bed," his voice boomed from a speaker in the floor of Tasha's platform.

"Let me out," she yelled. "You can't keep me like this. This is kidnapping. That's a fed—"

"Back on the bed or fall where you are."

She didn't know what he meant, nor did she care. She slapped the wall. "Let me out, dammit! Let me out right now!"

A hiss, like a bike tire being drained of air.

She twisted left and right, looking for the source, and froze when she saw a mist rising at the other end of the cell.

She had no idea what it was, but was sure it would put her back to sleep.

As she turned to the cot, the whole world went wobbly. She stumbled, her leg whacking against the cot's railing. For a second, she was convinced she would fall, but she willed herself forward and was able to tumble into the cot mere seconds before everything went black.

SEVEN

TONI MAHONEY GESTURED at a brick structure on the left side of the road. "That's the oldest building in town. The preservation society took it over about a decade ago. Good thing, too. It'd been close to collapsing at the time. They shored it up, and over the following years, they raised enough money to return it to its former state, with most of the funds coming from our new businesses. Now it serves as the city museum."

Hoping she sounded convincing, Ananke said, "What a nice story. I'll make a point of stopping by."

"They're not always open, but if you tell me when you want to visit, I can make sure someone's there."

"Great. Thank you."

Toni smiled and pointed again. "That two-story building is city hall. And the ones next to it are the fire department and the police department."

Ananke took special note of the police station. There were two squad cars out front, and an open area around the side she didn't have a good angle on, but where she guessed would be a few more department vehicles. "How many firemen and police officers does the city employ?"

"I don't know the actual number, but I think it's around twenty-five each. That would include office staff, too, of course."

"Of course."

After downtown, Toni drove Ananke through the new housing area where Patterson lived. All the roads had cutesy names like Binary Place and Motherboard Lane. Someone must have thought they would appeal to the tech transplants. Ananke had her doubts.

"Wonderful floor plans, and all the latest appliances," Toni was saying. "Solar, too, if you didn't notice. That's free of charge, by the way."

"Free of charge?"

"Scolareon provides free solar systems to everyone in Bradbury."

"Even the older homes?"

"Even the older homes."

"That's…generous."

"Just another benefit of living here. I believe they're currently installing a system at the new elementary school." She gazed out the window and pointed ahead. "Right up there is one of the houses we just listed. The one with the sign."

"That's actually the first for-sale sign in the neighborhood I've seen. How many homes are available here?"

"In this development, only three at the moment."

"What about the ones still being built?" Here and there they'd passed homes in various states of construction.

"Most of those are already spoken for, but don't let that concern you. Barry—he's the developer—is about to start phase four, which will nearly double the number of houses. By the time you and your employees arrive, we'll have plenty of new places to choose from." She flashed her Realtor smile. "I'd move into this neighborhood myself if I didn't already have a home."

Ahead was Cloud Drive, the street where Patterson lived. Ananke sensed Toni was about to go the other way, so as they neared the corner she said, "This street looks cute. Do you mind if we take a look?"

Perhaps in another setting, her request would have appeared suspicious, but it was perfectly natural for the kind of tour they were on. Toni said, "Of course," without batting an eye and turned right.

"It really is lovely," Ananke said a few minutes later.

In truth, she wouldn't be caught dead living here. While the homes did look well built and even upscale, the construction crews seemed to have been working from only five basic blueprints, creating a cookie-cutter neighborhood.

62

Ananke's least favorite kind.

As Toni droned on about the benefits of the area, Ananke searched the addresses until she spotted Patterson's place. Big for one person, but Patterson was a CFO, and at the lower prices in the area, she could have probably bought a home twice the size. Patterson had chosen blueprint No. 3, a faux craftsman two-story, painted medium gray with white and turquois trim. The only thing setting it apart from most of the other No. 3s was that Patterson's garage sat to the left of the house, not the right.

No car in the driveway or out front, but someone clearly had been taking care of the yard, because even with the new spring growth, everything looked trimmed and clean. A gardener service seemed a fair bet, but it would be worth having Shinji check that out.

I wonder if she has a maid, too.

"If any of your employees prefers more privacy," the Realtor said, "there are plenty of properties outside of town with a little land and no neighbors for as far as they can see."

"I'm sure a few will be interested in that."

"I could take you out that way now if you'd like, so you can get a feel for what I mean."

Ananke pretended to consider the suggestion. "Actually, what I'd love to see is…" She paused, as if trying to recall something. "I believe it's called Green Hills Estates? For our CEO, of course. I understand that might be an appropriate location."

Toni's eyes lit up at the potential commission for one of the high-end properties. "It absolutely would be. Be happy to show you that."

SINCE ROSARIO KNEW it would be the simpler task, she tackled checking out Officer Harris first.

The M on the woman's name tag stood for Morgan. She was thirty-two, and—except for a four-year stint in the army right out of high school—was a lifetime resident of Bradbury. Her parents had owned a hardware shop downtown that went bankrupt five years before the local tech boom took hold.

Patterson's father had taken odd jobs after that, and been seriously injured operating a forklift. After surgery, he obtained an infection that, two weeks later, claimed his life.

Young Morgan took a job at the local grocery store to help her mother out, and when she finished high school, joined the military and regularly sent a large chunk of her earnings home. When she returned to Bradbury, she moved back in with her mother and the two had lived together until the elder Patterson passed away two years earlier from cancer.

Officer Harris's military service records told of a competent soldier with plenty of commendations and no mentions of disciplinary actions or even minor trouble. After her service ended, she applied to the Bradbury police department, and was sent to a six-month academy program in Seattle. Since that time, she'd been one of the twenty-three officers on the Bradbury PD payroll. The first year, she filled in where needed, but since then had served almost exclusively on the graveyard shift. Her financial records showed her debts were contained to a $35,000 balance on the house she inherited, and about $500 due on a single credit card.

The only other items Rosario discovered were a handful of mentions in the local paper over the years. Nothing character revealing, just participation in this or that event, and the occasional appearance in the "Police Blotter" column as a responding officer.

All this boiled down to Harris being a competent public servant who had taken care of her mother until the woman died. Rosario knew Ananke would have liked more, but short of talking to anyone who knew Harris, this was all she'd get for now. Rosario didn't think Ananke would want her nosing around that much yet.

Rosario turned her attention to Natasha Patterson's phone.

She used a program that rendered her own phone number untraceable, and called Patterson's cell. Straight to voice mail. She went online and employed a well-used hack to get into the phone carrier's system. Sure enough, the phone was not currently connected to any network. Which usually meant it was either off or out of range of any cell towers.

Rosario set up a bug that would alert her the moment the phone reconnected. She then navigated to the company's records and found those for Patterson's number. The last tower contact was at 8:07 p.m. on April 5. After that, the phone was off the system.

The last call had occurred at 7:23 p.m. Reverse lookup revealed the receiving number belonged to Brian Patterson. The name was the same as the missing woman's brother. Rosario checked the address and confirmed the number belonged to him. The call had lasted for twelve minutes. Corresponding cell-tower information indicated Tasha Patterson had remained within an area covered by a single tower. Rosario coordinated that with a map of Bradbury, and confirmed the tower's zone included Tasha Patterson's house.

Rosario returned to the main records screen. Thirty-two minutes after the call to Brian Patterson ended at 7:35 p.m., the phone disconnected from the network and had not connected again. Rosario would have to dig a little deeper.

Getting into the company's raw data wasn't as easy, but soon enough she was awash in a sea of numbers that made no sense to the naked eye. She brought up a programmable computer worm she'd used under similar circumstances, modified it for her current needs, and sent it into the jumble of information to pull out what she wanted. It ran for eleven minutes before displaying the message it was done. Rosario opened the spreadsheet it had created and raised an eyebrow.

She had set the parameters to collect data on Patterson's phone from six hours before 8:07 p.m. to six hours after. As expected, there was a full list of tower check-ins and data use throughout the afternoon and early evening of April 5. What *shouldn't* have been there was any additional data after the cut-off time. And yet, there was data all the way up to 9:57 p.m.

She readjusted the parameters to cover the timespan from 9:57 p.m. on the fifth until a minute ago. This time the routine finished in only a few minutes. No spreadsheet was created because there was no information.

While Patterson's phone had definitely gone off network on April 5, it had happened nearly two hours after the processed records indicated. Which meant those records had been manipulated to cover up the true time.

She jumped back into the real records, to check on the phone's location for the phantom time. From 8:08 onward, Patterson's cell had moved progressively from one tower to the next. Given the number of zones covered and the distance between them, the woman must have been in a vehicle.

Rosario built a map from the data that showed Patterson heading northeast out of town on the highway for twenty miles, at which point she had stayed in a single zone for fifty-two minutes. After that, the phone headed north again, going an additional thirty-three miles before it abruptly stopped registering.

She brought up a satellite image of the area where the signal stopped.

"Huh," she muttered.

The last zone extended over the eastern half of the only bridge to cross the Columbia River between Bradbury and the Canadian border.

According to the raw data, the phone had been within the tower's operating sphere a bit longer than it had been in each of the previous five towers. Had Patterson switched it off and gone north to Canada? Or maybe west, eventually to Seattle?

Or maybe she jumped off the bridge.

The Administrator had not indicated the woman might be suicidal but it couldn't be ruled out. Rosario found photos of the bridge from several angles. It was high, but with the increased levels spring runoff would bring, not high enough to guarantee death unless a jumper aimed for the pilings. But that would not go unnoticed. Especially not for two weeks.

She searched for mentions of recent bridge suicides, but there were none. The last reported suicide attempt happened seven years ago, and the would-be jumper was talked out of it.

She checked for reports of bodies that had been found in the river between the bridge and the Coulee Dam to the south. There were more of these than jumpers, but not many. And again, none in the past few months.

Okay, she likely didn't jump from the bridge or get thrown over. Then why did her phone go off right there?

As Rosario considered the different possibilities, her phone rang. She picked it up, assuming Ananke was calling, but Ricky's name glowed on the display.

"What?" she asked.

"Hello to you, too."

"I am busy."

"And I'm not. I'm just sitting here in my room watching reruns of Judge Judy. A person can only watch her deal with these imbeciles for so long. I tried calling Ananke but she didn't answer. I thought maybe you could use some help. Ricky's here. Ricky should be doing something."

"Sorry to disappoint you. You are going to have to wait for Ananke. I really—"

"Rosario, for all that is holy! I'm finally off the boat and I gotta stay in this *room*? I can't do that! It'll drive me crazy."

"You were only on the boat for a few days."

"You're missing the point. You gotta have something I can do. *Anything.* Please!"

Rosario was about to tell him no again, but then an idea hit her, one she was sure Ananke would approve. "There actually might be something. How would you like to go for a ride?"

"A ride. Yes! I love that idea. Where?"

She gave him the location of the bridge and told him about the woman's phone. "Have a look around. If she jumped, then she would have left her car around there somewhere."

"You think she killed herself?"

"Unlikely but still a possibility."

"So you're sending me on a wild goose chase."

"I am sending you to investigate a lead. Or would you rather continue watching your Judge Judy?"

"Whoa, not complaining. Just making an observation. Count me in. What kind of car does she drive?"

Rosario consulted the information sheet Ananke had texted her. "A Prius. Light blue, 2016." She gave him the license number.

"Thanks, Rosy. Don't you worry about a thing. Ricky's

on the job!"

RICKY VOWED TO buy the Administrator a beer the next time he saw him, for hooking Ricky up with the motorcycle. It was a Yamaha SCR 950. Not a Harley but still a sweet ride, with a nice retro feel. Really, though, any bike would have been fine. To feel the motor between his legs...man, there was nothing like it.

He had to fight the urge to let the thing fly after he rolled out of the hotel parking lot, but while he was still in Bradbury, he had to play it cool. Once he reached the countryside, he let her rip.

The road snaked northward between the river on his left and the tree-filled hills on his right. There were few other vehicles on the road. He couldn't have asked for a more beautiful trip.

It took him forty-three minutes to reach the guardrail-lined ramp leading up to the bridge. The crossing was half trestle, half whatever the hell engineers called open air, with the latter being the side covered by the last cell tower to register Patterson's phone.

If the woman had jumped, there were plenty of spots to choose from. And if traffic had been as light then as it was now, she could have made her leap without anyone seeing.

Upon reaching the other end of the bridge, Ricky U-turned and headed back across. This time instead of driving all the way to the end, he stopped where the trestle and open sections met, and parked as far to the side as he could.

He stepped over a short guardrail onto a narrow walkway used by pedestrians wanting to cross. Along the outer edge of the bridge was a nearly continuous waist-high metal barrier. The only breaks came from parapets that flanked the bridge, one on each side, both sticking out three feet over the river. They were located right at the point where the two sections met. Solid concrete walls, same height as the barrier, on three sides, leaving only the sides facing the road open.

Ricky stepped onto the parapet nearest him and looked down. With the water rushing by below, this would have been a lovely place from which to take one's swan dive. He glanced at the east bank, thinking there was a good chance the cell tower's coverage reached this far.

Though he didn't expect to find anything, he spent a few moments looking around for signs that someone had been there recently, and then crossed to the parapet on the other side. He found nothing of value.

He remounted the bike and headed back to land. At the near end of Northport, he stopped at a restaurant and ordered the barbeque ribs and onion rings, hoping they wouldn't insult his taste buds. He was foolish to worry.

"How was the meal?" the waitress asked when she came to clear his dishes.

"If I'm being honest, I'd have to say your ribs have shoved their way into my top ten best-ever list."

"Not number one?"

"It's a pretty tough list."

When she finished picking up everything, she asked, "Can I interest you in some pie?"

"Don't tempt me. Just the check, please."

"Your loss."

She returned a few moments later with the bill.

He handed her more than enough cash to cover it. "Keep the change."

"Why, thank you. You have yourself a good day."

"Before you go, can I ask you a question?"

She smirked as if waiting for him to say exactly that. "Sorry, buddy. Married."

"You've broken my heart. But that actually wasn't my question."

She looked at him, waiting.

"If someone left a car parked around here for a week or two, what would happen to it?"

"You left a car here?"

"Not me. A friend. He was supposed to pick it up a week ago, but you know, things happened. Told him I'd check on it since I was heading this way."

"Oh, well, um…" The side of her mouth scrunched up. "If

no one reported it, I would think it would still be where he left it."

"And if someone had?"

"I don't know. Sheriff, I guess. There's a substation in the middle of town. You might try there."

"Thanks for your help."

He drove around the area, searching for a light blue Prius. He came across three of the hybrids, but none was the right color. He checked the plates anyway, in case the color info had been wrong. No match.

He did a drive-by of the sheriff's station, too. No Priuses in the lot. It could have been moved to a larger, countywide holding area, but he doubted it. In that case, it would be in the system and the Administrator would have been alerted. Ricky's hunter senses were telling him the car had never been left here. The most likely scenario was that Patterson—or someone—had tossed her mobile out a car's window as it drove across the bridge.

He reported his findings to Rosario and headed back south.

A MIDDLE-AGED Caucasian guard stepped from the hut at the entrance to Green Hills Estates, and leaned down to look into the sedan.

"Mrs. Mahoney. Good to see you," he said.

"Good afternoon, Joseph. Wondering if you could let us in for a little look around?"

Joseph noticed Ananke. The tightening of the muscles in his face was subtle, but Ananke picked up on it immediately. She'd experienced that look so many times she'd lost count. It was like he wanted to say, "What is *she* doing here?"

The joys of a world still peppered with ignorance and stupidity.

She beamed a smile and gave him a friendly wave, just to make him feel a little more uncomfortable.

"Um, of course, Mrs. Mahoney," Joseph said, flustered. "Let me get the gate for you."

As they drove in, Ananke stared at the guard, her friendly

smile morphing into an I'm-on-to-you glare only he could see. From the increasing discomfort on his face, her message was received.

"There are twenty-nine lots in the estates," Toni said, blissfully unaware of Ananke and Joseph's silent exchange. "The smallest are three acres, the largest over twenty. At this point, less than half the lots have homes." She switched to her sharing-a-secret whisper. "It's not cheap to buy in here, but that's what keeps it exclusive."

The road wound around a hill and dipped into a partially wooded valley, hidden from the highway. Ananke could see four mansions spread across the valley to the right, and the signs of several others scattered among the trees straight out and to the left.

"When I was a kid, this all belonged to the Lindens' farm. You see that pond over there?" Toni pointed way off to the left, where a small body of water sparkled in the daylight. "I was friends with Jenny Linden, and she'd throw swimming parties there in the summer. So much fun."

"Things look like they've changed a lot since then."

Toni laughed. "That's putting it mildly. When Scolareon moved here, I don't think anyone realized what was going to happen."

"They were the first?"

"Not quite the first, but they were the biggest to relocate here. They've grown even more since then. Mr. Scudder employs over three hundred people now. Back then it was probably a third of that. He's also helped the town entice several other companies to move here. You see that smoke?" She pointed at a thin column rising above the trees. "That's Mr. Scudder's house. Did I mention that he'll be at the meet-and-greet tomorrow night?"

"You said it was a possibility."

"Oh, I'm sure he'll be there. He never misses that kind of thing. It's going to be a really fun evening."

"I'm sure it is."

Toni drove them around Green Hills, pointing out the different houses, though more often than not, the only thing visible was a long driveway, a few of which were gated. Ananke nodded and commented as required.

As they headed up the hill back toward the main gate, Toni said, "And that's Green Hills Estates. What did you think?"

"It's beautiful."

"Do you think your CEO would be happy here?"

"I think anyone would be happy here."

"I couldn't have said that better myself. Anywhere else specific you'd like to check out?"

Ananke made a show of looking at the time on her phone. "Actually, I need to be heading back to the hotel. I have a conference call soon and some other work to deal with."

"Of course. We can finish the tour next time you're available."

"That works for me."

The gate opened before they reached it. As they drove out, Ananke looked at the guard hut, but Asshole Joseph remained hidden inside.

EIGHT

THE CHARTERED JET landed on a private runway fifty-one miles northeast of Bradbury, seven miles south of the Canadian border.

Three Range Rovers and a pickup truck waited next to the automated weather station that provided information for the few flights that used the field. When the plane came to a stop, the vehicles pulled up to its side.

Six passengers disembarked, all strangers to each other. Due to the nature of their trip, conversations on the flight had been basically nonexistent, a pattern of similar flights filled with other strangers.

A young man stood near the base of the stairs and directed each passenger to one of the waiting Range Rovers, while two other men loaded luggage into the bed of the pickup. The drive to the lodge took twenty minutes, and by the time the building came into view, the sun had set and stars had filled the sky.

The lodge was three stories tall and large enough to house at least fifty guests. From its pitched roof rose five chimneys. The place had the look of a quaint mountain hotel one might escape to for a weekend away from the city.

The SUVs stopped under a portico, and the same young man who'd been at the plane directed the guests to the main entrance. The ornate double doors opened onto a large room, two stories high. A fireplace roaring with flames sat in the center of the room. Facing it were several soft leather couches and chairs arranged in two arcs. A second-floor balcony stretched across the room, reachable at either end by a spiral staircase. There were several doors off the big room and a hallway to the left.

The new arrivals were the only people present.

"Hello?" the first man who entered said. He had made millions in Eastern Europe by cheaply converting old buildings into apartment complexes, and then renting them out at exorbitant rates. As for his name, they had all been instructed to leave identifications behind before boarding the flight in New York. They would be given temporary identities for the duration of their stay.

Another man, the second youngest in the group and heir to a large clothing company, spotted a bar beyond the arc of chairs and headed over to it.

When two of the others realized where he was going, they followed. Both were older than the heir, but their money was newer. One had struck it rich by playing the market, while the other had earned his cash from a growing network of fast-food franchises in the American Southeast.

The heir poured himself a whiskey, neat, and offered to do the same for the other two men. The fast-food magnate accepted, while the investor preferred making himself a rum and Coke.

"Hello!" the slumlord repeated, cupping his hands around his mouth.

The final two men, the oldest and youngest of the group, decided they too wanted something to drink. The oldest man, barely in his sixties, was the retired founder of a budget airline that operated throughout the Mediterranean. He now enjoyed a life of leisure funded by the millions he'd earned from paying his employees shit. The youngest guy was a new breed of entrepreneur who had started and sold three different companies for insane profits before his twenty-ninth birthday. Their drinks of choice were a glass of cabernet and a bottle of water, respectively.

The slumlord finally decided to join the others.

"Someone should have been here to greet us," he said as the heir handed him a whisky on the rocks. "It is very rude."

"You're right," a female voice said behind him.

They turned en masse to find a beautiful woman with long brown hair smiling down at them from the second-floor balcony. She wore a green calf-length dress that matched her eyes, and could have been anywhere from twenty-three to thirty.

"I'd like to welcome you all to Stanhope Lodge. I apologize for the delay, and I do hope you can forgive me. The nature of our gathering, as I'm sure you can imagine, requires us to limit the amount of people involved. This occasionally means having to do double duty." She descended the stairs nearest the men. "Perhaps one of you would be kind enough to pour me a glass of pinot noir."

The only two who didn't immediately spring into action were the retired airline CEO and the slumlord. Of the others, the heir won the day, laying his hand on the correct bottle before the others spotted it.

"Thank you," she said as he fulfilled her request. Glass in hand, she said, "Gentlemen, if you will please have a seat."

After the guests made themselves comfortable, the woman stepped in front of the hearth and faced them.

"We are so glad you are finally here." She walked over to the mantel and removed several envelopes from inside a wooden box. "These contain keycards to your rooms and approved areas of the lodge. If you lose your card, contact me immediately. Failure to do so will result in a nonrefundable termination of your stay."

The slumlord opened his mouth to say something, but she lifted a finger to cut him off.

"I know you all have questions, but I ask that you refrain for now as most of your queries will be answered in due course." She walked over to the entrepreneur and handed him the top envelope. "You are Mr. Welles, and you will be staying in the Nyyrikki Suite. South wing, upstairs." She gestured toward the appropriate stairs. He started to stand, but she touched his shoulder. "Please wait until everyone is ready." She moved on to the slumlord. "You are Mr. Huston, and will be staying in the Rundas Suite." She pointed the way and moved on again.

She handed out the rest of the cards and revealed their temporary names—Mr. Ford, Mr. Hawks, Mr. Wise, and Mr.

Reed.

After the last envelope was distributed, she said, "You are free to go to your rooms and freshen up. But please return here within the hour and fix yourself another drink. I will collect you when dinner is ready."

"Where's Mr. Lean?" Ford, the fast-food king, asked. Mr. Lean, they had been told after their participation fees were received, was the name of their host.

"Mr. Lean will join us at the first trial."

"What do we call you?" the heir, now known as Reed, asked.

"I am Miss Riefenstahl."

NINE

THE BRAZEN DINER filled the ground floor of one of the historic brick buildings on Main Street. While its name implied it possessed an unconventional menu, the choices were standard fare—french dips, patty melts, grilled ham and cheese sandwiches, and the old standby chicken fried steak. The most exotic item was the Caesar salad, but from the look of the one a customer was chomping on a few booths away from Ananke and Rosario, it wasn't worth the risk.

Ananke settled for the tomato soup and a side of toast, while Rosario opted for the roasted chicken breast with rice and green beans. Neither option turned out to be particularly impressive.

As Ananke popped the last bit of toast in her mouth, the bell above the main entrance dinged.

"Oh, great," she muttered.

Rosario raised an eyebrow. "Ricky?"

Ananke shook her head. "Officer Harris."

In contrast to Ananke's disposition, Rosario's expression brightened. "Oh, really?"

The cop, dressed in jeans and a nice turquois top, paused just inside and scanned the room for an empty table. When her gaze landed on Ananke, one corner of her mouth ticked up, and she started walking again.

Ananke groaned and said, her lips barely moving, "I think she's coming over here."

"Why?"

"How the hell should I know?"

Ananke tracked Harris's approach from the corner of her eye, and waited until the woman reached their booth before looking directly at her.

"Well, Officer Harris, what an unexpected pleasure. What brings you here?"

"It's dinnertime."

At that moment, Ananke and Rosario's waitress walked by. "Evening, Morgan," the woman said. "What'll it be tonight?"

"I'm thinking chicken fried steak."

"Spinach and onion rings?"

"You know me too well."

The waitress smiled and walked off.

"Sounds like you eat here a lot," Ananke said.

"Every night. Pre-shift ritual."

"Everybody's got to have a thing, right? Is there something I can help you with, Officer?"

Harris made a show of glancing down at her clothes. "I'm not in uniform. You can call me Morgan."

"Is there something I can help you with, *Morgan*?"

"I just thought I'd check to make sure you didn't have any problems finding your hotel."

"I would have thought you knew that already. I mean, since you followed me all the way there."

A small smile. "We try to be a full-service department."

"Is that so?"

Harris glanced at Rosario and then back at Ananke. "Are you going to introduce me to your friend?"

"I wasn't planning on it."

Harris held her hand out to Rosario. "I'm Morgan."

Rosario shook it. "Caroline."

"A pleasure to meet you, Caroline. So, what brings you ladies to our little town?"

"You part of the official greeting committee?" Ananke asked, forcing a smile.

"Just a local wanting to make sure you're enjoying your stay."

"We are. Thanks." Ananke stared at Harris, making it clear she wasn't going to add anything else.

Harris held her gaze for a moment before saying, "I'll let

you get back to your meal, then. Enjoy your evening."

"Appreciate that...Morgan," Ananke said.

Harris tilted her head and walked toward an empty table across the room.

"Can you believe her?" Ananke said as she watched the cop go.

"The pictures of her online didn't do her justice. She is stunning."

"Who cares what she looks like? I don't like the fact she seems a little too interested in us."

"Maybe she has a crush on you."

"Very funny."

"What's funny?" Rosario glanced over at Harris's table. "I would be flattered if she had a crush on me."

"Just...hurry up and finish. We've got things to do."

THE BIG ITEM on Ananke and Rosario's post-dinner agenda was getting a look inside Natasha Patterson's house. For this task, they needed Ricky's help.

Ananke called him as they were making their way back to the hotel. After she'd explained his role, he said, "What do you mean I don't get to go inside?"

"We need eyes on the street. That's you."

"*Booor*ing."

"I hope so."

"Come on, hon, you're wasting my talents."

She let the *hon* go without comment. As far as Ricky's terms of endearment went, it was the least offensive. "Ricky. Do you want to do the job, or do you want to go back to the ship?"

"Fine. If the boss wants to waste Ricky's talents, then Ricky will waste his talents."

"Good. I'm happy to hear that. Now get moving."

"Yes, ma'am."

ANANKE AND ROSARIO remained at the hotel until Ricky reported all the lights had gone off in the houses surrounding Patterson's place. They then set out on foot, passing behind the business district, crossing the high school baseball field, and finally hiking through the woods that separated old town from the housing development.

Patterson's home on Cloud Drive was near the middle of the tract. As best they could, they avoided the spill of streetlamps by creeping over front lawns, down alleys, and through the occasional backyard. By 10:27 p.m., they were in the alley behind the missing woman's home.

Ananke activated her comm. "Ricky, how's it looking?"

"I hate to tell you this, but there's an entire SWAT team surrounding the house, just waiting for you to make a wrong move."

"*Ricky.*"

He snickered. "I haven't seen a damn thing for almost half an hour. See, *boring.* Seriously, I'm dying out here."

"If only we could be so lucky."

"Funny."

Ananke peeked over the fence, confirmed everything was clear before she and Rosario climbed into Patterson's backyard. Crouching next to the flower bed lining the fence, they listened for anything indicating they'd been seen. All remained quiet.

Ananke led the way to a raised wooden deck attached to the back of the house, stopping at the base of the steps leading up. She scanned the home for signs of life, but everything was dark. Using her phone's camera, she zoomed in through one of the French doors. The only things she could see were the shadowy shapes of furniture. She lowered her phone and moved her finger toward the button that would turn the screen off, but before she pressed it, the cell's glow glinted off something on one of the steps.

She knelt down for a closer look.

Well, lookie here.

She motioned to Rosario and pointed out what she'd found. Rosario leaned in and then looked at Ananke, her eyebrows raised.

Thin monofilaments stretched half an inch above the center of each step, ensuring that even if someone skipped a step or two on the way up, he or she would still step on one of the thin lines, leaving behind evidence someone had been there.

Ananke checked under the steps in case the filaments were connected to silent alarms or, God forbid, explosives. They weren't.

Had Patterson been worried about intruders and put the traps there herself? That seemed pretty paranoid, not to mention out of character, for a typical CFO. But Ananke could think of no other reason.

With the stairs a no-go, she and Rosario climbed over the deck's railing and made their way carefully to the house. Ananke checked the French doors for any additional security devices but they were clean. She signaled for Rosario to do her thing, and waited while her colleague used a wand attached to her cell phone to scan for an alarm system.

When Rosario finished, she whispered, "She has one, but nothing too fancy. Doors and windows. Four motion detectors. And two interior cameras. This will not take long." She tapped on her phone for half a minute and then slipped it into her pocket. "Disabled."

Ananke dealt with the locks herself before easing the door open. Not a sound from inside. They moved across the threshold and shut the door.

"We're in," she reported over the comm.

"I and the empty streets surrounding you rejoice in your accomplishment," Ricky said.

The first order of business involved checking the entire house to confirm no one else was present, which they accomplished in under two minutes.

Task two, a more thorough search.

They started on the ground floor. A chef's kitchen, a sunken living room, dining room with a table large enough to seat twelve, and a plus-sized family room. Every item in each room had its place, with nothing extraneous lying around. Patterson clearly possessed a meticulous mind. The only thing that seemed off was the thin layer of dust everywhere. No maid service, then. Either that or service had been suspended for the last couple of weeks.

They checked drawers and cabinets but found nothing of interest, so they moved to the second floor. Four generous-sized bedrooms and an open area that served as an upstairs living room took up the entire space.

Their first stop was the master suite. Like the rooms on the ground floor, the bedroom was uncluttered and orderly. A look through the walk-in closet gave Ananke a sense of the woman's style—hip while a bit conservative. Patterson apparently enjoyed taking advantage of the local outdoor lifestyle because among the shoes sat two pairs of hiking boots—one brand new, the other with well-worn soles. No signs of any male clothes, so if Patterson was seeing someone, the relationship hadn't reached the leave-things-at-the-other-person's-place stage.

She checked the hamper. It was nearly filled, all with women's clothing.

Two of the other bedrooms were set up for guests, while the final one had been turned into a home office. They quickly dealt with the guest rooms and moved on to the office, knowing it would take more time.

After searching through the desk drawers and checking the closet, Rosario said, "There is a modem and a Wi-Fi router but no computer. Unless you've seen one somewhere else?"

Ananke shook her head. "Maybe she only uses a laptop and took it with her."

"Look at the desk," Rosario said. "The whole center area is open."

"Plenty of people use laptops and keep their desks clear."

Rosario knelt in front of the desk and checked underneath. "There is a power strip attached to the side. Very difficult to plug and unplug. Better to plug in once and leave it."

"Which again doesn't rule out a laptop. She could have multiple cords."

"Then where is the one she would have left here?"

"There's no cord?"

"I did not say that." Rosario slapped the female end of a white extension cord on top of the desk. "There is no *laptop* cord, but there is this one for a desktop machine."

"You knew that already, didn't you?"

Rosario shrugged. "Perhaps."

Ananke rolled her eyes. "Fine. So we have a computer cord without a computer."

"Yes."

"Do you know what type of machine it's for?"

"Not from this," Rosario said, lifting the cord a few inches. "It is generic. But when we get back to the hotel, I can use the modem's serial number to figure out what kind of machine accessed the internet from here."

Ananke looked around the room. Something else was bothering her. Patterson was in upper management of a tech firm that had relationships with companies around the country. There must've been deals going on all the time. Deals that needed the input of the company's CFO. It seemed likely for Patterson to be called upon to travel now and then. But—

"Have you seen any luggage?"

Rosario cocked her head. "No, I have not."

"If she went somewhere, she would have taken it with her. Maybe she took her computer, too."

"A desktop computer? It seems unlikely."

"But possible."

"I suppose."

"You finish looking around in here. I'll check the garage."

RICKY SCANNED THE neighborhood through his binoculars. The streets were as quiet and uninteresting as they'd been the other fifty times he checked.

Country towns, man. Early to bed and early to rise and all that crap. How can anyone live this way?

He was a big-city boy. An action guy. Bradbury was small-town USA and light on the action.

He lowered the glasses and shivered. His perch was on the second story of a house under construction, a couple of blocks from where Ananke and Rosario were. Being on a slight rise, it provided an excellent view of the area. What it did *not* provide was protection from the quickly descending nighttime temperature. He could not wait until this little foray was completed so he could go somewhere warm.

A flash of light to his right drew his attention. A car had turned off the highway into the development. Someone coming home late from work probably. He raised the binoculars, and smiled.

"Now we're talking."

The vehicle was no late-night worker bee cruising home in her hybrid. It was a police sedan.

It turned down the first cross street it came to, slow and steady. An officer on his beat.

Nice to see Mr. Law doing his job.

Ricky followed the sedan as it zigzagged through the neighborhood. When it neared Cloud Drive, he flicked on his comm.

"Ricky for Ananke."

ROSARIO THUMBED THROUGH the hanging files in one of the desk drawers. They were in alphabetical order—bank, gas company, sewage and water, etc. Old school. These days most people ditched hard copies for digital records in the cloud, if they kept copies at all.

She glanced in each file to make sure the contents corresponded to the folder's label. As she closed the drawer, she heard a very subtle *thuck.*

Being a master thief, Rosario recognized the sound right away. She opened the drawer again and pulled it all the way out of the desk. She reached into the vacated space and felt along the underside of the drawer above. Taped against it at the very back was an envelope, with a corner hanging down no more than an inch where the tape holding it had come loose. This flap had caused the noise when she closed the lower drawer.

She peeled the envelope free. It was about the length and width of a paperback book, and contained something maybe half an inch thick. She unclasped the flap and tilted the envelope, slid out a small Moleskine notebook.

What do we have here?

She pulled off the elastic band holding the cover in place and opened the notebook. The first seven pages contained dates followed by two columns. The first column held numbers ranging from one to seven, while the second contained twelve-character strings of letters and digits. The strings were repeated several times throughout the seven pages, but never in succession. Beyond these pages, the book was blank.

Rosario slipped it into her pocket. If it was important enough to hide, it was important enough for a closer look.

She picked up the drawer to slip it back in place as Ricky's voice came over the comm.

THOUGH NO VEHICLES currently occupied Patterson's garage, it possessed enough space to house two large cars, and that was even taking into consideration the wall of shelves that ran down the far side. Clearly labeled plastic storage bins filled most of the shelf space, while the rest was taken up by items too big or odd in size to fit in a container. Notably among these loose items were several suitcases.

Given Patterson's pattern of keeping things in order, Ananke would have expected to see an empty spot among the bags if the woman had taken one on a trip. But the suitcases took up all their allotted spaces. Right next to them were two tubs, one labeled SMALL BAGS and the other MEDIUM BAGS. She found each was filled to the brim, with no room for anything else.

Of course, none of this precluded Patterson from having used a suitcase or bag she'd kept in the house, but Ananke didn't get that sense. Everything had its place, and there had been no obvious storage location inside for a travel bag. If Ananke was right, the logical conclusion was that Patterson had not intended to be gone for any length of time.

She headed back toward the door into the house.

"Ricky for Ananke."

"Go for Ananke."

"Hey, boss, just thought you'd like to know there's a police car heading your way."

"I'm not in the mood for jokes, Ricky."

"No joke this time."

She paused. "How far?"

"I'd say it'll be turning onto your street in about fifteen seconds. So a block away, maybe."

Ananke raced back into the house. "What the hell, Ricky? What happened to a little heads-up?"

"Isn't that what I just gave you?"

"Son of a—"

"Relax," Ricky said, chuckling. "I said he's heading your way, not *heading your way*."

"What the hell does that mean?" she said, hurrying through the kitchen.

"He's patrolling the neighborhood, that's all. Nothing to get all freaked out about."

She stopped in her tracks. "I swear to God, Ricky. One of these days, I'm going to drop you down a deep, dark well and walk away."

"I will help," Rosario said as she stepped off the stairs onto the first floor.

"Got you running, didn't—"

Silence.

"Ricky?" Ananke said.

Another beat passed before he said, "We may have a problem."

"Define problem."

"The cop stopped in front of your house."

Both Ananke's and Rosario's gazes shot toward the front, but from where they were, the home's layout provided no direct line of sight to the street. Crouching, they hurried through the dining area into the sunken living room, and hunkered down by the sheer curtains covering the front windows.

The squad car was parked at the curb, headlights on.

"Are you sure we didn't trip an alarm?" Ananke asked Rosario.

"I am positive."

Ananke stared at the car. If the police had known Patterson was missing, they'd understandably send someone by her house every now and then, but unless the Administrator had been misinformed, the police had no idea there was a problem. So why the hell was one of their cars here?

The sedan's lights went out and the driver's door opened.
Oh, crap.

"Um, I think the cop's getting out," Ricky said.

"Yeah, we can see that."

Ananke figured if she and Rosario left at that very moment, they had about a fifty-fifty chance to make it over the rear fence without the officer seeing them. But that would mean not relocking the deadbolt or resetting the alarm, which would be even clearer signs than a tripped monofilament that someone had broken in. The safer play was to stay hidden inside.

The officer rounded the front of his car and started walking toward the house. At least he appeared to be alone. Ananke assumed he would turn down the stone path to the front door, but instead, he headed toward the garage and disappeared from sight.

"Go watch the rear," she said to Rosario.

With a nod, Rosario returned to the back of the house.

"Ricky, do you still have him?" Ananke asked.

"Yeah. He's looking at the garage door. Wait, he just crouched down at the west side."

"What's he doing?"

"I can't tell. His back is to me." A pause. "Okay, he's standing again…heading toward the front."

A light beam streaked across the stone walkway.

Ananke lowered herself as far as she could while still being able to see through the window. The officer came into view a moment later, his light turning him into more of a silhouette than before. When he reached the short set of stairs leading up to the small front porch, he squatted and played his beam along the first step.

The light bounced off the gray stone and illuminated the cop's face, causing Ananke to groan.

Not a male cop. Officer Harris.

After a few seconds, Harris stood and leaped over the steps onto the porch. Ananke quickly crawled away from the window and moved behind the couch, tucking herself up against it. She half expected to hear a key slip into the lock and the door open, but neither occurred. She heard nothing at all until Ricky said, "Anyone near the front window, hide now!"

Three seconds later a light shined inside and swept through the living room. Ananke pressed against the sofa, and watched the beam cut back and forth several times before disappearing.

"Status," she whispered.

"He's off the porch," Ricky reported.

"Not a he, Ricky."

"What? Really? Well, *she's* heading around the right side of the house. Hold on…she's opening the backyard gate. I'm going to lose her in a second."

Ananke hurried to the rear of the house and joined Rosario. From their hidden spot, they could see the deck and the grass area near the back fence.

The flashlight beam shot through the yard a moment before Harris walked into view. The cop played her light over the grass and approached the deck. When she reached the steps, she did the same thing she'd done out front—crouched and studied them.

Son of a bitch.

The monofilaments. Harris was checking them. Ananke was willing to bet another set had been strung across the front porch steps, and probably a third attached to the garage door.

Either Harris had put them there, or she worked with whoever had.

Not the police department, though. Stringing monofilaments was not standard policy for even the most advanced forces, so there was no way little old Bradbury's department would employ such methods. Besides, if they thought Patterson was missing, they'd be a lot more overt in their efforts to find her. A rogue officer involved in the woman's disappearance made much better sense. If Ananke had been that person, she would have wanted to know if anyone was snooping around her victim's house. Of course, Ananke would have used much more sophisticated methods, such as cameras and hidden microphones.

Officer Harris, you have moved to the very top of my persons of interest list.

When the officer stood back up, she shined her flashlight across the deck. Apparently satisfied, she went back the way she'd come and disappeared.

As soon as Ricky announced she had driven off, Ananke and Rosario left.

AFTER THEY ARRIVED back at the hotel, Rosario showed Ananke the notebook she'd found.

Ananke looked over the chart on the first several pages. "Maybe the right column is a personal code for a particular event or action, and the left one is…how many times that action occurred?"

"That is as good a guess as any. If you give me a little time, I can try to figure it out."

Ananke handed the book back with a nod. "Patterson's computer first. That's priority. Then the book. Better yet, shoot some pictures of it and send it off to Shinji. I'm sure he's dying for something to do."

While Rosario set to work, Ananke grabbed her own computer to write up a list of what they knew so far, and see if that would spur some other ideas. As the machine was booting up, Ricky called.

"I'm back," he said. "What's next?"

"Nothing else tonight. Get some rest."

"It's barely eleven p.m. There must be *something*."

"Go to sleep, Ricky."

"Why would I—"

She hung up.

"Just so you know, I checked the kit and there is more than enough sedative to keep him unconscious for the whole job," Rosario said.

"Don't tempt me."

THOUGH RICKY HAD been granted his release from Crestridge Federal Prison when he agreed to join the Administrator's team, he wasn't exactly free. Granted, detention on the *Karas Evonus* was considerably better than his days at Crestridge. On the ship, there was a video arcade, satellite TV, a private deck for lounging around, and a kitchen that served food a million times better than the crap the feds gave him.

But he was still in confinement. He couldn't even try to sneak off the boat. His new employers had injected him with subdermal tracking bugs that allowed them to always know exactly where he was. Anytime he came within a couple dozen feet of the gangplank, one of the ship's security personnel would appear to remind him it would be healthier to find somewhere else to loiter. Now that he was off the ship on another mission, there was no way he would go to sleep yet.

He was sure Ananke would be fine with him going out for a bit, but to be safe, he walked the motorcycle a block from the hotel before firing up its distinctive motor.

With the chilly wind rushing past him, he drove to a place he'd seen called the Blue River Bar, not far from the Brazen Diner. Though the sign had been turned off, he didn't give it much thought, until he walked up to the door and found it locked.

"Are you kidding me?"

Did the state of Washington have some sort of draconian law about alcohol-serving time? That didn't seem possible. Not in the twenty-first century. He figured the bar hadn't been busy enough to stay open tonight. What else could it be?

Their loss.

Bradbury might be small, but it wasn't *that* small. Surely someplace else would still be open. And, come on, was Ricky supposed to believe that a town with a sizable community of tech nerds didn't have, at the very least, a fancy cocktail place that served into the wee hours?

He googled *bars near me*, then gawked at the results. Within twenty-five miles of where he was, there were only five entries.

At the top of the list was Blue River. Weekday hours 11:00 a.m. to 10:30 p.m.

What a waste of real estate.

Another place, Max's, was also closed. It was more a bar and grill, off the highway just south of town. Of the three bars supposedly still open, only two were within city limits—the

Bradbury Brewery and the Cache Bar.

Ricky could imagine the décor of the latter—motherboards and floppy disks hanging from the ceiling, and portraits of Bill Gates and Steve Jobs on the walls. Definitely a location of last resort.

The Bradbury Brewery it was.

He found the place on the east side, in an old converted barn. A handful of cars sat in the lot and the lights still blazed inside. Feeling a sense of sweet relief, Ricky parked his bike as close to the entrance as he could and sauntered inside.

Three rows of picnic tables filled half the space. The other half was cut off by a serving bar running across the room, behind which lived the metal tanks and other accoutrements of the brewing business. It was a surprisingly large operation, making Ricky think they were likely selling beer up and down the river. Probably even had visions of breaking out nationwide.

Three hipster types manned the bar—a guy with a substantial beard and shaved head, and two girls sporting tattoo-sleeved arms. Spread out among the tables were several groups, most made up of twenty- and thirtysomethings. Scattered among them were gatherings of slightly older folks sharing a beer and a laugh.

"Evening," the female bartender with the darker hair said as Ricky approached. "What can I get you?"

"Evening to you, too," he said, flashing his Ricky grin. "Let me see."

He examined the beer list hanging behind her. Stouts, lagers, a double IPA, a hefeweizen, even a Belgian farmhouse. As impressive as the list was, its abundance of styles made him pause. Brewing was an art, each variety taking time to perfect. He questioned if this place had been in business long enough to create acceptable versions of all they were selling.

"Can I get a taster of the hef?"

"Of course."

She bopped over to the taps, poured a little of the wheat beer into a small glass, and escorted it back.

"Not bad," he said after a sip. It was not the best ever, but better than he'd expected. "I'll take a pint."

She poured him a glass and he paid with a ten, telling her to keep the change. That earned him a playful look that, were he not on a job, he'd have been tempted to investigate later.

Being about as far from an introvert as one could possibly get, Ricky took a seat between a group of youngsters and a couple of guys probably in their early forties, in hopes of working his way into one of the conversations.

The two guys were the first to look over when he plopped down. He raised his glass, but they didn't take the cue and returned to whatever it was they were talking about.

To hell with you, too, Ricky thought as he took a drink.

He turned his attention to the others, but they didn't seem to notice him at all.

Fine. Whatever. At least I'm out enjoying a beer and—

"I don't care," one of the older guys who'd blown off Ricky said, his voice suddenly loud.

"Relax," his friend whispered harshly.

Ricky listened in.

"I can't do this again," the first guy said.

"We have an obligation."

"You do it, then. I'm done."

"You can't just back out. You know they're not going to like that."

"Watch me." The I'm-done guy drained his glass and stood up. "Let's get out of here."

His friend rose and they walked out.

Small-town drama. A couple of aging computer geeks tired of pretending to be Nigerian princes, maybe.

When he snickered, one of the twentysomethings looked over.

Ricky smiled and said, "Any of you know a good place in this town to get a decent breakfast?"

Food. The ultimate conversation starter.

Ricky and his new friends talked until closing, and by the time he laid his head on his pillow, he had almost—but not quite—forgotten about the I'm-done guy and his friend.

Ten

The Next Morning
New York City to Washington State

DYLAN FOUND LIESEL already waiting at the JFK airport departure gate for their flight to Seattle. It had been only a few days since the team was last together, but he was still happy to see her.

Though he didn't want to admit it, working with the others probably meant more to him than any of them. As a driver/courier for hire, he conducted the majority of his work alone. It was nice to be part of a group he could count on. And even though they hadn't spent that much time together, he liked everyone. Well, the jury was still out on Ricky, but Dylan could tolerate him well enough.

"How was home?" he asked Liesel after a hug.

"Quiet," she said, in her brevity-of-words way. "How was Dublin?"

"Excellent, thanks. Dropped in on my family and surprised them." He patted his stomach. "Ate too much, I think."

On the plane, they sat together near the front. Liesel spent much of the flight sleeping, while Dylan watched a replay of an old Champions League football match on the tiny TV mounted in front of him.

In Seattle, they boarded a smaller plane for the flight east to Spokane. Upon arrival, they found their promised sedan waiting in the parking lot. In one of the bags in the trunk, they found their mission information packets, which included identifications for one Carl Lyne—American citizen originally from Cork, Ireland—and Andrea Kraus, a Swiss national. The biographies explained that Andrea, a novelist, was on a research trip to the Pacific Northwest for her next book, and Lyne, the publisher's representative, was assisting her. The other bags contained tools of the trade.

"Perhaps I should sit in the back," Liesel said.

"Why?"

"I am not sure Andrea Kraus is the kind of person to sit next to the help."

She reached for the back door.

"Don't you dare open that," Dylan said. "You're up front with me."

She allowed herself a small grin. "I suppose Andrea might make an exception. This time."

"Your kindness knows no bounds."

During the drive to Bradbury, Liesel read aloud from the mission brief so that Dylan would be as up to date as she was. When she finished, he said, "Missing woman that no one realizes is missing. Even money she ran off with a lover."

Liesel looked back through the pages. "There is no mention of a lover."

"Oh, sweet, innocent Liesel, there's always a lover."

"You are incorrect. I do not have a lover. And neither do you."

"And how would you be knowing that?"

She looked him up and down. "I know."

The fact she was right *and* was so sure about it annoyed him.

Sixty miles from Bradbury, traffic slowed to a crawl, and not long after that, it stopped. Dylan angled the sedan to see around the RV two vehicles in front of them, but all this revealed was the crest of a hill a hundred yards ahead. And more cars.

Five minutes passed with no movement on their side, and no cars coming from the other direction.

"I'll be right back," Dylan said and opened his door.

"Where are you going?"

"To see if I can figure out what's going on. Do me a favor,

if things start moving again before I get back, get behind the wheel and drive for a bit."

He hopped out before she could say no, and started up the slope.

His hike apparently signaled to other drivers it was okay for them to do the same. Before Dylan reached the top of the hill, half a dozen people were following him.

After cresting the summit and seeing the road ahead, he cursed under his breath.

The line of motionless vehicles stretched down the other side of the hill and into a large grove of pines. About a quarter mile farther on, among the trees, a dying pillar of smoke rose into the sky. If it had been a forest fire, the fire department had done a bang-up job of putting it out before it spread. More likely it had been a car.

A few minutes later, as the last of the smoke dissipated, cars in the opposite lane began moving out of the woods. Dylan counted twenty of them before the trickle stopped, and the vehicles in his lane, nearest the trees, started inching forward. The authorities were letting traffic through in alternating groups.

Dylan was back in the driver's seat in plenty of time to join the slow progress toward the woods. It took almost twenty minutes for Liesel and him to reach the front of the line. As they waited for the twenty cars coming from the other direction to pass, Dylan got his first good look at the problem.

Not a car fire, but a truck. A big rig, with a cargo trailer hitched to the back. The fire had consumed both trailer and tractor, collapsing the trailer into blackened slag, and turning the truck's cab into a charred ghost of its former self.

There were four fire engines, five state police cruisers, and two ambulances parked nearby. Since the ambulances were still there, Dylan guessed whoever they'd been intended to transport had either gotten out in time or were beyond help.

Death by fire. Dylan cringed.

He'd take losing his life by freezing over fire any day of the week. He'd take almost anything over fire, expect maybe drowning. Even then it would be a close call.

When they were finally allowed to drive on, he mouthed a prayer for the potentially departed and then increased speed.

Less than an hour later, they were in Bradbury.

ANANKE AND ROSARIO were in Ananke's room, both on their computers, when Liesel called and let them know she and Dylan had arrived.

The Administrator had arranged for the novelist and her assistant to stay in a rental house with a view of the river, two miles from the hotel. Liesel reported there was a back way onto the property that would allow the others to visit without anyone in the area seeing them.

"We'll be right over," Ananke said.

Before leaving, she called Ricky.

"Huh? What?" he said.

"Are you still asleep?"

"Oh, hey, bab—uh, Ananke. I was just, uh, lounging."

"You were sleeping."

"I, uh, might have dozed off. But what does it matter? It's not like you've given me anything to do."

"Well, I'm giving you something now." She relayed the instructions on how to get to Liesel and Dylan's house. "Be there in twenty. And bring drinks."

"Beer?"

"Water. Fruit juice. Maybe some iced tea."

"That doesn't sound like fun."

"It's not supposed to be fun, Ricky. Get moving."

She hung up.

THE RENTAL HOUSE sat on a large lot in an area of other large homes on large lots, spread across a bluff overlooking the Columbia River.

As instructed, Ananke and Rosario parked inside a work shed on the adjoining property. A path through the bushes led them to a hidden gate that opened into a trellis-covered passageway, which took them to the back deck of the house.

"Welcome to Casa de Artisa," Dylan said, standing in the threshold of an open sliding glass door.

The women greeted him with hugs, and then did the same with Liesel, who was standing just inside.

"Smooth journey?" Ananke asked.

"No problems for me," Dylan replied.

"Same," Liesel said.

"What do you mean, Casa de Artisa?" Rosario asked.

Dylan pointed at the living room wall, where old metal letters had been mounted, spelling out the phrase. "There's a lot of art on the walls, too. Seems to be a theme." He paused before adding, "Some of it's not that good, to be honest."

They sat around the large dining table, and Ananke and Rosario began bringing the other two up to speed. They had just finished describing their nighttime visit to Natasha Patterson's home when a buzzer sounded.

"The back gate is wired," Liesel explained. "Ricky must be here."

A few moments later, they heard steps on the back deck. Dylan pulled open the door and in walked Ricky, carrying an overstuffed cloth shopping bag.

"Morning, gang!" Ricky said. "Cool clubhouse." He walked over to the table and set the bag down. "I've got drinks."

"Put them all in the refrigerator," Ananke said.

"Bad enough I had to lug all this over on my motorcycle, and now you're going to make me put it away, too?"

"*Ricky.*"

"Again, not complaining. Just making an observation."

He carried the bag into the kitchen.

"Were you able to figure out the columns in the notebook?" Liesel asked, refocusing the conversation on where Ananke and Rosario had left off.

"Shinji's still working on that," Ananke said.

"What about her computer?" Dylan asked.

"That, we do know," Rosario said. "She had a top-of-the-line Dell Inspiron. That means monitor *and* tower."

"Not something you'd likely take with you on a whim," Ananke said.

Ricky strolled back into the room. "So, what are we

talking about?" He took a sip from the can he was carrying.

"What is that?" Ananke asked.

"Margarita in a can."

"You're *drinking*?"

He looked at her as if she were talking crazy. "Of course I'm drinking. I'm thirsty."

"Are you serious?"

"Hold on there, boss." He turned the can toward her and tapped the label. "Nonalcoholic."

Dylan looked as if he was going to be sick. "That sounds even worse."

"Anybody else want one? I got a six-pack."

Ananke took a deep breath. "Just sit."

"All right. You can serve yourselves." Ricky took the empty chair next to Liesel. "Hey, sunshine."

"My name is Liesel."

"Isn't that what I said?"

Ananke finished describing the rest of what they'd been doing, then said, "There are a ton of outstanding questions. What I'm hoping is that we can answer a lot of them today. Schedule-wise, Rosario and I have the mixer this evening that the city's sponsoring. My understanding is that there should be some important people in attendance, including Natasha's boss, Kyle Scudder."

"Ooh, that sounds fun," Ricky said. "Maybe it would be a good idea to have another pair of eyes there."

"Exactly what I was thinking."

Ricky leaned back, smiling smugly.

"I'll talk to the Administrator," Ananke said. "See if he can arrange for Liesel and Dylan to be invited."

Ricky went from self-satisfied to put out in a second flat. "Wait. What?"

"They have a good backstory. No one will question their presence."

"But-but I don't have a backstory. Just a stupid alias." Rudy Schmidt.

"Which makes you more flexible."

"All right. Good. Flexible isn't bad. What am I supposed

to do while you are all having fun?"

"What you do best. Hunt. I need you out there looking for Patterson, or anything unusual. In fact, that goes for everyone. Keep your eyes and ears open for anything weird in case there actually is something larger going on here."

"Do we have any new intel on Patterson?" Ricky asked.

"Rosario has created a map of her cell trail on the night she disappeared. I want you to check everywhere she went."

"You mean I get to ride around again?"

"You get to ride around again."

"See, if you'd told me that from the beginning, I'd have been fine."

"I will send you the information," Rosario said.

"Thank you, darling."

"Ricky," Ananke said.

"What? Oh, thank you, Rosy."

"*Ricky!*"

He took a breath. "Thank you, *Rosario*. Man, you guys are so uptight sometimes."

"So, are we to just wait around until the party?" Dylan asked.

"I've got something to keep you busy, too," Ananke said. "Scolareon gives tours every afternoon at one. You two are supposed to be here doing research. Go research."

ELEVEN

THE BIG RIG'S engine whined as it downshifted, sending a jolt through the trailer that earned cries of surprise from several of its occupants.

Eduardo felt Sonya stiffen as she jerked awake. "It's okay," he whispered.

A few moments passed before he felt her relax. "Are we stopping?" she asked. She had told him she was eighteen, which would make her two years his junior, but he suspected she was younger than that.

"I think so."

They'd been inside the metal box for two days and had stopped several times but never for long, and not once had the back door opened.

Eduardo didn't know how he got inside the trailer, but he recalled the events leading up to it. Jobs had been hard to come by as of late, and he'd taken to joining the dayworkers that hung out at the parking lot entrance to The Home Depot. A guy in a pickup had come looking for help clearing junk from a property and had picked Eduardo out of the crowd.

As they drove off, the guy—he introduced himself as Mr. King—asked Eduardo about his day, about the type of work he'd been getting, about where he liked to eat. They talked about family, too, Mr. King saying Eduardo was lucky he hadn't started one yet, that all his possibilities were still open. Then Mr. King asked if Eduardo was thirsty and nodded at the small chest between them, telling Eduardo to grab a bottle of water.

It had been a warm morning and he'd been standing around for hours, so Eduardo took a deep drink. He remembered feeling dizzy but nothing after that until he woke here.

There were five others with him—three men and two women. They'd been locked inside with three large ice chests that had been full of food and water when they started out, but were now getting close to empty. Against the wall was a chemical toilet booth, like ones at construction sites where Eduardo had worked. It probably stank to high heaven, but he couldn't tell anymore.

He hadn't known any of the others when he'd woken to find himself here. There had been a little talking at first, but no one knew where they were going, only that it couldn't be anywhere good. After that, most kept to themselves. When Eduardo heard Sonya crying that first night, he'd gone to her and held her and told her everything would be all right.

"What time is it?" she asked now.

"Not sure." The inside of the trailer was pitch-dark, though from the warmth radiating off the metal side he was propped up against, it must've been daytime. "Are you thirsty?"

"No. I'm okay."

He uncapped his water bottle and moved it to where he thought her hands were. "Take a little. You need to keep drinking."

A beat, then, "Okay."

He held on to the bottle until he was sure she had control of it, then he leaned back.

After she took a sip, she asked for the millionth time, "Where do you think they're taking us?"

And for the millionth time, he said, "I don't know."

The truck continued to slow. When it finally stopped, Eduardo could hear voices outside.

He wanted to scream and pound on the walls in hopes of getting help, but a voice over a speaker had warned them early on if they did anything to draw attention to the truck, the punishment would be severe and shared by all.

A few moments later, he heard the clink of a nozzle being put into a fuel tank.

Wherever they were headed, they apparently still had a ways to go.

TWELVE

USING ROSARIO'S MAP, Ricky started his hunt at the entrance to Patterson's housing tract and headed north, out of town.

Most of the data indicated she'd made steady progress all the way to the bridge. There was, however, an area about thirty miles past Bradbury where Patterson had remained within the confines of a single-cell town for nearly an hour. Could be she was visiting a friend, or having dinner at a café. Whatever the case, it was Ricky's job to figure it out.

Upon entering the zone in question, he slowed but did not stop until he reached the far end of the tower's range. No cafés or businesses or anything of that nature. Not along the main highway, anyway. There were several roads leading away from the highway—four along the west side, and seven along the east. Of these, only five were paved.

Ricky grinned. Options made a hunt fun.

Heading back the way he'd come, he turned down the first road on his right, one of the dirt ones. Scattered along it were a few homes set within the trees. Ricky stopped just long enough near each driveway to snag a quick, stealth picture of its mailbox, as all had addresses on them and most had names, too. Rosario could cross-check them against people who they knew had interacted with Patterson.

The next right turn off the highway—another dirt road— was a private driveway. He snapped another mailbox photo and moved on.

After exploring a few more streets, he had yet to come across a single business, and was beginning to think Patterson must have stopped at a house. It was the easiest explanation for why she'd remained in the area so long.

The next dirt road—on the east side—started off as more of the same, but soon he realized it was longer than the others. As he neared what he guessed was the outer edge of the cell tower's reach, he spotted another dirt road, heading north into the woods. It was wider than the other driveways, and had no mailbox standing sentry at the end.

He turned onto it, but kept his speed down so that the engine was only a low rumble. The route curled through the woods, right and left and right again. He came around this last bend, and let the bike roll to a stop.

A guard shack with an attached gate blocked the road thirty feet ahead. Standing just outside the shack was a man in a security uniform, his hand dangling very close to the pistol on his belt.

Ricky smiled broadly and said, "Howdy!"

Not moving, and definitely not smiling, the guard shouted back, "Sir, you're going to have to turn around and go back the other way. This is private property."

"What?"

"You need to turn—"

"Hold on, hold on. I can't hear you." Ricky revved the bike and glided it forward.

The guard tensed, his hand touching his weapon now.

Ricky stopped several feet away. "Sorry about that." He gestured toward his ears. "Too many rock concerts, know what I mean?" He let out a laugh. "Now, what did you say?"

"This is private property. You need to turn around and leave."

"Really? Well, that makes sense, doesn't it? I was wondering where the hell I was. My buddy Zander, he's terrible at giving directions. You wouldn't happen to know where I'd find the backroad to Harmony Creek, would you?"

"No idea. You need to leave now, sir."

"Bummer. Well, it was worth the ask." Ricky craned his neck and looked past the guard, as if there was something to see. There wasn't. "Some rich guy live back there?"

"Sir, I'm not going to ask you again."

"All right. I'm out of here. No need to go all gestapo on

me." Ricky wheeled his bike around. Before taking off, he looked back and said, "For someone who gets to sit in a beautiful place like this, you're awfully uptight."

He hit the gas and headed back the other way.

When he reached the main dirt road, he took it until he was sure he'd gone far enough for the guard not to hear his bike anymore. He made a U-turn, and drove back toward the turnoff as far as he thought he could without being detected. He turned off the engine and maneuvered the bike back into the trees, where it wouldn't be seen by anyone driving by.

He left his helmet on the seat and set off through the woods toward the guarded property.

In addition to the guard's aggression, Ricky had noticed something else that was odd.

The guardhouse hadn't been built on a permanent foundation, but sat on a leveled pad of dirt. *Fresh* dirt, that is. As a hunter, Ricky was trained to pick out those kinds of details, and the dirt hadn't looked weathered enough to have been exposed to open air for more than a week or two. Which meant the guardhouse had likely been erected *after* Patterson disappeared. This led to Ricky wondering if the two events were connected, which in turn led to a desire for a covert look around.

Once he caught sight of the guardhouse, he used his phone's camera to zoom past the trees and see through the side window. Mr. Aggressive was sitting in a chair, watching television. There were at least two monitors. The angle allowed Ricky to see only the screen of one and a sliver of a second. On the monitor he could see was a view of the intersection where the guarded road met the main dirt road. No wonder the asshole had been waiting outside his hut when Ricky turned the corner.

Ricky moved through the woods, passed the guard shack, all the way to where the trees stopped. Using a trunk as cover, he peered into the meadow beyond. About five yards away stood a fence that encircled the entire clearing. The cordoned-off area enclosed a construction site. Ricky could see the topsoil had been removed, and the exposed dirt had been leveled off. The cleared area was easily three football fields wide. Dotting this field in parallel lines were round, concrete pillars sticking maybe a foot and a half out of the ground. Each pillar had a metal bracket secured to the top.

Ricky had no idea what kind of building was being constructed. It certainly didn't look like the start of any he'd ever seen before. Call him crazy, but it appeared the structure would be supported on the pillars, like in a flood zone. Only this couldn't be a flood plain. If the Columbia ever rose this high, the whole planet would be screwed.

A rectangular building sat on the other side of the fence, about two dozen yards to Ricky's right. It was one of those mobile home-type offices used on construction sites. Like the rest of the site, it appeared to be deserted. Not surprising, given it was a Saturday.

Check that. Almost *deserted.*

A golf cart moved from behind a stack of building materials at the far side of the meadow, and continued slowly along the interior of the fence.

Ricky used his phone's camera again to get a better look. Even with the zoom, the cart was too far away for him to make out much, but Ricky had no doubt the driver was wearing a uniform identical to that of the guard at the gate.

Ricky conducted a more thorough camera scan of the site, checking for other guards, but it appeared there were only the two men. He lowered his phone. So, was this where Patterson had stopped?

Though whatever was being built here looked unusual, the construction site didn't seem particularly nefarious. He crept as close as he dared to the fence, and looked for anything that might indicate who owned the site, but there wasn't even a NO TRESSPASSING sign hanging on the chain link.

Stymied, he turned back to the woods, but went only a few steps before an idea hit him. He looked back and swore under his breath.

Jesus, Ricky. You're losing your touch.

What would one do with a large open field filled with rows and rows of stubby pillars topped with brackets?

Mount something on them.

What company did Patterson work for?

Scolareon.

And what business was Scolareon in?

Solar power.

What Ricky was looking at had to be the beginnings of a solar energy collection farm. He should have realized that right off. And if this was Scolareon's property, then the chances Patterson had come there just skyrocketed to ninety-nine percent.

Okay, but why*?*

Patterson was the company's CFO, so it seemed unlikely she was inspecting the construction. The site's plans and papers and that kind of stuff, though? That might fall under her responsibility. And where would that stuff be kept?

Inside the trailer.

Or she could have come here to meet someone, Ananke's voice said in his head. Why was it always her voice that came up with the good ideas?

Okay, either meet someone, or check something in the trailer.

What if it was both? Perhaps she met someone and together they did something in the trailer. Maybe she was having an affair, and it had been discovered, and—

"Slow down there, champ," he whispered. His imagination was getting a little too wild.

The trailer was the important thing. Something inside might help them find Patterson. As much as he wanted to hop the fence and break in, there was way too much daylight. Better if done under the cover of dark. And with someone watching his back.

He returned to his bike and phoned Ananke. When she didn't answer, he called Rosario.

"Where's the boss?" he asked.

"Busy. Did you find anything?"

"Ricky always finds something."

LIESEL AND DYLAN arrived at Scolareon fifteen minutes prior to the advertised tour start time. The receptionist directed them to a corner of the large lobby where three others—a man and two women, all over seventy—waited.

"Taking the tour, too?" the man asked.

"That, we are," Dylan said.

The man's eyes lit up. "Irish?"

"I am."

"Me, too. My grandfather came over from Dublin around the turn of the century."

"Is that so?" Dylan said. This was by no means his first trip to the States, and he'd come to realize almost everyone here believed they were Irish to some extent.

"I love Ireland," one of the women said. "Spent a wonderful three days in Cork." She turned to the other lady. "When was that?"

After a short pause, the other woman said, "Ninety-five. No, ninety-four."

"Right, ninety-four. Just lovely."

"I'm partial to it myself," Dylan said.

"Are you here on vacation?"

Dylan was saved from reciting his made-up backstory by the arrival of a smiling man in his early twenties, clad in khakis and a tucked-in, light-green polo shirt with SCOLAREON embroidered over his right breast.

"Good afternoon," he said. "My name is Casey, and I'll be your tour guide today. How is everyone doing?"

Not surprisingly, everyone was doing fine.

"A couple of business items and then we'll get started. The tour will last approximately forty-five minutes, and will take in our production, testing, and distribution facilities. Depending on what's being worked on when we go through, there may be some areas that we will not be able to enter. If you have questions as we go along, please don't hesitate to ask. And one final note, please, no photography."

"Well, that sucks," one of the women grumbled.

The guide pretended not to hear, said, "Follow me, please," then led them across the lobby and through a set of double doors at the far end.

As Dylan held one of the doors open for the others to pass

through, he tapped a finger against the pocket of his pants, depressing the remote switch that activated a micro camera concealed in the messenger bag he carried. Now everywhere they went would be recorded on high-definition video.

Their first stop was a conference room, where the walls were decorated with pictures of Kyle Scudder shaking hands with or standing next to celebrities and politicians. Prominent among the latter group were pictures of him with each of the last three US presidents, two UK prime ministers, a long-serving prime minister of Germany, and the Chinese premier. There were also certificates and proclamations that had been bestowed either on Scudder or the company.

"Scolareon was founded twenty-three years ago, right after Kyle Scudder graduated from MIT," Casey informed them. "What began as a consulting firm focused on alternative energy eventually evolved into one of the prime players in the solar energy field." Casey went into a detailed history of how Scudder's firm grew and moved west, first to Seattle, and then here to Bradbury. "Scolareon has been at the forefront of advances in solar technology over the past decade, and with the introduction last year of the Scolareon roof tiles, we continue to lead the way into the future."

Dylan couldn't help himself. He raised a hand and said, "Didn't Elon Musk's people come up with that idea?"

Casey's smile tightened. "A common misperception. It was actually Kyle Scudder, long before Mr. Musk mentioned the subject."

"Is that so? Didn't know that."

"Now, if you'll follow me, we'll visit the production facility."

Casey seemed eager to get moving again, which made Dylan think there was more than a smidgen of bullshit to the guide's answer.

Not being allowed within the production facility itself, the tour group observed the hangar-sized room from an elevated, glassed-in walkway.

Below, a combination of machines and humans worked to create the roof tiles that would both collect the sun's energy and act as a barrier against the weather. The human workers all wore white jumpsuits and matching hoods that covered their hair. The getups reminded Dylan of pictures he'd seen of computer-chip manufacturing facilities. Or of *Breaking Bad*.

He stifled a laugh at the idea of the space below being one giant meth lab.

Liesel elbowed him.

"Sorry," he whispered.

As Casey droned on, describing what was happening on the production floor, Liesel jabbed Dylan again.

"What?" he said under his breath.

This time when he looked at her, she glanced toward the ceiling of the hangar. He followed her gaze.

Crisscrossing just below the ceiling was a series of catwalks. Above these, spread across the roof itself, were four man-sized hatches. Dylan casually adjusted the strap of his bag so that the camera could record it all.

A few minutes later, Casey escorted the tour group down a set of stairs into the testing area, a space about a quarter the size of the production room. It had been divvied up into several work areas, some of which were blocked off by large, portable dividers, keeping whatever was being worked on out of sight.

"This is where we create the future," Casey explained. "Our research scientists are tasked with thinking about what alternative energy will look like in twenty years, and thirty, and even fifty. In this way Scolareon will secure its place as a continuing leader in the industry." He went on to spin more corporate PR without really saying anything specific about the latest products.

When Casey finished his look-how-great-we-are speech, he led everyone outside to a couple of waiting golf carts. Behind the wheel of each was a driver dressed in khakis and a company shirt that matched the guide's.

"Please, everyone, hop on one of the vehicles and we'll head over to our east building," Casey said.

The older folks filled one, and Dylan, Liesel and Casey hopped on the other.

As the carts circled around the back of the manufacturing

110

building, they passed through a small parking area filled with high-end cars in spots that had placards identifying who parked where. Dylan turned the camera and recorded the license plates and placards.

The real payoff came as they went by the spot nearest the door into the building. The sign in front of it read:

KYLE SCUDDER

Parked in his spot was a silky black Lexus GS Hybrid. Sixty-five grand just for the base model. Nice to be the boss.

The carts wove through the main parking area and across the highway into the lot in front of the Scolareon building on the east side. It was a mirror image of the building they'd just toured. The inside, however, had been designed to serve as the company's product storage, packing, and shipping center. Nothing much of interest, as far as Dylan could see. Though there was one little nugget that came to light as they were leaving, when the old man said, "You make the shingles over there," and pointed across the highway.

"We refer to them as tiles," Casey corrected him with a smile.

"Tiles, sorry. You make them there, and you haul them across the highway over here to ship? Why didn't you just build a bigger building over there? Or at least put the two buildings next to each other?"

"I see you're bucking for a position on our board of directors," Casey said, reciting what sounded like a line he'd used a lot. "In truth, that was the plan, but we were unable to secure enough property on either side of the road. But let me correct one misperception. We don't haul the tiles across the highway. There's a tunnel that links the two buildings, and an automated conveyor system that moves them from one building to the other."

That bit of knowledge was worth the previous fifteen minutes of tedium.

At the end of the tour, Casey gave each of them a two-inch-square piece of roof tile, a refrigerator magnet that said

111

SCOLAREON • STAR POWERED, and a brochure for the company that included a coupon for ten percent off solar installation. He then guided them into a small but well stocked gift shop. While the older crowd perused the wares, Dylan and Liesel made their way back to their car.

AFTER THE PLANNING meeting at Casa de Artisa, Ananke transferred into her backpack several items from one of the bag of tricks that had been in Liesel and Dylan's car, then drove Rosario to the hotel.

"I should be back in an hour or so," she said before her friend climbed out of the Mustang. "Text me if anything important comes up."

"Of course."

Once Rosario was gone, Ananke headed into the center of town and parked a block from the police station. Before starting in on the task that had brought her there, she called the Administrator.

"Any progress?" he asked.

"We haven't found her yet, if that's what you're hoping. But it does look like you were right to be concerned. I don't think Patterson's off on some kind of self-discovery vacation." She briefed him on their investigation so far.

"Do you think this cop is involved?"

"Unsure, but we're looking into her."

"What about Scudder?"

"I'm hoping to meet him tonight. The Bradbury Business Association is throwing a mixer this evening for me. He and a lot of other local bigwigs are supposed to be there."

"I know. Who do you think put that idea into their head?"

"Good, then you can definitely help me out."

"What do you need?"

"Rosario's coming to the party with me, but it would be great if you could pull a few strings and get Liesel and Dylan invited, too. The more eyes and ears, the better."

"Easily done. I'll text you with confirmation as soon as I have it. Anything else?"

"That's it for now."

After hanging up, Ananke grabbed her backpack off the rear seat and set it on her lap. Inside were the rectangular plastic cases she'd taken from the gear bag. They were nearly identical, about an inch high by an inch wide by four long. Each contained a different type of bug—tracking, listening, combo. There were also variations on adhesion—sticky back, magnetic, none. A two-letter code etched into the lid on each box indicated which kind was inside.

Ananke removed several Easy-Follow tracking bugs with sticky backs from their container and climbed out of her car.

The city of Bradbury had obviously been undergoing rapid expansion due to the tech-industry invasion. Some parts had been handled more successfully than others. An example of the latter was the police station.

The building that served as the department's headquarters might have been fine back when Bradbury had been a sleepy river town, but it was clearly too small for the city's current needs. Three temporary buildings that looked not so temporary anymore had been erected in the parking lot, leaving only a handful of spaces, all of which were filled with squad cars. Several more police vehicles were parked along the street, and the nearby spaces they weren't using were filled with other vehicles that Ananke guessed belonged to departmental employees.

She strolled down the sidewalk like a person with somewhere to go but in no hurry to get there. She moved her gaze casually through the neighborhood, the way one would while walking down a street. In reality, Ananke took in everything—the satellite dishes on top of the temporary buildings, the three men who'd just entered the diner across the street, and the pair of police station cameras, one above the front entrance and the other watching over the parking lot. The one covering the lot was clearly a relic from the pre-tech-boom era, much of its view now blocked by one of the satellite dishes.

There was no one in the truncated parking lot, nor did she see anyone looking out any of the small windows on the temp structures. Seizing the opportunity, she veered into the lot as she pulled out four tracking chips, removed the plastic covering the sticky back from one of them, and adhered the chip under the apex of the back wheel well of the first cruiser she passed.

A glance around confirmed she was still alone, so she moved to the next vehicle and repeated the trick. In less than a minute, she had all four cars in the lot bugged. It was, perhaps, overkill. The only car she was really interested in was the one Office Harris would be using, but Ananke was covering her bases. Of course, knowing where the rest of the force was at any given moment could turn out to be a nice side benefit.

The three squad cars parked in front of the station were trickier. Too many directions someone could see her from, and weaving around the trio of vehicles might provoke curiosity. She did her walk-by-wheel-well trick on the nearest car, but instead of continuing to the next one, she headed across the street and went into the pharmacy on the corner.

There she purchased toothpaste and shampoo, and then crossed back to the station side of the street. This time she walked down the gap between the two cars she hadn't tagged, and was able to stick a tracker in the rear well of one, and the front of the other.

She looked up and down the road and confirmed she hadn't missed any of the cruisers. Of course, there were ones out on patrol, but she could take care of them later if necessary. She headed back to her car, task one accomplished.

Twelve minutes later, she was driving into the hills east of Bradbury. Here, homes were scattered between large open fields and copses of pines. At Merrick Road, she turned again and started checking address numbers on mailboxes, finally locating the one she was looking for a mile and a half in. She continued down the road a few hundred yards until she found a grass-covered road—if you could call it that—that passed between two fields and disappeared into a copse of pines.

After hiding the Mustang, she grabbed a handful of Easy-Trak/Eavesdroppers—combination bugs that could both track and listen in on conversations—hopped out of the car, and moved into the woods.

Officer Harris's house sat at the end of a hundred-foot driveway, surrounded by a well-manicured lawn. The exterior of the house was gray stone on the lower third, and dark red-stained wood on the rest.

Parked in front was a Ford C-Max hybrid hatchback. That was unexpected. Ananke had guessed Harris drove a truck or at the very least a muscle car. She knew that was stereotyping, but that was the vibe the cop had given her. Maybe the car wasn't Harris's. Could belong to a friend or a roommate.

Ananke moved as close as she could get without leaving the woods. Though no lights were on that she could see inside the house, there was enough sunlight for her to identify the kitchen and the living room through the windows along the back. Both appeared to be deserted.

Just as she'd hoped.

Harris worked the graveyard shift, and probably didn't come home until close to seven a.m. And it was likely she hadn't gone to sleep right away. Even in a small town like Bradbury, a job like Harris's would require some winding-down time. Since it was barely past one p.m., Harris had probably been asleep for only five hours at most. If Ananke had the woman's job, she wouldn't open her eyes until three or four in the afternoon. She figured she had at least another hour before Harris woke.

She checked the yard for signs of a dog. No toys scattered about, no doghouse. On top of that, the lawn was a uniform green. A dog would have turned areas brown from repeated urination. Unless, of course, the dog was trained to go out into the woods.

She used her binoculars to scrutinize the house. No cameras, just several floodlights with motion detectors that would be a problem only at night.

Deciding the risk was worth it, she crept out of the woods and across the lawn.

No barks. No sound of running paws.

When she reached the house, she peeked through the nearest window into the living room. As she suspected, it was currently unoccupied. She turned her ear to the glass. Quiet.

She moved along the side of the house and up to the front corner, from where she scanned the front yard and driveway.

The C-Max was the only car in sight, and there was no garage. Well, there *was*, but it had been converted into a room, the door replaced by a wall and small window.

She padded over to the car and peeked inside. A police hat sat in the passenger seat.

Seriously? This was Harris's ride?

That kind of pissed off Ananke. She hated that a) she was wrong, and b) she'd pigeon-holed the woman in the first place.

Stay on task, she reminded herself.

Suppressing her annoyance, she stuck a bug against the lower front corner of the windshield where it could use the window as an amplifier, but would be out of sight and out of the way of the wipers.

She returned to the house, placing bugs in spots where she was sure Harris wouldn't look anytime soon. She was at the back, placing a bug on the frame of the kitchen window where it would blend in, when the curtain on the other side of the glass shook.

She dropped below the window frame a beat before the curtains swung open. From inside, she heard someone moving around—Harris, presumably. When there was no shout of surprise or, worse, a get-on-your knees, hands-on-your-head order, Ananke eased along the wall to the chimney.

The big problem: all retreats to the woods were in view of a window. The moment the cop spotted Ananke, she'd recognize her. There weren't that many tall, African-American women hanging around Bradbury, after all.

As Ananke contemplated her nonexistent options, the sliding glass door at the back of the living room opened. She pressed against the wall. If not for the protruding fireplace between them, she would have been in plain sight. And that advantage would disappear if Harris took more than a couple of steps outside. Ananke slipped quickly to the corner of the house and swung around it.

There, she allowed herself a quick, relieved breath, before pulling out her phone and a goose-neck camera she'd picked up when she grabbed the bugs. She attached the plug side to her phone and eased the camera end around the corner. At first everything appeared as it had before, the small back deck, the empty green yard, and the not too distant forest in the background. Then Harris stepped away from the house. She wore a pair of gym shorts and a sports bra, and held a coffee mug that had steam rising from it.

There was no denying it. Officer Harris was in great shape. With abs like hers, she must do a million—

Ananke didn't realize Harris was turning in her direction until too late. Her animal instinct was to pull the camera back and take off running, but years of experience kicked in and she kept it still, knowing jerking it away would make it more visible.

Harris's gaze swept along the side of the house, and turned out toward the woods as she lifted her cup and took a drink. Half a minute later, she sauntered back inside.

When Ananke heard the strong, steady flow of a shower from the other side of the bathroom window, she hightailed it back to the trees.

After reaching the Mustang, she sat behind the wheel for a few moments, catching her breath. She was even more confused about Harris now than she'd been before. The woman wasn't fitting neatly into the box Ananke had begun to build for her.

Her phone buzzed with a text from the Administrator.

Two additional party invites secured.

THIRTEEN

"I'M TELLING YOU, we gotta get in there and take a look," Ricky said.

Not wanting to chance exposure from a second in-person team meeting so soon after the first, Ananke had everyone on a video group chat so they could fill one another in on what they'd discovered. Ricky had told them about his trip north, and the discovery of the solar farm construction site in the area Patterson had spent extra time in on the evening she disappeared. Rosario had confirmed the site belonged to Scolareon.

"I don't disagree with you, Ricky," Ananke said. "What I'm saying is that we don't have the manpower to do it right this minute."

"Who said anything about right this minute? I meant when it gets dark."

"Great. Then there's no problem. We'll do it after the party."

"Whoa, whoa, whoa, whoa, whoa. How long is this shindig supposed to run?"

"I have no idea. A couple hours, I guess. Maybe more."

"And when does it start?"

"Seven."

"Seven? It'll be dark not long after that. We'll be wasting time."

"It's a long night, Ricky. It'll be fine."

"How about this?" he said. "You all go to the party, have your fill of Vienna sausages on a stick and spiked punch, and then, about halfway through, cut someone free. Liesel, Dylan, Rosario—I don't care. Anyone will do."

"Did you just insult us?" Dylan said.

"It did sound like an insult," Rosario replied.

"Cool your jets, Justice League," Ricky said. "I wasn't insulting anyone. I was saying that you're all *equally* good."

"That is not what it sounded like," Liesel said.

"The *point* is," Ricky went on, "three of you can stay at your fancy party as late as you want. Hell, go to the afterparty if there is one. While you're having fun, I and whoever you choose to join me can do some real investigating. See? Best of both worlds."

"I'll consider it," Ananke said.

Ricky's eyes narrowed. "Is that an *I'll consider it and probably yes*, or *I'll consider it and probably no*?"

"It's *I'll consider it.*" A pause. "Probably."

THE MIXER WAS hosted by a company called Digital Paste Unlimited. According to the info Shinji sent them, Digital Paste had been founded eight years earlier by Devon Rally and Elijah Chan, two software engineers who'd met at the University of Washington. The company had been one of the first to relocate to Bradbury, even before Scolareon. Their core business had evolved from time management software to a suite of organizational apps for smart phones. According to Shinji, three of Digital Paste's apps were consistently in the top twenty-five best sellers in both Android and Apple stores, with several other apps not far behind.

Since the party was ostensibly being held for Ananke's benefit, she and Rosario arrived at seven o'clock on the dot. The Digital Paste building was located in a converted Quonset hut, an arched structure that looked like a giant pipe sticking halfway out of the ground. The length of the building was covered in polished corrugated metal, while the front was entirely tinted glass.

As Ananke and Rosario walked up to the door, Toni Mahoney burst outside, smiling. "Right on time! Thank you so much for coming."

She pulled Ananke into a hug.

"Thank you for, um, organizing this," Ananke said as the

woman kissed the air above her cheek. When they parted, Ananke turned to Rosario. "This is my assistant, Caroline Cruz. Caroline, Toni Mahoney."

"Caroline, it is a pleasure." Toni hugged and air kissed Rosario.

"Nice to meet you," Rosario said.

Toni slipped her arm through Ananke's. "Come, come. There are some folks here already I'd love for you to meet before it gets crowded."

"How many people are you expecting?" Ananke asked.

Almost squealing, Toni said, "It's going to be quite the turnout!"

She hustled them through the entrance into a swanky waiting area filled with purple crushed-velvet seats, and a circular reception desk behind which sat a young man whose smile spoke of too many cups of coffee.

"Welcome to Digital Paste," he said. "We are honored to have you here. If you need anything, please feel to ask me. I am here for you."

"Thank you, Chad," Toni said as she fast walked Ananke and Rosario past the desk. Once they were beyond the half wall that separated the front area from the rest of the building, she stage whispered, "He's new. *Gay*, I think. But we're fine with that here now."

Ananke whispered back, "How progressive of you."

"It is, isn't it?" Toni said sincerely.

They'd entered a giant room that continued all the way to the back of the building. The immediate area was filled by long tables divided into side-by-side computer stations. Along both sides of the room were private, box-like offices built against the curved walls.

The party was happening in the back of the building. Digital Paste's Fun Zone. That wasn't a name Ananke thought up. It was written in pulsating neon on a sign hanging from the ceiling.

As corny as the name sounded, Ananke couldn't really argue with the description. The whole area was a monument to distraction. Pool tables, pinball machines, video games, to start with. There was also a soft-serve ice cream machine, a popcorn maker (the big kind, like at movie theaters), a gourmet kitchen, and a full bar that clearly wasn't there just for the party. Seating-wise, there were couches covered in the same purple velvet as out front, and high round tables with leather stools surrounding them. To finish it all off, high-end speakers hung from the ceiling, pumping out "Alone" by EDM artist Marshmello.

"How does anyone get any work done?" Rosario whispered only loudly enough for Ananke to hear.

"You got me."

The sixteen people present stood in groups throughout the area. Almost everyone held a glass of wine or a pint of beer.

Toni slowed as she looked around, then increased her speed again, and, with renewed energy, tugged Ananke along as she whispered in her special voice, "I'll introduce you to the mayor first."

The group they approached consisted of three men and a woman, none over forty-five. The guy on the left with the pretty-boy looks seemed particularly interested in Ananke. His devilish smile intensified as he tried to lock eyes with her.

She wasn't playing his game, however. Not yet, anyway. Maybe once she knew who he was and determined if he had information she needed, she'd string him along. Sometimes— *most* times—men were so easy. For now, she pretended not to notice his extra attention.

"Sorry to interrupt," Toni said, clearly not sorry. "I want to introduce you all to our guest of honor. This is Shawn Ramey and her assistant, Caroline Cruz." She gestured to the prematurely balding man on the right. "Shawn, Caroline, this is Mayor Paulson."

"Call me Zach," he said, holding out a hand and flashing a career-politician-in-the-making smile.

Toni motioned at the other three and said, "And these are the brains behind Digital Paste. Megan Brooks, the chief…um…"

"COO," Brooks said. She shook hands with Ananke and Rosario.

"Right, right," Toni said with a laugh. "So many corporate titles to remember. And these two gentlemen are Elijah Chan and Devon Rally, the company founders and our hosts this evening."

"Pleasure to meet you," Chan said.

"Thanks for throwing this," Ananke replied.

Rally, the pretty boy, beamed another smile. "Shawn. I've always liked that name."

Oh, boy. Bad bar pickup lines right from the start.

"I'm partial to it," Ananke said.

They spent a few minutes making small talk—"Are you enjoying your visit?" "Where are you from?" "Quite a change from Texas, yes?"—before Toni said, "If you'll excuse us, there's a few others I'd like them to meet."

Rally made a point of shaking Ananke's hand again. "I hope we have some time to talk more before the evening's over. I would love to hear about your company."

"Talking's what I'm here for," she said. She looked at Chan. "Again, thank you for having us."

THIRTY MINUTES LATER, the place was packed with at least a hundred people, including Liesel and Dylan, who, per instructions, spent the initial part of their evening far from Ananke and Rosario.

Though Toni limited introducing Ananke and Rosario to the higher-ups of the companies in attendance, every time she left them on their own, software engineers and coding monkeys and the like-minded stumbled over one another to meet them. Most of these worker bees were employed right there at Digital Paste, but a few represented other companies, including Scolareon. While Ananke acted interested in the Scolareon employees' conversations, Rosario remotely hacked into their phones—cloning all their information and setting up the devices to be used as listening bugs if needed.

"Ah, there you are."

At first Ananke didn't realize the comment was meant for her, but then a hand moved in front of her, holding a glass filled with ice and amber liquid.

"I hope you like mai tais."

She glanced around.

Pretty boy. Of course.

"Love them," she said, taking the drink.

"Gentlemen, you don't mind if I borrow our guest, do you?" he said to Ananke's gaggle of admirers.

She had a feeling they did mind, but none protested when Rally led her away. "Sorry it took so long to rescue you. Didn't realize you'd gotten trapped over here."

"I didn't realize I needed rescuing."

He smiled as if he knew she was joking. "I thought I might give you a tour and we could talk. About business."

"Business."

"Isn't that what this party's for? Give you a sense of what it might be like to relocate to Bradbury?"

"So I've been told."

"Then I am here to answer any question you might have. *Any* question." The creep factor ratcheted up another notch.

Rally led her out of the Fun Zone and toward one of the boxy offices in the center of the building.

"We have a relatively simple operation. App development and support is mostly handled in the Bridge."

"The Bridge?"

He pointed to the big open area with the long tables. "It's what we call the common workspace."

"Cute."

Upon reaching the office, Rally paused. "When we started, it was just Elijah and me, coding in our tiny, one-bedroom apartment. I still can't believe how big we've become."

He turned and opened the door. "After you."

She held her ground. "And what's in there?"

"My office."

She stifled a snort. "I think I should probably be getting back to the party."

"But we haven't really talked yet. I want to hear all about your company. See if there's anything I can do to help convince you to move here."

"I never said *I* would be moving here."

His brow creased. "Isn't that why—"

"We're a big company."

"Is that so? How big?"

Interesting, she thought. For the first time, she detected his interest had moved beyond wanting to get into her pants.

"Big enough," she said.

A mischievous smile. "You, Shawn, are a tease."

She allowed her own smile to match his, and then she turned and walked back to the festivities.

As she weaved through the crowd, someone moved up beside her.

"What was that all about?" Rosario whispered.

"Exactly what you think."

"Please tell me he is not coming to your room later."

"If he does, you have my permission to come in and shoot us both."

"Good. He is maybe handsome, but there is something…" She gave up trying to find the word and just shivered.

"Slimy?"

"Yes, exactly."

"Shawn! Shawn, over here." Toni waved to them from near one of the pool tables.

She was with the mayor and several others, one of whom was in a uniform. Ananke and Rosario made their way over.

"Having fun?" Toni asked.

"A great time," Ananke said.

"I'm so glad to hear that! Now, I have a few more people I'd like to introduce you to. This is our police chief, Ronald Yates."

The man in uniform gave Ananke and Rosario a curt nod, but didn't extend a hand until Ananke did it first. Clearly he was uncomfortable with the setting or Ananke, maybe both.

She turned on the charm. "What a pleasure. Thank you so much for coming."

"Um, sure. No problem."

"And this," Toni said, gesturing to the man whose back had been to Ananke as she walked up, "is Kyle Scudder, CEO of Scolareon."

Ananke turned to him with the appropriate sense of awe. "It's an honor, sir. I'm a big fan of what you and your company are doing. Not only for the energy solutions you provide, but for what you've done here in Bradbury. The community you've fostered by your presence is something to be proud of."

He chuckled. "You make me sound like some kind of saint. I'm just someone who wants a nice place to raise my family. Turns out a lot of others want that, too."

"Don't sell yourself short, Kyle," the mayor said. "To a lot of us here, you *are* a saint."

"So, we're all curious," Scudder said. "What company do you represent?"

The corner of Ananke's mouth ticked up playfully. "I'd be curious, too, if I were you. But I'm sure you can understand that until we formally decide where we'll be moving, we'd like to keep our name confidential. It's actually a board mandate."

"Makes it hard to offer any specific advice without some idea of what you're planning on doing here."

"What I can say is that our operation will be closer in size to yours than this place." She gestured at the building they were in. "But I can also say we're not one of your competitors."

"Even if you were, I wouldn't worry."

They talked about the benefits and drawbacks of working so far from a large city, and about what made Bradbury special. Twice during the conversation, Ananke's phone buzzed with a text but she ignored it.

Not long after eight p.m., a young woman approached the group and said to Scudder, "Sir, it's time."

He looked at his watch. "Wow, that went fast." He turned to Ananke and Rosario. "I apologize, but I need to return to the office."

"A CEO's day is never done," Ananke said.

"I have a feeling those words will be written on my tombstone. If you have any question you think I could help with, feel free to contact me." He pulled a card out of his wallet and handed it to her. "That's my cell number. I'm the only one who answers it."

If Pretty Boy had been the one to give her the card, it would have been done in an obvious attempt to hook up. But she received no such vibe from Scudder.

"Thank you," she said. "I appreciate it."

To both her and Rosario, he said, "Enjoy your evening."

As he and the woman started to leave, Chief Yates said, "I'll walk out with you. Ladies, good night."

And then there were only Ananke, Rosario, and Toni.

"I'm glad you had a chance to talk with Mr. Scudder," Toni said. "No matter how he downplays it, he's truly a hero here."

"I get that sense."

"I don't want to imagine what this town would have been like if he hadn't—" Her eyes suddenly widened as her gaze strayed past Ananke. Excited, she said, "Have you met the author yet?"

"Author?"

"We have a bona fide *New York Times* best-selling author at the party."

Ananke followed the woman's gaze, playing dumb. "Where is he?"

"Not he, she. That Asian lady over there." She leaned toward Ananke and whispered, "She's a foreigner."

"But she lives in Bradbury?"

"Oh, no. She's here on a research trip, I believe. Her publisher called the chamber of commerce, wondering if there were any events at which she could meet some of the locals. I didn't think it would be a problem for her join us." She paused. "Her last name is Kraus, I believe. Um…Andrea Kraus. The truth is, I don't read much so I haven't heard of her. Not a very Asian name, though, is it? Kraus?" This last was said, as Ananke had come to expect, in a hushed voice. "You should meet her." Raising her voice, she called, "Ms. Kraus! Ms. Kraus!"

When Liesel looked up, Toni waved her over.

"I HATE PARTIES," Liesel said, after she and Dylan had been escorted to where the party was held.

126

"You were a bodyguard," he said. "You must have gone to hundreds of them."

"Exactly why I do not like them. You have no real control in this kind of crowd. Everyone is extra friendly, even if you do not know them. Lots of close talking, bumping into each other. Too many chances for something to happen."

"Relax. You're not on bodyguard duty tonight. Have some food and a drink. Maybe two drinks. Enjoy yourself a little bit."

"We are not here to enjoy ourselves."

"Oh, for God's sake. We do need to *pretend* we're enjoying ourselves. You can at least do that, can't you?"

"It is what I am doing."

He snorted. "You're funnier than anyone gives you credit for, you know that? Because right now, you look like you're headed to a funeral."

"I do?"

"You do."

Her face relaxed a little. "Is this better?"

"Now it looks like you're going to apply for a loan. But I guess that's an improvement."

They met Toni Mahoney early on in their wanderings. Dylan had to work hard not to comment on the rhyming of her name. It was so ripe for the picking.

After that, they mainly tried to listen in on conversations for anything that might be useful. They picked up a few tidbits here and there, but nothing earth-shattering. Mostly it was general stuff on the local tech industry and life in Bradbury. Their eavesdropping came to a crashing halt when a group of programmers introduced themselves and went wide-eyed at Dylan's Irish accent.

Toni Mahoney calling out Liesel's fake name provided them with an excuse to extricate themselves from Dylan's group of admirers. But when he saw she was with Ananke and Rosario, he said, "Weren't we not supposed to mix?"

"I do not think we have much of a choice," Liesel said.

"MS. KRAUS," TONI said as Liesel and Dylan walked up. "I'd like you to meet our guest of honor. This is Shawn Ramey and her colleague, Caroline Cruz. Shawn, Caroline, this is the novelist Andrea Kraus and...I'm sorry, I forgot your name."

"Carl Lyne," Dylan said.

"That's right. Carl Lyne. He's with her publisher."

"It's nice to meet both of you," Ananke said. As they shook hands, her phone vibrated. Then again. And again. Annoyed, she pulled it out. "I apologize. I need to check this."

"Of course," Dylan said.

Ananke walked a few feet away and activated her screen. There were eight texts, all from Ricky.

First text:

> Sun's starting to go down.

Second text:

> I'm ready to go whenever.

Third:

> Is the party really THAT interesting?

Fourth:

> I'm starting to go stir crazy.
> Just thought you'd like to know.

Fifth through eighth:

> You can't possibly still need everyone there.

> I just need one person.
> Just send me one, I know you can.

> For the love of God, release me
> from this static torture!

> Too dramatic? Then give me

someone to work with. PLEASE!

Ananke stuffed the phone back into her pocket and returned to the others.

"Everything all right?" Toni asked.

"Just an associate who needs a little hand-holding now and then."

"Oh, I know what that's like," Toni said with a fake laugh.

I doubt you do, Ananke thought, but said, "I'll have one of my associates deal with him." When Toni wasn't looking, Ananke caught Dylan's eye and flicked her gaze toward the exit, then asked Liesel, "So, what kind of novels do you write?"

"Mysteries."

"I love a good mystery."

Dylan glanced at his phone. "My apologies, Ms. Kraus, I didn't realize how late it was. I have some work I need to do tonight."

"Then I guess it's time for us to leave," Liesel said.

"Already?" Toni said.

"I don't want to ruin your evening," Dylan said to Liesel. "Just call me and I'll come get you when you're ready."

"That's not necessary," Toni said. "I'd be honored to drive Ms. Kraus home once the party is over."

"Oh, that would be grand," Dylan said. He looked at Liesel. "I mean, if it's all right with you."

"Yes, that would be fine."

Dylan gave Toni the address.

"That's the Careys' place," Toni said.

"I wouldn't know," he said. "It's a rental."

"They're artists. Only here part-time. They do that Airbnb thing when they're away." She leaned forward and put a hand near her mouth. "The hotels hate that."

Ananke watched Dylan leave, wishing she could go with him. She was sure they'd learned all they could from the party, but, as guest of honor, taking off early would be poor form. She and Rosario talked with Liesel and Toni for a few more minutes, and then, claiming a need to visit the restrooms, left the two women to carry on without them.

As they neared the restroom entrance, a young man hurried toward them. "Ms. Ramey?"

"Yes?" Ananke said, turning. It was the chipper receptionist from up front.

He held out an envelope. "I was asked to give this to you."

"By who?"

"Mr. Rally."

How very junior high, Ananke thought. "Am I supposed to give you a reply or something?"

"I don't think so."

"All right. Thanks."

She waited until she and Rosario had entered the bathroom to open the envelope.

Shawn—

I just wanted to apologize for any misunderstandings earlier. I assure you my intentions were purely business related, and if it came across otherwise, then I'm truly sorry. I would have told you this in person, but I didn't want to make you feel uncomfortable.

I would love if you'd allow me to buy you a coffee while you're here. We can discuss the merits of Bradbury, and I can fill you in on where all the bodies are buried. Hahaha. Call me if you'd like to take me up on the offer.

Devon

She let Rosario read it. "Are you going to call him?"

Ananke grimaced as if she'd taken a drink of sour milk. "Not if I can help it."

Fourteen

RICKY HADN'T BEEN lying about going stir crazy. He tried sitting down. Pacing. Watching TV. And then he tried all those things again.

Nothing worked.

He looked over at his phone on the bed. "Screw it," he said, and grabbed the device to send Ananke another text.

His thumbs hovered above the screen for a full ten seconds before he moved them away.

Put the phone down, Ricky. She'll answer when she's ready.

He tossed the mobile back onto the bed and started pacing again, carving a path from the window, around the end of the bed, to the front door, and back. He was on his fifth lap, right in front of the window, when someone pounded on the door.

He sprinted across the room and peered through the peephole. With a grin, he pulled open the door and let Dylan slip inside.

"Party over already?" Ricky said, trying to sound nonchalant.

"Still going when I left."

So Ananke had listened to Ricky after all. He wanted to gloat, but there would be time for that later. Instead, he grabbed the spare helmet he'd bought that afternoon, tossed it to Dylan, picked up his backpack, and held it out. "It'll be easier if you wear this."

"I brought the car. Can't we just use that?"

Ricky snorted and shoved the backpack into Dylan's arms.

THE MOMENT THEY reached the open highway, Ricky let the

bike fly down the road. Dylan clung to the underside of the seat, praying to God he'd live through the next few hours, and wishing he'd put up more of a fight to use the sedan.

When they turned onto the dirt road, things didn't get much better. Though Ricky reduced their speed, Dylan now feared the next bounce on the rough surface would send him tumbling into the woods. He'd seldom been more thankful than the moment Ricky pulled to the side of the road and said, "We'll stow the bike and walk in from here."

The dark woods reminded Dylan of every demented fairy tale he'd been told as a kid: a child wanders into the forest, gets eaten by a wolf or a witch or a goblin or whatever and is never seen again. As Dylan and Ricky snuck through the forest, Dylan couldn't help but feel like the boy about to be served up for dinner.

They'd been going for less than ten minutes when Ricky snapped his head around and jammed a finger against his lips.

"What?" Dylan whispered.

Ricky silently mouthed something back.

Dylan frowned, having no idea what his colleague meant.

Ricky rolled his eyes, leaned in, and whispered in Dylan's ear, "You're walking too loud."

"I'm walking as quietly as you are."

"You're not. You're too loud. Watch your step."

Ricky started off again, not giving Dylan a chance to say anything else.

Though Dylan knew he hadn't been loud, he now took extra care with each step, not wanting to evoke another Ricky condemnation.

Somewhere to the left, an owl hooted.

Probably sending a message to its demon master that new morsels are on the way, Dylan thought.

He wasn't actually scared. Just uneasy.

He preferred the drone of traffic to the alien noises of the wilderness. Roads and alleys and highways were in his blood. Hiking through Narnia, not so much.

After another several minutes, Ricky paused again. He pointed ahead at a sliver of light between the trees.

"That's the guard shack on the road," he whispered, then led on.

Keeping a thirty-yard cushion between themselves and the light, they passed without incident. Another ten minutes and they reached the fence-enclosed clearing.

Pools of light created by a handful of flood lamps dotted the construction site, revealing several of the short concrete pillars Ricky had described. One of the lamps jutted out above the office trailer, lighting up the area in front of it that, at the moment, played host to a golf cart and two pickup trucks. The cart sat near one of the two trailer doors, while the cars were parked next to each other near the fence. These latter were likely the guards' personal vehicles.

The cart represented a problem. Parked by the door, it probably meant the guard assigned to patrol the fenced-in portion of the site was inside the trailer. Which was exactly where Dylan and Ricky wanted to be.

Ricky tapped Dylan on the shoulder and waved for him to follow again. Staying well within the trees, they moved parallel to the fence, past the mobile office, to a dark spot a few hundred feet behind the building.

Dylan eyed the barrier. Three strands of nasty-looking razor wire topped the chain-link. They could, of course, cut a hole through the fence, but the whole idea was to get in and out without being noticed. Digging *under* might work, but that would take a lot of effort, and would also leave evidence of their trespass.

"Tell me, how exactly do you plan on getting to the other side without being sliced up?"

Ricky grinned and motioned for Dylan to remove the backpack. From inside, he pulled out a folded piece of thick canvas and a looped bundle of climbing rope.

"Leave the bag and follow me," he said.

He led Dylan to the fence, where he grabbed the nearest pole and gave it a gentle shake. It swayed about an inch in either direction. He moved to the next pole and tested it. This one had barely any give to it.

Together they unfolded the canvas, stopping when they

had a double-thick sheet ten feet long and four feet wide. Using the unwavering pole as the center point, they worked one end of the sheet over the top of the razor wire until they had approximately equal sections of canvas hanging down each side.

Ricky created a loop in the middle of the rope, and gestured for Dylan to give him a boost up. Dylan raised Ricky high enough for him to scrunch a small section of the canvas down over the top of the pole. Ricky then placed the loop around it and pulled the knot tight. Back on the ground, he threw one half of the rope onto the other side, and used the other half to pull himself up and over the fence.

Dylan followed with a bit more reluctance, but was relieved when the canvas proved to be an adequate barrier to the razor wire.

Once he'd joined Ricky, they snuck toward the trailer.

Unlike the other side of the mobile office, the back had only one visible source of light, leaking from a high, narrow window that showed no sign of anyone looking out. Dylan and Ricky eased up to the side of the building and listened. Faint noises from a TV seeped through the thin wall. No live voices, though, or sounds of movement.

Again, Dylan created a hand cradle and lifted Ricky to the window. Ricky remained there, peeking inside, for nearly ten seconds before signaling he was done. Back on the ground, Ricky led Dylan several dozen feet away from the trailer.

"One guard," he whispered. "Looks like he's asleep."

"That's a problem."

Ricky smirked. "He'll have to do his rounds at some point."

"We just wait?"

Ricky patted Dylan on the cheek. "That's what I like about you. You're smarter than you look."

TWENTY-THREE MINUTES later, the faint beep-beep-beep of an alarm came from inside the trailer. Several seconds after that, the building groaned with movement. Nearly a minute later, a toilet flushed, more movement, and finally the squeak from one of the doors on the other side opening.

Ricky signaled for Dylan to stay put and moved over to the side of the building facing the fence. When he heard the whine of the electric golf cart moving, he chanced a peek around the front corner. The cart rolled across the parking area, toward the road that paralleled the fence. Though the angle prevented Ricky from seeing the driver's face, the size of the guard and the hairstyle matched that of the man he'd seen sleeping inside the trailer.

He waved for Dylan to join him.

"At the speed he's going," Ricky said, "it'll take him at least fifteen minutes to get all the way around to a spot where he could possibly see the tarp. If he makes any stops, it'll be even longer. You stay here and keep an eye on him. I'm going to go in and check around. Let me know when he's getting close."

"And how am I supposed to do that without comm gear?"

"Hey, I didn't have access to it. You guys have that stuff. Not me."

"And if we'd brought my car, we would have had it with us."

Ricky's eyes narrowed. "You'll just have to make do with the old-fashioned method. Two raps on the side and I'll get the message."

He headed around the corner and went straight to the closest of the two doors. Locked, of course. The second door was locked, too.

Great. A guard who actually cares about his job.

Using the scanner app on his phone, Ricky checked for an alarm. There was a system in place but it was currently inactivated. He revised his earlier thought. Apparently the guard's concerns about his job went only so far. Ricky picked the lock and slipped inside.

A long, waist-high counter ran across the back of the room, covered with stacks of blueprints and thick three-ring binders. A table and several chairs occupied the left end of the trailer. The guard had been sitting there, the small TV he'd been watching dark now. A desk sat at the other end of the room, on it a couple of stacks of paperwork, a telephone, and a computer.

If I were Patterson, what would interest me? The binders and blueprints?

He pulled out a random binder and flipped through the pages. Tech specs and drawings of hardware that Ricky couldn't identify. This could very well be exactly what the woman had come for, but he had no way of knowing that. He shot a few pictures just in case, and returned the binder to its place.

For a second or two, he considered taking random pictures of items in the other binders, but that would take forever so he dismissed the thought.

He looked around the room, his gaze stopping when it reached the computer. Were there files on it that couldn't be found somewhere else? That seemed inefficient, but not out of the realm of possibility.

He moved behind the desk and nudged the mouse. The screen came to life, asking for a password.

Dammit.

He stared at the screen and clicked his tongue against the roof of his mouth. He could try to break in. He wasn't the best at hacking, but he'd done his fair share. No way to know, though, how long it would take, or if he'd succeed.

He settled on taking a picture of the serial number on the back of the tower, and on the modem it was plugged into, and sent the shots to Rosario. Hopefully she or Shinji could hack in remotely.

He turned his attention back to the room.

AN ALERT POPPED up on a monitor at the Scolareon security office, located on the second floor of the company's manufacturing building in Bradbury. The officer on duty clicked the box to obtain more details.

The alarm had been triggered at an offsite facility, specifically the company's under-construction solar farm north of town.

The officer brought up the appropriate phone number.

The line rang three times before it was answered.

"Eldridge."

"John, it's Gary at the office. Did you just try to use the computer?" The only computer the guards were allowed to touch was the one in the guard shack down the road.

"Computer? I'm on rounds. I'm not even in the building."

"Please tell me you don't have someone there waiting for you." That was also a no-no, but a rule that had been broken more than once.

"Of course not. Are you telling me someone tried to log in?"

"No. Just screen activation." Rider hit a key on his computer. "Looks like it's gone dark again."

"Is that all? Probably just a glitch."

"Probably. But protocol says you need to go back and check."

Eldridge groaned. "Fine. I'll call you back when I'm done."

DYLAN'S GAZE NEVER left the cart as it slowly moved farther and farther away. While Ricky might have been a good hunter, Dylan knew vehicles, and based on the cart's current speed, the entire trip would take closer to twenty minutes than fifteen.

But hey, the more time the—

The cart's brake lights flashed. It sat motionless for a moment, and then made a Y-turn and headed back Dylan and Ricky's way.

"Shite."

He rapped twice on the side of the trailer, and after a few seconds, rapped again to make sure Ricky took him seriously. When he heard the door open, he stuck his head around the corner and saw Ricky slip out and give Dylan a what's-going-on look. Dylan nodded toward the returning cart. That got Ricky moving in a hurry.

"What the hell happened?" Ricky whispered once he'd joined Dylan around the corner.

"You're asking me? I haven't budged from this spot. You were the one doing all the moving around."

Ricky grimaced. "Let's go."

They ran to the tarp. Dylan went first. Ricky then climbed up and stopped at the top, a leg dangling on each side. He tugged at the knot holding the rope in place, but it didn't budge.

"Come on, you son of bitch," he muttered.

Dylan moved down the chain-link until the trailer no longer hid the cart's headlights. The vehicle was pulling up in front of the building. If luck was on their side, the guard would go straight into the building and not come out again until Dylan and Ricky had made it safely to the woods.

He hurried back to Ricky. "He just got there."

Ricky cursed again.

"Ricky, we've got to go."

"I'm not going to—"

Suddenly the knot slipped open and the loop popped off the top. Ricky, who'd been using his full weight to leverage the rope free, fell backward toward the forest side of the fence.

Dylan tried to catch him, but only succeeded in slowing Ricky enough so that the hunter hit the ground with a loud bump rather than a thundering crash.

ELDRIDGE PARKED THE cart near the trailer's east door and climbed out. He had no doubt the computer had sent a false alert. He'd just left the trailer and there hadn't been enough time for anyone to get inside.

As he slipped his key into the lock, however, he heard a dull thud coming from somewhere beyond the building.

He tensed and cautiously moved to the end of the trailer. Slowly, he stepped out so he could see the area behind the office.

The floodlight he'd been standing under screwed with his night vision, so everything appeared as dark shadows. He snapped up his flashlight, switched it on, and swung the beam back and forth. No movement, and everything as it should be.

He listened, hoping to pick up more sound, but the night was quiet.

Must have been a branch. Or a pine cone.

He moved the flashlight around for one last pass.

"What the hell?"

At the farthest reaches of the beam, he noticed something odd along the top of the fence. He took several steps toward it.

Trash? Kicked up by the wind? Maybe, but there hadn't been much of a wind that night.

A few more steps, and he could see the item was a cloth of some kind. Cloth draped evenly over both sides. What were the chances a gust of wind had done that?

Slim to none.

He moved the beam through the area near the fence on his side, but nothing was there. As he started to swing the light through the chain-link to the other side, his radio came to life.

CROUCHING NEXT TO the fallen Ricky, Dylan whispered, "Don't move."

The guard's shadow stood beside the trailer for a moment, before it began walking toward them, flashlight in hand.

"Coming this way," Dylan whispered.

"What do we do?" Ricky whispered back, not in the position to see anything.

Dylan didn't have a good answer. If they moved now, the guard would notice them for sure. If they stayed and the guard kept coming, they'd soon be in range of the man's flashlight.

Damned if you do, damned if you don't.

Dylan patted the air, indicating they should stay for now, and hoped the guard would stop.

Come on, buddy. Turn around. Just—

The light touched the tarp and stopped on it.

Oh, crap.

The guard studied the tarp for a moment, and then moved his light to his right. Dylan tensed, ready to run if the light swung back in their direction. Suddenly, a voice crackled from a radio on the guard's belt.

"John, come in."

The guard retrieved the device. "What is it?"

"Base just called me. Said you were checking on an alarm? They want to know what you found."

"Still checking."

"What the hell are they talking about? I didn't hear

anything."

"Computer alarm."

"Computer? Ah, Jesus. You weren't trying to log on, were you?"

"No, I wasn't trying to log on," the guard said defensively. "I'm not that stupid. I wasn't even there. But...there *is* something weird here."

"What do you mean, weird?"

"There's a blanket or something hanging over the top of the fence, behind the trailer." The guard covered the remaining distance to the spot and disappeared behind the tarp. "Feels like canvas."

"How did it get there?"

"Not sure. I was thinking the wind but this thing's pretty heavy. Hold on." The guard leaned around the end of the tarp and pointed his flashlight through the fence.

The beam wasn't aimed directly at Dylan and Ricky, but it was close enough to reveal they weren't part of the landscape.

"Oh, shit!" the guard yelled. "There's someone here! There's someone here!"

Dylan and Ricky jumped to their feet and sprinted into the woods, Ricky stopping only long enough to grab their backpack.

The guard, still shouting into his radio, said, "They're in the woods west of the trailer!"

Dylan had no plan in mind other than to get away. He ran between trees, on a path that took him straight out from where they had been. But within the first thirty yards, Ricky's hand clamped down on his shoulder, jerking him to a stop.

"This way," the hunter whispered, nodding in a direction that would take them on a diagonal toward the gate in the fence surrounding the construction site.

"Are you daft? They'll be coming from that direction."

"Exactly."

Dylan waited for more, but instead of elaborating, Ricky ran off.

"Ah, for the love of God," Dylan muttered. He took a deep breath and raced after him.

140

ELDRIDGE KEPT HIS flashlight fixed on the two trespassers until they disappeared into the forest. He relayed the information to his night watch partner, Samson, stationed out at the guardhouse along the entrance road, and told him to cut them off. Eldridge then hurried back to the golf cart and drove it to the main gate, pushing the electric motor as fast as it could go.

At the entrance, he entered his code into the control box a few feet from the fence. The instant the gate rolled open wide enough, he sprinted into the forest.

DYLAN NEARLY RAN into Ricky when the hunter stopped abruptly. Ricky grabbed Dylan's arm and moved to the left behind some brush, where they crouched down.

No more than three seconds passed before Dylan heard someone running in their direction. Closer and closer the steps came, until the person shot past right on the other side of the bushes. Dylan glimpsed a guard racing away. When the man disappeared, Dylan and Ricky continued in the direction they'd been headed.

Ricky's instincts had been dead on. The guards thought the intruders had gone in the other direction, and now that Ricky and Dylan were behind the guards, they'd be almost impossible to find.

They followed the landscape down a dip and up a shallow rise before reaching the entrance road.

Ricky leaned close and whispered, "We'll follow this. It'll be faster."

They hurried down the road, sticking to the left side where it would be easy to meld into the forest if need be. Another bend brought the guardhouse in sight. They crouched and slowed but did not stop.

Light bled from the open door of the shack, reflecting off the wooden gate blocking the way. Parked on the right edge of the road, directly behind the hut, was another golf cart.

Ricky crept up to the guardhouse and peeked in. He rose and waved Dylan over. The shack was empty.

They ducked under the gate and continued toward the main road. Less than a minute later, they heard a sharp voice behind them, like a curse. Dylan looked over his shoulder and spotted the dim glow of a moving light deep among the trees. His guess was that the guards were a hundred yards away, probably more.

As they neared the next curve in the road, Ricky stopped, his gaze locked on something on the ground.

"What are you doing?" Dylan asked. "We need to keep going."

"Look." Ricky pointed at the edge of the road, where two tire tracks had crushed the dirt at the edge and traveled straight into the woods.

"So what?"

"And there." Ricky jogged over to a tree at the side of the road, a few yards back.

Dylan looked down the road for the lights he'd seen before, but all was dark. If he and Ricky didn't get moving, though, the guards would catch up soon enough.

He hurried over to the tree to remind Ricky they needed to get out of there, but he noticed the gouge in the trunk a few feet above the ground. It had been made by something big, and not too long ago. Ricky picked something off the ground.

"That Prius—it was blue, right?" he asked.

"Prius?" It took Dylan a moment to realize Ricky was talking about Patterson's car. "Um, yeah, blue."

Ricky turned the item he'd found and held it up for Dylan to see. "That look blue to you?"

The object was about two by one-inch wide and had broken off a larger piece.

"It's night, Ricky. It could be green for all I know."

"I'll bet you breakfast it's blue."

"Okay. Sure. It's blue. We really need to keep moving."

"Just a moment."

"We don't have a—"

Rising, Ricky shushed him and hurried to another tree. It, too, had been hit. This tree led to another one, deeper in the woods, and then another, and finally to a pine that had been uprooted and was now leaning at an unnatural angle.

Ricky bent down and brushed away the top layer of

needles in front of it. "Check it out."

Under the top layer were two tire grooves. Dylan saw that the needles covering the area looked as though they had been brushed into place, instead of having fallen naturally.

"Whatever hit this," Dylan whispered, "didn't drive away." The vehicle would have needed to be a tank to survive the collision.

A glint of light off to their right. They both turned to it. A flashlight beam swept in an arc before disappearing behind trees. The guard was getting closer.

Dylan glanced at Ricky. "Shouldn't we—"

"We should."

They picked their way through the woods, and made it back to the motorcycle unnoticed.

ANANKE'S CELL PHONE rang.

"How was the party?" Ricky asked.

Barely eleven p.m., she had just finished taking a shower in anticipation of heading out again for some late night recon. "Interesting. How was your excursion?"

"The same. I have something you're going to want to see. I'll bring it right over."

"Ricky, wait! Don't you even think about—"

"Relax, Annie Stress Ball. I was kidding. I'm not coming over. I *do* have something you need to see, though."

"What it is?"

"A piece of a car."

"Okay. And?

"There's a paper bag behind the ice machine on your floor. Get it and take a look inside, then call me back."

He hung up.

Grumbling, she grabbed the ice bucket and exited her room. The community ice maker lived in a nook near the elevator. Unfortunately, when she arrived, a guy in gym shorts and a T-shirt tight enough to show off his beer belly was staring at a snack vending machine as if the choices might change at any second.

He glanced at her and grinned. "Never anything healthy

when you really want it."

She smiled back politely and stuck her bucket into the slot on the ice machine, angling herself enough to keep the man in her peripheral vision. He'd returned to staring at the vending machine. If Mr. Clean Living didn't leave before Ananke's bucket filled, she'd have to try again later.

Just take the candy bar.

As the last space in her bucket filled, she heard a clunk behind her and saw the man lean down to the extraction slot. She shook the bucket as if trying to make room for more ice.

"Have a nice night," he said.

She glanced over her shoulder. "You, too."

She tracked the sound of his steps as he walked down the hall. When she heard a door open and close again, she stepped over to the nook entrance and peeked around the corner. The hall was empty.

Quickly, she squeezed around the side of the ice machine. On the ground behind it sat a small paper bag. She snatched it up and returned to her room.

She knocked on the connecting door to Rosario's room, and then dumped the ice bucket in her bathroom sink. As she walked back into the bedroom, Rosario opened the door and leaned in.

"You wanted me?"

Ananke dangled the bag. "Ricky left us a present."

"What kind of present?"

"If he wasn't lying, it's a piece of a car."

"Not a very big piece."

"Not a very heavy one, either."

Ananke opened the bag and dumped onto her table a piece of plastic about the size of a crushed soda can. She picked it up and flipped it over. Blue on both sides.

She handed the piece to Rosario and called Ricky, putting him on speaker.

"Okay, we've got it," she said. "Where did you find it?"

"On the road into the solar farm, next to a tree that had been hit recently by something big. You know, like a car. A *blue* one."

144

"You're thinking it's from Patterson's Prius."

"Seems like a good possibility to me. Thought maybe Rosario could confirm car type."

Ananke looked at Rosario.

Rosario examined the piece for a few more seconds before saying, "Possible, but I am not sure."

"Oh, you're there," Ricky said. "Good. If you can't figure out exactly what it's from, you could probably rule out a bunch of models it doesn't belong to, right?"

"That is more likely."

"Did your scouting turn anything else up?" Ananke asked.

Ricky briefed them on his and Dylan's exploration of the solar site.

"You're sure the guard who spotted you can't ID you?" Ananke asked.

"One hundred percent positive. He only saw us for a couple seconds and most of that time it was just our backs."

"You said he came back to the trailer before he should have. Any idea why?"

"Not a clue. Maybe he ran out of coffee or something. Who knows?"

Ananke hit him up with a few more questions, then said, "Good job, Ricky."

"Did you just compliment me?"

"Don't make me regret it."

"You *did* compliment me."

"Good night, Ricky."

"Good night? But it's still—"

Click.

FIFTEEN

WHILE ROSARIO GOT to work on the car fragment and other info Ricky had turned up, Ananke headed out on her after-dark mission.

Via her tracking app, she located three of the Bradbury police cars she'd tagged earlier that were in use. Using side streets and approaching from behind, she eliminated the first car as the one she was looking for, and made her way to the second. At 10:40 p.m., she hit pay dirt, confirming the driver of squad car number two was Officer Harris.

Ananke had two goals for the evening. First: seeing if Harris made a return trip to Patterson's. According to the information Rosario had found, the graveyard shift started at ten p.m., therefore it was possible Harris had already visited the house, but Ananke's intuition told her no. The previous night the woman had arrived at the home around eleven p.m., meaning she had probably taken some time to settle into her shift first. There was no reason to think Harris would do anything differently tonight.

There was also no reason for Ananke to tail the woman herself.

She retrieved her phone.

Ricky answered on the third ring. "Hey, what's up?"

"I was wondering if you might still be up and willing to do a little something for..." She heard laughter and music in the background. "Where are you?"

"Bradbury Brewery. Come on over, I'll buy you a beer, then I can get on whatever it is you need."

"I'm a little busy. And you're about to be, too."

"Hey, didn't hurt to ask. What is it you need Ricky to do?"

"I want you to watch Patterson's house again. I have a feeling the cop from last night might make another visit. If so, I want to know what she does."

Silence, then, "Couldn't we just set up a camera to do that?"

"I apologize if I'm bothering you. I didn't realize that you were occupied with something that takes precedence over the *job*."

"Come on. It's not like—"

"Get your ass over there."

"Yes, boss. As soon as I finish this glass, I'll be on my way."

"*Now*, Ricky."

"All right. I'm going, I'm going."

RICKY HATED TO waste a good beer, and the Bradbury Brewery's Hidden Rapid IPA was a pretty damn good one. He considered downing the remaining half pint, but despite his rogue façade, he was a professional at heart, and knew the added alcohol would not aid his senses. Plus, there was the promise to Ananke.

He pushed the glass away, muttered his apologies to the drink he was leaving behind, and stood up.

"Where you going, man? It's still early," Magnus said from the other side of the table. He was a software engineer at someplace called Weedoo Noise. He and the two with him tonight—Kailee and Bennett—had been part of the group Ricky met at the brewery the previous evening.

"When work calls, what are you going to do?" Ricky said. He tossed a couple of twenties on the table. "Next round's on me."

On his way out, he noticed a copy of the *Bradbury Evening Independent* lying on one of the tables. Front and center was a picture of a burning big rig and trailer, with emergency personnel working to put the fire out. The headline read: TRUCK BLAZE CAUSES MAJOR BACKUP.

During the meeting that morning, Dylan had mentioned the accident had delayed his and Liesel's arrival. Ricky grabbed the paper. If nothing else, he could do some light reading while on stakeout.

ANANKE SWITCHED OFF her lights right before turning onto Merrick Road. The rising quarter moon provided just enough illumination to keep her from driving into a gully. When she reached Harris's driveway, she rolled to a stop.

No light on inside the house, and no C-Max parked out front. Though Ananke hadn't seen anyone else when she spied on Harris earlier, she had to assume, until proven otherwise, the cop didn't live alone. So, as much as she wanted to pull down the driveway, Ananke continued to the same forgotten road she'd used before.

She moved quietly through the dark on foot until she reached the edge of Harris's lawn. Using her camera, she checked the position of the sensors for the motion-activated floodlights, and discovered a narrow corridor between two that should allow her to approach the house without triggering any illumination.

She crept through the dead zone, ready to sprint back into the darkness if one of the lights came on. None did.

At the house, she paused and listened.

All was quiet on the Harris front.

Ananke worked her way to the back door and scanned for a house alarm. After a few moments, her app responded with:

NO SYSTEM DETECTED

A country house outside a small town that likely had a very low crime rate meant an alarm would be wasted money. Besides, most of the cops Ananke knew liked to take care of their own problems.

Harris had, however, invested in top-notch locks, which meant it took Ananke fifteen seconds longer than usual to pick each. After stepping inside, she found herself in a combo family/dining room. The furniture appeared to be at least a decade old. Utilitarian. Holdovers from when Harris's parents were still alive, perhaps.

Ananke crept into the hallway and checked the rest of the rooms. When she was sure no one else was present, she turned on her phone's flashlight, used her fingers to control its intensity and direction, and started a more in-depth search.

The only thing of remote interest in the front of the house was the mail on a side table in the dining room. Bills, mostly. She read the opened ones and noted none were past due.

Next stop, the master bedroom. She scanned it from just inside the door. The furniture here was a lot newer than that in the living room, and a hell of a lot more stylish. It felt almost like this room belonged to an entirely different house. It seemed that after Harris's mother died, the officer could bring herself to change only the room she slept in.

Two stacks of books and a lamp with a cell phone cord wrapped around its base covered the nightstand on the left side of the bed. Though the other nightstand had a matching lamp, only a single book lay beside it. Harris obviously slept on the left.

Since the right side of the bed was closer, Ananke approached it, intending to check under the box springs. But the cover of the lone book on the nightstand stopped her.

She picked it up. *Lab Girl* by Hope Jahren, with a bookmark about three quarters of the way through. The description on the back explained it was the memoir of a female scientist. Ananke flipped open the book to the marker and felt some give to the binding, telling her the book was indeed in the process of being read.

If Harris was reading it, why wasn't it over on the other stand? Had someone else brought it here?

She set it down and pulled open the nightstand drawer. A pad of paper and a pen, a hair brush, and an eye mask. She picked up the brush and noted long brown hairs in the teeth. Harris's hair was shorter and almost black.

A long-haired boyfriend? Or girlfriend?

Ananke touched the pad of paper and felt a bump. She pulled it out and ran her fingers over it. Indentations, several near the top of the sheet and in the middle. She removed the top three pieces of paper, slipped them unfolded into her jacket pocket, and returned the pad to the drawer.

She looked under the bed, found nothing there, then moved around to the left nightstand. No nonfiction here. Harris apparently had a penchant for mysteries with a medical bent. Ananke checked the drawer and found nothing unusual.

She headed into the master bathroom and noted two toothbrushes in a cup by the sink. A check of the shower turned up more of the long, brown hair.

Okay, Harris has a...friend. So what?

Ananke wasn't here to delve into the cop's love life. Her interest was strictly in any evidence of Harris being involved in Patterson's disappearance.

Ananke entered the walk-in closet. On one side were half a dozen police uniforms, and a whole bunch of shirts and pants and a few dresses that all appeared to be about Harris's size. On the other side were more woman's clothes, only Ananke didn't need to look at the tags to know they were too small to fit the cop.

A girlfriend, then.

Ananke started turning back to the bedroom when she noticed the two expensive-looking business suits tucked in among the smaller clothes.

Could it be...

She searched one of the suits and found a cough drop wrapper and thirty-five cents. In the inside pocket of the second suit, she found a small stack of identical business cards.

SCOLAREON, INC.
Natasha Patterson
Chief Financial Officer

Well, I'll be damned.

Harris didn't have just any girlfriend.

She had a girlfriend who'd gone missing.

THE DOOR TO Rosario's room still hung open when Ananke returned to the hotel.

A peek inside revealed Rosario studying her computer.

150

"Guess what I found out?" Ananke said.

Rosario looked up. "I have no idea."

"Come on. Guess."

"Um, okay. Harris has Patterson tied up in her basement?"

Ananke stepped inside. "Wrong, but not bad. But Patterson *has* been to her house."

"Really? Are you sure?"

"Positive. Patterson is, or was, Officer Harris's girlfriend."

Rosario stared at her. "You are serious?"

Ananke told her what she'd discovered.

"It would explain Harris's trip to Patterson's house," Rosario said.

"It would. And why she knew about the trip wires. Either she's involved in the woman's disappearance and wants to make sure no one comes snooping around, or she's wondering what happened to her."

"If she is not involved with those who took her, why would she not report it to the police?"

That question had occurred to Ananke, too, but she'd had time to think about it during the drive back. "We've pretty much established that Patterson is not AWOL of her own accord, and that whoever took her are the ones who've been sending the messages that claim to be from her, right?"

"Right."

"What if Patterson—or Harris, for that matter—wanted to keep their relationship secret and no one knew about them? Small country town. People might not be as understanding."

"Then whoever is sending the messages would not have known about Harris and would not have written her."

"Exactly. And Harris would have tried every means of getting ahold of her without success. Short of anything that might expose the women's relationship, since she couldn't be positive that Patterson was in trouble. And wouldn't want to damage her reputation."

Rosario grimaced. "Okay, but if I were Harris, I would have eventually tried to reach Patterson directly through Scolareon."

"*If* she's not involved, I'm sure she did. And they would have told her that Patterson was out of the office for a while. But Harris is a cop. A little more investigating, and she could have probably found out about the messages the company received. The problem would be that none of it was concrete proof that something was wrong."

"Sounds to me like you are convinced Harris had nothing to do with it."

"No, I'm not convinced either way. Both choices are equally possible."

"Perhaps we should ask her?"

"We might just have to do that, but not until we have a better handle on what's going on. For the moment, it's better if we keep an eye on her." She ran a hand across the back of her head. "I'm beat. Let's pick it up again first thing." She turned for the door, and stopped. "I totally forgot." She pulled out the notepad pages she'd found and handed them to Rosario. "There's something on these."

After running a finger across them, Rosario set them on the table and reached into her computer bag. As she rummaged around, Ananke's phone rang.

The display read RICKY.

"How'd it go?" she asked him.

"Your instincts were right."

"Harris is there?"

"Just left. Stayed about seven minutes and checked the house. Same pattern as last night."

"She didn't go inside."

"Nope."

"Okay, good. Thanks, Ricky. You're released for the night."

"Wait, there's something else."

"What?"

"I don't know if this means anything or not, but...you know that accident Dylan and Liesel passed on their way in this morning?"

"Uh-huh. What about it?"

"There's an article in the local paper, with pictures of the

152

two guys who died."

"I assume this is leading somewhere."

"I saw both of them last night."

She paused. "In person?"

"Yeah." He told her about overhearing the two men arguing at the Bradbury Brewery. "I thought they were talking about some stupid small-town crap they'd gotten messed up in. But I'm thinking now it had something to do with whatever they were hauling. The one guy sure didn't want anything to do with it anymore. I know, it probably has nothing to do with our gig, but you said to let you know if anything strange came up."

"I don't know if it has anything to do with it, either, but I appreciate you keeping your eyes open. Good work tonight, Ricky. Go get some sleep."

"Copy that."

As Ananke hung up, Rosario said, "Look at this." She held up one of the notepad pages. The white surface was covered by pencil rubbings that brought the indentations in the paper to life. Three lines in three columns: the first column contained strings of characters, the second numbers only, and the third dates.

"Like in Patterson's notebook," Ananke said.

"Yes."

The order of information was different, but otherwise it was the same.

"Duplicates?" Ananke asked.

Rosario shook her head. "The dates are after the ones in the book. Perhaps Patterson had not had time to transfer them yet."

"We need to know what they mean."

"I'll have Shinji help me work on that."

"Good."

Sixteen

ONCE AGAIN, RICKY was not ready to call it a night. The Bradbury Brewery wouldn't be closing for another hour, and having a beer to make up for the one he'd had to leave behind earlier sounded like a great idea.

He hiked through Patterson's housing tract back to the highway. He'd left his motorcycle next to a building just on the other side of the main road, as the bike would have attracted too much attention if he had ridden it into the woman's neighborhood.

As he lifted his helmet to pull it on, he heard the deep rumble of a powerful engine. He looked north down the highway, in the only direction he could see, but the road was clear. He moved up to the corner of the building and peeked south.

Headlights. A small convoy of them.

He grabbed the binoculars from his bag.

A police sedan led the parade. Behind it came a big rig pulling a trailer, another police sedan, and finally a pickup truck.

The convoy neared his position, so Ricky pulled back around the side and watched it drive by. As soon as the lead sedan came back into view, he realized he'd made a mistake. Though it had roof lights, it didn't belong to the Bradbury PD. Emblazoned on its door were the words SCOLAREON SECURITY.

Huh.

The big rig did not have identifying marks at all, nor did the trailer it was pulling. The third vehicle also belonged to Scolareon Security. Like the big rig, the white Ford F-150 pickup in the rear had no ownership markings. Four people rode inside it, and in the bed a tarp covered what appeared to be a giant, rectangular box.

A late-night delivery to Scolareon? Perhaps. But why the escort? Did the company experience a lot of hijacking around here? That seemed unlikely, especially within city limits. And what was the deal with the pickup truck?

Keep your eyes and ears open for anything weird.

"Dammit."

He really wanted that beer, but the convoy was exactly the kind of thing Ananke would expect him to follow up on.

He hurried to his bike, thinking he should be able to make sure everything was on the up and up and still get to the brewery in time for one last drink before closing.

Best laid plans...

YATES WAS ANNOYED.

Everything had been going so well for so long. Schedules had been kept, product had been easily obtained, clients had been satisfied, and money flowed in. And then that Patterson bitch had snooped where she shouldn't have been snooping. Thank God they'd caught her when they had, otherwise things would have gone into the toilet quickly.

The stuff she'd copied onto that jump drive he'd found on her...holy crap. That would have earned Yates and his brother and their cousin some serious jail time, not to mention the repercussions for their clients.

Yates had thought he'd been pretty sneaky hiding the docs on the Scolareon servers. Hell, for the last few years, he'd been right. How Patterson had figured it out, he had no idea. But she'd caused him to reconsider the setup, and within twenty-four hours of her capture, he'd removed everything and put it on a dedicated machine with no access to the web. It made work a bit more difficult, but they couldn't afford someone else stumbling on everything.

Patterson wasn't the only problem. In the early hours of that very morning, he'd been informed about the sudden resignation of two of the project's drivers. The thing was, no one resigned from the project.

Yates, as the enforcing arm of the organization, had dealt with them himself, placing an incendiary device inside the cab and a second inside the trailer. As of 8:53 that morning, the drivers were no longer an issue. In most places, such a device would be discovered by investigators, but Yates's dad—the chief of police—worked his state police contacts, and any traces of the device had disappeared.

Patterson would soon be taken care of, too, just in a more practical, killing-two-birds-with-one-stone way.

Yates checked the rearview mirror. The big rig continued chugging along behind him like it had been since they met up twenty miles south of Bradbury.

Transfer night. When the project was most vulnerable. Which was why they usually did it in the wee hours of the morning. Not tonight, though. The loss of the two drivers that morning necessitated a speedup of the schedule so they could get this truck emptied and back on the road within the next hour. A situation that added to Yates's annoyance.

And if that wasn't enough to up his blood pressure, his brother Slater wasn't happy with the product the two dead truckers had brought in. That's why Slater and his crew were following in their pickup, hoping the choices would be better on this delivery. If they weren't, there could be problems at the trials and no one wanted that.

When the convoy reached Scolareon, Yates pulled in first, stopping at the gate to the production building.

"Harry," he said with a nod to the guard.

"Evening, boss. What do we have here?"

"Hazardous materials shipment."

Scolareon security officer Harry Donovan swiped through some info on his tablet computer. "I don't have—"

"It's early. Wasn't supposed to arrive for another few hours, I believe."

More scrolling. "Ah. Okay, here it is. I'll let Receiving know you're here."

"Not necessary. Already called. The hazardous materials crew is the white truck behind us, so make sure they get through, too."

"Will do." The guard opened the gate. "Have a good night."

"Thanks, Harry. You, too."

Yates led the convoy to the delivery dock at the back of the building. He parked off to the side, walked over, and sent the two guards in the other car to the front of the building, where they were to return to the security office. He'd rearranged the schedule so that they would be on monitoring-room duty during the transfer, ensuring the cameras in all pertinent areas would not be recording. Though he'd been able to hire several members of his and his brother's secret organization into the Scolareon security department, not all the guards were his people.

Yates entered the building through the loading dock and was met by three other project members who worked for Scolareon—another guard and two warehouse workers. They'd brought several long carts usually used to transport solar panel parts.

"Status," he said.

"Not counting security personnel, only seven others in the building," the guard said. "Two up in administration, and five maintenance crew. They've finished this section already."

"And security?"

"Rounds have been altered per your instructions. We're good to go."

"All right. Let's make this fast."

RICKY CAUGHT SIGHT of the convoy again right before it turned into the Scolareon lot, west side of the highway—the manufacturing side, according to Dylan and Liesel.

He pulled off the road fifty yards shy of the business's property line, and rolled the bike down into a gully where it would be hard to spot. He hurried into the woods, paralleling the fence along the side of the property and then the back, until he spotted the convoy again near a loading dock. One of the security vehicles was missing, but the other three vehicles were there.

A man in a security uniform stood several feet away from the sedan, talking to two men dressed in jeans and light jackets. Every few seconds, the guard glanced toward the loading dock, as if waiting for something. Sure enough, a minute later, a guard exited the building and gave the others a signal.

The trio broke up, each jogging in a different direction. One of the men in jeans headed toward the big rig, the other to the pickup, and the security man to the loading dock where his colleague waited.

The semi's engine revved twice and the truck crept forward, until the back of the trailer faced the loading dock. With the security guards acting as guides, the big rig backed into place and shut down.

This turned out to be the cue for the white pickup, which reversed into the space next to the trailer. Once it had stopped, all four men exited the crew cab. Two headed toward the rear, while the other pair jogged out in front of the semi-tractor. There, they spread apart and then stopped.

"Okay, that can't be normal."

Ricky took a closer look at the pair through his binoculars. What had caught his attention were the rifles each man carried.

M4s. Serious hardware for a solar energy manufacturer.

Who were they guarding against? The place was behind a high fence and a guarded gate. The only people they'd likely run into would be other Scolareon employees, right? And at this hour, there couldn't be many of them around.

Ricky took pictures of the guards and the two trucks.

As he was switching back to his binoculars, one of the loading docks' big doors rolled up halfway. Shadows began moving across the dock into the building, but the trailer hid what formed them.

One of the men from the pickup truck moved behind the tailgate, reached over the side, and pulled up the tarp enough to expose the end of the box facing the building.

"Come on, dude. Help a guy out."

All the guy had to do was push the damn tarp back another foot, and Ricky might have been able to figure out what it was covering.

Obviously, they were going to take something out or put something in.

He increased to maximum zoom, and waited.

AS ALWAYS, THE sleeping drug had been pumped into the trailer prior to its arrival at the plant, rendering its human cargo unconscious.

Moving the bodies from the trailer to one of the carts was usually the job of the two warehouse workers, but since they were in a hurry tonight, Yates and the other guard lent a hand. Once all the product had been unloaded, Slater examined the haul.

"This one," he said. He placed a hood over the head of a young male, who appeared to be in relatively good shape, but not *too* good.

The warehouse workers moved the selection into a waiting wheelchair.

"Keep everyone else in the upstairs holding room," Yates said. "The van will be here within an hour."

As the warehouse workers wheeled the carts away, Slater pushed the wheelchair toward the loading dock, followed by his brother.

WITHOUT WARNING, THE man at the back of the pickup stiffened, his gaze now on the loading-dock door. For a moment, nothing happened, then the older guy emerged, pushing a wheelchair toward the white truck.

"Son of a bitch," Ricky muttered.

A bag covered the head of the person in the chair, but from the way he or she was drooping forward, the person had to be either unconscious or dead. Ricky raised his camera again, this time recording video. Upon reaching the end of the platform, the older guy locked the chair's wheels, then he and the security guard who'd been following him lifted the person out of the seat. They lowered the limp body into whatever was in the back of the truck. When they finished, the young guy waiting at the back of the truck pulled the tarp over the rear again and shut the tailgate.

You wanted weird, Ananke. I got weird for you.

The guard and the older man talked for a moment, then the older guy hopped off the dock and climbed into the driver's seat of the pickup. As his younger companion got in, the pair of armed sentries jogged over and did the same.

Ricky slipped his phone into his pocket and hurried as quietly as he could back toward his bike, hoping to follow the truck. He could see the southbound highway for most of his return trip and knew the pickup had not gone that way. When he reached his motorcycle, he headed north.

With each passing mile he drove without catching up to the other vehicle, his frustration grew. When he hit the ten-mile mark, he pulled to the side of the road.

Either the truck had turned off the highway, or was driving too fast for him to catch up.

ANANKE FELL INTO a deep sleep moments after climbing into bed, and was floating through a house that looked similar to, but not completely like, her home in Boulder. Birds chirped, and Emma Peel, full to the brim, told her the latest gossip on the neighborhood.

The knock on her door wrenched her back into consciousness. She grabbed her pistol off the nightstand, tiptoed to the door, and peeked through the spy hole.

Ricky stood in the hall, glancing back and forth nervously.

"You're not supposed to be here," she whispered.

He leaned toward the door and said in a low voice, "I know, but I got to show you something."

"Email it to me."

"That would take too much time. Come on. Open up."

Worried their conversation might wake other guests, she opened the door and yanked him inside.

"This had better be damn good," she snarled.

"I'm not sure *good* would be the right word." He moved past her into the bedroom and sat on the bed. As he pulled out his phone, he said, "You're going to want Rosario to see this, too."

The anger she'd felt when she first saw him subsided

quickly in light of his no-nonsense demeanor. She tapped on the common door and Rosario opened it within seconds, holding her own gun.

"I heard noise," she said.

"We have a visitor." Ananke nodded toward her bed.

Rosario took a step into the room and lowered her pistol when she saw Ricky. "He's not supposed to be here."

"I mentioned that."

"Should we shoot him?"

Ananke pretended to think about it. "Not quite yet."

Surprisingly, Ricky acted like he hadn't even heard them.

Rosario raised a questioning eyebrow, and Ananke replied with a shrug. They walked over to the bed and sat down on either side of Ricky.

"I was gonna grab a beer after we talked, you know?" he said. "Just to relax before coming back here. But then, well, I saw something *weird*."

"Something *else* weird?" Ananke said.

"I know, right? I'm like a weird magnet."

"What did you see?" Rosario asked.

"A parade of trucks and Scolareon security sedans."

"A parade?" Ananke said.

"Well, two trucks and two sedans."

"That's not a parade."

"Matter of opinion. But it's not important. It did seem kind of odd, though, so I followed them."

"And what did you discover?"

He grinned, held out his phone, and hit Play.

Ananke's eyes widened at the sight of the person being wheeled out and loaded into the back of a pickup truck.

"Correct me if I'm wrong," Ricky said, "but that doesn't seem like the kind of thing a solar panel plant would produce."

"Tell us exactly what happened."

He did.

"Do you know where the pickup went?" Ananke asked.

"I tried to get back to my bike in time, but I wasn't fast enough. I never found them."

"There might be satellite data," Rosario said. She hurried

into her room and returned a moment later with her laptop.

While she set to work, Ricky said to Ananke, "I want you to take a closer look at this."

He played the video again, this time zooming in on the back of the trailer. While that reduced the image quality, it wasn't bad enough to make a big difference.

He pointed at the shadows moving across the ground just beyond the trailer. "My first thought was that these were the people unloading contraband. You know, like drugs or who knows what. What I think now is that the cargo is *people*."

"And…what? They're storing these people at Scolareon?"

"Could be."

"For what purpose?"

"If they were a food manufacturer, I'd say Soylent Green."

No one laughed. Not even Ricky.

Rosario let out a breath and looked over at Ananke. "No luck. The only nearby satellite with the correct capabilities will not be in position for another ten hours. The best I can do is set up an automatic search for when it is overhead to look for white vehicles parked in the open."

"Do it," Ananke said, though that would be a crapshoot at best.

Rosario returned her attention to her computer.

"I took pictures of the men," Ricky said. "They were a little far, but maybe we can get IDs off them."

"What about license plates?"

Ricky showed her a picture of the pickup. No plates. "The big rig had one, though."

"Send me everything," Rosario said. "I will pass it along to Shinji."

Ananke tried to put all the pieces together. Human cargo. Patterson. Harris. Kyle Scudder. Scolareon.

"I know what you're thinking," Ricky said.

"You have no idea what I'm thinking."

Smiling, he leaned back and crossed his arms. "Oh, I know exactly what you're thinking. You're thinking we should go inside and have a look around."

He was right. It was exactly what she'd been thinking.

SEVENTEEN

2:55 A.M.

Bradbury was dead asleep, the only people out and about being Officer Harris and one other cop on patrol. And of course Ananke and her team.

According to the tracker, Harris was driving through the southeast part of town, while her colleague was doing the same up north in Green Hills Estates. Both were out of the way.

Ananke drew two parallel rectangles in the sand, with a line representing the highway running between them, and then looked at Ricky, Dylan, and Liesel. "Both buildings have the same camera setup." She dotted the dirt at the appropriate spots on each rectangle, the data collected from her and Ricky's recon before the other two arrived. "The only difference we saw was with the guard situation. The west building has four patrolling outside on foot, plus one at the main gate, while east only has two and one."

"And, naturally, we want to get into the west building," Dylan says with a smirk.

"Correct. And we need to do it without anyone knowing we were here. So that means no taking out of guards."

"Not even a sleeper hold here or there?" Ricky asked.

"Not if it can be avoided."

"You're taking all the fun out of things."

Ananke glanced at Dylan and Liesel. "I think we should go through the east building, and take the tunnel between the buildings you guys were told about. Do you have any idea where we'd find it?"

"We did not see it," Liesel said. "But the guide seemed to indicate that it is somewhere in this area." She drew an oval between the two rectangles, near the northern end.

Ananke asked Dylan, "Is that your sense, too?"

"It is."

"Okay, then that's where we'll go."

They spent a few minutes working out the plan, divvied up the equipment, and headed through the dark to the back side of the east building's lot. Just beyond the fence was a nearly empty parking area, lit by LED floodlights no doubt powered by stored solar energy. Unlike at Harris's house, there were no gaps between the lights for them to hide in while approaching the building. And though the cameras were spread apart, they were angled so that their fields of view overlapped, leaving none of the grounds unmonitored.

Ananke set Ricky, Liesel, and Dylan to work on creating a way through the fence that didn't involve cutting the chain link, and then contacted Rosario over their comm gear.

"We need two of the cameras blacked out for..." She paused, assessing the distance from the fence to the back of the building, and added some padding. "Forty seconds should do it."

"Show me."

Ananke aimed her camera phone at the back of the building. The device was currently linked to Rosario's laptop at the hotel. "This one," Ananke said, zooming in on one of the cameras. She switched to the other device in question. "And this one."

"A moment, please."

Ananke scanned the lot, knowing it was nearly time for one of the guards to take a walk across the back. No sign of anyone yet.

"Okay," Rosario said. "I am picking up several different Wi-Fi networks from the building. Most are pretty weak where you are, but I should be able to...yes, good. I am in. This will take a few minutes."

"Understood." Ananke glanced over at her colleagues. "How we doing?"

The others were working on one of the poles, and had already detached the lowest wire bracket holding the fence to

164

it.

"A couple more of these and we'll be able to lift it high enough to get under," Ricky said. "Should be ready by the time Rosario is."

Ananke caught movement at the far corner of the building. "Everybody down," she whispered.

A guard had come around the side and was now walking along the back of the structure.

He was about halfway across the back when Rosario said, "I am in Security and have control of the cameras. Just give me the word. And, Ricky, I believe that means I win."

"On a technicality," he whispered.

Ananke watched the guard meander along the structure until, finally, he reached the other corner and disappeared. If the pattern that she and Ricky had noted on their recon held, they had a good ten minutes until the next guard showed up.

"Let's get that thing open," Ananke said.

Thirty seconds later, the last bracket came free.

"Done," Ricky said, after testing to make sure he could raise it high enough.

"Rosario, whenever you're ready."

"Hold a moment," Rosario said. "Okay. Blackout in five, four, three, two, one."

As she said zero, Ricky lifted the fence again.

Liesel slipped under first and sprinted toward the building. Dylan followed, then Ananke and Ricky.

Once they were all at the building and out of the cameras' sight lines, Ananke whispered into her mic, "You can turn them back on."

"Copy," Rosario said. "Cameras back online."

"Are we all good?"

"I am looking at a feed from inside the monitoring room. The two men who are watching the screens seemed surprised at first, but have relaxed now that everything is working again."

"What about outside security?"

"Both men are still at the front of the building. One is at the main entrance, and the other has stopped by the guard shack at the vehicle entrance. They appear to be unaware that there was a problem."

"Keep tabs on them, and let us know when they head back this way."

"Copy."

Ananke turned to Ricky. "You're up."

WITH DYLAN PROVIDING the boost, Ricky climbed onto a wide ledge sticking out over the loading dock. He leaned over the side and helped pull up the others.

From there, they used a pair of pipes that ran up the side to scale the building all the way to the roof.

Ricky gave everyone a helping hand at the end of the climb, then asked Liesel and Dylan, "Where to?"

Liesel took a moment to get her bearings, said, "This way," and headed toward the right.

The building's roof was curved, not so much that they might slip off it, but enough to be a bit of a hike to the summit. Add to that the fact it was nearly all covered with solar cells, and it meant they had to carefully pick their way through the maze to avoid damaging anything.

Spaced evenly down along the apex of the roof were hatches, each about four feet in length and two and a half feet wide. Liesel led them to the one at the north end.

From the video Dylan had shot during the tour, Rosario had been able to identify the doors' manufacturer and learn they were primarily used for ventilation and could be remotely controlled.

"Okay, Rosario, we're here," Ricky said. "You want to let us in?"

"One moment."

A brief pause preceded the whoosh of air escaping from under the hatch as it crept open. When it stopped, the gap was only a bit more than eighteen inches wide.

"Can you give us a little more space?" Ricky said. "That's a little tight."

"The only way is if you remove a limit bar."

"This is fine," Ananke said. She glanced at Ricky. "Find someplace to tie off."

166

Ricky removed the rope from his backpack and attached one end to a large AC unit nearby. "All set, boss."

"Rosario," Ananke said. "How are we looking below?"

"All clear."

Ananke peeked through the gap before grabbing the rope. "Me first, then Liesel and Ricky. Dylan, don't get too bored."

"Bored? Sitting here, watching the stars, getting cold. What's boring about that?"

Ananke smirked and dropped out of sight.

Liesel glanced at Dylan. "No sleeping."

"Wouldn't think of it."

She vanished next.

"Okay, buddy," Ricky said. "If the bad guys show up, kill a couple for me."

"That's not funny," Dylan said.

Ricky grinned. "I'm not trying to be funny."

He slipped over the edge and lowered himself to the catwalk where Ananke and Liesel waited. He gave the rope a double tug and Dylan pulled it back through the gap.

"Clear," Dylan said over the comm.

Rosario lowered the hatch, sealing Ricky, Ananke, and Liesel inside.

ANANKE SURVEYED THE space below. This being the middle of the night, only a handful of the overhead lamps had been left on for safety purposes, turning the giant room into a spotty mix of shadow and light. Rows of boxes filled most of the floor, the only exception a clear area to the left.

"That seems the most logical place for the tunnel entrance," she said, pointing toward the spot.

"I agree," Liesel said.

"Rosario, we're ready to go down," Ananke said. "Are we clear?"

"One more minute, please."

While they waited for her, they moved to the end of the catwalk, where a wall-mounted ladder led down to the warehouse floor.

"Cameras are looped," Rosario said, letting them know

the feed would show previously shot footage of an empty parking area. "You can go now."

"Copy," Ananke said.

They climbed the three stories down to ground level, and quickly made their way through rows of boxes to the cleared area. Ananke's instincts had been correct. A conveyor belt, at least six feet wide, ramped out of a hole in the floor, then leveled off and ended at a boxing station.

Ananke peered into the opening, but it was too dark to see more than the faint outline of the conveyor system.

"Shall we?" Ricky said as he hopped up on the belt.

"I'll check first," Ananke told him. "You stay."

She pulled out her phone and flipped on her flashlight, climbed on the belt and followed the downward slope into the abyss. Though the ramp was steep, the semi-adhesive conveyer belt material kept her from tumbling to the bottom, which would have been even worse than she'd assumed since the ramp turned out to be twice as long as she'd expected. The belt must have gone down at least twenty-five feet before leveling off.

She shined the light ahead. The tunnel was about four feet wider than the conveyor, with most of that space on the left side, creating a walkway she guessed maintenance workers used. As for the height, it was about ten feet tall from the concrete floor to the ceiling, which meant around seven from the top of the belt.

"Come on down," she said.

She turned her light so that it illuminated the ramp. Ricky came first with Liesel a few steps behind.

"That was fun," Ricky whispered when he reached the bottom. "I wonder if anyone's ever tried to slide a cardboard box down that."

Ananke turned back to the tunnel and headed into it. Half a dozen steps in, she jammed on the brakes and doused her light.

"Rosario, there's a camera down here!"

"Are you sure? I do not see anything in the security system."

"I just flashed my light straight at it. So, yeah, I'm sure."

Rosario was silent for a moment. "No change in the security room. Hang on a moment."

Ananke didn't think they had a moment. Maybe the security guards hadn't noticed the unauthorized light pointing at the camera, but if their system was worth anything, an automatic alert would pop up at any second.

"It is not a security camera," Rosario said. "It is part of production monitoring, to make sure there are no problems in the tunnel. It is currently off."

"Are you sure?"

"Yes. You will encounter eight more before you reach the other end. They are also off."

While Ananke did trust Rosario, she felt uneasy as she turned her light back on and walked past the camera.

The conveyor stretched through the gray, utility pipe-lined walls, each section looking the same as the last. Here and there they passed one of the nonoperating production cameras. The conveyor seemed to go on forever before the team finally spotted another ramp ahead, ascending to ground level.

"Door," Liesel said.

Ananke looked to where Liesel was pointing her light. Tucked into a nook along the wall was a door with an attached sign that read MAINTENANCE. Ananke motioned for Ricky to check it out.

"Locked," he said. "You want me to pick it?"

"If we think it's important, we can hit it on our way back."

They climbed back onto the belt and headed up toward ground level. Just shy of emerging into the other building, Ananke stopped.

"Rosario, we're at the other side," she whispered into the comm. "Room check, please."

"Stop!" Rosario said. "Did you not hear me?"

"Hear you? What are you talking about?"

"Thirty seconds ago, I said do not leave the tunnel. Did you?"

"No, we're still in it. But we didn't hear anything. What's the problem?"

"There are two guards in the production room."

"Close to the opening?"

"Not yet, but they appear to be checking everywhere."

Ananke motioned for Ricky and Liesel to move back down the tunnel and then followed them. "Checking like they know there's a problem? Or checking like they are on rounds?"

"What? I…an't…Anan…"

"Rosario. Come in. Can you hear me?"

No response.

They moved past the bottom and continued down the tunnel. "Rosario? Rosario? Can you hear me? Rosario?"

"Ananke? Yes…hear…. Can you hear me?"

Ananke was a good fifty feet beyond where the ramp began. "Yeah, I can. There were a few seconds there when you disappeared completely."

"Same for me."

Ananke looked toward the tunnel exit, her eyes narrowing. "You said the guards were checking everything. Did you mean like normal rounds, or like they think something's wrong?"

"They do not seem agitated, just thorough."

That was good.

"They are getting closer to the tunnel entrance, though."

That was not good. If the guards descended the ramp, Ananke and the others would never make it to the other side without being seen, because there was nowhere in the tunnel to hide.

Hold on. Not *nowhere.*

"Ricky," Ananke whispered. "Get that maintenance door open."

THE MAINTENANCE ROOM turned out to be a large, shoebox-shaped space, with the long dimension running perpendicular to the tunnel. It contained very little in the way of maintenance supplies, though, just a single shelving unit, sparsely populated by cleaners and lubricants and tools. Except for that and a cart at the back of the room piled high with boxes, the rest of the space remained unused.

This left few options for cover if the guards decided to

come in.

"Keep an ear on the door," Ananke told Ricky. She motioned for Liesel to follow her and headed toward the cart.

Her plan was to move it from the wall so they could hide behind it.

As they neared it, Liesel pointed at the wall above the cart, near the ceiling. "Ananke, look."

Mounted there was a black, tubular electronic device about two feet long. Ananke knew exactly what it was—a Nakamura Systems 8500 signal jammer. Depending on the setting, it had a range between two dozen feet and nearly one hundred.

No wonder they had lost contact with Rosario.

"Why would there be a jammer in here?" Ananke said.

"I do not know."

When they reached the cart, Ananke gave it a tentative pull and found it lighter than expected.

"Squeeze around the back and make sure nothing falls off," she said. "I want to move it out a little more."

Liesel slipped between the cart and the wall. "Um, Ananke."

"Not enough room? Here, let me pull—"

"No, you need to come here."

Ananke moved behind the cart.

What the hell?

The cart hadn't been sitting in front of a blank wall. It had been blocking a door.

A metal bar lay across the door, held in place by thick hooks, clearly meant to prevent the door from being opened. *From the other side.*

"Okay, does that seem creepy to you?" Ananke asked. "Because it seems creepy to me."

"Creepy is a good word."

Ananke couldn't help but wonder if this was where the people from the big rig had been put.

"Hey," Ricky whispered. Since the jammer interfered with the comm, they could barely hear him across the room. "What's going on?"

Ananke leaned out around the cart and motioned for him to chill, then turned back to the door. "Shall we see what's on the other side?"

Liesel nodded.

Ananke performed an electronics sweep for any monitoring equipment on the other side. It detected no alarm, but did pick up electronic signatures of five cameras that, according to her app, were in sleep mode.

She lifted the metal bar from its brackets and eased the door open. The space beyond was pitch-black. She shined her flashlight inside. Another rectangular room, this one with three doors set at regular intervals along the wall on the left.

"Wait here," Ananke told Liesel, handing her the bar.

She removed her pistol from her shoulder holster and crept inside. She scanned the room with her light and spotted two of the cameras. Each was mounted on the wall to the right and aimed at the one on the left, presumably at the doors.

She approached the first door and slid the latch free. The door opened onto a sparsely filled storage room. Stacked along one wall were several giant, rectangular glass boxes that had one of the long sides missing. She walked over and tapped on one of them. Plexiglas. She took a few pictures, but had no idea what the boxes were used for.

Ananke moved on to the middle room. At first sight, it appeared to be completely empty. She stepped inside and swept her light through the space. Mounted against each side wall at approximately seven-foot intervals were electric outlets, each with four sockets. The outlet boxes were connected to one another via metal conduit.

A production room? Where identical workstations could be lined up one after another? If so, it would have a sweatshop vibe. Could that be the big secret?

As she snapped more photos, she noticed black scuff marks on the floor, under a layer of dust. Not from shoes but from wheels, like on a cart. She took a few shots of them, too, before exiting and proceeding to door number three.

RICKY PRESSED HIS ear against the door, listening for the

guards and shooting the occasional glance toward the cart at the back of the room.

What was taking Ananke and Liesel so long?

He wasn't even sure what they were doing back there. Was Ananke planning on bringing the cart over here to block the door? Or were they going to hide behind it? Sometimes it felt like people didn't tell him anything.

Footsteps outside. Distant, but growing louder.

He tensed, and for the umpteenth time made sure the door's lock had been reengaged. Not that it would delay the guards for more than a few seconds.

The steps kept coming, which meant they were definitely in the tunnel. Hopefully they would walk right past the door and head to the other building.

Tap. Tap. Tap. Closer and closer and—

The steps stopped right outside the door.

Ricky sprinted across the room. Whatever Ananke's plan had been, they were down to one option now: hide behind the cart.

As he neared it, he could hear the muted jangle of keys beyond the door behind him. He raced through the remaining distance and slid around the cart to join Ananke and Liesel.

Except the only one there was Liesel, standing, much to his surprise, in front of an open door.

"You are supposed to be monitoring the door," she said.

"Don't need to do that anymore. They're coming in."

As Liesel's eyes widened, Ricky picked up the faint sound of a key entering a lock.

He pushed Liesel through the opening, whispering, "Go, go, go."

He entered right behind her and closed the door until only an inch-wide gap remained.

For a few seconds, all was calm, and then a gentle whoosh of air pushed the door against him, signaling the outer entrance had been opened. He heard voices as the two guards entered. Nothing panicky, only the small talk of a couple of guys going through the same motions they did every day. They walked around the room for a few seconds, but never came as far back as the cart.

When the door finally closed again, Ricky held his position, alert for sounds of anyone who might have stayed behind. After several seconds, he said, "I think they're gone."

He turned but Liesel wasn't there.

Across the dark room, dim light seeped out of a doorway. He turned on his flashlight and walked over. Both Ananke and Liesel were in the room, down at the other end. Ananke's light lit up what appeared to be several low tables pushed together.

"In case anyone is wondering," Ricky said as he entered, "the guards are gone."

"Okay," Ananke said, not even looking at him.

"Okay? Would you have preferred them to join us?"

This time, she didn't answer at all.

He headed across the room to see what was more important than their freedom.

What the other two were examining weren't tables but wheeled platforms, the tops raised a few feet above the floor. They were rectangular, about five feet wide and ten long. The surface appeared to be some kind of polymer, with a deep groove running along each side about three inches from the edge.

Ricky asked, "So…what are we all enthralled about? It's a platform."

Ananke made a crude measurement of the width of the groove, using the barrel of her gun. "Follow me."

She led them to another room of the same size. Instead of platforms, this one held several stacks of clear, rectangular boxes. Huge ones.

Ananke placed her gun barrel against the edge of the opened end of one of the boxes. "See that? Perfect fit."

Liesel caught on a second before Ricky did. "You think these go on top of the platforms."

"Yeah, I do."

"Why?" Ricky asked. "To create monster-sized, see-through butter trays?"

"Cute. But no. But they would make convenient mobile holding cells."

174

Ricky blinked. He hadn't seen that coming.

"There would have to be a way to regulate air and temperature," Liesel said.

"There are hose ports under the platform, with hidden vents in the floor," Ananke said.

Ricky looked from one woman to the other. "Are you two crazy? Why would anyone use these as cells?"

"You were the one who suggested they were moving people. Seems like an innovative way of putting several people right next to each other while keeping them separate, and still being able to see what each prisoner is up to."

"Someone could just push it off," he suggested.

"Not if they are drugged," Liesel said.

"They wouldn't need to be drugged," Ananke countered. "There's a locking mechanism on the platforms, too."

Ricky stared at the boxes. "You're serious."

"What I think is that these things were intended for some other use and adapted."

"Jesus," Ricky said. "Then where are the people?"

"The middle room seemed to be designed as a holding space, but it's pretty dusty so I don't think it's been used for a while. My guess, they don't store anyone here anymore."

"Hold on," Ricky said. "I saw them unloading people just a few hours ago."

"You saw them unloading *something*. And then loading one guy into the pickup truck. But let's assume it was people. Keeping them here, at an active factory? That seems pretty impractical. But not quite as impractical if you think of this place as a late-night transfer point."

"So you think the trucks drop them off here and someone else takes them to their next destination?"

"I'm saying it's a possibility."

"Why wouldn't the truck go straight to this other place?"

"Could be any number of reasons."

"Maybe it is not practical," Liesel suggested.

"Right. Or maybe they want to keep the next destination a secret, and that would be a lot easier to do without a semi-truck showing up."

"So where is this other place?" Liesel asked.

"That's what we need to find out."

"And how are we going to do that?" Ricky asked.

"I think it's time for a more direct approach."

SURPRISE, SURPRISE. ANOTHER quiet night in the bustling metropolis of Bradbury.

About the only excitement Harris had encountered on her shift was the purchasing manager of one of the dot-coms drinking a little too much at the Cache Bar and making a nuisance of himself. Nothing a night sleeping in a holding cell wouldn't cure.

Dealing with him had knocked her off her normal schedule, though, and it wasn't until around midnight before she made it to Tasha's house. All the trip lines she'd set were still in place, and a quick look through the windows revealed no indication of anyone having been inside. She still wasn't sure if she should take that as a good sign or not.

She had spent the next several hours driving around town, "keeping the peace."

At a quarter to three, she turned onto Clearwater Drive and drove past the Collins Inn. Like she'd done every time her rounds took her by the hotel for the last two nights, she checked the parking lot for Shawn Ramey's Mustang.

Her foot eased up on the gas.

The Mustang was gone.

It had been there when she drove by about an hour and a half ago. Given the time of night, she'd assumed it would remain there.

She turned into the parking lot, thinking maybe Ramey had moved it for some reason. But a search through both the front and back lots confirmed the car wasn't there.

Had Ramey left town? If she'd had an early morning flight out of Spokane, leaving in the wee hours would make sense. But from what Harris had learned by quietly asking around, Ramey was supposed to be in the area for several more days.

Harris had that same feeling in the pit of her stomach she'd experienced the first night she saw Ramey driving around—

that the woman was up to no good. Ramey was supposedly here to look into potential locations for her company, but Harris wasn't buying it. There was something off about the woman. And in light of what had been going on with Tasha, Harris couldn't help but wonder if Ramey was involved.

She headed back to the main road, hoping to figure out where Ramey had gone. She glanced south and north. Both directions were devoid of traffic. She went south first, taking the occasional side street as she looked for the Mustang. When the car failed to turn up, she tried her luck to the north, but more disappointment followed.

Maybe she did *leave town.*

Harris could check with the night clerk at the Collins Inn, but she thought it safer not to have anyone wonder why she was interested. In the morning, she could make an anonymous call from the pay phone at the Brazen Diner to find out. She drove to the end of the block and turned back toward the highway, to take up where she'd left off on her rounds.

When she reached the highway intersection, she noticed headlights in the distance, coming from farther north. In her line of work, she was well versed in the differences between automotive light designs. While those heading her way were still distant, she could make out enough to eliminate several makes and models, but not Ford Mustangs.

She backed away from the intersection until she was hidden by the building at the corner, then turned off her headlights and killed the engine. She grabbed her bag off the floor, fished around until she found her phone, and after accessing camera mode, pointed it at the intersection.

It was a good forty-five seconds before she heard the motor. And another five when she realized there was not one but two vehicles.

Though she couldn't see anything yet, she began taking pictures, and didn't stop until after Ramey's Mustang and the nice-looking bike following it had gone by. Harris would have assumed they weren't together except the bike was driving very close to the car, and if it had wanted to pass, there had been plenty of space to do it.

She scrolled through the photos until she found the best one of the Mustang, and enlarged it to see inside the cab. As expected, Ramey sat behind the wheel, but Harris didn't recognize the Asian woman sitting beside her, or the Caucasian man in the back.

No sign of Ramey's friend Caroline. Unless she was the one on the motorcycle. Harris brought up an image of the bike. No, the rider was too big to be Caroline, and, from the silhouette, likely male.

She fired up the cruiser and turned onto the highway. She could see the other vehicles' taillights nearing the turnoff to the Collins Inn, but only the motorcycle went toward the hotel.

Leaving her lights off, Harris tried to cut the distance between her and the Mustang, but she was still three blocks away when the muscle car turned right and disappeared from sight. Harris raced to the intersection, but the other street was empty.

"Dammit."

She resisted the urge to search for Ramey, and headed back to the Collins Inn.

Upon reaching the hotel, she spotted the motorcycle parked in front of the east wing. She had no doubt now its driver knew Ramey.

Harris found a concealed spot in a lot across the street and waited for the Mustang. When it showed up, Ramey was alone. Harris watched her park and walk into the hotel.

Supposedly, Ramey's only colleague in town was her friend, Caroline Cruz. But it seemed the woman knew at least three others.

Yep. Definitely something fishy going on. Harris was determined to find out what it was.

EIGHTEEN

THE GUESTS ATE breakfast at the banquet table in the lodge's dining room, choosing from an assortment of eggs—scrambled, fried, and boiled—sausage, bacon, pancakes, french toast, fruit, yogurt, and cheese and meats spread down the center.

Unlike when they'd arrived two days before, those present talked easily with one another, recounting events from the previous day, when they had all gone through training on the various weapons and methods they might use when the trials began.

As they were finishing their meals, the kitchen door opened, and a smartly dressed man who looked to be in his early forties emerged. Fit, with a bright smile and perfectly styled short brown hair, he exuded a confidence the gathering's attendees could relate to. He was one of them. A member of the elite. A mover and shaker. A man at the top of the power pyramid.

"Good morning, gentlemen. It's a pleasure to finally meet you. I am your host, Mr. Lean."

Greetings were returned in kind. Even the grumpy Mr. Huston, the slumlord, managed to sound almost kindly. They had all been wondering when they'd meet their host.

"I understand training went very well yesterday," Mr. Lean said. "I'm happy to hear that. I'm told you're a particularly talented group." He smiled. "I trust you all had a good night's sleep, because today is not a day to be low on energy."

There were a few chuckles and knowing laughs. Today was the start of the trials.

"Is everyone done with breakfast, or do you need a bit more time before we get started?"

"Hell, no. Let's do it," Mr. Welles said.

A few eyes turned to Mr. Wise, who had still been eating when Mr. Lean arrived. When he noticed the attention, he pushed his plate away and said, "All done."

Mr. Ford, the other slow eater, made a similar gesture.

"Fantastic," Mr. Lean said. He lifted a bell off the buffet table behind him and rang it.

The kitchen door opened again, this time admitting three young men who began removing plates and glasses and serving dishes. Once the table had been cleared, table cloth included, the servants exited. Mr. Lean took his place at the head of the table but remained standing.

"I know you are all anxious to get underway," he said.

That was an understatement. A sense of excitement and anticipation filled the room as if it were the very air they were breathing.

"So, let's begin. Today's schedule will be broken up into two parts. This morning you will put to use your training from yesterday, and partake in a series of tests to gauge your individual skill levels. This will make it easier for us to provide help where needed, and to match you to the trophy best suited for you. After lunch, we will commence the first trial."

The men grinned like kids on Christmas morning.

Mr. Huston raised a hand. "How will it work? I mean, do we all go at once, or is it one by one? Is there a time frame?"

"An excellent question. The short answer is, each trial has a different method and time frame. But don't you worry, we'll go over the details of today's event this afternoon before we start. Any other questions?"

There were a few, but all were answered in the same quick, efficient manner.

Mr. Lean rang the bell again, and Miss Riefenstahl entered. "Gentlemen, if you will please follow Miss Riefenstahl, she will take you to the testing facility now."

AS THE GUESTS filed out of the room, the host smiled in a

gracious, happy-you're-here kind of way. But as soon as he was alone, the grin disappeared.

What he and his two cousins had created here amounted to a sociologist's dream on so many levels. Of course, Slater and Yates didn't quite see it that way. They were small-time thinkers, who used their portion of the profits to fund the so-called "initiatives" they thought would bring about their dream of a pure world. It wasn't that the host didn't sympathize with their goal, but he knew the world was too far gone to ever see that dream realized. He humored them because he needed them to deal with the logistics of the trials.

What he was interested in was power. Real power. That's what the trials meant to him. Every gathering helped move him that much closer to his goal. Having the cream of the cream participate in the trials gave him a giant lever to manipulate them in the future, when the time came for him to make his move to the top.

He walked down the hallway to the basement entrance, and placed his fingers against the screen next to the door. The pad scanned his prints and released the lock. At the bottom of the stairs was a second door. This time the associated pad required his other hand. Again, the lock disengaged and he passed inside.

The lodge had been a resort back in the mid-twentieth century, catering to families looking to spend a week in the wilderness without having to rough it. It was based more or less on the resorts back east that had sprung up at roughly the same time.

Its glory days lasted about fifteen years, but it had clung on for another decade, going through a series of ownership changes until it was shut down and boarded up in 1979. In the ensuing years, hunters and adventurers and more than a few transients had found their way inside and stayed for a night or a week or month.

The host's late father had come into possession of it in 1992. When he was killed for being the asshole he was, title for the property had passed down to the host. He'd been in college then, having moved away from Bradbury with his mother when he was only eight. After his own company was up and running, he decided it was time to go back. It took a bit of manipulating to convince all those with an interest in his company to see the merits of the move, and it had paid off. No one but his cousins, of course, knew about his ties to the town. That was something he kept secret even now.

Upon his return to Bradbury, he spent a lot of cash refurbishing the lodge. He'd tried to rent it out to other companies for business retreats and the like. Unfortunately, it didn't attract nearly the number of customers he needed. Add to that a few financial setbacks at his company, and he was looking at shutting everything down and selling off the pieces.

It was around this time when his cousins had come to him with their idea for the trials, and their projections on the money they could make.

They'd underestimated. Each attendee paid two hundred and fifty thousand US dollars to be here. That was one and a half million for the five-day affair, against an event cost of less than fifty thousand. Since he was the one providing the location and the initial seed money, he received fifty-five percent of the profit, while Yates and Slater split the remaining.

To ensure they had enough product for events, extras were brought in, meaning once the monthly trial was complete, they could make even more cash selling the surplus to interested parties outside the US.

All in all, the host had been clearing five million a year, and would be doubling that this year. The only reason he didn't close his company was he needed a front.

He navigated the maze of basement hallways, occasionally passing through other security doors, until he reached the prep room.

As expected, Slater was there alone, his men upstairs cleaning the dishes and helping with the morning activities. A small, trustworthy crew was the key to the gathering's success.

"Is everything ready?" the host asked.

Slater opened one of the equipment lockers and pulled out several items. "Will be."

"Problems?"

"Think they hit the new one we brought over last night a little hard with the gas. He'll have to be the alternate." As alternate, the man would be used only if one of the other two trophies didn't perform as needed. And if he wasn't needed, he'd have a place in the rotation the next day.

"But the other two are good?"

"See for yourself." He nodded at a door across the room that led to the prep room.

The host walked over and entered the room. Though it was smaller than the one he'd been in, it was more than large enough for the six mobile holding cells present. Male trophies occupied three of the Plexiglas enclosures. Two were awake and standing at one end of their cells.

Though the nearest guy had been cleaned up and given a haircut, there was no removing the homeless aura he exuded. The host had seen enough like him since the beginning of the project to recognize his type: the furtive eyes, the over-aged skin, the facial ticks, the swaying, the look of resignation. He was white, which saddened the host. It pained him to see how low some people sank when they should have had it all. But a person who was a drain on society was a boon to the project.

The man stared at the host for a moment, looked away, and turned back, rocking side to side the whole time.

The other conscious man did not share the homeless guy's sense of futility. He pounded the box, yelling, but the host could hear only the dull thuds the man's fists made.

This one was of the much more common brown skin. Latino, definitely. The host figured him for Mexican, but the host had been wrong on that front before. Ultimately, it didn't matter. The man was just another illegal, now fattening the host's pockets. At the base of the Mexican's neck, like with the homeless trophy, was the familiar red mark signifying Slater had tagged him with a tracking bug.

The third man, as Slater had mentioned, lay on the floor of his cell, dead asleep. Another Latino. And young, too. Maybe twenty or twenty-one. He was a real find. He'd make an excellent participant, and would provide the kind of experience attendees enjoyed the most.

Satisfied, the host exited the room.

"What about tomorrow's stock?" he asked his cousin.

"I'll be heading over to the barn after I'm done here to make the final choices," Slater said.

The old barn was behind the host's house near Bradbury, and was where they held inventory until it was needed.

"I was thinking that tomorrow might be a good day to send in the woman," Slater said. "Maybe the midnight trials?"

The host considered it for a moment. "I love that idea."

NINETEEN

ROSARIO GRABBED THE mobile off the nightstand without looking, and pulled it under the covers with her. She checked the screen and hit ACCEPT after she saw who it was.

"This had better be good."

"Were you asleep?" Shinji asked. "It sounded like you were asleep. I can call back...but..."

She groaned. "I am awake. What is it?"

"I ID'd some of the guys Ricky saw at that delivery. I, um, sent you an email with the details."

"You called me to tell me you sent me an email?"

"No, no, no. That's not why. I, um...well, uh...see, I got to thinking about the delivery, and it reminded me of the link you sent from the *Bradbury Evening Independent*."

"What link?" she asked, still half asleep.

"The one about the accident." He paused. "The truck." Another pause. "On the highway?"

"Oh. Right."

"Two trucks, in odd circumstances, and on the same day? I thought it might be a good idea to see if there's a connection."

She pulled the covers off her head and sat up. "That's not bad, Shinji. Is there a connection?"

"The first thing I did was see if I could get some kind of ID numbers off the trucks, see if maybe they were owned by the same people, or came from the same place. It took a bit, but I got them. Only..."

"Only what?"

"Well, when I saw the numbers, it reminded me of something else. I double-checked, and it turned out my hunch was right."

"Shinji, you are giving me a headache. Just tell me."

"Patterson's notebook. The long string of characters. Those are *truck* IDs. In fact, the IDs for both the burned-out rig and the one Ricky saw are on the list."

She jumped out of bed and hurried over to her computer. "Send me the ID numbers."

"Already did."

She opened her email program.

"Any other surprises for me?"

"No. Sorry, that's it."

"Do not say sorry, Shinji. This is excellent. You have my permission to call me anytime you have something like this."

"Really? Well, uh, okay."

"I'll talk to you later."

She hung up and began verifying what he'd told her.

ANANKE'S ALARM WENT off only a few minutes after Rosario's phone had rung.

She killed it and lay still for a moment, wishing she could fall back to sleep. But she'd told the others they'd reassemble at Casa de Artisa at 8:30, and it wouldn't look good if she showed up late. Plus, she needed to talk to the Administrator before she left.

She climbed out of bed and grabbed her phone.

"There have been some developments," she told him after he answered.

"Tell me."

"We don't have a complete picture of what's going on yet, but it's coming into focus. We're pretty sure the something strange going on you were worried about involves the involuntary transportation of people."

Silence, then, "Explain."

She told him about the very long day she and the team had experienced, ending with their adventure at Scolareon.

"If I'm understanding correctly, the human trafficking assertion is still speculation," he said.

"Technically, I guess. But it's hard to ignore."

"What would Scolareon's purpose be in undertaking this

kind of thing?"

"That's one of those things we still need to work out."

"Then I repeat—speculation."

"Not for long."

"All right, tell me your plan."

EVERYONE HAD ARRIVED at Casa de Artisa by the appointed time. Dylan had been kind enough to have coffee ready, and Ricky, unprompted, had picked up croissants, donuts, and a big bowl of chopped mixed fruit.

"Anybody come up with any ideas why Scolareon might be into shipping people?" Ananke asked.

"Could be smuggling in cheap labor," Ricky suggested.

"We didn't see anyone who looked forced to work there when we walked through," Dylan said.

"Do you really think they'd expose you to them?"

"Maybe not, but I can't believe they could hide something like that from their regular employees. And there'd be no keeping it quiet then, would there?"

Dylan was right. The biggest enemy to a conspiracy was the number of people who knew the truth. The larger the group, the more likely someone would spill the beans.

"They could have a different facility," Liesel suggested. "Off...away?"

"Off-site?" Ananke asked.

"Yes, off-site."

"It's possible," Ananke said. "Anyone else?"

"Whatever the reason, they have been doing it a while, *and* at a pretty steady pace," Rosario said.

Ananke looked at her. Rosario had been surprisingly quiet on the drive over, as if lost in thought. "What do you mean?"

"Shinji cracked the code Patterson used in her notebook. The character strings are truck identification numbers. One in the list belongs to the truck Ricky saw. Another belonged to the truck that burned on the highway."

"The one we passed?" Liesel asked.

"Yes."

Ananke stared at her. "How long have you been sitting on

this?"

"He called me not long before we drove over here."

"And you couldn't have mentioned something then?"

"If I did, I would have had to repeat myself."

"What about the other numbers on the list?" Dylan asked.

"I do not know for sure, but it seems likely the dates are delivery dates. And the number could be how many people in a specific delivery."

"We should have Shinji track down the other trucks on the list," Ananke said.

"He's already doing so."

"Damn," Ricky said. "Good job, Shinji."

Rosario nodded. "There is one more thing."

Ananke said, "The floor is still yours."

"The white pickup Ricky saw is owned by a man named Dalton Slater."

"You're like Santa Claus," Ricky said. "Please tell us you have an address, too."

"Of course I do."

Ananke looked at Rosario. "Is that it?"

"For the moment."

"Well, then, I guess in the spirit of Shinji and Rosario, today's the day we find answers."

Ricky grinned. "I like the sound of that. Are we going after the Scolareon guy?"

Ananke shook her head. When they went after Scudder, she wanted to be armed with as much information as possible. "I have someone else in mind first."

"WAKE UP."

It wasn't so much the voice that pulled Harris from her dream as the squeezing of her foot.

She blinked, her mind still processing what was happening. The moment she realized a hand was tugging her, she yanked her foot away and shoved her hand under the spare pillow.

"Sorry, it's not there."

Shawn Ramey stood at the foot of her bed, dangling the

pistol Harris always kept nearby. The woman had not come alone. Caroline Cruz stood close to the bed also, as did the two others Harris had seen in the Mustang the night before. The only person she didn't recognize was a man standing by the empty side of her bed.

Every single one of them was armed.

"Sorry for waking you early," Ramey said. "I know how it is. Night shift. Already a pain in the ass to sleep during the day. The problem is, we don't have time to waste waiting for you to get in your eight hours."

"Give me back my gun and get out of my house!"

"Good. Get that out of your system."

Harris's brow furrowed. "What?"

"You're angry. You wake up and find a bunch of strangers in your bedroom. That would irritate the best of us. So let it out. You'll feel better."

"This is breaking and entering! Of a *police officer's home*, in case you forgot! You are in deep shit."

Laughing, Ramey said, "Oh, my God. You are a pro at this. Keep going if you need to."

Harris threw back her covers and started to get out of bed, but the man she didn't recognize grabbed her shoulder and firmly pushed her back down.

"Better if you stay where you are," Ramey said.

Harris tensed. "Can I at least sit up?"

"That's a reasonable request. Make yourself comfortable."

Harris propped herself against the headboard. "Am I allowed to ask what the hell you're doing in my house?"

"Morgan—may I still call you Morgan?" Harris just glared at Ramey. "We're going to ask you a few questions. How you answer them will determine how we treat you."

"Screw you!"

"That would be an example of a wrong response. I'll give you a pass this time." Ramey smiled. "I know your instinct will be to lie and cover yourself, but trust me, that never works. Not with us. Here's the first question. Where's Natasha Patterson?"

WHEN ANANKE ASKED the question, she thought things would go one of two ways: Ramey would get defensive and claim to know nothing, or she would withdraw into herself for a second, surprised by the question, and then try to give an answer that put her participation in her girlfriend's disappearance in the best light.

What happened instead was, Harris shot toward Ananke like a missile, her hands extended to latch on to Ananke's face.

Ananke started pivoting to redirect Harris to the floor, but the cop never reached her. Ricky and Dylan dove at her from both sides. Ricky caught her in the hip, while Dylan wrapped his arms around her ankles, sending her plummeting back to the mattress. Her head hit the bedframe with a whack.

"I think we have a wild one, boss," Ricky said. "Back on the bed, lady." He started pulling Harris toward him.

"Ricky, wait," Ananke said. She crouched next to Harris's head. The woman's eyes were shut and her face had gone slack. Ananke lifted an eyelid. "Well, that's just great. You knocked her out."

"Would you have preferred we let her tackle you?" Dylan said.

Ananke almost said yes, because she would have subdued the cop without Harris losing consciousness, but Ricky's and Dylan's instincts had been good and she couldn't fault them for protecting her.

"Help me turn her over," she said.

After they got Harris onto her back, Ananke examined the woman's head. The cop would have a nice welt right above her ear, but the cut wasn't bad enough to need stitches.

"Dylan, wet towel," Ananke said. "Rosario, see if there's any Neosporin or antiseptic and a Band-Aid. Ricky, chair and rope. And Liesel, help me with her."

They got Harris cleaned and bandaged, then tied her to a dining room chair Ricky brought in. In addition to the other items she'd been sent to collect, Rosario found a bottle of aspirin, so they had that and a glass of water standing by. Liesel grabbed a kitchen towel and filled it with ice, which she now held gently over Harris's wound.

After a few minutes, Ananke began to wonder if the injury was worse than she'd thought, but finally the woman began to moan, a hushed hum deep in her throat. As it grew louder, her head slowly tilted from side to side. Her brow creased with the first signs of pain.

When her eyes opened, Harris looked confused again, but then she saw Ananke. She tried to jerk away but the ropes held firm.

"Let me go!" she screamed, rocking the chair. "Get this off me!"

"Relax," Ananke said calmly. "The rope is for your protection, not ours. I'm worried my friends won't be quite as gentle if you tried something stupid again."

Harris yelled in frustration and strained against her bindings. She rocked again, this time tipping the chair far enough that she started to fall. Liesel caught and righted her.

Harris huffed and puffed and glared at Ananke.

"We get it," Ananke said. "No one likes to be unprepared for guests. They always catch you when you haven't had a chance to clean the house." Harris didn't laugh. "Like I said before, the more cooperative you are, the quicker and easier this will go."

"Go to hell."

Ricky leaned in from behind and whispered in the cop's ear. "We're going to get our answers one way or another. If you want this to be difficult, we can do difficult."

Keeping her face neutral, Ananke resisted the urge to slap Ricky on the side of his head. His comment had not been part of the script. *She* was the one who was supposed to do the talking. No one else.

His words seemed to have some effect, though, as Harris got her breathing under control and quit fighting her restraints. The glare remained.

"Shall we start again?" Ananke asked.

Zero change in Harris's expression.

"Where's Natasha Patterson?"

Harris's breathing deepened and sped up again, her nostrils flaring, but her mouth stayed shut.

"It's a simple question."

Harris's eyes narrowed.

"Where's Na—"

"Like you don't already know," Harris said through clenched teeth.

"If we did, I wouldn't be asking you."

"Bullshit! You're the ones who took her!" She rattled her chair again.

"Why would you think we have her?"

"You don't want to play games? Great. Let's not play games. I know you're not who you say you are. You don't work for a company thinking about coming up here. And I'm sure your friends don't do whatever it is they've been telling everyone they do, either. I checked on you. And though I don't have enough to prove it yet, I know there's no such person as Shawn Ramey. Not the Shawn Ramey you are, anyway."

"You've checked on me, have you? Have you shared that information with the people you're working for?"

"I sure did. And when the chief realizes something's happened to me, he'll call in the FBI. Meaning you're screwed. The only thing you can do is untie me, tell me where Tasha is, and then get as far away from here as possible before they start looking for you."

"I'm not talking about the police," Ananke said. "We both know I'm talking about the people you really work for."

Though the fury remained on Harris's face, a touch of bewilderment passed through her eyes. "People I really work for? I don't know what you're talking about."

All four of the others snuck looks at Ananke. They had clearly heard the same thing she had in Harris's voice. The truth.

"I'm talking about the people who took Tasha," Ananke pressed. "The people you helped."

"Why in God's name would I help someone take Tasha? I—" She took a deep breath. "You're just trying to trick me."

"Into what? Saying you and Tasha were having a relationship? We know that already."

An instant of shock, followed by a look of guarded denial.

"It was a ruse, though, wasn't it?" Ananke said. "You were ordered to get close to her, weren't you? She had no idea you were scamming her."

"I would never do that to her! I…"

"Sure, you would. It would have been a perfect cover to keep an eye on her. You would have then been in position to deal with her when the time came."

"Are you serious? I could *never* hurt Tasha! You're the ones! You've done something to her! Where is she?"

More glances from Ananke's colleagues. Even Ricky appeared to be rethinking the woman's involvement in Patterson's disappearance.

Ananke thought for a moment before saying, "If you were in a real relationship with her, why did she contact others but not you after April fifth?"

"How did you know that?"

"That's not the question."

"The hell, it isn't. If you didn't take Tasha, then who are you and why do *you* care?"

Rosario and Liesel gave Ananke a nod, encouraging her to tell Harris the truth.

"We're here at the request of a friend of Tasha's who's worried something happened to her."

"Friend? What friend?"

"Scott Davos."

"Davos," Harris said, not like she was surprised, but like it made sense. "If that's true, then we want the same thing."

"Not so fast. You still haven't answered my question."

"About being contacted?" Harris let out a short laugh. "Bradbury might be modernizing, but it's not so progressive yet that a relationship between…someone like her and me would be universally accepted. We've kept it quiet. No one, and I mean *no one*, knows. We set up a special email account that we use only for each other. Whoever sent out those messages pretending to be her must have used the contacts from her main email account. I'm not on that list, so they knew nothing about me."

That made sense. "When you suspected she was missing,

why didn't you report it? You're a cop."

"The answer isn't any different. If I did, and it turned out she really wasn't missing, I, for sure, would be forced out of town. My *home*town. And Scolareon would be pressured to fire Tasha. I have no proof other than my gut, but I'm the only woman cop in the whole department. Even if I pretended Tasha was just a friend, do you really think my bosses would listen to me?"

"So that's why you put the wire traps around her house?"

Harris's eyes widened. "How do you know about those?"

"Because we've seen you check them."

Harris was silent for a few seconds. "Look, Tasha told me that if anything happened to her to contact Scott Davos, so the first thing I did was email him. If he really sent you here, it's because of me."

"Why would she think something was going to happen to her?"

"I honestly believed she was joking when she told me. It was about two months ago, maybe a little less. She didn't make a big deal of it, but she did tell me not to forget."

Ananke nodded, and looked at Liesel and Ricky. "Untie her."

After the cords had been removed, Harris stretched her arms and gingerly touched her head.

"Uh, yeah, about that," Dylan said. "We weren't trying to crack your skull open or nothing, just keep you from ripping the boss's eyes out. Sorry."

"I would have if you hadn't," Harris said.

"You would have tried," Ananke corrected her.

Harris looked as if she wasn't so sure.

"How was Tasha before she disappeared?" Ananke asked. "Was she acting strange? Different?"

Harris looked around. "Is that aspirin?"

Dylan handed her the glass of water and opened the pill bottle. "How many?"

"All of them?"

"How about we go with four. That sounds like an excessive but not too excessive amount, if you know what I mean."

She downed the pills, then said to Ananke, "I'm not telling you anything else until we have an understanding."

"We do have an understanding. If you don't cooperate, we tie you back up and leave you here until we've completed our mission."

"You won't do that."

Ananke said nothing.

"I share what I know and you share what you know," Harris said. "That's the deal."

"No."

Harris stared at Ananke as if she expected her to change her answer. But Ananke remained silent.

"Fine," Harris said. "You don't have to tell me everything, but from this point forward you keep me updated on your progress. And when you find her, I'm the first to know."

"Officer Harris, *Morgan*, I respect and understand your desire to remain engaged in the search. Here's my deal, nonnegotiable. You will answer all our questions, and when necessary, provide any assistance we might require. This could range from using the police department's resources, to giving us rides, to anything else we might think of. In return, I will inform you first when we find her. There will be no updates or sharing of information. With the exception of what I've already told you, this is a one-way street, you to us."

Ananke held out her hand. After a moment, Harris shook it. "Fine."

"Good. Now, about Tasha's mood before she disappeared."

"Something was definitely bothering her. She had a hard time sleeping and was more frustrated than usual."

"What do you mean by frustrated?"

Harris thought for a moment. "Like she'd lost something she couldn't find."

"What about struggling with something she couldn't figure out?" Ricky asked.

"That's it! Yes."

"Did you ask her about it?" Ananke said.

"All the time, but she just said it was work stuff, and not to worry. I assumed that's what it was."

"And she never told you anything else?"

"No."

Ananke looked around the room. "Did she leave anything else here other than clothes and the book on the nightstand?"

Harris glanced at the memoir. "She'd bring her briefcase, but would always take it with her when she left. That was about it."

"Do you know if she ever had problems with Kyle Scudder?"

"Not that I'm aware of. As far as I know, they got along well, and he was happy with the job she was doing."

"Is there anyone she might have mentioned that she was having an issue with?"

"No, no one."

"Who were you trying to catch with the traps at her house?" Rosario asked.

Some of the strength drained from Harris. "I'm not sure. I guess I thought if someone *had* taken her, maybe they would come to search her place. But I can't deny there was a part of me that also wondered if this was some kind of ploy to break things off, and maybe I'd catch her sneaking back."

"I gotta say, that's verging on stalker territory," Dylan said.

Ricky shrugged. "I've done worse."

"I wasn't going to *do* anything if it were true," Harris said. "I just wanted to know where I stood and didn't want to be ghosted."

They clarified a few more points, but gained little new information.

"Can we trust you not to blow our cover?" Ananke asked.

"If I say no, will you kill me?" Harris asked. "No, I won't turn you in. Unless I find out you've been lying to me."

"We'll be in touch."

TWENTY

THE LAST THING Eduardo remembered was the *clunk-clunk, clunk-clunk, clunk-clunk* of the big rig's wheels and the sway of the trailer lulling him to sleep. But as his consciousness returned, he realized not only were both gone, so were the rumble of the truck's engine and the snores of his traveling companions.

Everything was quiet. Deathly quiet.

He pried his eyelids open, both feeling as if they weighed a million pounds, and had to quickly shade his eyes from the glare of light. After they adjusted, he saw he was in a gray-walled room.

He tried sitting up, but an intense swirl of vertigo kept him down. Eyes squeezed shut, he waited until the world stopped spinning, and tried again. His head swam again, but not as badly, and he made it all the way up.

His bed was a cot, sitting on a platform a few feet above the room's floor. The disturbing discovery was the large transparent box containing him.

He rose unsteadily to his feet and put a hand on the wall. Not glass, but thick plastic.

He tried to push it but it was anchored in place, and all he managed to do was rock the whole thing—cover and platform—an inch or two in either direction.

He scanned the room. His wasn't the only boxed-in platform. There were six others, lined up against two of the walls. Though the room had a heavy-looking door on the far side, there were no windows.

He turned his attention to the other—enclosures? Cells?—looking for Sonya. He'd promised to protect her. All but one of the boxes were empty, however, and the one that wasn't held a man sitting on his cot, facing the other way.

Eduardo slapped the wall. "Hey! Hey! Over here!"

The man didn't move.

"Sir, please!" Eduardo yelled louder. "Behind you!"

Not a twitch.

Eduardo hit the wall harder, but the man remained motionless. Eduardo attempted to rock his cell into the adjacent one, hoping to start a chain reaction that would bump the man's platform, but as much as he pushed, he couldn't get his platform to move enough.

He cupped his hands against the plastic and repeatedly yelled, "Over here!"

When the man stood, Eduardo thought he'd finally gotten through to him, but then Eduardo noticed movement in his periphery.

The door had swung open, and two men had entered. Both were Caucasian, the older one in his forties at least, but the younger one looked to be around Eduardo's age. They both wore blue jeans and long-sleeved, buttoned work shirts.

They headed straight for the other guy's cell, but as they crossed the room, the older man noticed Eduardo watching them. He said something to his companion. The young guy continued to the other caged man, but the older one changed course toward Eduardo.

As the man neared Eduardo's cell, he grinned.

Eduardo shouted, "Where's Sonya?"

The man pointed at his ears, signaling he couldn't hear.

Eduardo hit the transparent wall. "Where's *Sonya*?"

The man's eyebrows rose, and he held up a hand in the universal signal to wait. Kneeling in front of Eduardo's platform, he fiddled with something underneath. Suddenly there was a low buzz in the cell.

The man stood again and said, "Sorry, I missed that. What did you say?" His voice came from under the cot and sounded distant, like the guy was standing too far from a microphone.

"Where's Sonya?"

"Sonya? No women in this room, amigo."

"Where is she?" Eduardo demanded.

"Now, hold on. Let's see. You came in last night, right?"

"Tell me where she is."

"She, uh, older or younger?"

"Younger. Eighteen."

"Eighteen?" The man shook his head and whistled in surprise. "Sorry to tell you this, but she's probably a thousand miles from here by now. Don't you worry, though. I'm sure her new owners will treat her in the way she deserves." The man laughed.

Owners? What the hell did that mean? "Where is she, goddammit?"

"Better you worry about your own hide."

Across the room, the young guy said, "Ready."

The older man looked over his shoulder and then back at Eduardo. "You might want to get a little more rest. If we need you this afternoon, you'll want to be sharp."

"You can't hold me like this! Let me out! Let me out!"

Somewhere in the middle of Eduardo's rant, the man had reached down and turned off the communications system.

But Eduardo kept yelling.

SLATER AND HIS assistant, Bryan, rolled the holding cell into the work room, and set about prepping the prey for trial number two. Trial one's soon-to-be trophy was in his cage on the other side of the space, sitting on his cot, stunned.

This was the most common reaction. Slater had seen it dozens of times. The this-can't-be-happening cloud that descended after a prey had their tracking chip embedded at the base of their neck and been told what was going to happen. The second most common reaction was enraged pacing and shouting. Little did this latter group know that, by using up so much energy, they were only making things worse for themselves. Members of this group seldom ever lasted more than the first hour, whereas someone who'd reacted with shock might make it two hours or even three before they found themselves in the crosshairs.

Once number two was ready, Slater said, "Let Monica

199

know the prey are ready to go. I'll be back later."

"Yes, sir."

Slater headed upstairs and exited at the back of the lodge. His cousin's car was gone, the man no doubt putting in an appearance at his day job. Slater was glad he didn't have to worry about anything like that, and could concentrate on the bigger picture.

Between trials, he was free to plan where his and his brother's cash would be used to further the cause. Slater was the one who'd picked out the land they'd bought in northern Montana, which would someday be the heart of their glorious free state, where like-minded people would find none of the crap the rest of the country had been collecting.

He whistled as he climbed into his truck, and started the drive to Green Hills Estates.

TWENTY-ONE

WHILE THERE WAS no concrete evidence Kyle Scudder was involved with the human trafficking scheme, it was hard to believe he wasn't somehow part of it. Tasha Patterson worked for him. She disappeared after visiting one of his facilities. Secret shipments of, presumably, people were processed through his factory by his employees. And, from what Ananke and the others had discovered at his facility, the people may have even been stored there at one time.

It was time Ananke had a little talk with Scolareon's owner.

Unlike with Officer Harris, they couldn't just break into Scudder's house or office and wait for him. Nor would it be wise to tie him to a chair and pepper him with questions until he broke. Not yet, anyway.

Fortunately, Ananke had a legitimate way to get to him.

She pulled out the business card he'd given her at the party and called his cell.

"Kyle Scudder." True to his word, he answered his own line.

"Good morning, Mr. Scudder. It's Shawn Ramey."

She expected him to take a moment to recall her name, but there wasn't even a beat before he said, "Shawn, nice to hear from you. And, please, if I didn't say it last night, you should call me Kyle."

"Thanks. I'm calling because you mentioned being willing to talk about your experiences here in Bradbury. I was wondering if we might get together. I know this is short notice, but are you free for lunch?"

"Hold on a second." The line went quiet. When Scudder

came back on, he said, "I'm supposed to have lunch with one of my production managers, but between you and me, I'd love an excuse to cancel. So, I'm definitely free. Twelve-thirty?"

"That would be great."

"Have you tried TJ's Grill yet? It's on Pine Avenue, just off Main Street."

"I have not."

"Let's meet there."

"Sounds great. Thank you for making the time."

"My pleasure. I'll see you then."

"See you then." Ananke hung up, filled in the others, then said, "Liesel and Dylan, I want you nearby, monitoring the meeting remotely. Rosario and Ricky, find Dalton Slater and see if you can get a tracking bug on his truck."

ANANKE ARRIVED AT TJ's Grill at exactly twelve-thirty. In place of her normal comm mic, she'd equipped herself with a Spedzine 23XT concealed microphone that was guaranteed to evade ninety-nine percent of electronics sweeps by shutting down the moment it picked up any detection equipment.

Dylan, who had eaten at the restaurant thirty minutes earlier, had attached a signal booster under the diner's lunch counter before he left. During the meeting with Scudder, he and Liesel would be strolling the neighborhood, "researching her novel" while listening in on wireless earpieces.

At the start, though, they waited in their rental car across the street, keeping an eye out in case Scudder brought any muscle with him. There was no reason to believe he knew Ananke wasn't on the up and up, but plenty of missions had been blown by similar assumptions.

As Ananke climbed out of her car, she whispered, "Test, test."

"Loud and clear," Liesel said in her ear.

"Your date's already inside," Dylan chimed in. "I recommend the roast beef sandwich. It was pretty tasty."

Ananke silenced her phone so that she wouldn't be distracted while questioning Scudder, and entered the restaurant. Scolareon's CEO had claimed a table along the wall. If it was a big deal for the founder of Bradbury's largest company to be gracing the small café with his presence, there was no sign of it.

He rose as she approached and pulled out her chair for her.

"Thank you," she said as she sat. "Sorry I'm late."

"You're not. You're right on time. I had some business on this side of town so I arrived a few minutes early."

"I didn't realize Scolareon was so spread out."

"Not Scolareon. I have investment stakes in a few of the smaller firms that have moved here."

She raised an eyebrow. "From before or after they arrived?"

A small grin. "Let's just say I've provided the encouragement for a relocation or two."

"Convenient."

He acknowledged this with a smile and picked up his menu. "You really can't go wrong with anything here. The burgers are good. The barbeque chicken's delicious, but messy. If you're vegetarian, their cobb salad is tasty."

She perused her menu. "What are you getting?"

"The salad. I've got a busy afternoon, and if I eat too much, I'll want to take a nap."

She laughed because she knew it was expected. "The salad sounds perfect."

They made small talk until the waitress took their order. After she was gone, Scudder said, "So, how can I help convince you Bradbury is the place to be?"

Ananke started in on a series of questions she and the others had come up with, aimed at putting Scudder at ease. The truth was, he appeared relaxed from the start. If he was heading up a notorious smuggling operation, he certainly didn't seem concerned about it.

He had given her the lowdown on why he'd picked Bradbury for his company, telling her how it reminded him of his childhood, how he loved that it was close to nature, and how it had an unmatched quality of life. When he finished, Ananke decided it was time to move toward the stuff that really mattered.

"One of my company executives used to work in California with someone I believe works for you now."

"Is that so? Who?" No suspicion in his voice.

"Natasha Patterson."

The look on his face changed to veiled sadness, but there was no hint of wariness.

"I'm sorry," she said. "Did I say something wrong?"

"No. Not at all. Tasha's great. One of my best employees. I'm lucky to have her. It's just that she's away on a family emergency."

"Oh, I'm sorry. What happened?"

"She's a very private person." Nice cover.

"I didn't mean to push."

"No, you weren't. To be honest, I have no idea what's going on. Like I said, she's a private person and has kept the details to herself."

"Of course. Well, when you *do* see her, please tell her Noah Markle says hi."

"I will."

Lunch came, and as they ate, Ananke asked a few more generic questions about life in Bradbury while trying to figure out what her next move should be. The problem was, the vibe she was getting off him—like the vibe she'd gotten from Harris—didn't fit Ananke's preconceived narrative. Perhaps he was an accomplished actor—one didn't get as far as he did without faking it at least a little sometimes—but Ananke was an expert at seeing through that kind of bullshit. If she wasn't, she would have been dead a dozen times by now. With Scudder, her internal lie detector stayed silent.

She decided to test the other thing that might get a reaction out of him.

"What about zoning laws and regulations? Any issues there?"

"Both the county and the city are very accommodating to new businesses. There's even a joint commission made up of government officials and several local CEOs, including myself. I'm sure you'll have little problem with anything, as long as it is within reason, of course."

"Without going into too much detail, there's a shipping and receiving component to the facility we're planning. At times, it might get a little high volume."

"Not a problem. As you can imagine, we do a lot of shipping ourselves. Might I suggest, though, finding a spot just outside of town to prevent any noise complaints."

"Have you experienced that?"

"A bit at the beginning, but we adjusted our schedules and we haven't had any problems since."

"Even with your late-night deliveries?"

Scudder looked at her. "I'm sorry?"

"Like last night."

"Last night?"

"My colleague and I were coming back from having a drink, and a truck drove by escorted by a couple of Scolareon security cars."

Scudder's confusion continued. "I guess there's a chance a truck was behind schedule. We cut off all shipping traffic by eight p.m., but occasionally there are exceptions."

"Of course."

Like before, she detected no indication he was trying to mislead her. She asked a few more questions so that the truck matter wouldn't be the last thing they discussed, and then said, "I know you're a busy man so I won't keep you any longer. I can't thank you enough for meeting with me."

"Absolutely my pleasure. We're building something special here, and I take it as my personal mission to make sure that continues. If you have any further questions, now or in the future, you have my number."

Ananke offered to pay but Scudder insisted on doing it, so she thanked him again and left after a handshake.

She waited until she was back in the Mustang, pulling out of her parking spot, before she said, "Did you guys hear all that?"

"Every word," Dylan replied.

"It sounded like he knows nothing about what is going on," Liesel said. "Of course, we could not see him. What is your sense?"

"The same. If he's involved, then I need to retire."

"But Ricky saw the truck *at* Scolareon," Dylan argued. "It's on the list Patterson made. And she works for Scudder. How can he not know?"

"I don't know the answer to how," Ananke said, "but I don't think he does know. Someone else at the company must be running things, or working with whoever is."

She signed off with them and called Shinji.

"I need to know more about the people working at Scolareon. Start with the security people Ricky saw at the delivery. Then look into management. There's got to be something off about someone there."

"Scudder didn't pan out?"

"We can't close the door on him, but I don't think he's part of the problem."

"I'll get right on it."

BEFORE DYLAN AND Liesel shadowed Ananke on her lunch date, Ricky and Rosario stopped by their rental to pick out some gear. The latter two then headed out on Ricky's motorcycle toward Dalton Slater's address, a good five miles north of Green Hills Estate.

Interesting fact number one: the place was a ranch of at least two hundred acres on an old country road. The house sat about a quarter mile from the highway, and was reached via a long driveway. Ricky and Rosario only knew this because the fields surrounding the house were clear of trees, giving them a good view of the place as they drove by.

Fact number two: a six-foot-high electrified fence, topped with two strands of razor wire, surrounded the entire property. In addition to signs hanging from the fence, warning of its shocking nature, there were other signs reading: THE ONLY GOOD TRESSPASSER IS A DEAD TRESSPASSER, and TO ALL POTENTIAL TRESSPASSERS—WE SHOOT FIRST AND ASK QUESTIONS LATER, and GO AHEAD I DARE YOU. The last was accompanied by a cartoon of a stereotyped Mexican in sombrero and poncho staring bug-eyed into the barrel of a shotgun.

Friendly folks, these Slaters.

Getting on the property would be tricky, but that didn't mean they had to leave without getting a decent look at the place. Ricky picked out a hill on the opposite side of the road, two hundred yards past the driveway, and parked the motorcycle around the back where it would be out of sight.

From there, they climbed the hill.

At the summit, Rosario pulled her binoculars out of her backpack, took a look toward the Slaters' home. Ricky retrieved his own set.

At maximum magnification, the view made him feel like he was standing in their front yard. The house—four bedrooms at least—was a decent size for the area. It had a wraparound porch and a sloped roof with a pair of chimneys. Beyond the house was a barn and a stable with a fenced-off corral.

He scanned the rest of the property. To the right of the house was a large, closed garage. In addition to whatever vehicles were stored in it, five cars were parked between the building and the house.

"No white truck," Ricky said, lowering the binoculars.

"It will be here eventually."

"If I'd known this was going to turn into a stakeout, I would have brought a bag of pork rinds."

"Pork what?"

"Skin, you know. Deep fried." He smiled. "Tasty!"

She gave him a glance over the top of her lenses, then went back to scanning the area.

They'd been sitting there for nearly half an hour when she suddenly tensed. "Is that the truck?"

He tried to follow where she was pointing her glasses. "Where?"

"Way to the left. On the highway."

He aimed the binoculars west. The highway was about a quarter mile away. When he found the vehicle she'd indicated, the skin on his forearms tingled.

A white pickup, crew cab, Ford headlights, and something in its bed covered by a tarp the same color as the one he'd seen.

"That's it," he said, smiling.

He kept the binoculars on the vehicle. Another few seconds and it would be turning onto the road to the farm. He was so sure of this that it took him a second to register the truck had driven right past the intersection.

"Son of a bitch!" He jumped to his feet. "Come on!"

They half slid, half ran down the hill back to the Yamaha, and seconds later were racing down the road. When they swerved onto the highway, Ricky jammed the accelerator and flew down the asphalt.

The highway curved and dipped and curved again, thwarting efforts to see far ahead. Finally, they crested a ridge and the truck was there, about half a mile away. It wasn't quite to Bradbury yet, but getting close.

"It is slowing," Rosario yelled.

It sure as hell was, Ricky saw. A moment later it turned left off the highway and disappeared.

"I think that is the entrance to Green Hills Estates," Rosario said.

Ricky nodded. He'd driven this way enough by now to know the entrance to the exclusive housing area was the only road in that area. He decelerated, and by the time they drove past the entrance, the bike was under the speed limit.

A quarter mile on, he spotted a dirt road on the same side as the estates and veered onto it.

"Do you know where you're going?" Rosario asked.

"We'll find out soon enough."

To their left, rolling hills separated them from the estates. Ricky kept an eye out for a trail that might lead over them. He stayed on the dirt road until it petered out.

He stopped for a moment, foot on the ground, and scanned the hills for the best way over.

"What about over there?" Rosario said, pointing to a pass a little farther ahead.

It was as good a choice as any. Ricky said, "Hang on," and steered the Yamaha off the road into the hills.

When they reached the top of the pass, he stopped again.

Green Hills Estates stretched out below them, nestled in a gentle valley. He could see the main road that circled the entire estates—Grand Way, according to the maps—and several of the luxury homes built along it. The road was deserted, which, given how few lived in the area, wasn't surprising. Between it and their position grew a large grove of pines.

Rosario examined the valley through her binoculars. "I do not see the truck."

"It's gotta be there somewhere."

She put the glasses away and grabbed on to Ricky's waist. "Let's go find it."

Letting gravity do most of the work to reduce the noise of their engine, Ricky steered the bike through the woods.

When they reached Grand Way, he said, "Left or right?"

"Right?"

"Why not?"

Long driveways intersected Grand Way in a seemingly random pattern. Some led to homes already built, while the majority appeared to end at properties still waiting to be developed. No sign of the white truck on any of the lots.

Had Slater left while they were looking for a way into the valley? That would suck.

The next driveway was gated off about a hundred feet in. Ricky stopped just past it.

"Scudder's place," Rosario said, after consulting a map on her phone.

Given that Scolareon's CEO was at the top of their list of potential evil masterminds, chances were very good Slater would be there. Unfortunately, too many trees prevented them from seeing the house or the grounds.

"We could hike in," he suggested.

"If Slater leaves while we are on foot, we will lose him. I think we should continue checking other places, in case this is not where he is. But if he is and he leaves before we can come back, he will drive right by us on his way out."

Ricky wasn't crazy about leaving the most likely place Slater would be, but first making sure he wasn't at one of the other places was the right move. He pulled them back onto the road.

They passed another driveway, and another, and another.

None had a white truck parked in sight.

At the next driveway, Ricky stopped again. Like at Scudder's place, a gate blocked the entrance, this one a brushed-metal monstrosity.

Rosario aimed her binoculars past it.

Ricky asked, "Anything?"

"Part of the house. Two stories. Looks big. Large attached garage. Um…."

"White truck?"

She was quiet for a moment before lowering the binoculars. "No."

They headed to the next driveway. No gate here. As for a house, they couldn't tell. The drive weaved up a small wooded hill and disappeared. Ricky turned into it, thinking they'd go only far enough to get a look at the property. But by the time they could see it was an empty lot, they were near the top of the rise.

"Take us all the way up," Rosario said. "We should have a good view from there."

Ricky did as requested. Rosario was right—they did have an excellent view of the nearby properties. They hopped off the bike and separated to scan more ground quickly.

Ricky could see as far as the roof of Scudder's place. No sign of the truck in the land around it. He moved the binoculars over the other homes they'd passed, ending at the property next door to Scudder's, hidden behind the garish, brushed-metal gate.

Rosario had been right—the house *was* a monster, as wide as four normal houses set side by side, and with two perpendicular wings jutting out the back. What she hadn't been able to see from the road was the pond a hundred yards behind the house, and the barn near it. Surprisingly, the barn looked to be decades old, its white siding and gray roof faded with age. If that was the case, it had been there long before the house had been built, long before Green Hills Estates had been an idea in some developer's mind.

As he scanned the barn, he saw something sticking out

from the far side. Ricky jogged across the plateau until more of it came into to view.

"Rosario," he called, waving her over. The thing sticking out from the barn was the back end of a white pickup, with a tarp-covered box in the bed.

When she joined him, he directed her where to look with her binoculars.

"¡Ay! So, he did not go to Scudder's."

"Nope." That surprised Ricky, too.

Rosario scanned the area. "I don't see anyone."

"Probably inside the barn."

She pointed the binoculars at the land between their position and the barn. "Fence. No barbed wire, though."

He lifted his binoculars. The fence was about six hundred yards from their position.

"You up for a little hike?" he asked. They might never have a better chance of getting a tracker on the truck.

She grinned. "We should let Ananke know what we found first."

"Allow me."

He pulled out his phone and typed:

Found the truck at a property in Green Hills Estates.
No address visible, but near the north end of the
big circle road. The only place with a pond.

He hit SEND, gestured to the rear slope, and said, "After you."

TWENTY-TWO

THE GUARD AT Green Hills Estates raised the entrance gate as soon as he saw Slater's white truck turn onto the road. Slater gave him a wave and a "Afternoon, Owen" as he passed by.

"Afternoon, sir."

A good boy, that Owen. Smart. Slater had big plans for him. Owen, like all the guards who worked the estates, was a member of Slater and his brother's organization.

When Slater reached Grand Way, he went left along the loop, taking it to the property where the Lindens' old farmhouse used to be. Though the pond and the barn were still there, the house had been replaced with one of the mansions that made up Green Hills.

Back in the day, the whole area had been part of the Lindens' farm. But agriculture had held no interest for any of Artie and Fran Linden's children, and after their parents passed away, the kids sold the property to Jack Williams, who sat on it for a decade before turning it into the estates.

While Slater firmly believed dividing the farm into a multimillion housing tract was a waste of good land, it had its upside. Mainly that his cousin owned the house by the pond. And, most importantly, the barn.

When the three men first started the project, they'd kept the illegals—and other riff-raff their agents had picked up—in an unused storage area at Scolareon. With Yates as head of security, their activities went unnoticed. That had been okay when there had been only two or three people who needed to be put on ice for a bit. But as the trials grew in scope, so did the need for more product and the risk of discovery.

That's when Slater had his brilliant idea. Why not

expand the old Linden barn to accommodate their needs? Their cousin had needed a little convincing, but in the end he'd gone along with it.

It addition to the main level, the barn had a basement. Using only their own people for labor, Slater and Yates expanded downward to a second underground level, where they created a secret holding area. Now, the trucks still came into Scolareon, but the product was soon transferred to one of their customized delivery vans and relocated to the barn.

All nice and tidy and no one the wiser.

Slater used his remote to open the gate to his cousin's place, and drove around the unnecessarily massive house down to the barn, where he parked near the door.

He rolled his head over his shoulders, working out a little kink, as he walked to the barn. A gentle push against a board near the doorframe released the latch holding it in place. Behind the board was a fingerprint-activated screen, identical to the ones at the lodge. A scan and the door unlocked.

Despite the secured entrance, the ground level of the barn was used as storage space only for things like landscaping equipment and fertilizer and grass seeds. Nothing that would strike anyone as unusual.

The basement was reached via a rectangular opening, fifteen feet long by five wide, in the floor at the other end of the building. A protective handrail surrounded most of it, missing only at the entrance to a set of stairs at one end and to a simple platform elevator at the other end. Slater took the former.

The only change to the original basement was the floor. Back in the Lindens' day it had been dirt. Now it looked the same, but underneath was a steel-reinforced cement floor.

To those not in the know, this was where the building appeared to end. To the few who knew better, the entrance to the lower level was behind a shelving unit that looked as if it were part of the wall.

Slater pulled the hidden release handle, and the unit moved smoothly out of the way, revealing the elevator entrance. Another fingerprint scan opened the lift's door, and soon he was traveling down.

The secret basement looked nothing like a barn. It was wall-to-wall concrete that had been divided into three large rooms. The elevator let out in the central space referred to as the lobby. A desk protruded from the wall on the right, and was always manned by one of Slater's personally trained guards.

On duty today: Vander Keane. Like a good foot soldier, the kid was standing at attention in front of the elevator when the door opened.

"Good afternoon, sir."

"Afternoon, Van. At ease."

Vander widened his stance and put his hands behind his back, army style, though he'd never been in the service.

"Anything to report?"

"Nothing more than the usual, sir. The new people wanting answers, the old ones quiet and mostly asleep." They had an overlap of shipments at the moment. Seventeen bodies currently being stored there, nearly double the product they usually kept at one time. And more was due that night. But that's what happened during the trials. Always had to make sure they had plenty of prey available, since inevitably some of the product would turn out to be defective.

"I need to pick out five participants for the midnight trials. Any suggestions?"

"There's the Mex in tank sixteen who seems pretty spunky."

"The one from the first shipment?"

"Yeah."

It was a good call, but the product was also a perfect fit for one of their Arab clients. Size and facial structure just the way the sheik—or whatever the hell he called himself—liked them.

Slater grabbed a sheet of red stickers off the desk and headed into the holding room. When staff wasn't present, they kept the room near dark, though the guard in the lobby was still able to monitor activity via a night-vision camera. As Slater stepped inside, he touched the wall switch, turning on the floodlights.

The room held twenty-five of the Plexiglas moveable cells, or tanks, as Slater and his men called them. The eight empty ones were scattered among the seventeen containing product. Within the latter group, most were on their feet, shielding their eyes and blinking. A few others lay on their cots, sleeping or pretending to.

Slater walked down the central aisle, glancing in each cell for a few seconds as he passed. He dismissed anyone still in bed. What he wanted were the ones who still had fight in them, the feisty and the defiant.

He put a sticker on cell five, where a twentysomething mixed-breed woman was pressing herself against the wall and yelling at him. Hispanic and white, maybe? Who knows? An abomination nonetheless. He then tagged a black guy in his late thirties. A bit older than Slater usually liked for the trials, but the man looked like he was in decent enough shape to put in a good showing.

Next, Slater came to the Mex in tank sixteen. The kid definitely had the right stuff for the trials, but if someone else fit the bill, there'd be no sense in throwing away the money the product would bring from the Arab.

Slater skipped the Mex and tagged his neighbor, an ugly woman in her late twenties. She probably wouldn't last long, but there had to be at least one easy trophy for the hunters who weren't as good as they thought they were.

The occupant of the final cell was lying down. Slater rapped his ring on the Plexi and smiled at the woman when she looked at him.

"How you doing today, Miss Patterson?" He knew she couldn't hear him, but it amused him to ask anyway.

She stared for a moment, and then closed her eyes.

He laughed, stuck a sticker on her cell, reached under the platform, and turned on the gas that would render her unconscious. The time had come to get rid of her.

He looked back through the room. He'd placed stickers on four of the cells, but he needed five bodies. None of the others were up to snuff.

Reluctantly, he tagged the Mex's cell. It pained him to miss out on the extra cash, but the trials demanded a certain quality, and the last thing they needed was one of the participants going apeshit because of inferior product.

Slater had his five.

RICKY AND ROSARIO descended just north of a rocky formation at the back of the rise, and worked their way to a section of the wire fence separating the properties. Unlike the fence at Slater's ranch, there were no signs hanging from this one.

It was also not electrified, so they climbed over at a post, and took a circuitous route through the woods to a hidden spot within spitting distance of the pond. Ricky surveyed the barn area through the binoculars. Still no movement.

"Wait for my signal," he whispered, then sprinted across the open space between the trees and the side of the barn at the opposite end from where the truck was parked. When it was clear he hadn't been noticed, he waved for Rosario to join him. They moved down the building toward the pickup.

He peeked around the corner, using a goose-neck camera attached to his phone. The pickup was parked near a door at the center of the wall. The door was closed, and no one was about. He put his ear against the building but couldn't hear anything.

He held his hand out to Rosario, whispered, "Trackers."

"I will do it."

"This was my find. I should do it."

She grimaced, but retrieved the trackers from her pocket and shoved them into his hand.

"Thanks. Be right back."

Staying in a crouch, he sneaked over to the front end of the truck and placed a tracker on the underside of the fender, high on the right. Keeping the truck between him and the barn, he moved to the rear of the vehicle and affixed a second bug inside the wheel well.

Job completed, all he needed to do now was get back to Rosario and they could get out of there. But he was painfully aware how close he was to the box in the truck bed. He *really* wanted to see what it was.

Screw it. It would take only a second to check, and he would hate himself if he passed up on the opportunity.

SLATER REENTERED THE lobby.

"I tagged the cells I want," he told Van. "Move them to the prep room. I'll send the boys over later to pick them up."

"Yes, sir, Mr. Slater."

"I'll take one with me now so I'll need your help." The van could transport only four at a time. No sense in making two trips when he was already here.

"Of course."

"I just gassed her so grab some masks."

Van pulled a couple of high-end, air-filtration masks out of the desk and followed Slater back into the holding room. At Patterson's cell, they donned the masks and removed the Plexiglas box.

Slater checked the woman's vitals. Her pulse was nice and strong, her breathing steady.

"We're good. Get the cart."

Van had retrieved the mobile metal table from the other room, and on the count of three, they hoisted Patterson onto it.

"Who's on after you tonight?" Slater asked as they rode up in the elevator.

"Colton, sir."

Colton was relatively new, and still in need of discipline. "Leave the tanks for him to clean. It'll be good practice."

Van tried to suppress a grin. "Yes, sir."

The elevator stopped, and the door to the upper basement level opened.

RICKY ROSE SLOWLY, ready to duck back down at the first sign of movement.

When he cleared the top of the bed, he grabbed a handful of tarp and pulled—but the canvas didn't cooperate. The damn thing was fastened to the floor of the bed.

He moved around to the tailgate and checked the tarp

again. It was fastened there, too, except unlike the clips holding it at the side, here the connectors were easy-to-release snaps. Ricky unhooked three of them and lifted the tarp.

The rectangular box underneath was made of metal, and appeared to be bolted to the bed. But for a few holes drilled here and there, the sides of the box were solid. The door at his end could only be opened when the tailgate was lowered. It was also held in place by a latch and padlock. It kind of reminded Ricky of those animal shows he'd watched as a kid, where lions and other fierce creatures would be transported in cages in the backs of vehicles.

He lowered the tarp, and had two snaps reconnected when the barn door rattled.

Leaving the third undone, he made a beeline for the closest side of the barn, which was opposite the one Rosario was on, and reached it just as the door opened. He continued to the back corner and ducked around it. Rosario was already there, waiting for him. He pressed against the barn and grinned.

"That was close," he whispered.

"Too close," she replied, not nearly as happy.

"We needed to know what was in the back."

"So, what was it?"

"A box."

"We already knew it was a box."

"A metal box, with breathing holes and a big lock."

A loud rattling from the other end of the barn. Ricky touched a finger to his lips, reattached the goose-neck cam, and stuck it around the corner.

SLATER AND VAN rolled the cart out of the barn and over to the rear of the pickup.

Slater helped Van undo the straps holding the cargo in place, then reached into the truck's bed and unhooked the snaps holding the tarp down. One of them had come undone. That happened on occasion, especially on the dirt road to the lodge, so Slater thought nothing of it. He piled the tarp on top of the box, lowered the tailgate, unlocked the padlock, and opened the transportation crate.

The steel tray mounted inside the box pulled out smoothly, and clicked to a stop when it reached the end of its track. Slater and Van unstrapped Patterson and maneuvered her onto the tray.

"You have any problem with the others, you let me know right away," Slater said.

"Yes, sir. I will."

Slater shoved the tray back into the box until it locked in place, then closed the door and engaged the padlock.

After he reached in and snapped the tarp down, he said, "Need help with the cart?"

"No, sir. I've got it."

Slater gave Van a nod, climbed into the cab, and started the engine.

THE MOMENT RICKY saw the body, he knew they needed to get a look inside the barn. He hurried over and turned down the side of the barn they'd originally approached the pickup from.

Rosario caught up to him and whispered, "Where are you going?"

"No time. Hurry, hurry."

When they reached the front corner, Ricky used the goose neck to peek around the side. Slater and his companion were removing straps that held the body to the cart, their backs to him. And, as he'd hoped, the barn door was open.

He slipped around the corner and crept to the door, moving inside as the last strap was removed.

Rosario followed closely, and whispered as soon as they were inside, "What the hell?"

"Don't you want to get a look around? I mean, you just saw what they wheeled out of here, didn't you?"

She grimaced, but before she could say anything, they heard Slater's voice. "Need help with the cart?"

"No, sir. I've got it."

The rattle of the cart's wheels started up again.

Ricky and Rosario moved deeper into the barn and ducked into a stall, hiding behind a stack of seed bags.

Outside, the pickup roared to life and drove away. A moment later, the cart rolled inside and the door shut. The clattering wheels continued down the center of the barn, passing Ricky and Rosario's stall, and moving all the way to the other end, where they finally stopped.

A few footsteps, and then the whine of an electric motor and the creaking of cables.

When the motor stopped, the cart rattled again, only the sound was distant now.

Ricky eased out from behind the bags and moved to the end of the stall. Slater's companion and the cart were nowhere to be seen.

"Clear," he whispered.

He crept to where the motor sounds had come from. Cut into the floor was a wide rectangular gap, lined on two sides by a railing. On one of the open ends was a set of stairs to a basement level. On the other, an open space for a lift that was currently on the floor below.

Ricky lowered the camera into the opening, and saw the young guy rolling the cart away from their end. Ricky glanced back to make sure Rosario was looking at the feed on his phone, too. She was.

"We should go down," he said.

She hesitated, and then nodded.

They crept down the stairs, their gazes affixed on the guy's back. They were still a few steps shy of the bottom when the cart turned left.

They froze, knowing they were in the man's peripheral vision, but the cart rolled on and out of sight behind a set of shelves without any indication the guy had seen them. They completed their descent and moved to the aisle where the cart had turned.

Hiding against the end of the shelves and using his camera, Ricky watched the guy roll the cart into an elevator. When the doors closed, the shelving unit along the wall began moving over the elevator entrance.

Ricky sprinted down the aisle and jumped in the path of the closing shelves, bracing his hands against it to stop it.

"Hurry," he whispered.

As Rosario rushed over, he created room between himself and the unit while still pushing on it.

"Sneak through," he said. "It looks like there's enough space behind this thing for both of us."

She slipped under his arms into the gap. Ricky did the same and let the shelves close, plunging them into total darkness.

"A hidden elevator?" he whispered. "Tell me this isn't getting exciting."

The doors began to part. Ricky tensed, thinking the kid must have realized he was being followed and had come back. But it was Rosario pulling the doors apart. He lent her a hand, and they shoved the doors all the way open.

Rosario turned on her flashlight and shined the beam down the shaft. The top of the car sat motionless about eight feet below.

"We can climb down there," Ricky said, pointing at a section of the metal structure lining the shaft.

Rosario grabbed a support and went first. When he joined her on top of the car, she was kneeling next to the roof maintenance door, listening for sounds.

"Empty, I think," she whispered.

Ricky pulled out his gun, aimed it at the door, and nodded for her to open it. She lifted the hatch, and swept her flashlight beam through the dark interior. Empty, as she had thought.

Ricky lowered himself into the car, and helped Rosario down.

"I'll open the door a little," he said. "You take a look."

He pulled at both sides until a half-inch gap opened between them. Rosario crouched and peeked through.

"A little wider," she whispered.

He separated the doors another inch.

"More."

"At some point he's going to notice," Ricky said.

"I do not see anyone."

Ricky increased the gap another inch.

Rosario checked again, and looked up at Ricky. "Unless

he is standing right outside the elevator, he is not there."

Ricky opened the doors until there was enough room for them to squeeze through. No one was waiting for them.

They found themselves in a large room that stretched the width of the basement level above and at least a third of its length. In the right and left walls were wide double doors. Muffled sounds drifted through the ones to the left. Ricky and Rosario crept over and each placed an ear against the door.

Ricky heard someone walking around and the occasional clang against a metal surface. He wanted to peek inside but that might be pushing things too far, so he suggested they check the other door.

Faint machinery noises this time, but no steps or anything indicating someone was inside. He grabbed the handle and started to open one of the double doors, but Rosario grabbed his arm and whispered, "Wait."

She tapped on her phone for a few seconds before giving Ricky a you're-an-idiot look. A few more clicks, then she said, "There was a camera. But it's off now. Go ahead."

Ricky pushed the door, intending to create only a wide enough gap to peek through, but then they heard the door of the other room start to open.

He and Rosario rushed inside, and he shut the door behind them. The room was dark, though not completely. Scattered throughout were what appeared to be several floor-level lights, each putting out illumination so low that it didn't help Ricky and Rosario see anything. Ricky had come across similar lighting schemes throughout his career and knew their purpose. Apparently, the camera Rosario had detected had a night-vision setting, for which the dim glows provided the necessary light.

Ricky turned on his flashlight so they could find someplace to hide, but what he saw made him momentarily forget all about their safety.

The room was dominated by—if not quite filled with—giant transparent boxes. The exact same kind of boxes he, Ananke, and Liesel had discovered at Scolareon. Only these boxes had been flipped over and mounted on top of the exact same type of platforms they had also seen.

He and Rosario took a few steps farther into the room.

Every box contained a cot, and most were occupied. Fifteen boxes—no, *sixteen*—held people.

"Holy shit," he muttered. "I think we've found the mother lode."

Rosario pulled out her phone. "We need to tell Ananke about this." When the screen lit up, she swore in Spanish. "No signal."

A low thud inside the room, off to their right. Ricky turned his light toward the sound and lit up one of the captives, standing at the end of her box. She looked right at them, her mouth moving, but they couldn't hear a word. She slapped the box, creating another thud.

Ricky glanced back at the main door, hoping the sound didn't carry that far.

Thud.

Rosario ran over, so he followed.

The woman was yelling, or at least looked like she was.

"We cannot hear you," Rosario said, cupping her ear and shaking her head.

The captive said something else and pointed toward the floor. Ricky and Rosario looked where she indicated, but saw nothing. Another thud drew their eyes back to the woman. She spoke again and pointed down, this time adding a hooking motion.

She meant under her cell.

He knelt and felt under the end of the platform. "There are switches here." He lowered his head until he could see them. There were five switches in all, each with a different label: O2, AUX1, AUX2, COMMUNICATIONS, SPKER VOLUME.

He flicked the communications switch and straightened back up. "Can you hear me?"

"Yes!" the woman said, her voice coming out of a speaker by the switches. "Yes! Oh, my God! Get me out of here, please!"

"We will," Rosario said. "We prom—"

"They're going to kill us!" the woman said. "You have to get us out!"

"We understand. Just calm down and let us—"

From across the room came the clunk of metal slipping into metal.

VANDER KEANE PUT the empty cart in the prep room. He then took a few minutes to lay out the instruments and set up everything he and the others would need to prepare the remaining participants for that night's trials. After he finished, he returned to the lobby and sat down at the desk, intending to enter the events of the last half hour into the log.

A message was flashing on the computer screen.

CAMERA MALFUNCTION – HOLDING ROOM

He frowned and brought up the feed. The image was only digital noise. He scrolled back, trying to find out when the problem had started. Turned out it was only about a minute before, but that wasn't what commanded his attention. In the image, a crack of light ran partway up the wall, right where the doors to the lobby were.

He looked over at them, thinking one of them had somehow slipped open, but both doors were shut tight.

He rose and moved to the doors. As he reached for the handle, he heard voices coming from somewhere deep in the room. A conversation that could not happen unless one of the talkers was outside the tanks.

The hairs on the back of his neck stood on end.

One of the prisoners must have gotten out. That wasn't possible, but what other explanation could there be?

He rushed back to the computer, turned on the holding-area emergency lock, and activated the escaped-prisoner protocol.

RICKY AND ROSARIO ducked behind the woman's cage.

But instead of the door swinging open in a blaze of light, they heard a low hiss.

"Gas!" Rosario said.

They raced across the room, no longer worried about

concealing their presence. Ricky reached the door first and tried to yank it open, but it didn't budge.

He whirled around and shined his light through the room, focusing on the walls. "There has to be another way out."

Rosario made her own scan and shook her head. "There's not."

"Dammit! Dammit! Dammit!"

He began feeling woozy and knew they didn't have much time. Perhaps they couldn't do anything to save themselves for now, but they could protect their friends. He threw his phone on the floor and stomped on it, breaking it apart. He dropped to his knees and sifted through the debris until he found the SIM card.

Before he snapped it in half, he looked at Rosario. She was standing there, pointing her light at him. "What are you waiting for?" he asked.

"Would you rather do that in the dark?"

"Oh, right," he said.

As soon as he broke his SIM card, Rosario popped out hers and destroyed it, too.

Ricky, closer to the floor, began coughing uncontrollably. A few seconds later, Rosario convulsed in her own fit. She cocked her arm and let her phone fly.

Ricky watched its light shine until the phone crashed against the wall. He heard its shattered body fall to the floor only a few seconds before Rosario did the same.

VANDER WAITED TWO minutes after the gas cycle had completed before turning on the exhaust system. Once the green light came on, he entered the room, holding the M4 rifle he thought he'd never need down here.

Having heard the pounding on the door, he knew he'd find the attempted escapee not far inside. What he hadn't expected was to discover two bodies, neither of which was one of the prisoners.

He checked to make sure both were knocked out before he ran back to his desk and called Mr. Slater.

SLATER MARCHED OUT of the elevator exactly eleven minutes later.

Vander was waiting for him once more near the door, this time clearly nervous.

"Where?" Slater said.

"In the holding room, sir. I put them in two of the empty tanks."

Slater veered toward the holding room and flung the doors aside. "Lights, goddammit."

"Right. Yes, sir. Sorry, sir."

The flood lamps lit up, and a few seconds later, Van joined Slater inside.

"Which ones?"

"I'll show you."

Vander led him to a transparent box a couple of spots from the door. The cot had been removed so the body inside lay directly on the platform. The man was what some might call Caucasian, but his tanned skin and Mediterranean features spoke of inferior blood. Six foot. Maybe six two. And three or four days past due for a shave. His hair was neatly trimmed, however. He wore dark blue jeans, a leather jacket over a black T-shirt, and black boots.

"The woman's two down."

A Mex, or whatever she wanted to call herself. From somewhere south like that. Tiny. Five one, if she was lucky. Dark hair and dark clothes.

"Did they have anything on them?" Slater asked, his eyes still on the intruder.

"He had some loose cash, two hundred and forty-four dollars. And these." Van moved around the side of the tank and picked a few things off the floor.

In one hand, he held several small black squares Slater couldn't immediately identify. In the other was something he knew well—a Beretta pistol and attached suppressor.

Slater grabbed the gun. Brand new, with a full magazine. He could tell the suppressor was high quality.

Who the hell are these guys?

When Vander had called, Slater had assumed the intruders

were FBI or ATF. But a fed wouldn't snoop around with equipment like this. CIA? Maybe, but he doubted it.

Could be private investigators.

Maybe someone actually cared about one of the unwanted and had hired these two to find him or her. But even that seemed far-fetched. Not only were the collection teams trained to take only those who wouldn't be missed, but Slater and Yates had also taken great pains in setting up the organization so that it would be nearly impossible to connect the different segments.

Someone had found them, though.

"This was it? No IDs? Nothing else?"

Vander hesitated.

"What?"

"They both had phones. But—"

"Phones? Goddammit, give them to me!"

Vander looked like he was going to say something else, but instead he jogged back into the lobby and returned a few moments later with two plastic bags.

"What are those?"

Vander held out one of the bags. "Their phones, sir."

Slater grabbed it and looked inside. The broken remains were gathered at the bottom. "What the fuck happened?"

"I'm...I'm not sure, sir. I found one on the floor near the guy, and the other lying next to the wall."

The intruders must have destroyed their phones on purpose. "Did you dig out the SIM cards at least?"

"They're in there, too. Um, both snapped in half."

"Are you shitting me?"

"I-I'm not, sir."

Slater swore under his breath and looked at the other bag. More plastic items, but these appeared intact. "What's in there?"

Vander handed him the second bag. "I found these on them. I'm not sure what they are."

Slater pulled out one of the items. It was a small plastic square that had a sticky surface on one side, covered by a thin protective sheet. He knew exactly what it was. A tracking bug.

"At least tell me you know how they got in," he said.

"I don't know for sure, sir. But-but-but I would guess it happened when we were-were loading the product onto your truck."

As mad as Slater felt, he was clearheaded enough to realize Van was probably right. He also realized the other potential ramification. If the captives had been able to get into his truck while he was in the barn, they may have bugged it. He kept the bag of bugs, but handed the other one back to Van. "Get rid of this crap."

"Yes, sir." Vander hesitated. "What do you want me to do with them?"

Slater thought for a moment. Whoever these two assholes were, they were problems that would only get bigger if they were let go. The only sound option was to get rid of them. He walked over and pulled the red sticker from the tank of the Mex kid whom he'd wanted to sell to the Arab. He did the same on the tank holding the twentysomething, mixed-blood woman, as they'd be able to get a little cash for her, too.

Slater transferred the stickers to the tanks of the intruders. "Send them over with the others tonight."

"Yes, sir."

Slater hurried back topside, conducted an exhaustive search of his truck, and found two bugs. He put them into the bag with the others, stomped them with his boot a couple of times, and tossed the whole lot into the pond.

TWENTY-THREE

ANANKE CHECKED HER phone as she returned to her hotel room after her lunch with Scudder.

Ricky had texted her about fifteen minutes earlier, while she was talking to Scudder.

He and Rosario had found the truck at Green Hills Estates. Ananke's immediate thought was to wonder if she'd misread Scudder. *Was* he involved?

She hurried over to her computer and brought up a satellite image of Scudder's property at the estates. Ricky had mentioned a pond, but there was no pond at Scudder's.

She zoomed out until she had a view of the entire development. She spotted a body of water several properties west of Scudder's place. As she magnified the area, she remembered her conversation with Toni Mahoney when the woman had told her about swimming in a pond at the farm that used to be in the valley. It seemed likely they were one and the same.

Near the pond stood a big building. A garage or barn, or perhaps even a guesthouse. The main house sat to the south, a mansion bigger than most of the others in the development.

She opened a video chat window and called Shinji.

"Hey, boss," he answered.

"Something I need you to check out right away." She described the house and told him its location. "I need to know who owns it."

"Shouldn't take more than a minute or two. Do you want me to give you the info on the people in Ricky's pictures first?"

It took her a second to remember what he was talking about. The pictures would be the ones Ricky had taken while witnessing the delivery the previous evening. Rosario had asked Shinji to ID the security personnel.

"You've got names?"

"Of course I've got names. This is what I do, remember?" She rolled her eyes. "All right, Mr. Hotshot, let's hear it."

She heard him click a key, and his face was replaced by one of Ricky's pics, cropped close to focus on one of the guards. "This one's name is Patrick Monroe. He is twenty-four, and has worked for Scolareon for three years. His personnel file is nice and clean, regular yearly raises in line with company norms and no mentions of trouble."

The image switched to another guard. "This is Ryan Porter, twenty-five, also been at Scolareon for three years. Clean record, regular raises. Though it's not in either of their company files, he and Monroe are first cousins. Their family has been in the Bradbury area since the early 1900s."

"Related? That's interesting."

"It *is* a small town."

"True."

The picture changed to a guard a couple of decades older than the other two. "Man number three is named Leonard Yates. He is forty-four, and has been with Scolareon for nearly five years, and, get this, he's their head of security."

"Yates? I met a Yates at the party, but he was a lot older."

"Let me guess. He was the chief of police."

"Yeah, he was."

"He's Leonard Yates's father."

"Well, I'll be damned."

"I know, right? But that's not all. Though Leonard isn't related by blood to Porter or Monroe, he is via his brother's wife, Katherine Porter, who is Porter and Monroe's aunt. You want to guess her married name?"

"I don't know. Scudder?"

Shinji laughed. "That would have been good, but no. Slater."

"Slater? As in Dalton Slater?"

"One and the same."

"They're brothers?"

"Technically, half brothers. Same mom, different dads. Slater's older by two years. Yates's dad basically raised them both."

"Holy crap."

"I'm not done. Before Yates the younger was hired at Scolareon, he and his brother started a security company called Riverside Trusted Security. Still up and running, ostensibly with Katherine Slater in charge. RTS provides security services, including guards, to many of the businesses in town, such as U-Jay Soft, Klay Tone, Digital Paste, Remakers 2100, and—given what you just asked me to find out, you're going to love this—all the guards at Green Hills Estates."

Ananke said nothing as she processed what this all meant. Clearly, the Yates/Slater family was like a fungus infecting the entire area. "Excellent work, Shinji."

"Thanks, boss. Now if you give me a minute, I'll track down who owns the house."

"Take two if you need it."

While he worked on that, Ananke called Ricky for an update. The line didn't ring even once before "Ricky ain't here, but Ricky will get back to you when Ricky can. Only if you leave a message, though."

After the beep, she said, "It's me. Call back."

She tried Rosario but was also sent to voice mail. Thinking maybe they'd been able to get a bug on Slater and were following him, she opened her tracking program. The only bugs that showed up were the ones she'd put on the police cruisers.

"Got it," Shinji announced from the computer.

It took her a moment to remember what she'd tasked him with. "Whose house is it?"

"It's owned by a corporation."

"A corporation?"

"I believe you've heard of them. Digital Paste?"

WITHIN SIX MINUTES, Ananke was parked in the lot next to Digital Paste's headquarters, mentally transforming herself back into Shawn Ramey. When she was ready, she headed inside.

Perky Chad was behind the reception counter again. "Welcome to Digital Paste. How can I—oh, Ms. Ramey, so good to see you again. Were we expecting you?"

She smiled apologetically and said, "Not exactly. I was hoping maybe Devon might have a moment to chat."

Chad's own smile faded. "I'm so sorry. Mr. Rally isn't feeling well so he didn't come in today."

"Oh, no. I hope it's nothing too serious."

"He gets migraines sometimes. I'm sure he'll be back in a day or so. Is there someone else who could help you?"

She hesitated a moment before saying, "Is Elijah in?"

ELIJAH CHAN ROSE as his executive assistant ushered Ananke into his office. "Good to see you again. Please, have a seat."

"Thank you." She settled into one of the chairs in front of his desk.

"Can we get you something to drink? Coffee? Tea?"

"Water?"

"Of course." Chan looked at his assistant. "A water, please, Chloe. Actually, make that two."

Ananke casually surveyed the room. It was more cluttered than what she remembered from the glimpse she'd gotten of Rally's office. Not messily so, but in a way that denoted someone who was elbows deep in a lot of different projects.

"I hope I'm not disturbing you," she said.

"Not at all."

"Are you sure about that?" she said, nodding at the thick, three-ring binder opened in the middle of his desk. It had little Post-it flags sticking out from the tops of dozens of pages.

He chuckled. "We have a new app that goes live next month. There's always a few last-minute glitches that need to be sorted first."

"Don't you have people to do that?"

"Sure, but another set of eyes never hurts."

"Plus, it's your company."

"And there's that. Well, mine and Devon's, of course."

"Confession time," she said. "I actually came by to see

232

him. He'd mentioned that if I had any questions he'd be happy to answer them, but I understand he's out today."

"He is. Sorry about that. Is there something I can help you with?"

"If you don't mind."

"Of course not."

"Thank you." She leaned forward. "One of the things I'm concerned about is housing. I've been told that a new phase of the tract north of downtown is about to start, which is great, but I'm wondering if I'm just having smoke blown up my ass or it's really going to happen."

Chan laughed again, louder this time. "You don't beat around the bush, do you?"

"That wastes too much time."

"True. I don't know the specifics of their timeline, but I can say that Barry Hurst—he's the developer—is an up-and-up guy. I have nothing but good things to say about him."

"That's a relief. I'm guessing that's where a majority of our people would be living if we relocate here."

"They'll love it. I know my wife and I do."

"You live there?"

"Yep. On Circuit Circle." He smirked. "Cheesy, I know. But it's a nice neighborhood."

"I kind of thought you'd be one of the folks out at Green Hills Estates."

"You'd have to ask Devon about that. That's where he lives. We're much more comfortable where we are."

Ananke asked him other questions about the area, repeating some she'd asked Scudder at lunch. When she felt enough time had passed, she said, "Thank you. I appreciate you taking a break to talk."

"My pleasure. And if you still want to ask Devon anything, I'm sure he'll be back tomorrow."

"I'll keep that in mind."

As soon as she was back in her car, she called Shinji. "It's Devon Rally's place."

"That's the slimy one Rosario told me about, isn't it?"

"Find out everything you can about him."

TWENTY-FOUR

MORGAN HARRIS HAD not gone back to bed after Shawn Ramey and her friends made their unexpected visit.

If what Shawn and the others had told her was true, Tasha had inadvertently gotten mixed up with something big and bad happening right here in Bradbury. Morgan might have been scared for her girlfriend before, but she was terrified now.

Her first thought was to go to Scolareon and lock Kyle Scudder in a room until he told her everything. But she knew if Shawn and her friends were really here to help—and Harris's gut told her they were—then doing that might screw things up for them.

She paced through her house, overflowing with energy that needed release. This pent-up anxiety gnawed at her, screaming that she needed to do something, until she got it in her head that shadowing Shawn would be a good idea. She justified the plan by telling herself she'd only be making sure Ananke hadn't fed her a pack of lies, but in truth, she was hoping to be close by when they found Tasha.

She grabbed her keys and headed out the door, but made it only a few steps before she realized the flaw in her plan. Shawn would know her car. Morgan thought for a moment, and pulled out her phone.

"Hi, Sarah," she said, when her old high school friend answered. "I've got the day off and was wondering if I might borrow your pickup to run some errands?"

As she knew would happen, Sarah said yes.

Her next call was to Travis Blake, one of the junior officers who was always looking for extra shifts. "Travis, it's Morgan Harris. Would you be interested in covering graveyard for me tonight?"

MORGAN PARKED DOWN the street from the Collins Inn, and picked out Shawn Ramey's Mustang in the parking lot through her binoculars.

She settled in, ready for a long wait, but only eight minutes passed before Shawn exited the inn and walked to her car. As the Mustang drove away, Morgan followed at a discreet distance.

Turned out to be a short drive, as Shawn parked a few blocks away near TJ's Grill. She entered the restaurant at half past noon. Morgan found a parking place half a block away, and toyed with the idea of walking by the café to see if Shawn was meeting anyone.

That thought vanished the moment she noticed two of Shawn's associates, the Asian woman and the Irish guy, strolling down the street, looking in shops. Though they avoided walking by TJ's, their presence in the area couldn't be a coincidence. When it seemed they might be heading her way, Harris pulled back onto the road and made a quick U-turn to avoid being seen.

Her new vantage point was farther down the road, but she still had a decent view of the café's entrance. Shawn reemerged almost exactly an hour after she'd entered. As she headed toward her car, her two friends, who'd continued roaming the neighborhood the whole time Shawn was inside, quickly made their way to another vehicle.

Morgan was worried the other two would follow Shawn and spot Morgan if she tried to do the same, so she let the Mustang pull onto the road and waited to see what the others did. When they headed in a different direction, she pulled out and took off after the Mustang. As she passed the café, she nearly hit the brakes in surprise when the door opened and Kyle Scudder walked out.

Was he the one Shawn had met? Did that mean Shawn was actually working *for* Scudder and the people Tasha had tangled with?

Morgan followed Shawn back to the Collins Inn. Again,

the woman stayed inside the hotel for only a short time before returning to her vehicle. Her destination this time was Digital Paste, one of the star tech firms that were transforming Bradbury.

What did Digital Paste have to do with Tasha? Morgan couldn't remember her girlfriend ever mentioning the company.

She chanced driving by the entrance soon after Shawn had gone inside, and caught a glimpse of her standing in the lobby, seemingly waiting for someone.

Twenty minutes later, Shawn returned to the Mustang, and Morgan followed.

TWENTY-FIVE

LUNCH WAS LIGHTER than breakfast, enough to replenish the energy expelled during the morning's testing session and fortify everyone for the initial trial that afternoon. Much to the chagrin of several of the participants, no alcohol was served.

As soon as the meal was completed and the dishes removed, Miss Riefenstahl entered the room, carrying an envelope.

"Congratulations to you all for your work this morning," she said. "Your scores have been tabulated, and your individual levels determined. These have been used to appropriately tailor the groupings for today's trials, and determine the equipment best suited for each of you."

As she opened one of the envelopes, Mr. Welles said, "Aren't you going to tell us our levels?"

Miss Riefenstahl paused. "The levels are unimportant, and only have bearing on our preparation. We've found that sharing this information can, frankly, be disruptive. That said, if you wish to know yours, you may approach me after the final trial, at the end of the gathering."

Satisfied looks graced the faces of a few participants. These were the ones who would ask later. Each would be told the same thing, that they had ranked at or near the top of the group. Sugary words meant to ensure their satisfaction with their visit, and none of them true.

Miss Riefenstahl removed a card from the envelope. It was all for show, of course. She knew the groupings already. "Mr. Welles, Mr. Hawks, and Mr. Ford, you will be the first grouping. And Mr. Huston, Mr. Wise, and Mr. Reed, you will go next." She lowered the card. "Now, if you would all follow me."

She led them to the armory, where two of the young men who did double duty as meal servers outfitted each participant with the weapons chosen for them. Mr. Welles, Mr. Hawks, and Mr. Ford received identical Smith and Wesson 9mm pistols, Mossberg Maverick double-barrel shotguns, and Remington Sendero hunting rifles. Mr. Huston, Mr. Wise, and Mr. Reed were given the same types of pistols and shotguns, but instead of the rifles were provided Ravin R15 crossbows.

After the assistants ensured each participant could properly operate his weapons, they gave the men their specialized vests. Traditionally, hunters donned bright, reflective outerwear to cut down on the possibility of being shot. The trial vests performed the same tasks, though they were not reflective or made from brightly colored material. Instead, sewn into the padding were transponders that would activate a beeping signal on a weapon anytime it pointed at a vest.

Miss Riefenstahl escorted them to a pair of off-road transports that looked like tricked-out golf carts. The drive from the lodge took ten minutes, followed by a short hike led by Miss Riefenstahl down a well-worn path to a clearing in the woods.

The meadow was V shaped, with the path letting out at the point where the two sides met. Mr. Lean stood seventy-five feet away on a steel-reinforced platform approximately two feet high, with ramps leading down on the three sides not facing the bottom of the V.

"Mr. Huston, Mr. Wise, and Mr. Reed, if you will please take a seat in the waiting area." Miss Riefenstahl gestured to the eastern edge of the clearing, where two rows of bleachers had been set up. As they walked off, she turned to Mr. Welles, Mr. Hawks, and Mr. Ford. "Gentlemen, this way, please."

She led them to an area in front of the platform and had them stand in a line, facing it.

"Welcome, gentlemen, to the first trial," Mr. Lean said. "Each group will have two hours to complete the task. Once both rounds are completed, you will return to the lodge for a quick meal, and then your next few hours should be spent resting for the midnight event. The sooner you finish this afternoon's trial, the more rest you will have for tonight's. Is everyone ready?"

"Hell, yes," Mr. Welles said.

"Let's do it," Mr. Ford threw in.

Mr. Hawks, however, was trying to keep from shaking and said nothing.

Mr. Lean looked past the group and nodded.

A moment later, a middle-aged man the participants hadn't seen before and one of the younger assistants escorted the game—a disheveled but nervous Caucasian man—onto the platform.

"Gentleman, your trophy," Mr. Lean said. "I want to reiterate that the object is to work together to bring it down. If you try to go solo, it will be noted by our observers and you will be disqualified from this event. Are there any questions?"

"Yeah, I got one," Mr. Welles said, leering at the target with a hunter's lust. "What's the fastest anyone's completed this trial?"

"Twenty-seven minutes."

Mr. Welles's smile grew, as if he had every intention of breaking the record.

"Anyone else?" Mr. Lean asked.

The men shook their heads.

"Very well, then. For this trial, the prey will be given two minutes after they reach the woods before the hunt begins. If you leave before I have released you, you will be disqualified."

"Does the record timer start when he—I mean, it is released, or when we go?" Mr. Welles asked.

"When you go."

"Okay, good. Just wanted to make sure."

Mr. Lean looked at each hunter to make sure there was nothing else, then said, "Prepare the trophy."

While the young assistant held on to the trophy's arms, the older man pulled out a knife and sliced through the bindings holding the prey's wrists behind his back. The two turned the captive to face away from the hunters and toward the ramp at the back of the platform. The older man whispered something to the prisoner that ratcheted up the terror in the prey's eyes.

"Group one," Mr. Lean said. "The first of your trials begins now."

The young assistant released the prey's arm. The older one slapped the prisoner on the back and yelled, "Run!"

The man stumbled down the ramp but somehow caught himself from falling. He glanced back, his face dark with fear, before racing toward the woods.

When the prey reached the trees and two additional minutes had almost passed, Mr. Lean said, "Prepare yourselves. Five seconds. Four. Three. Two. One. Hunt!"

SOMETHING HARD PRESSED against Ricky's cheek. But that was nothing compared to the headache raging in his head.

It took a herculean effort to pry his eyelids open a fraction of an inch, but the effort was wasted, as his surroundings were as dark as they had been when his eyes were closed.

He tried to recall what had happened.

The transparent cages. The woman yelling at him to get her out.

The sound of gas filling the room.

Rosario coughing. And him coughing, too.

Oh, crap.

He shoved himself up, the sudden rush of adrenaline keeping most of his pain at bay.

He ran a hand over his body to make sure nothing was broken. Thankfully, other than the sore cheek and the headache, he seemed to be okay.

He slowly rose to his feet and reached for the pocket where he usually kept his phone.

"Right," he muttered, remembering.

He'd destroyed his phone. It had been the right thing to do, but it sure would have been nice to have use of its flashlight.

He extended an arm, intending to shuffle forward until he found a wall, but he hit a flat surface without having to take a step.

Good. This is good. Just need to follow it to a door and

I'm in business.

He moved down the wall, keeping a hand on it, but went only a few steps before he reached a corner. He turned down the next wall. Two steps, another corner.

Dread rose in his chest as he headed along the third wall. When he quickly reached yet another corner, he raised a hand above his head. Two feet up, it hit a ceiling.

He hadn't woken on the floor of the room where he'd collapsed. He was in one of those crazy Plexiglas cells.

His first instinct was to hit the walls and scream at the top of his lungs, like the woman he and Rosario had found. But he knew, from being on the other side, it would only get him a whole lot of nothing.

He began a tactile examination of the cell, paying special attention to the seam where the box met the platform. As he feared, they fit tightly together. Without any tools, he had no way to lever the box out.

He tried pushing up on the roof. Nothing.

Thinking maybe he could dislodge the box by tipping the whole thing over, he threw his weight against the side over and over, but the enclosure remained rooted in place.

He stood in the center, his shoulder sore from beating it against the wall, and tried to come up with another method. Before another idea came to him, the overhead lights flickered on.

He blinked, and for a few seconds, could see nothing but white. Then things started coming into focus. He wasn't in the room he'd blacked out in.

There were only three other transparent cells here. And unlike the other space, this room had a wide, stainless steel workbench running along two of the walls, plus several stainless steel tables scattered around. But the most disturbing things were the restraint-equipped dentist chair—there was no other way to describe it—in the center of the room, and the heavy-duty hoist hanging above it, attached to tracks that ran across the ceiling.

He checked the other cells. They were all occupied, but like his, none had cots. Rosario was in the cell farthest from him, apparently still unconscious. In the containers between them were an African-American man and another woman, both also out.

From across the room, the door opened. For a brief second, he considered dropping to the floor and feigning sleep, but he was pretty sure they already knew he was up. There'd been a camera in the other room, so one was probably here, too.

He moved to the end of his cell and stared toward the entrance.

The young guy who walked in was the same one Ricky and Rosario had seen helping Slater. Ricky watched him pull a full-length leather apron off a peg on the wall and put it on. Next, he donned a pair of heavy-duty rubber gloves that extended all the way to his elbows.

If Ricky didn't know any better, he would have thought the kid was about to slaughter a cow. Though there were no cows in the room, Ricky worried he wasn't too far off about the slaughtering part.

The kid spent some time at one of the workbenches, pulling things out of drawers and fiddling with them on the counter. He faced the other way, preventing Ricky from seeing what he was doing. After he finished, the kid carried a metal tray over to the table next to the dentist chair, and reclined the chair as flat as it would go, swinging its arms to the side.

He pulled a thin rectangular box from a pocket on the apron and tapped it. The hanging harness moved toward Rosario's cell. Another push on the remote brought the rig to a halt above her.

Slater's man walked over, peered at Rosario, and reached under her platform. Ricky couldn't see what the guy was doing, but he knew it must involve the buttons beneath.

When the kid straightened up, he studied Rosario again. From all appearances, whatever he'd pushed had done nothing, but Ricky didn't believe that for a second. He was willing to bet more invisible gas had just been released in her cell to make sure she stayed asleep.

Slater's man stepped over to the other woman's box, checked inside, and flipped something under her platform. He repeated the process at the box of the man next to Ricky.

He then walked up to Ricky's cell.

The asshole locked eyes with Ricky and smirked. If the wall hadn't been between them, Ricky would have smacked the look right off the kid's face. Since that was currently not an option, he simply stared back, his expression blank.

The game of don't blink went on for nearly a minute before the kid snorted and leaned down in front of Ricky's cell. Ricky guessed it was his turn to be put under, but instead of the whoosh of gas, he heard the echoing sounds of the room beyond the Plexiglas.

The kid stood up again. "Buddy, I don't know who you are, but you sure broke into the wrong place."

A whole list of smartass retorts played through Ricky's mind, not the least of which was "Do you always talk in clichés, or is this a recent problem?" But he held his tongue, his expression unchanged.

The kid's smugness cracked a little at Ricky's non-reaction. With a tad more venom in his tone, the guy said, "If you think you're getting out this, you're sorely mistaken."

Sorely? Who taught this guy to speak?

"By this time tomorrow, it'll all be over. I hope you're ready to meet your maker, scum."

Video games. That has to be it. He watches too damn many video games.

The kid reached under the platform and flicked off the speaker. Again, Ricky assumed he was about to be gassed, but his jailer walked away without the air in the cell changing.

Ricky watched as the guy opened Rosario's cell and transferred her into the harness.

A motor raised her into the air, and the rig transported her to the dentist chair. After she was strapped into the seat, the kid picked up a gun-like device from the tray and placed it against the base of her neck.

"Son of a bitch," Ricky muttered.

Though the instrument was crude, he'd seen its type when one was used on him.

The kid pulled the trigger, and the gun recoiled off

Rosario's skin. He ran a finger over the contact point and smiled.

When Ricky had been recruited to join the Administrator's organization, one of the conditions had been that he agree to be implanted with tracking bugs so that the Administrator would always be able to find him. Five bugs, in fact, a few inserted in places Ricky couldn't reach on his own. The device that had implanted those bugs was a more advanced version of the one the kid had used. Why the prisoners would need tracking bugs, Ricky didn't know. But he didn't like it. Not one bit.

Over the next twenty minutes, the guy performed the same task on the two other captives. Then he approached Ricky's cell.

He pointed at Ricky, then at his wrist, like he was wearing a watch.

Your turn, he was saying.

He laughed, and reached under the platform again.

This time, the whoosh of gas was unmistakable.

TWENTY-SIX

ANANKE CHECKED HER phone as she walked from the Mustang back to her hotel room.

Still nothing from Ricky.

She tried calling him. Voice mail again. She tried Rosario. Same thing. She sent them both a text—CALL ME ASAP—and kept the cell in her hand as she walked. The device remained silent. She checked for active bugs again, but nothing new had appeared.

When she reached her room, she opened her laptop and started a video chat with Shinji. "Can you get me a location on Ricky's and Rosario's phones?"

"What's wrong?"

"They should have checked in by now."

"Give me a second."

She stared at the computer while he worked.

"That's weird," he said several moments later.

"What?"

"Their phones are gone."

"What do you mean, gone?"

"Neither registers on the network."

"Try the satellite link." The phones could use either cell or sat tech.

"I did. Not there, either." He tapped his keyboard. "The last cell tower they connected to is the one covering Green Hills Estates."

"None after that?"

"No. The signal cut off while within its coverage, forty-seven minutes ago."

The worried look on his face mirrored what Ananke felt.

Keeping Shinji on the computer, she called Liesel.

"We have a problem." She told Liesel about their friends being MIA. "Meet me in the parking lot next to the Cache Bar, then we'll go together from there."

"On our way," Liesel said.

Ananke looked back at Shinji. "Anything new on Rally that could help us?"

"Haven't figured out who he really is yet, but he wasn't born Devon Rally."

Her brow furrowed. "Are you sure?"

"Oh, he's created a pretty elaborate cover, but it's still a cover. No doubt in my mind."

"Contact me the moment you have anything new."

"Will do."

As she headed out of her room, she knew there was one thing she needed to do before she rendezvoused with her friends. She had intended on ignoring the problem, but with Rosario and Ricky missing, it seemed a good idea to turn it to her advantage.

MORGAN LOWERED HER binoculars just far enough for her to see the Collins Inn over the top of them. She was starting to think she was spinning her wheels by following Shawn, and that she was deluding herself in thinking the woman would lead her to Tasha.

But she couldn't go back home and sit around waiting again, either. She would go crazy.

What, then? Approaching Scudder could still screw things up for Shawn, so it was best to keep that off the table for now.

What about Scott Davos?

He certainly wouldn't be easy to get to, but she'd already contacted him once so he knew who she was, and if he really was worried about Tasha, Morgan was sure he would talk to her. At the very least, Davos could confirm whether Shawn was on the level or not.

She raised the binoculars again. The hotel was still quiet, the Mustang right where it had been the last time she looked.

I'll give her thirty minutes. If Shawn didn't show up by

then, Morgan would work the Davos angle. And if she struck out with him, she'd—

Something thumped against the passenger door.

Morgan snapped her head around while reaching for her service weapon, which was tucked between the seat and the console.

Shawn waved from the other side of the window. "Are you going to unlock this or what?"

Morgan cursed under her breath, then triggered the electric lock.

Shawn hopped into the other seat and fastened the belt.

"What are you doing?" Morgan asked.

"You have heard of global warming, right? I figured if you were going to keep following me, we should share a vehicle. Now, come on. We're wasting time."

"Hold on. I'm not—"

"Let's go, let's go. I've got two people in trouble and two waiting for us. Or would you rather I drive myself and keep pretending I don't know you're behind me?"

Morgan started the engine. "Where are we going?"

"Cache Bar. Fast."

Morgan headed back to the highway and turned north.

"Why are your friends in trouble?"

"That's a good question. I don't know."

"What happened?"

"Same answer."

They rode in silence for half a minute.

"Did you learn anything from Scudder?" Morgan asked.

Shawn looked at her and smirked. "Only that he's not involved."

"Are you sure?"

"A hundred percent? No, but close enough."

More silence.

"Not going to ask me about Digital Paste?" Shawn said.

"I was thinking about it. Why did you go to Digital Paste?"

"Because I'm pretty sure Devon Rally is involved."

"Rally, that prick?"

"I see you've had the pleasure."

"We've received a complaint or two, but no charges filed."

"Let me guess," Shawn said. "He's all smiles and hands."

Morgan nodded. "And unfortunately has the cash to make his problems go away. What makes you think he's involved?"

"You'll find out soon enough."

A few minutes later, they turned into the Cache Bar's parking lot.

"Over there, far end of the lot." Shawn pointed at a sedan sitting by itself.

Morgan recognized it as the one she'd seen Shawn's associates use when Shawn was at TJ's Grill with Scudder. Morgan parked next to it, and she and Shawn took seats in the back of the sedan. The Irish guy was behind the wheel and the Asian woman in the passenger seat.

They both glanced at Morgan suspiciously before looking at Shawn.

"Under the circumstances, I thought we could use some extra help."

"Not a bad choice," the Irish guy said. "So, any word from—" He glanced at Morgan again, not sure if he should continue.

Shawn frowned, said, "Right," and turned to Morgan. "Okay, here's the deal. My name's not Shawn Ramey. It's Ananke. My friends here are Dylan and Liesel. The two who are missing are Rosario, who you know as Caroline, and Ricky. He's the one who helped Dylan split open your head."

"Which, if I may remind everyone, wasn't on purpose," Dylan threw in.

Ananke said to him, "The answer is no. I still haven't heard from them."

Morgan was not surprised the Shawn Ramey name had been a cover. She wouldn't be shocked if the new names were false, too.

Ananke turned to her again. "Are you familiar with Dalton Slater?"

Morgan's face tightened. "I went to school with his daughter."

"You don't sound too happy about it."

"Let's just say they're not a very tolerant family."

"Did you know that he's your chief of police's stepson?"

"What?" She had *not* known that.

"And half brother to your chief's other son, Leonard Yates?"

"Is that really true?"

"We haven't performed a DNA test, but, yeah, it's true. Last night there was a…delivery at Scolareon that we think involved the involuntary transportation of people."

Harris's brow furrowed. "You mean trafficking?"

Ananke nodded. "Present were both Slater and Leonard Yates. Today I sent Rosario and Ricky to plant a tracking bug on Slater's truck. They followed it to Devon Rally's house in Green Hills Estates, and that's where their phones went dead."

"You think they're still at the house?" Harris said.

"I don't actually know if they got all the way there," Ananke said. "I only know they were nearby earlier this afternoon. That's what we're going to go check right now. The thing is, I'd rather not use the main entrance to the estates, so please tell me you know another way in."

MORGAN DID INDEED know another way.

Back when she was a teenager, in the days before the valley became Green Hills Estates, she and her friends had explored pretty much every square inch of the county. In small and dying Bradbury, there had been little else to do.

In the hills between the highway and the valley where the estates were now was a hidden place high school kids had been using as a party hangout for years.

Morgan directed Dylan through wide gulches and barely visible roads into the hills.

"Are you sure this is the right way?" Dylan asked, not for the first time.

"Did *you* grow up around here?" Morgan said. "No, you didn't." A few minutes later, she pointed ahead. "See that tree up there on the right? The one that's half dead?"

"I see it," Dylan said.

"The turn's just after it. It'll be a little steep at first, so you'll need some speed to get over the hump, but trust me."

As they neared the target tree, Dylan pressed down on the accelerator. As soon as they passed the marker and he saw the road, he whipped the car to the left and raced up a short slope. After cresting, the sedan thudded down, right in line with a pair of tire ruts carved through a grassy meadow.

They crossed the clearing, reentered the woods, and soon were headed upward again. This time, the pseudo road looped back and forth so that the climb was not so difficult. Not long after it finally leveled off, the road ended in a clearing, with no other visible exits.

"Where next?" Dylan asked.

"Stop. We walk from here."

They piled out of the car and Morgan started toward the trail that would take them down into the valley.

"Wait a minute," Ananke called.

Morgan glanced over her shoulder and saw the others gathered at the open trunk of the sedan. She jogged back to them. In the storage space were two black suitcases sitting side by side. One was open, revealing a rack of pistols, a section of ammo magazines, several cylindrical devices, a few rifles with folding stocks, and at least half a dozen boxes of ammunition.

Ananke handed weapons out to her friends, took a pistol for herself, then grabbed a cylinder and attached it to the end of the barrel. A suppressor, Morgan realized.

Ananke glanced at her. "You're not getting one."

"It's okay. I brought my own." She opened the side of the zip-up hoodie she was wearing and flashed her service weapon.

"Yeah. You're leaving that here."

"What?"

"This is our operation. If there's any shooting going on, we'll be doing it. And if that's not reason enough for you, remember, you live here. You need to keep your hands as clean as possible."

"I'll be fine."

"I'm sure you will be. Now give me the gun."

Though Morgan didn't like it, she handed over her

weapon.

Ananke put it in the case with the unused weapons, closed the top, and opened the second suitcase. Inside were several containers and a row of compact binoculars. She handed out the glasses, giving Morgan a pair, too.

"If it comes to it, you can whack someone on the head with this."

"Gee, thanks," Morgan said.

Items she didn't recognize were removed from some of the containers and divvied up between the three others. Lastly, Ananke pulled out four palm-sized leather pouches and tossed one to each of them, once more including Morgan.

"Put it on," Ananke said.

"What is it?"

"Radio. The disk is a microphone. Take off the protective backing and stick it on the inside of your collar. I'm sure you can figure out where to put the earpiece yourself."

Ananke shut the trunk, donned her radio, and looked around. "Everyone set?"

"Set, boss," Dylan said.

"Set," Liesel said.

Morgan nodded. "Set."

"All right," Ananke said. "Lead on."

ANANKE, LIESEL, AND Dylan followed Harris through the woods along a single-file trail that led over the summit and down into the valley.

As they passed through a gap between trees, Harris pointed to the northeast. "See that water? That's the pond near where the old Linden farmhouse used to be."

Ananke raised her binoculars. "And the white building near it? That's the barn?"

Harris checked through her own glasses. "Yeah. And to the right of it and a little farther away, you can see part of Rally's house."

Ananke picked out the mansion and scanned Rally's property. "Anyone see Ricky's motorcycle?"

For nearly half a minute, they silently examined the valley

below.

"Found it," Liesel said.

"Where?"

"You see that rise about a quarter mile southwest of the pond?"

Ananke moved her binoculars. The top of the rise in question had been cleared and leveled, but currently was house-free. "I see it."

"It is on the downslope that is facing us, near the right corner."

Ananke scanned the slope until she spotted it. It was definitely a motorcycle. Ricky's? Too far to know for sure.

"Dylan, swing over there and check it out. The rest of us will head for the woods north of the barn."

Dylan nodded and headed down the slope, on a line that would take him farther south.

With Harris still leading, the women hiked down the hill toward the pond. When the slope became more gradual, they made better time, and soon were on flat land.

"Hold up," Ananke whispered.

Harris looked back, a question on her face.

"Fence," Ananke said, pointing past her. About thirty yards farther on, among the trees, a shadowy line traveled from left to right as far as she could see.

Harris searched a bit before she saw it. "There wasn't a fence there when I was a kid. But that was a long time ago."

"Stay behind me," Ananke said.

Moving forward, low and slow, she led them to a covered point twenty feet shy of the barrier, where they crouched down. While Liesel used the electronic signal detection app to check for cameras, Ananke scanned the fence through her binoculars. The barrier was five feet high, made of large gauge wire in a box-like pattern, strung between four-by-four wooden posts, and did not appear to be electrified.

"No signals for at least fifty meters," Liesel said.

Ananke lowered her glasses. "You two stay here."

She crept up to the nearest fence post, and examined it to make sure she hadn't missed a connector that would allow a

252

portion of the wire to be charged. There was nothing.

She waved the others over and clicked on her mic. "Dylan? You reach the bike yet?"

"Just a few seconds ago," he said. "It's Ricky's bike, all right."

"Any sign of him or Rosario?"

"No one here but me."

"Footprints?"

"Checking." He was silent for several seconds. "One set heading across the slope, toward the Rally house." A short pause. "Two sets now. Second set smaller. They head down the slope." The sound of sliding dirt and a whispered curse came over the line.

"You all right?"

"Word of warning. These pine needles are pretty damn slippery. Rode on my arse all the way to the bottom."

Liesel snorted.

"Yeah, yeah, hilarious," Dylan said. "Okay, got the trail again. They're still heading toward Rally's house."

"Follow them as far as you can, then meet us in the woods behind the barn. There's a fence around the property, but no sign of surveillance."

"Copy."

Ananke, Liesel, and Harris climbed the fence and made their way through the forest until the barn came into view. Remaining in the safety of the trees, they scanned the area. There were no cars parked in back of the structure, or any doors or windows on the side of the building they could see.

"You guys go right as far as you need and get a look around that side. I'll check the one to the left."

The east and west ends of the barn were shorter ends. Ananke found a spot where she could see the one to the east. No cars were parked along that side, but there was a door smack dab at the midpoint of the wall.

"I've got an entrance over here," she said into her comm. "What about you guys?"

"No, just a flat wall," Liesel reported.

"Come to where I am, then."

Ananke raised her binoculars. The door was shut and had no obvious locks. She made a sweep of the barn area to make sure she hadn't missed anything.

Tire tracks creased the dirt about twenty feet away from the barn. They paralleled the building and looked recently made. The tracks also looked wider than those made by a standard car, like they were created by tires on an RV.

Or ones on large pickup trucks.

Ricky had said he found the pickup on Rally's property, but hadn't said where. She'd assumed it had been parked at the house, but it could have been here at the barn.

She focused on what she could see of the back of the mansion. No lights were on in any of the visible windows, nor did she detect any movement. But as she knew from the satellite image, the place was big. She couldn't be looking at more than a third of it, so the rest of the house could be filled with people.

Dammit, Ricky. Where are you guys?

When Liesel and Harris reached her, she lowered the binoculars and said into the comm, "Dylan, ETA?"

"How about now?"

All three of them turned to find Dylan emerging from the trees behind them.

"Afternoon, ladies," he whispered as he crouched next to Ananke. "So, what's the plan?"

Ananke said, "You and Morgan will stay here and watch the barn, while Liesel and I check the—"

"I hear a motor," Liesel said.

Ananke cocked her head and heard it, too. It was hard to tell where it was coming from, other than the general direction beyond the mansion.

"How far is the road that runs through the estates from here?" she asked Harris.

"Grand Way? It's got to be at least a couple hundred yards beyond the house."

The rumble grew louder and louder.

"Then it must be coming up the driveway," Ananke said.

Though they were well hidden already, Ananke and the

others backed a few feet deeper into the woods as the roar increased. A cargo van came into view as it rounded the side of Rally's mansion.

Ananke sensed Harris tense. "Do you recognize it?"

"I've seen a couple just like it in town before," Harris said.

"Who do they belong to?"

"I've never had to stop one so I don't know."

"No logos or company name on them?"

"Not the ones I saw."

As the van continued toward them, Ananke's phone vibrated with a call. She reached into her pocket and pushed the button that sent the call to voice mail.

She trained her binoculars on the van. "Two men in the cab. They look fairly young."

Harris, looking through her own glasses, said, "The driver's Justin Keller and his friend is Aaron Sherwood. They graduated high school two or three years ago."

"Trouble?"

"They spent more than their fair share of time at the station when they were still in school, but I don't think they've been back since they started working for Slater."

Ananke's phone vibrated twice with a text, but she kept her eyes on the van as it pulled up next to the barn, parking in the same area where she'd seen the tire tracks.

Keller and Sherwood hopped out. While Keller headed to the barn door, Sherwood disappeared around the back of the vehicle.

Ananke kept her eyes on Keller. He touched the wall near the door, released a hinged panel, and tapped something within the recess several times. He then shut the panel and pulled the barn door open. Clearly the building was more than it pretended to be.

"They are not alone," Liesel whispered.

Ananke looked back at the van. Sherwood had stepped out from around the back end, accompanied by two more young males.

Harris grunted. "Caleb Fredericks and Orel Johnson. Two more of Slater's screw-ups. They both graduated last year."

255

"Which one's which?"

"Johnson's the taller one."

"Is it just me, or do they look like they could all be brothers?" Dylan said.

It was true. All four were Caucasian, within an inch or two on either side of six feet, and had similar brown hair, cut military style. They were dressed identically, too, in jeans and gray T-shirts.

The group talked for a moment in front of the barn door, then three of them went inside while Fredericks jogged over to the back of the van and moved out of sight again. When he reappeared seconds later, he carried an M4 rifle. He jogged back to the barn door and took up sentry duty.

"Liesel." Ananke nodded toward the trees on the other side of the van. "Work your way over there and see if you can get a view into the back of the van."

Liesel nodded and vanished into the woods.

Ananke kept her attention on Fredericks, knowing he would give them the first indication the others were returning.

Two minutes passed.

Three.

Then...

"In position." Liesel's voice, soft over the comm.

"What do you see?" Ananke asked.

"Racks on both sides of the van, with two wide shelves each."

Ananke did not like the sound of that.

"Movement," Dylan whispered.

Fredericks had turned to face inside the barn, and appeared to be talking to someone. Though they couldn't hear what was being said, Ananke did pick up the faint rattle of wheels on wood.

A few seconds later, Fredericks stepped to the side and Keller exited, followed by a kid who hadn't been in the van but shared the group's compulsion to dress alike. He, too, was carrying an assault rifle.

"Vander Keane," Harris whispered.

Another one of Slater's rescues, Ananke assumed.

Keller said something to Keane that directed him to the back of the van, where he took a guard stance, rifle ready. Fredericks assumed a similar position near the front of the van, facing the direction of Ananke and her team.

Keller disappeared inside the barn momentarily and then walked back out in reverse, pulling one end of a metal cart. Stretched on top was the unconscious body of a man. The other end of the cart was being pushed by Sherwood.

Ananke focused the binoculars on the prone man. An African-American, around forty, clothes smudged with dirt. His chest moved up and down so at least he wasn't dead.

"Do you know the guy on the cart?" she asked Harris.

Harris shook her head, frowning, and lowered her glasses. "You weren't lying about the trafficking thing, were you?"

"We weren't lying about anything."

"Except our names," Dylan said. "Oh, and why we were here. And—"

Ananke glared at him.

"What?"

She focused back on the van and the two men wheeling the cart to the rear. When they moved out of view, she said, "Liesel, what do you see?"

"The person on the table is being moved into the van. Now they are putting him on one of the shelves."

When the transfer was complete, Sherwood pushed the cart back into the barn, with Keller following. After a short pause, a second cart rolled out with Keller once again in front, only this time with Johnson pushing.

"Uh, Ananke. Are you seeing what I'm seeing?" Dylan asked.

Ananke's grip on her binoculars had tightened. She was indeed seeing what Dylan was seeing.

"What is it?" Harris asked.

"That's Ricky," Ananke whispered through clenched teeth.

The men rolled Ricky behind the van.

"They are loading him in," Liesel said. "Top spot on the right."

When cart number three came out—pushed by Sherwood—Ananke knew exactly who would be on it.

"Say the word and we can take them down right now," Dylan said, when he realized the unconscious passenger was Rosario. "They're a bunch of kids. They don't stand a chance."

He was right. Two quick shots would take down the sentries, and the team could neutralize the two men at the cart before the assholes realized what had happened. They might have to work a little to get Johnson, who'd headed back into the barn, but it would be easy enough. If Ananke and the others mounted a rescue right now, however, they would likely damage the chances of taking down everyone involved and uncovering the full scope of the operation.

"I wish we could," Ananke whispered. "But we need to find out where they're going first. I want you to go back to Ricky's bike and follow them on it. We'll catch up to you as soon as we can."

She could tell Dylan was a bit disappointed, but he nodded and headed into the woods.

"They are putting Rosario on the shelf below Ricky," Liesel reported.

The men returned to the barn, and Keller and Johnson rolled out a fourth cart. Ananke was watching through her binoculars so she didn't notice Harris move until she heard the crunch of leaves under the woman's foot. Ananke grabbed Harris by the waist and yanked her down behind a bush.

"Where the hell do you think you're going?"

"Let me go. That's Tasha."

Harris tried to break free, but Ananke had more than enough strength to hold her where she was.

"Stop. It's not her."

"Your friends are there. It has to be her."

"Use your binoculars."

Harris lifted her binoculars. When she lowered them again, she looked crestfallen.

"I thought…I mean…"

"You wanted it to be her. Our friends were there so why not Tasha, too."

258

"Maybe she's in the barn."

"Or maybe she's wherever the van's going. She could be anywhere."

"She's alive. I know she is."

"I believe you," Ananke said, meaning she believed Harris believed that.

Harris took a few deep breaths. "You can let me go now."

"You promise to stay with me?"

A beat. "I promise."

Ananke let her go. As Harris tried to right herself, her hand slipped on some needles and she fell forward into the brush.

"Freeze," Ananke whispered.

Fredericks's gaze had whipped in their direction at the sound of the branches rustling. He stared into the woods for a moment, and took a few tentative steps toward them.

Having finished returning the fourth cart to the barn, Keller, Johnson, and Sherwood came outside again, this time not pushing any cargo. When Keller realized Fredericks had moved from his position, he walked toward him.

"Problem?" the driver asked, his voice raised just enough to carry into the woods.

"I heard something."

"A person?"

"Not sure. Something moving around in the bushes."

Keller stared into the woods. "I don't see anything. Do you?"

Fredericks frowned. "No."

"Has there been any more noise?"

"Nothing after that first time."

Both men were silent for a few moments.

"Probably a bird or something," Keller said. "Come on. We need to keep to the schedule."

Keller turned and walked back to the van. After a moment's hesitation, Fredericks did the same. All four men who'd arrived in the vehicle climbed back inside it, while Keane reentered the barn and closed the door.

"Dylan, tell me you're ready," Ananke said into her comm.

"Having a little…problem…getting—" The roar of an engine erupted over the comm. "Yep. All set."

"Get out to the highway. They're leaving now."

"Copy."

Across the way, the van made a Y-turn and drove toward the house.

"I'm sorry," Harris said.

"You slipped. It happens. Just let it be the only time."

"It will be."

Once the van disappeared behind Rally's mansion, Ananke said, "Everyone back to the car."

TWENTY-SEVEN

DYLAN DIDN'T WASTE time finding a way through the hills back to the highway. Instead, he took Grand Way to the main exit, and sped past the guard shack before the guy inside had a chance to look out the window.

At the highway, he found a spot just to the south, where he could see the start of the entrance road to the estates, but was hidden enough that the guys in the van wouldn't notice him when they drove out.

Not much more than a minute later, the van stopped at the intersection with the highway. Instead of turning south, as Dylan had anticipated, it went north.

Dylan eased back onto the highway and settled in a comfortable distance behind the van.

He activated his mic and shouted over the noise of the road. "Ananke, come in." When he received no response, he tried again.

"Go for Ananke." Her voice swam in a river of static as it challenged the range of the comm.

"On the highway, in pursuit of the van, northbound."

"Dylan...ou repeat?"

"In pursuit of the van, northbound on the highway."

"Dy...ease...an...wa...ound?"

"North," he yelled. "Go north."

Dead air.

"Ananke?"

No answer.

"Ananke?"

He'd have to use his phone once he had the opportunity to stop. Until then, his mission was clear. Don't lose the van.

Onward they went, paralleling the river, along the same path Ricky had brought Dylan the previous night when they visited the solar farm. It wasn't too long, in fact, before they neared that very turnoff. Dylan thought there was a good chance the van's destination lay somewhere in the farm's direction, but the other vehicle blew right past the road and continued northward.

The setting sun had begun to cool the air that rushed over Dylan's gloveless hands. But his knuckles weren't the only things that ached. His arms and chest felt the chill, too. While Ricky's helmet had been with the bike, his leather jacket and riding gloves had not. Dylan wasn't dressed for a long motorcycle ride through the country, so he did the only thing he could—grit his teeth and try to not think about it.

Twenty minutes beyond the solar farm turnoff, in the middle of what looked like nowhere, the van slowed. Its brake lights glowed in the twilight. Dylan, a few hundred yards back, contemplated slowing, too, but that might make the guys in the van suspicious. So he continued at his current speed and eased into the other lane as he neared them. Though he really wanted to glance over, he kept his face forward as he passed, like he had no interest in them at all.

For a few moments, the van's headlights lit the road as Dylan headed away from them, then they disappeared. He glanced over his shoulder. The van was no longer there.

He squeezed on the brakes, made a U-turn, and raced back to where the vehicle had been. He spotted an entrance to a road leading into the woods. He'd missed it because he'd kept his gaze forward as he passed by.

He pulled onto the shoulder, parked the bike, then jogged over to the turnoff. The road had been blacktopped once, portions of the old surface visible here and there. Now it was mostly dirt. About a hundred feet down, it veered to the right, explaining why he couldn't see the van now.

He returned to the motorcycle, but before continuing his pursuit, he retrieved his mobile and texted Ananke the GPS coordinates of the turnoff.

Back on the bike, he headed down the dirt road, his lights

off and his speed no more than fifteen miles per hour. The forest thickened the farther he went, turning the twilight into night. On and on he drove with no sign of the van. He'd been keeping an eye out for intersecting roads and hadn't passed a single one, so he knew the vehicle had to be still in front of him somewhere. The situation finally changed after he'd been going for nearly fifteen minutes.

A new road led only to the left. He parked where it began and scanned it. It was almost a carbon copy of the one he'd been on. *Almost.* The major difference was the fifteen foot-tall secured gate straddling the road, approximately fifty feet away. Attached to each side was a matching fence. There didn't appear to be any guards, but he had no doubt there were cameras.

Though he was sure he was in the right place, he pulled out his flashlight and checked the intersection for tire tracks. Several showed up in the beam, the top set matching the ones he'd seen back at the highway turnoff.

With the van beyond the gate, his tailing mission had come to an end. But that didn't mean Dylan had to sit on his hands until the others arrived.

He rolled Ricky's motorcycle into the woods, parked it where it wouldn't be seen, and set out at an angle toward a part of the fence fifty yards away from the gate. When the wall of wire mess came into view, he knelt and studied the area beyond it via the night-vision mode on his binoculars. He didn't spot any cameras, but that wasn't proof they weren't there. He changed the binoculars' setting again, this time to thermal.

Whoa!

He'd been hoping to pick up heat generated by any active cameras, but instead the whole fence lit up.

The damn thing was electrified.

Great.

He concentrated on the trees beyond the fence. They all remained cool, so probably didn't contain any working electronics. This wasn't particularly shocking, now that he had a better sense of the fence. Why waste a good camera on unnecessary surveillance when you had an electrified fence?

Getting to the other side was a problem he couldn't solve on his own.

He texted Ananke again, updating his GPS location. She replied immediately, telling him they were twenty minutes out.

Deciding he might as well do something useful in the interim, he began walking the fence, hoping to find a weakness.

ANANKE, LIESEL, AND Harris hiked quickly back into the hills where they'd left the sedan. As they climbed the slope, they heard Dylan's voice on the comm, his words coming through in bits and pieces that most of the time made no sense. Twice Ananke heard the fragment "orth," and thought he was telling them to go north. Confirmation of this came soon after they began driving out of the hills, when Dylan's text arrived with GPS coordinates for where they should turn off the highway.

A second set of coordinates came in as they raced north. Liesel, acting as navigator, input the info on her phone and said, "It is approximately seven miles east of the highway."

"What is it? A town?" Ananke asked.

"According to the map, there is nothing there. Switching to satellite." A pause. "There *is* a structure about three-quarters of a mile northeast of the coordinates."

"A house?"

"If it is, it is a very large one."

"May I see?" Harris said from the backseat.

Liesel passed the phone to her.

"Do you know that area?" Ananke asked, looking at Harris in the rearview mirror.

The cop shook her head. "Driven by on the highway, but never been that far out."

"Are there a lot of isolated buildings like that?"

"A few cabins here and there. For hunting mostly, I think. I don't know of anything this big."

Ananke glanced at Liesel. "Send Shinji the coordinates. See if he can dig up a more detailed image."

Liesel took her phone back and shot off the message. A few seconds later, her phone rang. "It's Shinji."

"Put him on speaker," Ananke said.

Liesel accepted the call. "Hello, Shinji."

"Liesel, thank God. Are you guys all right? Do you know where Ananke is?"

"I'm right here," Ananke said.

An irritated Shinji said, "Um, hello? I seem to remember we talked about you answering your phone."

Ananke recalled the vibrations she'd felt when they were watching the van at the barn. "Calm down. Sometimes I *am* busy."

"Busy? Okay. Sure. I understand that. But you sent me directly to voice mail. I thought the same thing happened to you that happened to Ricky and Rosario."

"I'm fine. We think we know where Ricky and Rosario are now. Those coordinates Liesel sent, there's a building just to the north I need you to—"

"I already know about the building. That's one of the things I was trying to call you about. It used to be a resort. It was purchased decades ago by Devon Rally's father."

"Devon Rally's *father*? Rally's from this area?"

"He was born there, but he and his mom moved back east when his parents split. He apparently came back in the summers to visit family."

"I've never heard of anyone here named Rally other than Devon," Harris said.

"Uh, who is that?" Shinji said.

"Morgan Harris," Ananke said.

"The *cop*? Are you guys under arrest? Or do you have her tied up in the back?"

"She's helping us, Shinji. Pretend she's part of the team."

A pause. "You're sure you're okay?"

"Shinji!"

"All right, all right. You're okay. Well, um, she's right. I mean, you're right, Ms. Harris, um, Officer Harris."

"Morgan," Harris said.

"Morgan. Uh, nice to meet you."

"Get on with it," Ananke said.

"Sorry. Where was I?" Shinji said. "Oh, right. There is no Rally family in the Bradbury area. Because Rally isn't Devon

Rally's real name. It's Robert Seiver."

"Seiver?" Harris said.

"Yeah, that's a name you probably know, isn't it? His dad was Michael Seiver, brother to Sharon Seiver. Seiver is her maiden name, of course. She's been married twice and is the mother of two boys."

Glancing in the rearview, Ananke saw both surprise and realization on Harris's face. "What am I missing?"

"Her name is Sharon Yates now," Harris said. "She's married to my boss. Which means she's Leo Yates and Dalton Slater's mother."

"Which also means Devon Rally is Leo Yates and Dalton Slater's cousin," Ananke said.

"Bingo," Shinji confirmed. "And Devon now owns the old resort near those coordinates."

Ananke said nothing as the new information sank in. A clearer picture of what was going on here began to surface. "We need plans and whatever other info on the resort you can get."

"I found some plans that are, like, fifty years old," Shinji said. "If there are any more recent, I haven't come across them."

"Send us those, but keep looking."

"Will do."

As Liesel hung up the phone, Ananke checked Harris via the mirror again. "You all right?"

Harris was staring at the back of Liesel's seat. Without shifting her gaze, she said, "I remember him. I was about six, I think. Robert...I mean, Devon would have been fifteen or sixteen. I saw him beat up this kid, a boy a few years younger than him. Chris something, I can't remember. I don't know why he beat him up, but I remember a few weeks later finding out Chris and his family had suddenly moved away. I doubt he did anything to deserve what happened to him. Robert was this mean son of a bitch who showed up every summer. I don't remember seeing him with Yates and Slater, but I bet they were around." She shook her head. "Devon Rally is goddamned Robert Seiver. That bastard."

Ananke and Liesel said nothing, letting Harris work things out in silence.

After they made the turn onto the dirt road, Liesel texted Dylan, informing him they were close. It took an additional eleven minutes to reach his GPS coordinates.

Dylan walked out from the pines as they pulled to a stop. Ananke rolled down her window, and he leaned in.

"The entrance road is right up there," he said, pointing at a turnoff a few dozen feet away. "It's blocked by a big gate just a little ways in. There's a matching, electrified fence to go with it. I followed it down one side, thinking I could find out where it turned, but by the time you texted me, I hadn't reached it."

"Let's have a look."

"If you back down the road a bit, I found a spot you should be able to squeeze the car into."

With Dylan's help, Ananke eased the sedan into the woods. Then they all worked together to create a blind of branches and loose brush to obscure the vehicle's presence.

Next, they geared up, taking more specialty items since they weren't sure what they might come up against. Unlike at Green Hills Estates, Ananke gave Harris a pistol and suppressor.

Once everyone was ready, Dylan led them into the forest to a point where they could see the gate.

"You weren't kidding about big," Ananke said.

Even if one of them stood on another's shoulders, they wouldn't reach the top. Not that they'd want to, given the strands of razor wire. The gate appeared to have some kind of electronic lock, maybe even an electromagnetic one. They might be able to roll it open if they could kill the power source, but that was undoubtedly on the other side.

They moved west to get a better look at the fence. It hummed with the current running through it.

"Did you notice any weak points?" Liesel asked.

Dylan shook his head. "What you see is what you get."

Ananke walked up to the very edge of the tree line, gave the barrier a closer look, and then walked back to the others. "The way I see it, we only have a few options. One, we hike around the perimeter until we find a weak spot."

"And if we don't?" Harris asked.

"That's the risk."

"What is option two?" Liesel asked.

"We wait until someone comes out, and we recruit them to let us in."

Harris looked dubious. "You really think any of those people will help us?"

Dylan leaned toward her and whispered loudly enough for everyone to hear, "I believe you're taking the word *recruit* too literally."

Her eyes widened. "Oh, you mean…"

"Yes," Ananke said.

"What if no one comes out until morning?"

"Then we'll need to come up with a fourth option."

"Fourth? Did I miss the third?"

"The third is splitting up and doing both options one and two."

"I vote for that," Liesel said.

"Three makes sense to me, too," Dylan agreed.

"Three," Harris said.

"Good," Ananke said.

SINCE DYLAN HAD already scouted part of the fence to the west, Ananke assigned him to continue checking for weak spots in that direction. Liesel set off to the east with the same instructions.

Ananke led Harris back toward the gate.

"So, we just sit around and wait?" Harris said.

"Unless you have a deck of cards. Or we could discuss what we're going to do when someone comes out."

"Do you have a plan?"

"Of course I have a plan."

TWENTY-EIGHT

JUSTIN KELLER AND the rest of the transfer team off-loaded the participants for the midnight trials and ferried them down into the basement, where Mr. Slater would finish the preparatory phase.

On a cart in the holding room was the body of a man Justin had transferred to the lodge just the day before. The homeless guy. From his gunshot wounds, it looked like he'd either made a pretty good game of it, or the trophy hunters had been bad shots. Likely it was both. In addition to the large shotgun blast center chest, he had wounds in his arm, shoulder, and thigh.

After Justin and the transfer team brought the last of the new prey down, Slater said, "Just got an update on tonight's shipment. They're on time for 2:30 a.m. Grab some supper upstairs, then get back to the ranch, grab a little sleep, and make sure your asses are at Scolareon when the truck arrives."

"Yes, sir," Justin said.

He and the others went up to the kitchen, where they had a quick meal. They then returned to the van and started the fifty-minute trip to Slater's farm.

The road was iffy enough in daylight. Now that night had fully fallen, the drive out was slower than the drive in. Per procedure, when they stopped at the gate, everyone but Justin exited with their rifles and took defensive positions to prevent anything other than the van from passing through.

When his friends were in position, Justin pushed the remote.

Four floodlights mounted in trees on either side of the gate blazed on, illuminating an area of nearly a hundred square feet, ensuring nothing could approach the gate without being seen.

The lock disengaged and the gate rolled to the side.

After it opened all the way, Justin and the others had exactly twenty seconds to get the van and themselves to the other side before the gate slammed shut. Justin sped through the gap and stopped, still within the halo of the floods. He heard the bang of the gate shutting a few seconds before the others scrambled back into the van.

Justin drove to the intersection and turned down the main dirt road that would take them back to the highway.

"Oh, shit," Sherwood said as someone ran onto the road, at the far reaches of their headlights.

"Who the hell is that?" Justin asked as he lifted his foot off the accelerator.

Whoever it was, he was waving his arms over his head, trying to get their attention.

Justin let the van creep forward until he'd cut the distance between them in half, and then stopped. The person dropped his arms and jogged toward them.

Wait. That's not a man, Justin thought as the figure neared.

It was a woman with short hair. A *familiar* woman.

"Isn't that that lady cop from town?" Sherwood said.

It was. Justin didn't know her name but he'd seen her, mostly at night, on patrol. His hand slid down to the pistol he kept next to the seat.

The cop smiled as she moved to the driver's-side window and jumped onto the running board. "Man, am I glad to see you!" she said.

She motioned for Justin to roll down the window.

"Be ready," he whispered to Sherwood without moving his lip.

Slowly, he lowered the window.

"I didn't think I was ever going to see anyone!" the cop said. "I was out on a hike and it got late and I got lost, and somehow came out on this road. Oh, and you both might want to take your hand off your guns."

Justin's brow furrowed. "What?"

"If you don't, my colleague will put a bullet in your

buddy's head before either of you can make a move." She nodded across to the other side of the van.

Justin and Sherwood turned. An African-American woman smiled at them through the passenger window, in her hand a pistol pointed at Sherwood's head.

She tapped the glass with the muzzle. "Let's get this window down, too, hon."

Sherwood raised his hands in the air.

"Appreciate the surrender," the woman said. "Still need the window down."

"What? Oh, um, sure." He rolled the window down and put his hands back up.

"Thanks. How you boys doing tonight?"

"What do you want?" Justin asked.

"Okay, if you'd rather cut the small talk, we can get right to it. The first thing I want to know is, are your friends in the back again or is it just you two?"

"No," Justin said, way too quickly. "It-it's just us."

She sighed. "Justin. It is Justin, right?"

His eyes widened, but he said nothing.

"Justin, I have a bullshit meter that goes off at the slightest lie. So why don't we try that again. Are your friends in back?"

He licked his lips and nodded.

"Thanks. Now, which one of you bozos is in charge?"

"He is," Sherwood said, without hesitation.

"I appreciate the candor."

In a flash, the barrel of her gun shot through the window and connected with the side of Sherwood's head. He slumped toward Justin, unconscious.

"I have a confession," the woman said. "We already knew you were in charge. And unfortunately for you, we don't need your help just yet."

Before Justin could figure out what she meant, pain spiked across his skull.

"WHAT'S TAKING SO long?" Fredericks said under his breath, after the van had been sitting still for several minutes.

He and Johnson had heard faint voices from up front but

those had stopped. Due to the insulated construction of the rear compartment, they couldn't make out anything that was said.

"Probably something in the road," Johnson said.

"Like what?"

"I don't know. A tree, or maybe a dead cow."

"A dead cow? Have you seen any cows up this way?"

Johnson shrugged. "One could have wandered up."

Fredericks rolled his eyes. Johnson was a good guy and a dedicated member of the organization, but he was far from the smartest in the group.

Fredericks knocked on the wall between the back area and the cab, and then placed his hands against it and yelled, "Hey. What's the holdup?"

He didn't really expect one of the guys to shout back, but he thought he'd at least get a knock. There was no response at all.

He was silent for a moment. "We should check."

"Aren't we supposed to stay here?"

"Not if there's a problem."

Fredericks grabbed his rifle and headed down the narrow aisle to the rear of the vehicle. After a brief pause, he heard Johnson follow.

Fredericks pushed open the double doors. All was quiet behind the van, the road dark and empty as far as he could see. All was quiet from around front, too. That was disturbing. He'd thought they would hear Keller and Sherwood moving around.

He motioned for Johnson to go right, then he moved onto the rear step near the left corner. He glanced back at Johnson. His partner was staring at him, a tremor in his lower lip. Fredericks tried to smile reassuringly, but he felt uneasy, too.

He turned back to the corner and yelled, "Justin? Aaron? You guys out there?"

The only response was a breeze sweeping through the trees.

Fredericks cursed under his breath, looked back at Johnson, and whispered, "On three. One. Two. Three." He swung around the end of the van.

"Hello."

At the same moment he registered the black woman standing in front of him, he heard a scream from back in Johnson's direction. The next thing he knew, his rifle had been ripped from his hands and he was on his knees, the woman's arm wrapped around his neck.

His vision began to collapse, like an iris closing.

And soon he saw nothing at all.

ANANKE DRAGGED HER target behind the van and laid him on the ground, a moment before Harris appeared with her own unconscious Slater disciple.

"Any problems?" Ananke asked.

"Other than him screaming like a baby?"

Ananke glanced at the guy at the cop's feet. "You know, technically what you just did is called assault, Officer Harris."

Smirking, Harris said, "I kinda liked it. Do you think that's bad?"

"You're asking the wrong person."

They loaded all four bodies into the back, and strapped them into the shelves with the attached restraints.

They climbed into the cab, Ananke in the driver's seat.

"We need someplace, not too far from here, where we can have a private conversation with our new friends."

Harris thought for a moment. "There's an old campground a couple miles to the north that's been closed for a few years. A few people use it now and then, but it's usually deserted."

"Sounds lovely." Ananke dropped the van into drive.

EIGHTEEN MINUTES LATER, Harris directed Ananke down an old winding road off the highway and into a canyon. Soon they came to a sign that read NEEDHAM CANYON CAMPGROUND, at the bottom of which was another sign proclaiming CAMPGROUND CLOSED NO TRESSPASSING.

Ananke drove past the mangled mess of a gate that had once been chained across the road, and through the entire campground to make sure it was empty before choosing the spot farthest from the entrance.

After she parked, she looked over at Harris. "I should

probably do this alone. It could get…messy. Better if you have deniability."

"I don't give a shit about deniability. These people took someone I love, and God only knows what they've done to her or the others they've taken. Would it go easier if I helped you?"

"Probably."

"Then what are we waiting for?" Harris opened her door and climbed out.

When they opened the back of the van, Ananke wasn't surprised to see the two assholes they hadn't smacked in the heads had woken up.

One was glaring at the women as they moved between the shelf beds. He probably thought he looked tough and scary. The other one looked as if he was about to soil his pants—eyes wide and terrified, his whole body shaking.

"One of you is going to tell us what we need to know," Ananke said. "So who's going to volunteer?"

Glaring Boy looked like he wanted to bite her head off, so she turned her attention to the nervous Nelly.

"Don't you say a word," Glaring Boy warned.

Ananke twisted back around. "Did I give you permission to speak?"

The smartass opened his mouth to respond, but was only able to get *fu* out before Ananke's fist connected with his jaw, rocking his head sideways. He lolled against the pillow, groaning.

"Well, that's disappointing," Ananke said. "I was really hoping that would have knocked you out."

She punched him again, this time achieving the desired result.

She swiveled back to the other guy. "Are you going to be a problem, too?"

"N-n-no. Not a problem."

"Good. How do we get past the gate?"

He licked his lips and looked worried.

"You said you weren't going to be a problem."

"Th-there's a remote. I-i-i-it opens the gate."

"And where will I find this remote?"

"M-m-mounted under the dash. But...but..."

"But what?"

"It's, um, fingerprint activated."

"Will your finger work?"

"No, just..."

"Justin's?"

He stared at her, surprised, then nodded.

"So all I need is his finger."

The kid's face went white. "Oh, God. You're not going to cut it off, are you?"

COLD WATER ARCED through the air and splashed into Keller's face. He sputtered and gasped, his head swinging back and forth, until the water had all run off.

He sat back and tried to move his arms, but discovered he'd been tied to a tree. His gaze fell on Ananke and Harris, standing in front of him.

"Welcome back," Ananke said.

"What's going on? Why am I tied up?"

"Because I want to make sure you understand your situation before you agree to assist us."

"Fuck you, bitch. I'm not helping some nig...someone like you."

"Hey," Harris said. "Be respectful, asshole."

He glared at her. "I'm not listening to a dyke cop, either."

Ananke could sense Harris tense, and wondered if she would have to restrain the woman again, but the cop held her ground. Ananke stepped over to Keller and leaned down until her face was less than a foot from his.

"I don't think you fully appreciate what's going on here."

She could tell he was planning to spit the moment the thought entered his mind, so she grabbed his nose and pulled his face forward.

"I know you think you're tough, but you don't know tough. You, Justin, are a delivery boy. You want to know what *I* do for a living? I'm an assassin. I kill people, a lot smarter and a lot tougher than you, all the time."

She pinched harder, then twisted until she felt the cartilage crack. She then palmed his face and shoved his head into the tree, not hard enough to knock him out, but enough to leave a mark.

"I ask questions. You answer truthfully. Nod if you understand."

He took several rapid breaths, his chin resting against his chest.

"Don't make me ask again."

Without looking at her, he nodded.

"Good boy. Where did you take the four people you picked up from Devon Rally's barn? Be specific."

He looked like he was trying to come up with the courage not to answer, but it turned out he wasn't completely stupid. "The lodge."

"The lodge. That's the big building on the other side of the gate."

He nodded.

"Where in the lodge?"

"The holding room. In the basement."

She tapped him on the cheek. "Excellent, Justin. Keep it up. Are they all still alive?"

"For the moment."

"But not for long?"

He shook his head, not in disagreement, but confirmation.

"What are they going to do to them?"

"Put them in the…the trials."

Ananke glanced at Harris, but the cop clearly didn't know what that meant, either. "And what are the trials?"

"A-a-a competition."

She grabbed what she could of his short hair and yanked his face up. "Look at me."

Wincing, he pried his eyes open.

"You do not want to frustrate me. And right now, dribbling out little pieces of information like you are, that's exactly what you're doing. What kind of competition?"

"H-h-hunting. The people we took are the…the…."

Ananke's blood turned cold. "Spit it out."

"Prey."

Ananke didn't even try to hide her disgust. Though she might not yet know the why, she now knew what was going on here.

"What about Natasha Patterson?" Harris said. "Did you take her to the lodge, too?"

Keller looked confused, then figured out what she meant. "I didn't take her. Mr. Slater did."

"When?"

"This morning."

Harris could barely contain her anger. "Is she already dead?"

"No. She goes at midnight with the others."

"You bastard!" Harris yelled.

If Ananke hadn't been between them, Harris would have ripped Keller apart. As it was, Ananke barely got her arms around the cop in time to keep her from clawing a chunk of his face off. She marched Harris away, the woman huffing in anger as she stared over Ananke's shoulder at Keller.

Ananke said, "Calm down and remember what you promised me."

"Did you hear what he said? They're going to kill them!"

"They're *planning* to kill them. And if we're going to stop them, we need his assistance. Can you control yourself, or do I need to leave you behind?"

Harris's nostrils flared a few more times before some of the tension in her face eased. "I'm okay."

"Promise me you're not going to attack him, no matter what he says."

"I promise I won't until you say I can."

"I can live with that."

Ananke slowly let her go, ready to grab Harris again if the woman made a wrong move. She didn't.

Ananke returned to Keller. "Officer Harris isn't particularly happy with you. As long as you continue cooperating, she's agreed not to kill you. If you don't, I won't stop her next time."

Keller's gaze flicked to Harris and returned to Ananke. He nodded.

"The trials start at midnight?"

"The ones your friends will be in…I think."

"You *think*?"

"I don't work the trials. I'm transportation."

"So, you're done for the day?"

He glanced away before looking at her again. "Yeah, that's right."

She grabbed his nose again, pressing on the fracture point. "You're lying again."

He screamed. "Please! Let go! I'm sorry, okay? I'm sorry!"

"The truth," she said, still hanging on.

"We-we're heading home, but we're not done."

"Then you did lie."

"I lied. I'm sorry!"

She let go. "I forgive you. Now tell me, what else do you have planned for tonight?"

TWENTY-NINE

"GOOD EVENING, ANANKE," the Administrator said. "Are you still making progress?"

Ananke stood beside the open driver's door of the van, looking across the dark campground. "You could say that."

"Have you located the Patterson woman?"

"We have."

"That's excellent news."

"Not quite. We know where she is. We don't have her yet."

"Perhaps you should fill me in."

"I'd love to, but there's not a lot of time now. I'm calling because I need your help with something."

"What can I do?"

"There's a truck that will be arriving at Bradbury tonight between two and two-thirty a.m. It'll be met south of town by at least one Scolareon security sedan and escorted to the Scolareon facility, where it will drop off its cargo. I need you to arrange for the shipment to be intercepted. But not by local cops. It's got to be the FBI."

"You and your team were sent there to handle whatever was happening. Shouldn't you be dealing with this?"

"Trust me, it's going to take a while to unravel everything here, and I don't think you want us hanging around that long. So, the feds are going to have to be involved at some point. Might as well be now. Besides, we're going to be busy elsewhere."

"It's already eight o'clock. That kind of operation may prove difficult to arrange."

"You don't need a whole squad of agents. A handful

would be enough in a pinch. I'll text you the coordinates where the truck will rendezvous with its escort."

"The FBI won't act simply because they are asked to. They'll need a reason."

"You can't tell me you don't have a few strings you could pull. But fine, tell them it'll be the tip of the iceberg to one of the biggest cases they've had in years."

"That's still not very inform—"

"Human trafficking. Tell them it's about that. Oh, and premeditated murder on what I believe is a massive scale."

The line went silent for a few seconds. "I'll make sure they show up. Is there anything else?"

"Yes. When we were flying back after the last job, Ricky mentioned the bugs you implanted in him."

"Purely a precautionary—"

"I'm not questioning why you did it. What I need is real-time access to his tracking information."

SLATER LOOKED UP as his daughter and Devon Rally entered the prep room. He and one of his assistants had just finished moving all six prey into individual wheelchairs—the five they'd brought over from the barn and the unused alternate from that afternoon. The trophies were all unconscious and would remain so until Slater administered adrenaline injections prior to the start of the midnight trials.

Rally sauntered over and walked slowly in front the chairs, as if he were a general inspecting his troops. "These the two you told me about?" He gestured at the duo who'd tried to cause problems at the barn. Like the other prey, they were held in place by restraints, their heads drooping forward.

"That's them."

Rally frowned at the woman. Hair cascaded down both sides of her downturned face, and her small frame made her look almost like a child in the chair. "Pretty scrawny. Do you really think she'll last very long?"

"She'll do all right," Slater said.

"If you say so. Though I'm sure I could find more…interesting uses for her."

Slater swallowed his disgust. He didn't share his cousin's lust for women of inferior breeding. He thought it made Rally weak. But there was no sense in saying anything. It was an illness, and words were useless.

Rally continued his inspection, stopping again in front of the last wheelchair. "This one's not so bad, either. Not great, but good enough for a little spin." He patted Natasha Patterson on the cheek as if she were a baby, and glanced back at Slater. "Did I tell you I gave her a shot once? Thought she'd be an easy pickup but she blew me off." He squeezed her chin. "Nobody blows me off, bitch."

Slater said to his daughter, "Are we still on schedule?"

"Ahead, actually."

Good. That meant the participants were already in their rooms, resting for the midnight session.

Slater's brother would be happy to hear that when he arrived. If they'd had to adjust the start by more than an hour, he'd have to miss it, as there wouldn't be enough time for him to get back to Scolareon to oversee tonight's delivery.

Rally walked over to him. "A decent crop. The guy you caught today looks like he should provide a nice challenge."

"I was thinking the same thing."

"Well, if I'm not needed for anything else, I think I'll go take a little nap."

DYLAN AND LIESEL met the van on the dirt road, half a mile before the turnoff for the lodge, at 8:44 p.m. After she outlined her plan, Ananke obtained the specialty items Liesel had in her backpack, and then Liesel and Dylan climbed into the back of the van with three of the restrained delivery boys.

Ananke drove to the intersection with the lodge road and stopped. She turned to Keller. He was kneeling in the gap between the front seats, Harris's gun jammed into his ribs.

"You do anything to screw this up, you're dead," Ananke said. "Do I make myself clear?"

Keller winced as Harris ground the muzzle into his side.

"Yes, clear," he said.

Ananke continued to stare at him.

"I won't screw up. I promise," he said.

She took her foot off the brake and made the turn.

When they reached the gate, Ananke said, "Okay, now."

Keller reached two fingers under the dash and touched the special screen on the remote. As he'd described, four floodlights switched on, turning the area surrounding the entrance into daylight. The gate began rolling to the side. Ananke drove through.

When they were out of the glare of the floodlights and surrounded by trees again, Ananke stopped the van, turned back to Keller. "Tell me again. The road leads to…"

"The east side of the lodge."

"And there are no guard posts or cameras between here and there?"

"No."

"I'm starting not to believe you again."

"I-I-I—"

"It's okay," Ananke said. "It's not really that important." She unzipped the palm-sized, leather case Liesel had given her, and withdrew a preloaded syringe. "Your usefulness has run its course."

She stuck the needle into his arm and depressed the plunger. Within seconds, Keller's eyelids drooped and his body tilted forward, his head knocking against the dash as he lost consciousness.

Ananke and Harris transferred Keller into the back, where Liesel and Dylan had already given similar injections to Keller's associates. When the van started moving again, Liesel stood on the running board beside Ananke's door, holding on through the open window, while Dylan did the same next to Harris. Ananke kept their speed slow as all four searched for somewhere they could stow the van.

A creek running into the woods provided their best opportunity. Ananke carefully guided the van down the slope and into the hubcap-high water, then followed the stream a good hundred yards around a bend before killing the engine. In the daylight, the vehicle could probably be spotted through the trees, but at night, not a chance in hell.

Ananke climbed out of the cab and joined Liesel, Dylan, and Harris on the other side. "Let's go find our friends."

YATES WAS RUNNING late. He'd been planning on getting to the lodge by eight so he could help Slater with the final preparations, but it was nearly nine by the time he used his remote to open the gate to the lodge.

There'd been a small snafu on that evening's Scolareon security schedule. Flynn Hart, a newbie Yates had been forced to hire because the guy was some bigwig's nephew or something, had been assigned to graveyard. But it was delivery night, and the last thing Yates wanted was some Goody Two-shoes accidentally seeing what he shouldn't.

Yates had come up with some mandatory training bullshit to explain the last-minute reshuffling of personnel, and then had to figure out what that training would be. That's what he got for delegating. Of course, it didn't help that it was a trials week, when his attention was always pulled in several directions.

He drove onto his cousin's property and down the entrance road at a pace faster than was safe. But he'd taken the road so many times that he knew every dip and hole and turn. When he was about halfway to the lodge, he caught a flash of red lights through the trees. Apparently, another car was on the road ahead of him. He kept expecting to catch up to it, but he made it all the way to the lodge without seeing anything.

It had probably been one of Slater's men out on a 4x4, doing a security check.

After parking his sedan, Yates walked over to the lodge and headed around back to use the kitchen entrance. When he rounded the corner, he saw the transport van parked by the opened doors to the basement lift. Light glowed from the shaft, and he could hear the hum of the electric motor. A few seconds later, the platform reached the top, carrying his brother and Bryan Evans and two warm bodies in wheelchairs.

Apparently, Yates wasn't as late as he thought.

"Hey, let me give you a hand," he called as he jogged over.

ANANKE AND THE others had barely set out when they heard a car drive past on the road, moving pretty fast given the conditions. It had come from the gate and was heading toward the lodge.

For a moment, she wondered if its speed meant the van had been spotted driving off the road, but it seemed highly unlikely. They'd been walking by the time the sedan was anywhere nearby. The driver was probably one of the hotshot kids who worked for Slater, exercising his God-given teenage right to ignore common sense.

Keeping the distance between themselves and the road at a hundred feet at least, they hiked on a northern heading that should take them straight to the lodge. Any cameras would likely be concentrated on the road rather than scattered in the wilderness. But just to be safe, Ananke tasked Dylan with making periodic binocular sweeps on thermal setting, and Liesel doing the same with the electronics detection app.

It took eight minutes before they caught their first glimpse of the lodge. Three stories and as wide as a city block.

Light oozed out from several windows on the first and second floors, while on the third, only two were lit. Those glowing on the second floor were grouped together near the middle, and on the first spread from end to end. Five chimneys rose from the roof. Though it was too dark to see any smoke, one of the fireplaces must have been in use because Ananke could smell the burning wood.

A well-manicured lawn fronted the building, creating a wide gap between the lodge and the woods. Off to the right, where the entrance road let out, was a dirt parking area containing several cars.

Ananke examined the building through her binoculars. The open lawn area and the parking lot were illuminated by floodlights similar to those back at the gate. But unlike at the gate, an electronics scan revealed at least half a dozen devices, presumably cameras, attached to the lodge.

Ananke opened the tracking map on her phone, and used the information the Administrator had given her to locate Ricky. The dot representing him sat squarely in the building, the dimensional callout putting his vertical location eleven feet below ground level—in the basement. That jibed with what Keller had told them.

She led her team to the right, and circled through the forest to the other side of the lodge. As the back came into view, she saw that here, too, a clear area separated the structure from the trees, only it was mainly dirt, not grass. What caught her attention was the van parked next to the building, its back doors open wide so she could see inside.

She signaled the others to stop and raised her binoculars.

The vehicle was the same make and model as the one she and Harris had hijacked, but it wasn't identical. It had a ramp leading from the back to the ground, and the four metal beds the other van contained were missing here. Instead, four people in wheelchairs occupied the space. The chairs appeared to be locked against the walls, two per side, facing the middle. Their occupants were all leaning forward, heads bowed. Unconscious or close to it, she guessed.

Ananke couldn't see any of the people's faces, but the small person in the chair on the left, farthest back, was the same size and had the same long dark hair as Rosario.

After a closer look at the others, she held her glasses out to Harris. Before the cop could raise them, Ananke touched her hand. "Remember, you promised to do what I say and not act out on your own."

Tensing, Harris began lifting the glasses, but once more Ananke stopped her.

"Tell me you remember."

"I remember."

Ananke let go of her hand. "There are four people in the back of the van. I want you to look at the one on the right side, closest to us."

Ananke knew the moment Harris located the correct passenger by the way the cop suddenly squeezed the binoculars.

"It's Tasha, isn't it?" Ananke asked.

"Yes." Harris packed more anger into a three-letter word than Ananke thought possible.

A faint hum emanated from the area behind the lodge. Ananke grabbed the binoculars from Harris and aimed them at the noise.

Light shot out of the ground adjacent to the lodge, and a few moments later, two men rose into view, standing behind two more occupied wheelchairs. Ananke recognized three of the people. The standing pair were Dalton Slater and his half brother, Leo Yates. One of those sitting was Ricky.

Ananke checked her tracker, just to confirm. Ricky's dot and his vertical location matched what she was seeing.

Slater and Yates wheeled the chairs up the ramp into the van, where they anchored them with straps, one on each side. As they were doing this, two more men rose out of the hole. Young guys. More members of Slater's youth brigade.

When Slater and Yates exited the van, the younger men removed the ramp and slipped it into a slot below the floor of the rear compartment. Then they hopped in back, and Slater and Yates closed them inside. The two older men walked to the front.

When the brake lights flashed on, Ananke lowered the binoculars but kept her eyes on the van. Keller had told them the "trials" were held farther north within the forest that belonged to the lodge. If he hadn't lied, the truck would head in that direction instead of south, back toward the gate.

The van slowed as it reached the far end of the lodge, and turned left.

North.

She grinned.

THIRTY

10:17 p.m.

BUILT INTO THE backside of a small crest, fifty yards from the clearing that served as the trials' starting point, was the concrete building containing the final holding cells for the prey. The front portion was essentially a long, hallway-like room, from which there were entrances to ten individual cells. The only ways in and out of the rooms were through thick, steel-reinforced doors that had handles only on the outside.

The highest number of cells ever used at one time had been eight, though plans were for nine to be put to use for this session's final trial in two days, depending on the quality of product from the shipment due in that night.

For the upcoming midnight trials, they were using six cells, starting from the right. Each of the prey had been laid out on army cots, and were still unconscious.

That would change in one hour and twenty-eight minutes, when they would each be administered a jolt of adrenaline, and then at 12:03 a.m., paraded into the meadow and presented to the trial participants.

Yates entered the building, shoving his phone back into his pocket.

"Still on schedule?" Slater asked.

"Yup," Yates replied. "Truck's about two hours south of Spokane. So, unless they blow a tire, we're good."

"Ready for a fence check?"

"Let's do it."

USING RICKY'S TRACKING bug to guide them, Ananke and the

others caught up with the van thirty minutes after it had left the lodge. More specifically, what they caught up to was a concrete building half buried in the side of the ridge. Ricky's dot glowed from inside the structure.

The team hid among a rock outcropping about seventy-five yards away and surveyed the site. A door in the middle of the building was the only access point. Yates paced outside, near the door, talking on the phone, while the two young guys who'd ridden in the back of the van stood sentry with M4 rifles at opposite ends of the ridge above the building. The only other details of note were the three 4x4 ATVs sitting next to the parked van.

"No cameras attached to the building," Liesel whispered.

"Nothing in the trees, either," Dylan added.

Security here was undoubtedly a delicate situation. The last thing they'd want would be to have recordings of their activities end up in the wrong hands. Better not to have any at all. Besides, even if a prisoner escaped, he or she would make it only as far as the fifteen foot-high electric fence. Probably not even that far, given what Keller had said about the tracking bugs they implanted in everyone.

Poor Ricky. He must feel like a pin cushion.

Yates lowered his phone as he reached for the door. For two seconds, Ananke had a view inside, but all she could see was another wall not too far beyond the entrance, and part of a door set in it.

She lowered her binoculars and motioned for everyone to gather around.

"Keller said there's a clearing where the trial starts," she whispered. "It can't be far. Dylan, find it and learn everything you can about it. Liesel, I want you and Morgan to stay here and keep an eye on that building. If I'm right, nothing should happen until closer to midnight, but if I'm wrong, report right away. I'm going to scout out the area where this…hunt is supposed to take place." She checked the time. "It's ten-eighteen. We rendezvous back here in one hour. Questions?"

From back toward the building came the sound of the door opening, then a voice, followed by a laugh, and another voice, younger.

Ananke, Liesel, Dylan, and Harris all brought up their binoculars.

Slater and Yates had exited the building, and Slater was talking to one of the guards on the ridge. When he finished, Slater and his brother walked toward the van. But their destination turned out to be the ATVs. They each climbed onto one, started it up, and sped past the building into the forest.

Ananke glanced over at Dylan. "Try not to let them catch you."

"A little confidence, please," he said. "I'm not Ricky."

They headed off in opposite directions.

DYLAN THOUGHT THE easiest way to find the meadow was to locate the path leading there from the building.

There had to be a path, right? If the building was where they kept the…victims—God, it made him sick every time he thought about it—then there had to be an easy way to take them to their deaths.

Moving through the woods in an arc that never took him closer than a hundred and fifty feet to the ridge, Dylan looked for the path. Not far past the ninety-degree mark, he found it. While the ground wasn't so beaten down that grass and clover stopped growing on it, someone had cleared away the six foot-wide strip of trees and large bushes.

Not knowing if any other of Slater's people were around, Dylan paralleled the path from a dozen feet inside the woods. It went basically straight for maybe a hundred feet before it took a gentle dip into a depression. Another fifty feet on, he found the meadow.

It was shaped almost like a baseball field—one end coming together at a sharp point, with the meadow flaring out wide until it was swallowed again by the forest about a hundred yards away. Near the pointed end, a little farther than where a pitcher's mound would be, sat a platform that had ramps leading off it on all sides but one.

Using the binoculars on thermal mode, Dylan scanned the clearing for human-sized heat signatures, but it was clear. He trained the lenses on the woods surrounding the clearing. He couldn't see through the trees, but could confirm no one was standing between them.

Still not ready to step into the field, Dylan walked down to the rounded point. There he found another trail, wide enough for a vehicle. He followed it away from the clearing. It was nowhere near as long as the one that had brought him here, as it ended after fifty feet at a wide dirt area, sprinkled with footprints and tire tracks. It didn't take a genius to figure out this was where the vehicles that brought the hunters parked.

Dylan returned to the meadow, and continued around the "home plate" end to the other side. In a nook within the trees, he found what he could only describe as a spectator area—two rows of benches, the back ones set up on a mound of dirt so those sitting there could see over the heads of those in front. The idea of spectators here repulsed him even more.

He searched through the woods all the way down the side, and continued doing the same across the far end of the meadow and back down the side from where he originally arrived. Though he discovered no other man-made items, he did note several potential ambush spots and hiding places.

Upon completing the search of the surrounding woods, he checked his watch and saw he had just enough time left for a closer examination of the meadow.

AT THE BEGINNING of her scout, Ananke used the sound of the ATVs to guide her, thinking Slater and Yates would be checking the grounds where the trial was to take place. This led her into a densely wooded area, north-northwest of the meadow Dylan was checking.

What she really wished she had was a pair of night-vision goggles. She'd have to talk to the Administrator about including them in future missions.

Future missions? Am I really considering that?

Refocusing on the task at hand, she buried the thought.

She may not have had night-vision goggles, but her binoculars were equipped with an adequate night-vision setting. The only problem was that she had to be farther away from her target than if she were using goggles, not to mention she'd need to raise the glasses whenever she wanted a more detailed look.

A sweep through the trees ahead revealed several items of interest. She proceeded to the first, a pine tree about thirty feet away with an almost oval chunk of bark missing. She ran a hand over the spot, and found the exposed wood splintered and ripped and riddled with dozens of tiny holes. She was tempted to shine a light into one of the holes, but the risk of exposure was not worth it. Besides, she knew a shotgun blast when she saw one.

Moving on, she saw other trees had also been marred by firearms. She didn't want to imagine what might have happened here, but it was impossible not to. A captive running for his or her life. Some entitled asshole stalking him with a shotgun and a tracking device showing exactly where the prey was. A series of blasts as the hunter flushed the runner out of a hiding place. Then somewhere, probably not far from where Ananke was standing, the shot taking down the innocent. Blood splattering the ground. A shout of triumph from the hunter. The prey either dead or reeling in pain. Perhaps there was a final shot to put the victim out of his misery. Or maybe the hunter and his colleagues stood around and waited for the prisoner to take his last breath.

Ananke's face hardened.

She picked up her pace, and squeezed out every second she had to scout the area before it was time to head back.

AT 11:00 ON the dot, a four-note musical alert repeated three times from speakers in the suites of all the participants. This was followed by the voice of Miss Riefenstahl. "Good evening, gentlemen. I hope you have had a pleasant rest. In twenty minutes, please join me by the fireplace for some quick refreshments."

All the participants were in the main room well ahead of time. The hostess entered at exactly 11:30, followed by two young men carrying trays of hors d'oeuvres. The men set the appetizers on a table next to the bar, and began pouring flutes of champagne.

As soon as they were done, Miss Riefenstahl grabbed one of the glasses. "Gentlemen, please."

When they each had a flute, the hostess raised hers.

"May the coming trial provide challenge, excitement, and, most of all, success."

Everyone drank.

"Help yourselves," she said, gesturing to the appetizers. "But I'd advise against eating too much. You won't want to be sluggish on the field. There will also be a full breakfast once the trial is finished."

At first no one approached the food, but soon, one by one, the men made their way to the trays, taking two or three of the treats before moving on.

The hostess moved through the room, sharing a word of encouragement with each man and wishing them all good luck. At 11:35, a young man appeared briefly in the dining room doorway and gave her a subtle nod.

The hostess returned to the front of the room. "Gentlemen, it is time. If you would follow me, we will pick up your weapons and return to the carts."

DYLAN HAD RETURNED by the time Ananke got back.

"Any change?" she asked Liesel, glancing at the half-hidden building.

"Slater and Yates drove back about ten minutes ago and went inside. That is about it."

To Dylan, Ananke said, "Tell us about the meadow."

After he described what he'd found, Ananke did the same about her recon, and then laid out how she wanted to proceed.

When she finished, Dylan grinned. "I like the way you think, boss."

"You'll be okay with the rifle?" Ananke asked Liesel.

"Of course."

Ananke turned to Harris. "Last chance for you to get out of this."

"No, thanks."

"Then I guess it's time to get into position."

292

They each grabbed the equipment they required and set out for their assigned spots.

THIRTY-ONE

11:45 p.m.

RICKY'S EYELIDS SHOT open and he gasped for air. He tried to sit up, but quickly discovered he wasn't going anywhere. Straps across his chest, waist, and thighs held him down, while thinner ones secured his wrists and ankles.

"Deep breaths," a voice said.

Ricky twisted his head toward the sound.

"Welcome back," Yates said, smiling.

Ricky kept his expression as blank as possible.

"You're a tough one, aren't you? That's good. You might even be the last one standing." Yates leaned in and whispered, "We could make it a little easier on you, you know. Make sure you don't suffer too much. All you have to do is tell us who you are and who you're working for."

Ricky snorted.

"Your call," Yates said. "But in about twenty minutes, you're really going to wish you talked."

Ricky burst out laughing, as if it were the funniest thing he'd ever heard.

ROSARIO WOKE TO find Slater standing over her, an empty syringe dangling from his hand.

Every cell in her body tingled as if each had received an individual jolt of electricity. She glared at her captor, jaw tense.

"*Hola, chica,*" he said. "You'll have to forgive me. That's about the extent of my *hablo espanyol*. You speak English?"

She didn't reply.

Shrugging, he said, "Well, if you do, I'd advise you not to

try to break free. It'd be a waste of energy you're going to wish you still had later. I've seen it happen before." He turned for the door. "We'll be back in a bit."

Rosario watched him leave and then looked back at the ceiling. She didn't know what they had planned for her, but she wasn't going to sit back and let it happen.

THE OFF-ROAD golf carts brought the participants back to the trial's starting point, where the men were once more escorted onto the field. Lights mounted in the trees lit the clearing from one end to the other. Like that afternoon, Mr. Lean waited for them on the platform, only this time he held a long, cloth-covered object in his hands.

"Good evening, gentlemen," Mr. Lean said. "Welcome to the midnight trials. Some of our past guests consider this to be the most difficult and rewarding event on the schedule. I'll leave that for you to decide, though.

"Tonight, you will all take the field at the same time. Six prey will be released. You are each allowed one kill. Once you've bagged your trophy, you will return here to await the others. As an added incentive, whoever takes down the one we have determined to be the most difficult target will receive this."

He removed the cloth covering the item he was holding. Underneath was a gold-plated Mossberg shotgun mounted on a long, black plaque.

Though each participant was more than wealthy enough to commission hundreds of such prizes for himself, their eyes lit up at the sight of the prize.

One of the assistants took the shotgun from Mr. Lean and carried it off the field.

"You have each been assigned an observer," Mr. Lean continued. "They are available to provide limited assistance. The actual tracking and eliminating of your prey will be up to you, of course."

As he spoke, six young men emerged from the woods and took spots behind the hunter they would be shadowing.

"Are there any questions?" Mr. Lean asked.

No one spoke.

"Excellent. Then let's get things started." Raising his voice, he said, "Bring out the prey!"

ROSARIO HEARD THE rattle of metal beyond the door to her room. A *lot* of metal. When it stopped, the noise was replaced by footsteps and a door opening. Not hers, though. Silence for a minute, and then another door. And another.

And then hers.

"Time to play," Slater said as he entered.

Yates came in behind him, with a young guy who looked like another knockoff of the proto-adult she'd seen at the barn. The clone took a position halfway between the cot and the door, holding a Mossberg shotgun, while the two older men approached Rosario.

They strapped a leather cuff around each of her legs, just above the ankles. The restraints were connected to each other by a two-foot length of chain. The men hooked up a similar rig to her wrists. The only difference between it and the one between her ankles was a three-inch metal hoop at the chain's midpoint. Slater wrapped a final cuff around her neck. This, too, had a chain extending from it, only it wasn't connected to anything.

After they removed the straps holding her to the bed, Slater yanked on the throat-cuff chain. "Get up."

Rosario rose to her feet.

"This way," Slater said, giving her another tug.

He and Yates led her out of her room, into a long hallway where another one of the young clones was standing watch over three people who, like Rosario, were in cuffs and chains.

Yates hurried ahead and grabbed the end of a long chain off the floor. The other prisoners were already attached to it, so it was no surprise that Yates threaded the chain through the hoop between her wrist cuffs, and clipped them together once she was three feet behind the nearest other captive.

"Stay," Slater ordered.

He and Yates and the kid with the Mossberg disappeared inside the cell next to Rosario's, emerging a minute later with

Tasha Patterson in tow. The chain was played through the woman's hoop, and she was clipped in place behind Rosario.

When the asshole brothers and their minion entered another room, Rosario snuck a peek at the guard who'd been left behind. He scanned the lot of them back and forth, his gaze never stopping. When his eyes had moved off her, she chanced a very low "Tasha" over her shoulder.

The woman continued to stare at the ground, apparently not having heard her. Rosario was about to say her name again when a shout came from the room Slater and Yates were in.

The hallway guard rushed to the door and looked inside.

Rosario turned and whispered more loudly, "Tasha. Tasha Patterson."

Patterson blinked at Rosario.

"We're here to get you out. But you need to stay strong and alert."

Patterson said, "Get me out?"

"Yes. Whatever happens, stay close to me."

"I don't…know you, do I?"

"No. We are friends of Scott Davos."

That got through. "Scott?"

"He asked us to find you."

Confusion again. "Who is *us*?"

Another roar from inside the room, followed by a body staggering out and smashing against the wall. Ricky turned and faced the way he'd just come, smiling. "That was good. You're pretty strong, you—"

The chain attached to his neck cuff jerked forward, yanking Ricky to the ground.

"*That* is us," Rosario said.

ON THE LIST of things Ricky did not like, being restrained was right there near the top.

His anger had been building since he woke, and had skyrocketed when the cuffs and chains were put on him.

But Ricky waited, holding on to that fire. When Slater tugged on the leash and told Ricky to get up, Ricky did. Only instead of stopping once he was on his feet, he launched himself at Yates, aiming to head-butt him in the nose. But Yates turned his face away a second before contact, taking the brunt of Ricky's thick skull in the cheek.

The shout of pain Yates let out was glorious, and Ricky would have sworn on a stack of Bibles he'd heard the guy's cheekbone crack.

Slater pulled the chain again to get Ricky away from his brother, which was exactly what Ricky was expecting. He went with it, using the momentum to swing over toward the punk with the shotgun. He came within inches of getting his hands on the weapon before Slater rushed over and shoved Ricky to the side, sending him shooting out into a hallway.

Ricky twisted back around and grinned at Slater. "That was good. You're pretty strong, you—"

Slater tugged on the chain again.

One second Ricky was standing, the next he was on the floor. Hands grabbed his arms and hauled him back to his feet. Slater and the clone marched Ricky over to where several other cuffed people were standing in a line.

When Ricky saw Rosario two places in front of him, he was relieved. He'd been wondering what had happened to her after the gas. He winked at her, and she gave him the tiniest of smirks. She then flicked her gaze at the woman standing between them.

Tasha Patterson. How about that?

Looks like we wrapped this case up.

He laughed, earning him a hard shove in the back.

"What?" he said. "You got something against good moods?"

Slater grabbed the shotgun from the kid. "I'll tell you what." He walked past Ricky and Patterson to Rosario, and stuck the double barrel under her chin. "Any more trouble out of you and your friend pays for it. So, you got another smartass comment, funny man?"

Ricky glared at Slater. "I do not."

"Good." Slater lowered the shotgun. "Next time I'll just pull the trigger. No warning. Got it?"

The rancher took a couple of steps away from the line and

said in a loud voice, "We are going to walk out of here in a nice, obedient line. Anyone who causes a problem—walks too slow, weaves out of place..." He looked at Ricky. "...opens his mouth—will immediately be removed and shot. Are there any questions?"

There were none.

DYLAN ACTIVATED HIS comm. "They just came out of the building. All six prisoners are chained together, like in one of those old prison movies. Yates and Slater are with them, plus three of their lapdogs." He watched for a moment through his binoculars. "They're heading for the path to the meadow."

"Copy," Ananke said. "Go ahead and reposition."

"Copy."

EDUARDO GLANCED AT the others in the line ahead of him as they were marched through the woods. He had no doubt they were being taken to their deaths, and there was absolutely nothing he could do about it. The chain holding him to the others prevented any chance of running away, but even if it hadn't been there, the weapons his captors held would take him down before he could move more than a few steps.

But he would not give in to hopelessness.

He had to believe there was still a chance of survival.

DEVON RALLY HELD his arms out wide, like the ringmaster of a traveling circus who'd just introduced his main act.

From out of the woods marched the prey for that night's festivities—six unwanted members of society, chained together.

The hunters eyed their soon-to-be quarry, each calculating which prey he should go after. The most skilled hunters, Mr. Wise and Mr. Reed, settled their gazes on the big white guy Slater had caught at the barn that day, while the least skilled, Mr. Hawks, seemed unable to decide between Tasha Patterson, the little Mex girl, and the older black guy.

The prey were led onto the platform and told to face the hunters.

Rally turned to the prisoners, and in a voice loud enough for everyone to hear, said, "Welcome to the midnight trials. In a few moments, your shackles will be removed and the event will commence. I'm sure you are wondering what I mean by that. The trials are a tournament of sorts, a test of skills, if you will. These gentlemen"—he gestured back at the hunters—"have paid a great deal for the honor of participating. They are all skilled hunters, and you are to be their prey."

Rally took particular pleasure in this moment, that beat before his words were fully absorbed, followed by the realization of what was about to happen to them. The horror on their faces was electrifying. At most of the previous trials, all the prisoners displayed the same piss-in-their-pants expressions. Tonight, however, four did not react in the expected manner.

Tasha Patterson looked as if she'd already given up, which was understandable. She'd been their guest for over two weeks now, and had been living the whole time with the realization things wouldn't end well for her. The Mex guy looked more pensive than fearful. Perhaps he was contemplating his demise, or planning to attack one of his captors. Most annoying, however, were the two intruders from that afternoon. They stared at Rally, their faces impassive.

Rally's eyes narrowed. There was something familiar about the woman. But whatever it was, he couldn't place it, so he continued with the script. "You see the forest behind you? Go ahead. Take a look."

All the prisoners looked over their shoulders, save the two intruders who continued to stare at Rally.

"When you are given the signal, you will run into those woods. Three minutes after you reach the trees, my friends behind me will..." It suddenly hit him. The woman was Caroline Cruz, Shawn Ramey's assistant. Why had she broken into the barn? "...um, will come looking for you."

Clearly Cruz was not who she'd said she was, which meant there was a good chance Ramey wasn't, either. But it didn't matter. Within a few hours at most, Cruz would be dead. As for Ramey, she needed to be eliminated in case she *was* involved. Rally would instruct Yates to make sure she would not see another sunrise, either.

With renewed strength, he said, "If you will please turn back around." The prisoners did. "The good news is that somewhere in the woods is a way to freedom. I'm not saying it's easy to find, but if you do, your life will be yours again. As long as you never breathe a word of what happened here to anyone. If that happens, we will come for you and your family and everyone close to you."

Though there was still fear in several of the captives' eyes, Rally could see his words had given them hope. *False* hope, of course. There was no way out. The only freedom waiting for them would come from the business end of one of the hunters' weapons.

He looked at Slater. "Have the prey been ranked?"

"Yes, sir," Slater said.

"Please reveal the rankings."

Slater went down the line, stopping in front of each prey to announce his or her difficulty level. The ugly Caucasian woman was proclaimed the sixth hardest, Tasha Patterson fifth, the black man fourth, the woman who went by the name Caroline Cruz third, the Mexican man second. The man who had been with Cruz at the barn was awarded the distinction of being judged hardest to kill, meaning whoever claimed him as trophy would receive the golden Mossberg.

Rally turned back to his paying guests. "Gentlemen, if you will raise your rifles. We will now remove the prey's restraints. If anyone makes a move to get away or try to hurt one of the attendants, you are free to kill them here and now." Rally then said to his cousins, "You may begin."

LIESEL WATCHED THE meadow through the scope attached to her collapsible Accuracy International AWM sniper rifle. Devon Rally had arrived, and then the hunters assembled before him. Though Rally was facing away from her, and too far away to hear, his hand gestures made it obvious he was giving a grandiose speech meant to inspire his guests.

After a few minutes, the captives were led in. Liesel

picked out Rosario, Ricky, and Tasha Patterson at the end of the line. When the hunters raised their rifles, she wondered if Keller had misled them and the prisoners were to be executed where they stood. But then Slater and Yates and a couple of their men began to unfasten the chains binding each captive.

Once the chains were removed and Rally's people had stepped out of the way, Rally lifted an arm into the air.

Liesel whispered into her comm, "Looks like things are about to start."

"Copy," Ananke said. "Dylan, you ready?"

"Ready."

"Morgan?"

"Ready."

"GENTLEMEN, PREPARE YOURSELF. It is now time to start the midnight trials." As Rally swung his arm down, he said, "Release the prey!"

Slater, Yates, and several members of the youth brigade shouted, "Run! Run!" and "Get moving!" and "You stay, you die!"

It didn't take much prodding to get the captives racing toward the woods. Even the defiant intruders wasted no time hanging around.

The moment the first of the runners reached the trees, Rally said, "The three-minute countdown begins now."

"RELEASE THE PREY!"

Rosario grabbed Tasha by the arm and yelled, "Come on," as she ran for the far end of the clearing.

Sprinting beside them, Ricky said, "Some hills to the right. We should head that way."

Rosario saw the rise in the terrain. "Good idea."

While Ricky moved in front of the two women to lead the way, Rosario glanced over at the other prisoners, who were fanning out to her left. The Latino guy was by far the best runner of that group, and had already surged several yards ahead of the other two. Rosario, Ricky, and Tasha were pretty much keeping pace with him, though Tasha's strained breaths made Rosario unsure how long the woman could keep up.

"We'll slow down when we get into the trees," she told Tasha.

Tasha managed only a nod.

The Latino guy hit the woods first, followed by Rosario, Ricky, and Tasha seconds later, all painfully aware that in less than three minutes, the hunters would come looking for them.

LIESEL WATCHED THE prisoners spread across the meadow and race toward the woods where she was set up.

"Rosario and Ricky are with Tasha," she reported. "They will leave the meadow farthest east. The other three are each running alone. The first one to reach the forest will be a man, coming in a dozen meters west of center point. The other two are about half a minute behind him. One will enter right at the center, and the other, five meters west of the first man."

ANANKE ADJUSTED HER position based on Liesel's information, and hunkered down again. She was in the woods approximately a hundred feet from the meadow.

"First one in the woods," Liesel announced. A short pause. "Rosario, Ricky, and Tasha, in." The next pause lasted nearly three times as long. "The last two, in."

Footsteps pounded the dirt, faint at first, but growing louder by the second. Ananke raised her binoculars and scanned the area between her and the meadow. The body-sized heat signature of the first man flickered between trees.

"Dammit," she said under her breath.

If he'd kept on the straight line he'd been on while crossing the meadow, he would have run right past her, but he was now on a diagonal path heading farther east, closer to where she'd been set up before.

Her original idea was to grab him as he ran by, but there was no time to reposition so she took off on an intercept course. Though the man was young and in decent shape, Ananke's superior conditioning allowed her to quickly narrow the gap, getting to within twenty-five feet of him before he realized she was there.

He panicked when he saw her and increased his speed, changing direction again.

"Slow down," she called. "I'm not going to hurt you."

This only seemed to heighten his fear. Why should he believe her? He'd been told he'd be hunted, and would perceive anyone as a threat.

She raced after him, the chase taking her farther from where she was supposed to be.

DYLAN HAD BEEN tasked with grabbing whichever captive entered the forest farthest to the east. This turned out to be the African-American man, who was obviously running out of energy. The moment he transitioned from the meadow into the woods, his all-out sprint turned into a staggering jog. By the time he neared Dylan, it couldn't even be called a jog anymore.

Dylan was close enough that he simply reached out and wrapped his arm around the man's arms and chest.

"Hold on there, my friend," he said.

The man tried to twist away but didn't have the strength. When he realized this, he slumped in Dylan's grasp. "Please, don't kill me. I'll do anything. Please. I'm not ready. I'm not ready."

"It's okay, it's okay. I'm not one of the bastards who want to shoot you. I'm actually here to make sure they don't."

The man blinked. "I-I don't understand."

"Come on. We need to get you somewhere safe."

Suspicion clouded the man's vision. "You're just going to take me to them, aren't you?"

"I'm not. But if I was, you're in no condition to stop me, are you?"

The man shook his head.

"All right, then. The faster we get going, the faster you'll see I'm telling the truth."

MORGAN HEARD THE woman's staccato breathing before she heard the woman's steps. The captive's trajectory was west of Morgan's position, but not by much.

Morgan eased behind a tree along the woman's path,

waited until the captive was within ten feet, and stepped out.

The woman skidded to a stop across the needle-covered ground, her eyes wide.

"Don't worry," Morgan said. "I'm a police officer. I'm here to help."

"Police?" The woman sounded as if she wanted to believe it but wasn't sure she could.

"Yes, ma'am. We have the place surrounded. Nothing is going to happen to you. I promise."

"You-you're really with the police?"

"I am."

The woman threw her arms around Morgan, crying. "Oh, thank God. Oh, thank God."

Morgan pulled herself free and put a supportive arm across the woman's back. "This way."

LIESEL WAS CLOSEST to where Rosario, Ricky, and Tasha entered the woods, but not close enough to signal them. Since she had an entirely different job to do, she silently wished them good luck and returned her eye to the rifle's scope.

"TEN SECONDS, GENTLEMEN," Rally said. "Remember, only one trophy per hunter!" He looked at his watch again. "Five, four, three, two, one. Hunt!"

"THE GUNMEN HAVE been released," Liesel announced. "ETA at the woods, thirty seconds."

"Copy," Dylan said. "I've got my man and am en route to safe zone."

"Copy," Morgan said. "Me, too."

A few seconds passed before Liesel said, "Ananke?"

Another couple of beats. "I copy," Ananke said. "My target's being a little uncooperative. But don't wait for me. Stick to the plan."

"Copy," Liesel said.

She followed the hunters via her scope for a few seconds, and then looked back at the other end of the meadow, where Rally, Slater, Yates, and the men who weren't accompanying the hunters remained. Rally was talking to his cousins, waving one arm dramatically in Liesel's general direction. She memorized everyone's position, and took her eye off the scope to check on the hunters' progress.

They were approaching the woods, only seconds away. She continued watching them until they disappeared.

After double-checking that the suppressor was properly mounted, she nestled against the rifle stock, did a quick practice run, and reset to position one.

"I'M SURE," RALLY said, annoyed. "I just met her last night! Her name is Caroline Cruz. She was introduced to me as the assistant to Shawn Ramey."

"Ramey?" Slater said.

"You know, the woman in town looking at locations for her company."

"The black one."

Rally nodded.

"Do you think they might be the feds?" Yates said.

"Hell, yes, I think they might be the feds," Rally said. "That's why you need to get back to Bradbury and eliminate Ramey before she can cause us any more problems!"

While Slater agreed the woman had to be dealt with, they needed to be smart about it. "*After* we bring her in and talk to her first."

"Bring her in?" Rally said. "Are you crazy?"

"Robbie," Slater said. "Hear me out."

Slater had used Rally's childhood nickname on purpose, not only to get his attention, but as a subtle reminder that Slater was the oldest member of the family present.

"Cruz and Ramey obviously didn't come here alone," Slater continued. "Who knows how many more friends they have with them. The only way we're going to find out is to make Ramey tell us. Unless you want me to pause the trial and collect Cruz and her friend."

He knew full well Rally would never agree to removing a third of the prey from an active trial event.

Frustrated, Rally said, "Okay. Bring her in. But as soon as

you get what you need, get rid of her."

"No problem." Slater looked at his brother. "Do it."

Yates nodded. "Give me two hours and I'll have her back here."

"No," Rally said. "Not here. Take her to the—"

Without warning, Rally pitched forward toward his cousins, screaming in pain. Slater caught him, and as he was lowering Rally to the platform, Yates said, "Jesus. He's been shot!"

Rally's knee had been ripped apart. The two brothers dove off the platform, and then reached up and pulled Rally down with them.

Their cousin's screams were joined by someone else's. Slater looked to his right and saw Joey Wilson rolling on the ground, his right pant leg torn and dark with blood.

Rally clutched his leg and continued howling. Slater knew if they didn't do something quick, their cousin would die of blood loss.

Slater removed the shoelace from one of Rally's boots and gave it to his brother. "Tie off his leg!"

Another person screamed.

And another.

"Where are they shooting from?" Yates asked. "I don't hear anything."

"We need to get out of here!" Rally said.

A fifth wail, this one to their left.

If they moved from behind the platform, Slater and Yates would be shot next. What they needed was a cover for their escape, and Slater knew just what that could be. He twisted around, looking for someone who could help. Most of his men lay in the field, writhing. But then he spotted sandy blond hair peeking over the benches in the observation area.

"Cory!" he yelled.

Cory Reese lifted his head enough to see over the bench. "Mr. Slater. I-I-I thought they got you."

"Listen to me. Get the van from over by the cells and drive it out here!"

"I don't have the keys."

Slater had already pulled the keys out of his pocket. "Here," he said as he tossed them toward the benches. They landed with a jangle, five feet shy of the tree line.

Cory looked at them and back at Slater, clearly not wanting to go back into the meadow.

"Pick them up and get the van!"

"Y-y-yes, sir."

When Cory moved out of view, Slater expected him to reappear seconds later, at the edge of the trees nearest the keys, but the boy remained out of view. Behind Slater, Rally moaned, and seemed on the verge of passing out. He'd lost a lot of blood before Yates tied the leg off. They had medical supplies within the lodge, with plasma Rally needed for a transfusion, but they didn't have the facilities or the expertise to deal with the minced meat that was once their cousin's knee, so ultimately they would need to take him somewhere that could deal with it. If he didn't die first.

"Cory! Goddammit! Where the hell are you?"

"I'm coming!" Cory shouted. "Just a second."

A few moments later he appeared among the pines, on his stomach. But instead of rushing out to grab the keys, he reached out with a large branch and tried to drag the keys to him.

The tree trunk right above Cory's head exploded as a bullet slammed into it. To the kid's credit, it made him pause for only a second before he continued fishing for the keys. Another bullet hit the ground next to the branch, but Cory kept dragging.

Though Slater couldn't see the keys, it appeared the boy was making progress. When they were within a foot or two of Cory, Slater yelled, "Just grab 'em and go!"

LIESEL SWEPT THE scope across the meadow. She'd disabled Rally and all the young men who'd been holding rifles. That left only four—the woman who had disappeared into the woods, a young man off to the side near the benches, and Slater and Yates, pinned down behind the platform.

She saw Slater toss a set of keys toward the remaining young man. No mystery there. They wanted a vehicle close so they could get away in a hurry. The only question was, which one would it be?

She got a better look at the man when he started trying to drag the keys to him with a branch, and realized *man* was a generous term. He couldn't be much more than eighteen.

Though she could have easily taken him out, she aimed for the tree just above him to keep up appearances. She sent another shot into the dirt near the keys. The idea was to divide and subdue, so she wanted him to hurry. It would be great if she could take out Slater and Yates, but chances were the standoff would be prolonged, in which case many of the men she'd already taken down would die from lack of medical attention. The sooner the kid fishing for the keys got Slater and Yates out of there, the sooner she could do the bare minimum needed to keep the others alive. It wasn't so much an act of kindness as a desire not to lose a potential information source.

When the man-boy leaned out from what he must have thought was the safety of the trees, she tilted the barrel ever so slightly and pulled the trigger.

The ground a few feet in front of him erupted in a spray of dirt. The kid dove forward, grabbed the keys, and scrambled back into the woods.

Liesel sent a final shot in his general direction to keep him on his toes, and then activated her mic. "You were right, Dylan. They have sent one of their men for a car."

"Ha!" Dylan said. "I believe that means you owe me dinner."

MONICA SLATER, KNOWN during this month's trials as Miss Riefenstahl, ran through the woods.

At first, she had no direction in mind except away from the meadow, but once she had some distance on the gunfire, she stopped to get her bearings.

Her father had told her long ago that if anything ever went wrong, she was to get out of the situation as fast as she could and head back to their ranch. He'd made her promise that under no circumstances would she stay in harm's way.

She glanced back toward the meadow, worried about him.

She wanted to go back, see if he was all right, but he would be furious if she did.

What she didn't have to do was hike all the way back to the lodge. There were ATVs sitting unused near the building with the holding cells. She veered to the west, avoiding the main trail, and hurried over the small ridge, down to where the vehicles were parked.

As she started to climb onto one of the ATVs, an Irish man's voice said behind her, "Beautiful night, isn't it?"

THIRTY-TWO

EDUARDO WAS UNDER no delusion that an escape route out of hell actually existed. What he did know was that the people who'd taken him and the others were insane. Hunting *people*? How could that not be crazy?

So there might not be a real escape route, but he knew the longer he avoided the hunters, the better his chance of finding a way out of this. As plans went, it was light on details, but better than just rolling over and letting them kill him.

He'd worked all of this out on the sprint from the platform to the woods. Seconds later, when a woman came out of nowhere to chase him, everything flew from his mind except running for his life.

He had no doubt she was part of the setup, there to slow him down. Her words to the contrary were so transparent, he dismissed them immediately.

Racing through the dark forest, he thought he'd be able to lose her. He'd always been a good runner, and she looked older than he was, so she should have quickly fallen behind. But not only did she keep pace with him, his multiple directional changes never threw her off.

He scanned ahead for anything that might assist his escape. When he saw a patch of trees and brush thicker than the area surrounding it, he decided to turn behind it. If he could use the cover to double back and throw her off, he would be in the clear.

When he rounded the trees, he realized he'd lucked onto something even better than he'd hoped. The growth had been hiding a streambed sunk into a ten yard-wide mini arroyo, the bottom a good four to five feet below ground level.

He jumped over the side and landed on the bank. He'd seen enough movies to know that the way to throw off a tracker was to obscure one's trail in a river, so he ran into the water. After a few steps, though, he realized he had a bigger problem. While he wasn't leaving any visible steps behind, the water sloshing was just as much a giveaway of his whereabouts.

He swung left and right, looking for some other solution.

There!

The near vertical walls of the arroyo twisted and turned, creating dozens of little nooks. Hoping one was large enough for him to hide in, he hopped onto a slab of rock that stretched all the way to the wall, and rushed toward the nearest crevasse.

ANANKE LOST THE man she was chasing when he made a hard turn to the right into a thick stand of trees. When she reached the point where he'd disappeared, she discovered trees had been hiding a creek flowing down a ravine.

The man's footprints showed he'd jumped into the depression, so she followed. She found a few more steps along the creek's bank and then nothing.

If the guy had used the water to cover his trail, then she either should have heard splashing or been able to see him, because he would have had to move slowly to mitigate any sound.

She spun around. Though only about five feet high, the side of the ravine undulated like a twisting ribbon set on edge. Some of the crags looked large enough to hide in. But there were no footprints in the bank leading to them.

She scanned along the stream and smiled. About ten feet farther down, a slab of half-buried rock extended from inside the water all the way to the ravine's edge, and on it, water spots in the distinct pattern of steps. The wet footprints continued a good two-thirds of the way toward the wall, decreasing in intensity the farther from the stream they went, until the last were barely visible.

She studied the wall, and counted at least four different recesses in which the man could be hiding.

"Just come on out," she said. "I swear I'm not going to

hurt you. I'm here to help."

She cocked her head, listening for movement. Only silence.

She took a step toward the wall. "The last thing I want is for those assholes to put a bullet in you. But that's exactly what's going to happen if I don't get you someplace safe in a hurry."

Still nothing.

Dammit.

Guessing he was in one of the two recesses closest to the rock slab, she moved another few steps toward them. "Listen, if I wanted to kill you, don't you think I would have shot you when we were running? The answer is, yes, I would have. And I could have done it a dozen times, but I didn't."

The babble of the creek but nothing else.

"Seriously, buddy. We're running out of time here."

EDUARDO HAD BEEN hoping to hear the woman splashing down the stream away from him, and though he did hear a few watery steps, they soon fell silent. He could see nothing from the nook he'd slipped into, and had no idea what she was doing.

Stay calm. She'll be gone soon enough.

"Come on out. I'm not going to hurt you."

His breath caught in his throat. She hadn't left, and was, in fact, close to the wall of the arroyo. She tried tricking him again with her words, but he still wasn't buying it.

He heard her take another few steps closer before she pleaded with him again.

"Seriously, buddy. We're running out of time here."

On that point, he agreed. The other hunters were still out there, and every second he remained in the same spot they gained ground.

The woman stepped forward again, giving him a much better idea of where she was. He still had a chance, he realized.

He took a deep, quiet breath, and then eased toward the alcove's entrance.

ANANKE WAS ONLY five feet from the wall now, the entrance

to one crag directly in front of her, and the other a few feet to her left.

She took a careful step forward, not wanting to make any noise, and then leaned a little to the right to peek inside the niche. Empty.

She moved to the left and leaned forward to look inside the other crag.

EDUARDO STEPPED TO the very edge of his nook and peeked out. The woman was about ten feet away, her back to him.

He slipped out of his hiding place and sneaked down the riverbank, away from her. His stealth mode lasted only a few steps before his fear got the better of him, and he began running down the side of the stream.

THE INTERIOR OF the niche was coming into view when Ananke heard someone running behind her. She spun around and saw the man racing away from her.

"Oh, come on!"

She took off after him.

Though the side of the ravine where they'd jumped down was too steep to easily climb back up, the man found a gentler slope a dozen yards farther on and was soon back at the forest ground level. Ananke huffed up the side, worried she might lose him again. But there he was, racing through the trees.

In the most dangerous direction he could have taken.

"No! Not that way!"

EDUARDO RAN OUT of the arroyo and into the woods. Without stopping, he looked around and tried to figure out which way to go.

The stream had bent a bit, hadn't it? He thought so, but wasn't sure. Nor was he sure if he was heading toward the meadow or away from it.

Behind him, he heard the woman reach the top of the ravine.

"No!" she yelled. "Not that way!"

He lost a step, wondering if she was right until he

reminded himself her job was to trick him. The days in the trailer behind the semitruck, the drugs they'd given him to keep him knocked out, the sheer disbelief when he learned why he and the others had been brought there, and the constant running since then had turned his mind into mush. The only thing he knew for sure was that if he stopped, he would die.

ANANKE HAD TO admire the guy's determination to live. But since her warning had done nothing to change his direction, that same determination was going to get him killed.

Somewhere beyond the man, she heard the snap of a branch.

Oh, crap.

One—or more—of the hunters was closing in. Or worse, waiting for the runner to come to them.

Ananke hit her afterburners, and all but flew between the trees.

MR. HUSTON KNELT behind the fallen tree, his crossbow propped on the trunk.

"You're in perfect position," his observer whispered. The man looked at the handheld tablet that tracked the prey's location.

Mr. Huston scanned the woods through the scope. It wasn't true night vision—that would provide too much advantage, he'd been told—but it did have heightened nighttime abilities, so he was able to partially make out the landscape as far as a hundred and fifty feet away. Nothing was moving out there yet.

"He should be about five degrees right of straight ahead," the observer said.

Mr. Huston adjusted his aim.

"Any second now."

EDUARDO HEARD THE woman gaining ground. He tried to increase his speed, but he had nothing more to give. Keeping his head down, he pressed on, knowing he was unlikely to live through the next few minutes.

ANANKE WAS SO close now, she could hear the man's panicked breaths. She looked past him for any sign of hunters, but all she could see were trees and more trees.

They had to be there somewhere, which meant there was no more time. She closed the gap and launched herself forward.

"ONE HUNDRED AND sixty-five yards," the observer said. "One hundred and sixty…one hundred and fifty-five."

Mr. Huston saw movement at the far edge of his vision, man-shaped. Before the observer could update the distance, Mr. Huston pulled the trigger, letting the bolt fly.

EDUARDO HAD A moment of confusion when the sound of the woman's steps suddenly stopped. He started to look over his shoulder to see what had happened when—

ANANKE SLAMMED INTO the man's back, knocking both of them to the ground, her on top. Before the guy could react, she heard something whiz over their heads, *thwack*ing into a tree. She looked back and saw a crossbow bolt protruding from a trunk.

The man struggled under her.

"Stay down," she whispered.

"Let me up."

"Do you want to die that much? Because there's a guy out there with a crossbow who is more than willing to help you with that. And if you don't believe me, look."

She twisted his head a little so he could see the tree that had been hit.

"That whitish thing sticking out of the trunk? That's called a bolt. And I'm pretty sure he doesn't have just one. Do you believe me now?"

He looked confused. "Who are you?"

"I'm the woman who's going to save your life."

"I GOT HIM!" Mr. Huston declared. "Did you see that? I got him!"

"The target is down," the observer said.

316

"I know. I got him!" Mr. Huston looked through his scope at the shadowy hump on the ground. It moved a little, but showed no signs of getting up again. "I think he's still alive."

"May I see?"

Mr. Huston handed the bow to the observer. The young man sighted downfield.

"You're right. Would you like to finish it off, or let it bleed out?"

"I'm here to hunt, not sit around."

The observer handed him back the crossbow. "Then let's go do it."

ANANKE SAW TWO silhouettes emerge from the woods and head in their direction.

"You're not going to like this, but I need you to do something," she whispered.

"What?"

She told him.

"No way. Let me up. I'd rather run."

"Your way will get you killed. My way won't."

"Are you crazy? Of course it will."

"That's fine. You don't need to believe me." She checked the two hunters. "But you're smart enough to know if you try to run now, they'll kill you before you reach safety."

The man looked toward the silhouettes and cursed.

"So, do you want my help, or should I leave you to deal with them yourself?" she asked.

He took another peek at the approaching hunters and whispered, "Help me."

"Good. Stay right here and don't move or make a sound."

She slipped off him and belly crawled into the bushes a few feet away.

THE DARK LUMP of the downed prey seemed to be writhing on the ground as Mr. Huston and his observer began their hike across the field.

They were nearing the midpoint when the trophy appeared to roll onto its back and lose half its height. Mr. Huston paused,

317

waiting to see if the prey was preparing to attempt an escape, but the shadow stopped moving.

He grinned. Perhaps his initial shot had been enough and the trophy was dead. One shot, one kill. That sounded pretty damn good. Mr. Huston bet few of his fellow hunters were that skilled.

They were about thirty feet away when Mr. Huston began to see details in the shadow. It was one of the male targets. Maybe Mr. Huston had just won himself the golden Mossberg! But then he realized the man on the ground was too small to be the guy ranked most difficult. Probably the Hispanic guy, who'd been number two. That was nothing to sneeze at.

Mr. Huston crept forward, his crossbow raised in case the prey was playing possum.

Movement.

The prey's chest. Up and down. Up and down.

Mr. Huston frowned. So much for a one-shot kill. It would have to be two.

He sighted down his weapon.

ANANKE WATCHED THE hunters approach. There appeared to be only two—a balding, middle-aged guy holding a crossbow, and one of the young lookalikes.

She let them come closer, in case others might reveal themselves. None did.

She took a breath, let it halfway out, and held.

EDUARDO HEARD THE crunch of pine needles under the approaching steps.

His pursuers were close. *Way* too close.

What was the woman doing? She'd said she would help him.

She was never here to help you.

The voice in his head sucked away the last of his hope. As he'd assumed at the start, she had only meant to make him an easier target.

Another crunch, no more than ten feet away.

He braced himself for the inevitable.

Thup.

MR. HUSTON AIMED at the trophy's head and prepared to pull the trigger.

Pain exploded from his left leg. He screamed and fell to the side, the bow dropping near his feet.

The moment he hit the ground, he heard another scream and saw his observer go down.

Mr. Huston felt along his leg. His pants were torn apart, and underneath was a gooey mess of tissue where his knee should have been.

He tried to roll so that his knee wasn't on the ground, but stopped when something hard smashed into his ribs.

"How do you like that, asshole?!"

The prey glared down at him, looking as if he hadn't been struck by the bolt at all.

The next kick caught Mr. Huston in the cheek, rocking his head to the side.

"Does that feel good?" the prey said, clearly winding up for another strike.

Before he could lash out again, a calm but commanding female voice said, "That's enough."

"THIS *PENDEJO* WAS going to kill me," the man Ananke had rescued said.

"He was, but he's not now."

"He wanted me dead. I want him dead."

"Understandable. But let's let him suffer for a little while first, shall we?"

The guy's chest heaved up and down with rage, but eventually his breaths slowed and he took a step back without delivering another kick.

"What's your name?" she asked.

A hesitation. "Eduardo."

Ananke pulled out several heavy-duty zip ties from her bag and held out a few to him. "Do you know how these work, Eduardo?"

"Sure."

"Good. Take them." She nodded at the younger guy she'd shot. "Secure his hands behind his back and tie his ankles together. Then use a couple to create a tourniquet on his thigh above the wound."

Eduardo gawked at her. "Why would you want them to live?"

"Let me ask you a question. Do you know how far this operation spreads? Because if you do, then, please, by all means, stomp their heads into the ground. If not, wouldn't it make more sense to keep them alive until we know who knows what?"

Eduardo glanced away.

"Damn," Ananke said. "I guess that means you don't know. Looks like you're going to have to tie him up."

While Eduardo worked on the younger guy on the ground, Ananke knelt next to the older man—the hunter. "How's that leg feeling?"

He muttered something under his breath.

"I'm going to tie off your leg so you don't bleed to death. That sound like a good idea to you?"

He blinked. "Yes. Tie it. Don't let me die."

She connected three ties together and created a loop around his thigh. He winced as she tightened it.

"You should still have enough blood in you to keep you going," she said, smiling. "Of course, the shock might kill you. Sorry."

With Eduardo's help, she dragged both men to separate trees and used more zip ties to secure them to the trunks.

"Gentlemen, it's been a pleasure," she said. She started to turn away, but then stopped. "It'll probably be a while before anyone gets out this way to collect you, which means, at best, you're likely going to lose those legs. Something to think about and start adjusting to while you wait." She looked at Eduardo. "You want to stay alive, follow me."

She headed into the woods.

THIRTY-THREE

MR. WISE, MR. Reed, and Mr. Welles moved through the woods with their observers, in a north-northeasterly direction. They had not planned on traveling together, but both Mr. Wise and Mr. Reed had marked the big Caucasian guy as their target. Mr. Welles, ever the opportunist, had watched the big guy stay with the two women when they ran for the woods, so he felt confident the two other hunters would lead him to at least one potential trophy. And who knew, maybe he'd get lucky and bag the number one prey himself.

Mr. Wise and Mr. Reed seemed to have silently declared a temporary détente and were working together to find the prey. Since they were superior trackers, Mr. Welles let them lead but stayed right behind them.

Mr. Reed let out a low double hiss before waving everyone in his direction. At his feet, a spotty line of disturbed ground cover ran to the north.

"Is it fresh?" Mr. Welles asked.

Mr. Wise and Mr. Reed looked at him as if he was an idiot, and then started along the trail without saying a word.

Apparently it was fresh.

Assholes.

The tracks went nearly two hundred yards before they disappeared. The men searched around, trying to pick them up again, but the ground in the immediate vicinity revealed nothing.

"We should split up and look farther out," Mr. Reed suggested. "We can meet back here in ten minutes."

"Right," Mr. Wise said. "Then you find something and keep going while we wait here for you to return."

"I give you my word."

Mr. Wise snorted.

"Maybe we should search together," Mr. Welles said.

"That'll waste too much time," Mr. Reed said.

"More time than standing here arguing about how we should do it?"

Mr. Reed didn't look happy, but said, "Fine."

RICKY, ROSARIO, AND Tasha's immediate goal was to put as much distance between themselves and the meadow as fast as they could. Unfortunately, they weren't far into the woods when it became clear Tasha wouldn't be able to keep up for much longer. Easing back a bit, Ricky slung an arm around Tasha's back to help her, while Rosario took over at point.

Knowing they were leaving a clear trail but unable to do much about it, they continued into the woods for nearly ten minutes before Rosario stopped and pointed to their right. "Look."

A rocky ridge poked above the treetops about fifty yards away. High ground.

Ricky said, "I like it."

Instead of immediately heading toward it, Rosario studied the surrounding area before saying to Tasha, "Watch me carefully. Light steps, along the same path I take."

Tasha nodded, looking too tired to say anything.

Rosario picked her way around the spots where the pine needles were densest, and avoided all dead branches and anything else that might leave a sign of their passing. By the time they reached the top of the ridge, she was confident they'd left little to no tracks.

They climbed through the rocks and stopped just on the other side.

"You can rest here," Rosario told Tasha.

Tasha leaned against one of the boulders.

"They're still going to be able to find us," Ricky said and tapped his shoulder where it met his neck.

Rosario looked at him, confused.

"Trackers," he said. "We've all got them."

She touched her own neck. The skin was tender, something she would have noticed sooner if she hadn't had other things to worry about. Underneath, she could feel the tracking bug.

Her anger, already high, flared. To Ricky, she said, "See if anyone is following us."

While he snuck up between two of the rocks, she searched the ground, picking up stones and setting them down again when she found something better. Her final selection had a corner that came to a point, and a somewhat tapered edge. It wasn't perfect but it should do the job.

She sat on a rock, and moved her finger over the spot where the bug had been implanted. The device was the size of a small ball bearing, and about a quarter inch below the surface.

Using the rock, she dug into her skin, creating a slit half an inch long. Since the bug had been put in only that afternoon, the path it had carved through her tissue hadn't had time to heal, and she was able to quickly work the ball out the slit.

As she dropped it into her palm, she felt Tasha's eyes on her.

"That's in me, too?" Tasha asked.

"Apparently."

Tasha searched her own neck until she found the bug. She hurried over to Rosario, her head cocked to the side. "Get it out! Please, get it out."

"It's going to hurt."

"I don't care. Get it out!"

Ricky crawled back down the rocks as Rosario finished up operating on Tasha.

"They're down there around where we stopped running," he whispered before he noticed what Rosario was doing. "Uh, is that thing sterile?"

"Sit down and shut up," Rosario said. "You are next."

MR. WISE, MR. Reed, and Mr. Welles completed an arc of approximately one hundred and eighty degrees without finding any signs of the prey.

"We do it again," Mr. Reed said. "Wider."

"Wait a second," Mr. Welles said. "How do we know we're not wasting time? Maybe they went the other way."

"This is a *hunt*," Mr. Wise said. "This is how you do it."

"Maybe that's how *you* do it," Mr. Welles said. He hadn't made his fortune by always sticking to the rules. He walked over to the observers. "You guys know where they are, don't you?"

After the young men exchanged looks, the one assigned to Mr. Welles said, "Of course."

"Then which way do we need to go?"

"We can't tell you that."

"Okay, can you at least tell us if we're spinning our wheels here? I mean, none of us want to waste time looking for things that aren't there, right?"

The observers huddled for a moment of hushed conversation. Then Mr. Welles's observer said, "You are not spinning your wheels."

"Good. Thanks for that. No hints on direction, though?"

"No."

Mr. Welles grinned. "I'm a good tipper."

While his observer replied, "I'm sorry, Mr. Welles, but as you know, those are the rules," his colleague at the back—Mr. Reed's observer—locked eyes with Mr. Welles and purposefully moved his gaze to the right and turned his head a little. And then he did it again.

Another smile from Mr. Welles. "No problem. I understand."

As he headed back to his fellow hunters, he glanced in the direction Mr. Reed's observer had indicated and spotted a ridge of rocks through the trees.

"Gentlemen. If you'll follow me."

"THIS LOOKS LIKE a good spot," Ricky said.

They'd hiked about seventy-five feet farther north, along the ridge.

Rosario scanned the area. "I agree."

She tossed the trackers into a bush.

MR. WELLES LED his reluctant colleagues up the slope to the top of the ridge, pausing right before the crest.

He glanced back at the others, pretending to check their positions when in reality he was looking for Mr. Reed's observer. The man checked his tracking tablet then nodded to the left and held his thumb and forefinger close together.

Mr. Welles acted like he was listening for a few seconds. "Did you hear that?"

Mr. Wise and Mr. Reed looked unsure.

"Yeah, footsteps," Mr. Welles said, his head cocked. "Up the other side a ways, I think."

He took them over the apex and followed the ridge to the north. Additional check-ins with his observer-in-crime homed him in on the spot where the prey should be.

As Mr. Welles raised his Mossberg and prepared to creep forward, Mr. Reed grabbed his shoulder and shoved past him. Mr. Wise tried to do the same, but Mr. Welles stuck out a well-timed elbow and held on to second position.

The men stepped around the rock with their weapons up, ready to claim their prizes.

No one was there.

Though Mr. Wise and Mr. Reed were disappointed, they didn't share Mr. Welles's surprise since they hadn't possessed the information indicating this was the spot. Mr. Reed continued north along the rocks. As they rounded a big boulder, Mr. Wise attempted to pass Mr. Welles again. This time, Mr. Welles didn't put up a fight. He was more interested in finding out why the observer had led him astray.

He paused, as if to catch his breath.

Mr. Wise's observer came around the big rock next, and Mr. Welles's man followed. Mr. Reed's, however, did not appear.

"Where's your friend?" Mr. Welles said to his observer.

The guy looked around. "He was right behind me." They waited for a few moments, but when the third man still didn't show up, Mr. Welles's observer said, "I'll go check on him."

He headed back the way they'd come.

Mr. Welles grimaced. He knew what had happened. The

missing observer had been feeding him bad info and was now trying to avoid a confrontation.

No tip for you, asshole.

Mr. Welles waited a moment longer, but when neither observer returned, he decided it was time to catch up with the others. He didn't want to miss his opportunity for the kill.

ROSARIO LAY THE unconscious kid next to the first one. Like his friend, this one had a pistol and computer tablet. Before Ricky left, she'd given him the other guy's weapon. She took this one and continued her pursuit.

The six-man hunting team was now down to four.

AN OUTCROPPING OF rock blocked their path, forcing Mr. Reed to lead the others down the slope a bit to move around it.

As they hiked back to the summit, he glanced over his shoulder. Mr. Wise was right behind him. The man was the closest thing Mr. Reed had to a competitor. Mr. Reed, however, had no intention of letting Mr. Wise claim the ultimate prize.

A dozen feet behind Mr. Wise came the opportunist Mr. Welles. While the man wasn't even close to being in the same league as Mr. Reed and Mr. Wise, the bastard could get lucky.

The observers were apparently much farther back, as none of them had come around the low end of the outcropping yet.

A crunch.

Mr. Reed whipped his head back around. It had sounded like something pushing down on pine needles, just on the other side of the rocks.

Crouching, he quietly approached the ridge. The rock face directly in front of him was too steep to climb, but a little farther on, the surface was broken into a dozen smaller chunks he could use to scale the formation.

He ascended to right below the top, then raised his head to peek down the other side.

ROSARIO STOOD WITH her back against a tree, as if she were part of the pine itself. The last of the three younger men had finally noticed his friends were missing.

He paused near the low end of the rocky spur the hunters had just gone around, looking back the way he'd come. For a moment, he seemed torn on which way to go, but his concern about his buddies won the day.

He hiked right by her position, not even glancing at the tree, allowing her to easily slip in behind him and smash him on the side of his head with her pistol.

Three down. Three remaining.

ANOTHER CRUNCH. THIS time from the woods just beyond where the rocks ended.

Mr. Reed brought his crossbow around and looked through the scope. Someone was there, hidden by the trees.

His gut tingled in excitement. This was it, the moment of closing in that would culminate in the bagging of his trophy.

Mr. Wise crept up beside him and peeked over the rocks. "Where?" he whispered.

"Not sure," Mr. Reed told him. "Might have been an animal."

"They're all animals, aren't they?"

"True."

Mr. Reed looked down the ridge for a good place to make a quiet descent. A fissure between boulders about ten feet to the right looked to be the best choice. He wished he could take it without Mr. Wise following, but that wasn't going to happen.

It looked like winning would come down to who was the better shot. Which, of course, he was.

He moved sideways across the rocks to the fissure, and slipped into it without raising his head above the ridge.

Mr. Wise stayed right behind him.

MR. WELLES WAITED at the bottom of the rocks, while the other two hunters climbed to the top and look over. No reason to waste energy.

When the two men moved sideways and disappeared into a crack, however, he knew it was time to get going.

He started scaling the rocks.

MR. REED REACHED the bottom and slowly stepped out of the fissure.

The trees where the noise had come from were about ten yards away. All was quiet now, which made him think the prey was hunkered down, hiding.

He pulled his crossbow up again, holding it rib high so he could get off a quick bolt if necessary, or raise it to his shoulder for a more accurate shot if he had the time.

As he stepped toward the trees, he heard Mr. Wise exiting the fissure behind him.

Another step, then—

"Drop the bows, boys."

Both Mr. Reed and Mr. Wise jerked in surprise and turned to the voice.

One of the prey stood behind them, shielded by a chest-high slab of rock. The big guy. The ultimate prize.

At the same moment Mr. Reed saw Mr. Wise adjust the aim of his crossbow, he realized the prey was holding a pistol.

A gunshot echoed off the rocks before Mr. Wise could let his bolt fly. The man dropped to the ground, a bullet hole in the center of his forehead. Mr. Reed stared, wondering how in God's name the prey had obtained a weapon.

"I did warn him," the prey said. "Are you going to try to shoot me, too?"

If Mr. Reed pulled his trigger now, the bolt would slam harmlessly into the rock. But if he tried to readjust, he'd suffer the same fate as Mr. Wise.

What he needed to do was buy time until Mr. Welles and the observers could do something. The gunshot would have alerted them, and Mr. Reed was sure they were getting into positions to take out the prey.

"I believe I said drop it," the prey said.

Mr. Reed lowered the bow and let it gently fall to prevent any major damage. He'd need the weapon again soon enough.

"Take three steps back," the prey said.

After Mr. Reed did as asked, the prey came around the rock and picked up the crossbow.

"This is sweet," the man said as he examined the weapon.

He set his pistol on a rock surface and pointed the crossbow at Mr. Reed. "So tell me, how does this feel?"

Mr. Reed took a breath. *Where the hell is everyone?*

"Not too good, does it?" the prey said.

Mr. Reed shook his head, shooting a sideways glance at the rocks.

"Bad news, my friend," the prey said. "Your hunting partners aren't going to rescue you."

Though the big man didn't look like he was bluffing, he had to be. The two women he'd been with couldn't have taken out the other four on Mr. Reed's team. That idea was ludicrous.

"I have to say I admire that you came after me, with my ranking as most difficult." The prey grinned. "Clearly it was well deserved, wouldn't you say?"

"I am just a guest here," Mr. Reed said. "I-I-I did not realize when I came what was going to happen."

"Oooh." The prey winced. "Really? You're going straight for the blame-others defense? That's pretty crappy. And to be honest, makes me hate you just a little more."

Mr. Reed heard a scrape in the rocks behind him.

Finally! With renewed hope, he said, "No, no. I was not going to shoot you. I was going to stop the others from doing so."

"You're saying you would have shot your friend there and not me?"

A step this time. Definitely a step.

Trying to keep the smile off his face, Mr. Reed said, "Yes, exactly."

"Now *that* is funny."

MR. WELLES HAD pulled himself up to the crack and started to lower himself inside when he heard the gunshot. He paused, surprised.

Though Mr. Reed and Mr. Wise were carrying pistols, they had both made clear their weapons of choice were their crossbows. Obviously one of them decided to use the easier weapon.

But as Mr. Welles took his first step down, he heard

someone say, "Are you going to try to shoot me, too?"

The voice did not belong to Mr. Reed or Mr. Wise.

Mr. Welles stretched forward and sneaked a peek around the edge of the fissure and down into the area below. A man he was pretty sure was Mr. Reed was standing still. It took a moment before Mr. Welles noticed Mr. Wise lying on the ground, his crossbow beside him.

"I believe I said drop it."

Mr. Welles followed the sound of the voice and spotted the large prey, half hidden by a rock, pointing a pistol at Mr. Reed.

Mr. Welles pulled back inside the crack. The prey was *armed*?

Oh, shit. Oh, shit. Oh, shit.

Mr. Welles knew he could get a shot off if he propped his back against the side of the crack, but was less confident about his ability to hit the mark. The way he figured it, his shot would miss, the prey would kill Mr. Reed, and then come after him.

Nope. This is not *what I paid for.*

The observers should take care of this, not him.

He climbed back up the crack and pulled himself onto the rock on the other side.

"Hello."

He leaped backward at the sound of the woman's voice. An unfortunate reaction, considering his location. Right before he tumbled down the side, he caught sight of her. It was the small prey, the Hispanic, crouching next to the crack. He'd hoped she'd be his trophy.

As he fell, she waved.

The first few hits against the rock broke his arm and at least two ribs. Then, three-quarters of the way down, his head slammed into the surface, not quite blacking out the world but close.

It was his neck breaking when he reached the bottom that accomplished that mission.

RICKY HAD HEARD the sounds behind the hunter, too. He had also seen Rosario stick her head out from the break in the rocks and give him a thumbs-up.

The hunter clearly was expecting reinforcements. Ricky let him live in his delusion for a few moments longer. "So, how were you going to explain killing your friends and not us? I mean, I gotta think the assholes who run this place probably wouldn't have liked that."

"It-it-it does not matter. It would have been the correct thing to do."

Rosario eased out from the fault.

"If that's so, you are way more noble than I gave you credit for," Ricky said.

The hunter attempted to look self-effacing. "It is no more than anyone would have done."

"Everything else wrapped up?"

The hunter looked unsure how to answer, but that was because the question wasn't for him.

"One dead, and three who won't be waking up for a while," Rosario said as she moved around the hunter to join Ricky.

Ricky focused back on the now pale man. "Did you really think you'd get away with hunting people? With hunting *us*?"

"I-I-I told you, I—"

Ricky pulled the trigger.

He and Rosario relieved the two dead hunters of their remaining weapons before rejoining Tasha where they'd left her to wait.

The Scolareon CFO eyed the guns and crossbows. "We're okay?"

"We are okay," Rosario said.

"What now?"

Rosario and Ricky shared a look. Rosario said, "We help the others, if they are still alive. Then we get you out of here."

THIRTY-FOUR

DYLAN LAY ON the roof of the building where the holding cells were, looking through his binoculars. He scanned the area between where the vehicles were parked on the side and the woods back toward the meadow where the trials began.

It was only a short wait before the silhouette of Slater's man separated from the trees and sprinted across the open ground to the van.

Dylan clicked his mic twice to let the others know the guy had arrived. He could have easily taken the kid out, but his gun remained at his side as he watched the guy rush up to the vehicle and jump into the driver's seat.

When the engine started, Dylan said, "Prepare to reposition."

"Copy," Morgan said. She was really getting the hang of things.

Dylan was off the roof and ready before the van started moving. There was a chance the guy would decide to screw his bosses over and head for safety. If that was the case, they would let him go. But scared as the kid probably was, he was also well trained, as he headed for the path toward the meadow.

"Coming your way, Liesel."

"Copy."

Dylan moved to the hidden spot he'd picked out earlier, close to where the path to the meadow exited the trees. "In position. Morgan?"

"In position."

He glanced toward the eroded ditch she would be in. He couldn't see her, but that was the point.

"Liesel?" he asked.

LIESEL EYED THE opening to the path via the rifle's scope. "He has paused just inside the trees."

It didn't take a lot of thought to know the driver was scared of getting shot. The irony was, she could shoot him dead where he was sitting right now.

Though she couldn't see Rally, Slater, or Yates hiding behind the platform, she did hear one of them yelling. Since it was all anger and no pain, she figured it was one of the brothers, urging the guy in the van to get his ass in gear.

It took a second shout to finally get the vehicle moving. It crept forward, but as soon as the front bumper cleared the trees, the driver slammed on the accelerator. The van raced onto the field, took a sharp right turn that nearly toppled it, and skidded to a stop on Liesel's side of the platform.

"Loading now," she said.

THE MOMENT THE van stopped, Slater and Yates hauled their cousin up between them. Rally was barely conscious. Slater thought they'd stopped the bleeding in time, but he didn't know for sure.

While Cory had been thinking enough to park the van on the other side of the platform, he had not been smart enough to stop at a point that would have allowed them to walk around the side of the structure without putting them in view of the gunman. They had to maneuver Rally back onto the raised surface, and then help him across it and down the ramp on the other side, the same ramp the prey had used when they fled.

"Open the goddamn door," Slater yelled as they neared the vehicle.

Cory, who'd been sitting motionless in the driver's seat, sprang to action and unlatched the passenger side door. Yates went in first, then pulled on their cousin while Slater pushed from the other side. Given his injury, Rally needed to stay in the seat, so Slater climbed over him, yanked the door closed, and twisted around until he could join his brother in the middle area.

"Go!" Yates said to Cory.

As if to emphasize the order, a bullet pinged off the back

of the vehicle.

Cory sped toward the path. More bullets hit the van but they stopped once the vehicle reached the trees.

When they came out the other side of the path, Slater sighed with relief and—

Bang.

The van began fishtailing.

"Keep us on the road!" Slater said.

"I'm trying," Cory replied.

Bang.

The front driver's side dipped, pulling the vehicle to the left.

Bang.

The front passenger's side dropped, and they heard the *flap-flap-flap* of loose rubber.

Someone was shooting their tires out.

Bang.

Now all four were gone.

In somewhat of a miracle, Cory kept them from crashing. But he was also slowing.

"No!" Slater said. "Keep going."

"The tires are gone."

"I don't care. If you stop, we're all dead!"

The kid stepped on it again and headed down the road to the lodge, the van weaving left and right.

"DAMMIT, THEY'RE NOT stopping," Dylan said.

He pointed his gun at the back of the van but didn't pull the trigger. They needed the brothers and cousin alive.

"What's going on?"

"Ananke?" he said. They hadn't heard from her since not long after the people being hunted had been released. "Are you back?"

"Two minutes from the rendezvous. Give me an update."

As Dylan and Morgan made their way back to the cell building, he and Liesel took turns filling in Ananke. By the time they finished, Dylan and Morgan and Ananke had all reached the building. With Ananke was the Hispanic male former captive.

"Liesel, go find Ricky and Rosario," Ananke said.

"I have not checked the men I shot in the field yet."

She was supposed to provide first-aid once it was safe, so that no one would bleed out.

"Take care of that as quickly as you can, and then find our friends. But be careful. I incapacitated one of the hunters, but the other five are still out there."

"Copy."

Ananke looked at Morgan. "I need you to stay here and watch over everyone. This is Eduardo. He'll help if you need it."

Morgan nodded and shook hands with Eduardo.

"I think the best plan would be to barricade yourselves inside the cell building until we come back."

"Makes sense," Morgan said.

"You know we already have someone locked up in there," Dylan said.

"Who?" Ananke asked.

"The woman working with Rally and Slater. She showed up over here and I led her to a cell."

"Oh. If only they were all so easy."

"Tell me about it."

"Come on, you're with me."

She ran toward the ATVs Slater and Yates had used earlier. As Dylan followed, he could hear Eduardo say to Morgan, "Who are you guys?"

THE FLAT TIRES made the going considerably slower. Slater cursed silently for not having taken the wheel, but knew it was better to let Cory continue to drive than to stop and make the switch.

The van banged over a pothole and pulled left.

"Watch it!" Yates yelled. "You don't want to get stuck!"

Cory turned the wheel to the right and kept the van on the road. Barely.

Several similar incidents occurred before they finally spotted the glow of the lodge lights.

Slater patted Rally on the shoulder. "Almost there."

When Rally didn't respond, Slater checked his pulse.

"How is he?" Yates asked.

"Weak," Slater said.

"Pick it up, Cory," Yates ordered. "Faster!"

ANANKE AND DYLAN sped over to the meadow parking area and down the road back to the lodge.

They were about halfway to the building when she spotted a flash of brake lights in the forest ahead that had to belong to the van. Riding on rims and the remains of tires had slowed it considerably.

Ananke kept on the road until she caught the first direct sight of Slater's vehicle. With Dylan close behind, she veered into the woods and carved a path between the trees that would take them to the lodge.

THE VAN CAME up the gentle slope leading to the parking area next to the lodge.

"Take us around back," Slater said.

"We've got to get him to a doctor," Yates argued.

"No, shit. But he needs blood."

Given the nature of the trials, the lodge had a supply of standard and nonstandard first-aid supplies, including pouches of blood plasma.

Cory drove the van behind the lodge and stopped near the kitchen door.

"Bring your car over," Slater said to Yates. "I'll get the blood. Cory, you stay here with Mr. Rally. Don't wait for me to get back before moving him into the sedan."

"WHICH ONE DO you want?" Ananke asked.

"I'll take Mr. Security Chief," Dylan replied.

"Shout if you need help."

"I won't."

THIRTY-FIVE

RICKY LED ROSARIO and Tasha through the forest in the general direction he'd seen the other captives run. After they'd been going for several minutes, Rosario let out a low *psst*. Ricky looked back and she motioned for him to stop and get down. As he did, she and Tasha moved up beside him.

"I saw something," Rosario whispered.

"Where?"

She pointed ahead to the left.

Ricky surveyed the forest, but didn't spot whatever she'd seen. "A person?" he asked.

"Not sure. Big enough, I think."

"I'll circle right, and you…" He remembered Tasha was there.

"I'll be okay," Tasha said.

Ricky looked at Rosario, unsure.

Rosario said, "Give her your gun."

Ricky had a pistol and a crossbow. He handed the gun to Tasha, butt first. "You know how to use this?"

"Point and pull the trigger," Tasha said.

"Right. Will you be able to use it?"

A moment before she nodded. "If I need to."

"Good." He smiled. "Just try not to use it on us."

He and Rosario went their separate ways, leaving Tasha hiding in some brush. Ricky went as wide as he thought necessary, and arced back around toward the point Rosario had indicated. Every twenty feet or so, he paused and listened, but whatever Rosario had seen was either gone or had stopped moving.

Onward he went, closing in on the spot, until he was only

a few yards away. Nothing there but the trees and the ground and a few bushes. As he stepped closer, he saw Rosario coming his way. He headed toward her, but then spied movement out of the corner of his eye. He twisted around and brought the crossbow up to his shoulder.

"I would appreciate it if you did not pull the trigger," Liesel said. She held a rifle, pointed at the ground.

"Holy crap," Ricky said. "What the hell are you doing here?"

Rosario hurried over and the two women hugged. "We are very glad to see you."

"Damn right we are," Ricky said. "Where are Ananke and Dylan?"

"A little busy at the moment."

"But you all came for us?"

"We did."

"That is *so* sweet!"

Liesel looked around. "Did something happen to Tasha Patterson? I saw her run into the woods with you."

"Oh, right. Tasha. Hold on." Ricky hurried back to where they'd left the woman. As he neared the bushes, he noticed the muzzle end of the pistol sticking out between branches. "Take it easy. It's me. Don't shoot."

He escorted a relieved Tasha back to the others.

Rosario said, "I told Liesel about the hunters following us."

Liesel did not look happy.

"What's wrong?" Ricky asked her.

"Ananke did not want us to kill anyone and lose a potential information source, unless it was absolutely necessary."

"I think we can chalk up those three assholes as absolutely necessary. I mean, they *were* trying to kill us." He paused. "If it makes you feel better, Rosario did leave their guides alive."

Liesel didn't look like his words made her feel much better.

"There were three other hunters, and guides, I presume," Ricky said. "Tell me you took them out."

"Ananke took care of one, and we were able to remove the

people they were hunting."

"Did you remove their tracking bugs?"

"I do not know."

"Then the hunters are going to find them wherever you took them."

"Which is why we need to hurry." Liesel started walking toward the southwest.

Ricky jogged up next to her. "Wait. What about Slater and his people? We need to do something about them, too."

"Ananke and Dylan are handling Slater, Yates, and Rally right now. As for Slater's people, they are no longer a problem."

Ricky grinned. "Now that's what I like to hear."

PER ANANKE'S INSTRUCTIONS, Morgan and the three former captives barricaded themselves inside the building where Eduardo and the other two had been held less than half an hour before. Given that there was only the one way out, and their survival was completely contingent on Ananke and her team being successful, it was a gamble. But if they'd stayed outside and tried to make it off the lodge property on their own, they would have never made it.

After the door was secured, they searched for anything they could use as weapons. They found an unlocked rifle cabinet, but the only things in it were several sets of shackles. They took these, thinking they could be swung at an opponent if necessary.

Morgan took up position at the door and pressed her ear against it. The thing was thick and heavy, and she had no real hope of hearing much of anything through it, but she could think of nothing else to do.

"They are coming back for us, right?" the female captive—Claudia—asked.

"They'll be back," Morgan said.

"Are you sure? Maybe we should see if we can find the way through the fence."

Gerald, the African-American guy, frowned. "There *is* no way through the fence."

"You don't know that. How could you? You didn't have time to look."

"He's right," Eduardo said. "They just said that so that we would keep running and not just sit down and wait for someone to shoot us."

"That can't be true. There's got to be a way out."

Morgan looked back at them. "There is a way out. Through the front gate. We'll use it when my friends come back."

No one said anything for several seconds.

"They *are* coming back, right?" Claudia said.

"Absolutely," Morgan said. She had seen Ananke and her people at work, and knew they'd be a match for groups ten times their size.

Ten quiet minutes passed before she heard a faint scratch coming from the other side of the door. Morgan pressed harder against the door, and closed her eyes to concentrate. The door handle rattled. She jumped back, surprised, but then shoved her shoulder against the door in case whoever was on the other side somehow opened it.

Eduardo joined her a second later, and then Gerald, and finally Claudia.

More rattling, then someone pounding on the door, and a muffled "Open up!"

MR. FORD BANGED the butt of his rifle against the door again, and repeated his demand that those inside open up.

Tracking the prey had been difficult at first. That changed when Mr. Hawks's observer had hinted at a possible solution to the hunters' problems. A price was agreed upon that would be split between the two guides, and from there, it had been a simple task of following the men's instructions.

It was a surprise to everyone that the prey turned out to be holed up in a building not far from the meadow where the trials had begun. According to the observers, it was used as the holding area for the prey, and this was the first time any had ever come back to the building. More importantly, they said it had only one way in and out.

Mr. Ford hit the entrance again. "Open the damn door!"

LIESEL COULD HEAR the man yelling before she, Rosario, Ricky, and Tasha had reached the far side of the ridge. The question was, was the hunter alone? Or was the remaining fellow killer with him?

They had a quick huddle, then Ricky headed around to the north end of the building and Liesel around the south, while Rosario stayed with Tasha.

Liesel circled wide to the rocky outcropping where she, Ananke, Dylan, and Morgan had watched the building from earlier. She unshouldered the sniper rifle and put her eye to the scope.

She counted four people. Two hunters and two escorts.

They were trying to get the door open without any success.

She checked her watch, and waited until go time.

When the second hand hit zero, she picked her target and pulled the trigger.

"ENOUGH!" THE MUFFLED voice on the other side of the door yelled. "If you don't open this now, we will blow it open, and there will be nothing left of you!"

Claudia's eyes went wide. "Do you think they can do that?"

"Who cares if they can?" Eduardo said. "If we open the door we will be just as dead."

"You have one minute. If I were you, I'd—"

An odd sound, almost like an animal screeching. Followed by more of the same, then everything went quiet.

Morgan put her ear against the door again.

"What's going on?" Claudia asked.

Morgan shushed her. She thought she could hear something but wasn't sure.

Thirty seconds later someone knocked on the door again, only it was more a rap than pounding.

"Morgan? It is Liesel. You can open the door."

Relief flooded through Morgan. She reached for the bar that locked the door, but Eduardo put his hand over hers.

"Are you sure it's one of your friends?" he asked.

"I'm sure."

"Maybe they are using her to trick us out."

"If they are, then it means my friends have failed and it doesn't matter what we do."

She pushed the bar out of the way and pulled the door open.

Liesel stood on the other side, a rifle in her arms. "Is everyone okay?"

"Yeah," Morgan said.

She and the others came outside.

Four men writhed on the ground, clutching their legs. Two had metal bolts piercing their knees, while the other pair appeared to have been shot by more conventional means.

"Hey, Lady Cop." Ricky, one of Ananke's colleagues who had gone missing, smiled and nodded at Morgan.

She looked around. "Tasha was with you, wasn't she? That's what Liesel said. W-w-where is she? Where—"

Two figures emerged from the south end of the building. Rosario, the other missing team member, and Tasha. When Tasha saw Morgan, she stopped and stared, clearly not expecting her to be there.

Morgan ran over, smiling bigger than she ever had in her life. She threw her arms around her girlfriend, lifted her off her feet, and planted her lips against Tasha's. Joyful tears ran down their cheeks.

"I thought I was never going to see you again," Morgan said once they stopped kissing.

"I was sure you wouldn't. But you're here." Tasha sounded like she still couldn't believe it.

"I'm here."

They kissed again.

Liesel, Rosario, and Ricky checked the injured men and knocked out the ones who weren't already unconscious. Then everyone pitched in dragging the men into the separate cells and locking them in.

When they were finished, they began hiking toward the lodge.

THIRTY-SIX

DYLAN LET YATES get all the way to the sedan before closing in. As Yates climbed into the driver's seat, Dylan rushed over in a crouch, yanked open the passenger door, and hopped in.

Yates dived for the center console, obviously going for a gun. Dylan poked him hard in the forehead with the suppressor end of his own weapon, stopping the head of Scolareon Security in his tracks.

"Hello, Mr. Yates. Now why don't you just sit back?"

Yates leaned back, rubbing his forehead.

"What's in the compartment?" Dylan asked. "Wouldn't be a gun now, would it?"

Keeping both his gaze and his pistol aimed at Yates, Dylan opened the center console and extracted a Glock G43 9mm.

"Well, lookie here. I was right."

"What do you want?" Yates said.

"What do I want? To be honest, I'd love to be back in my room, asleep. But that's not what you meant, is it? It's not a matter of want, Mr. Yates. It's matter of what we are in the process of doing. Go ahead. Ask me what we're doing."

Yates did not oblige.

"Fine. I'll ask, then. What are you doing, man holding the gun? Thank you for asking, Mr. Yates. What we're in the process of doing is shutting down your little killing factory."

"You're never going to get out of here alive."

"Why? Because you have an army of men beyond the ones we've already taken out? Well, we know there are a few still out there. You do have that delivery coming into Scolareon tonight. But you're in luck. The FBI is helping you out on that."

The color drained from Yates's face. "You're…you're

FBI."

"Do I sound like I'm FBI?" Dylan said, playing up his Irish accent. "Of course we're not FBI. They've got too many rules."

"Then who are you?"

"You know, that's a good question. We really could use a name. We'll have to get somebody working on that. For now, you can think of us as a group of individuals who do not approve of what you're doing."

"Which means you're here to kill me."

"You're in luck. I'm not here to kill you, only to make sure you don't go anywhere. But if you force my hand, I will do it. Now, if you could please toss your keys over here, that would be grand."

Dylan had to waggle the gun to get Yates moving, but eventually the keys landed at his feet.

"You *are* going to kill me."

"Mr. Yates, I already told you I wasn't. And I'm a man of my word. I am, however, going to have to hobble you."

Dylan shot Yates in both ankles. Yates screamed and tried to bend toward his injuries, but was thwarted by the steering wheel.

"Do you feel that's enough to keep you here, or do I need to take out one of your knees, too?"

Dylan was pretty sure Yates hadn't heard him.

"You're right. No sense in wasting the bullet."

Dylan smashed the still hot silencer against the side of Yates's head. The man crumpled against the door but didn't black out. A second hit did the job.

Dylan was sorely tempted to spit on him, but decided it would be a waste of good saliva.

He attached zip-tie tourniquets to both of the man's legs, then climbed out and headed back around the side of the lodge toward the van.

SLATER ENTERED THE lodge cautiously. Whoever had attacked them at the field could have colleagues waiting inside.

The kitchen was unoccupied, as was the hallway to the

basement entrance. He put his fingers against the basement security screen and yanked the door open.

He took the stairs down two at a time, touched the security screen at the bottom, and hurried to the other end of the floor where the medical room was located.

In addition to several packets of plasma, he grabbed two infusion kits, half a dozen rolls of gauze, a bottle of hydrogen peroxide, and two rolls of medical tape, throwing everything into one of the duffel bags hanging on the wall.

By the time he returned to the upper hallway, four minutes had elapsed. He jogged back to the kitchen door, pushed it open, and was four steps inside before he realized he wasn't alone.

A tall, black woman sat on the edge of the prep table, smiling at him. Though he'd never seen her before, he knew she was Shawn Ramey, the associate of the Mex woman he'd prepped for that night's trials.

"There you are," she said. "I've been waiting for you."

Slater dove back at the door and rushed into the hall. What he really would have liked to do was head down into the basement again, where there was not only another way out of the building, but also weapons he could use to deal with the bitch. But he knew he didn't have enough time to perform the security scan, so he raced to the end of the hall and took the servants' stairway up to the second floor.

"UGH," ANANKE SAID after Slater reversed course back into the hallway. She'd done enough running for the evening, and *really* didn't want to partake in another chase.

It was her own damn fault. She should have waited in a spot where he wouldn't have seen her so soon. Another two steps into the room and he wouldn't have gotten away.

She pushed herself off the table and jogged over to the door. She'd checked out the hallway earlier when he was downstairs, and she'd seen the fingerprint-scan protected door. She expected to find him there now, trying to head back to the basement. But instead he was way down at the other end, disappearing around the corner that led to an upward set of stairs.

She ran after him and hustled up the steps.

Upon reaching the second-floor landing, she could hear him on the next flight, heading up to the third level. She followed.

The new landing let out into a long hallway moving down the center of the floor. Slater was about thirty feet away, running for his life.

Ananke thought about shooting him, but he was moving around so much she was worried she'd kill him. Not that the asshole wouldn't deserve it, but besides the need to preserve the information he had, killing him would be letting him off easy. He and his relatives deserved to spend decades locked away in a deep, dark cell.

SLATER HEARD THE woman run onto the third floor behind him.

Dammit.

No way he could let someone of her kind catch him. Maybe the project was finished, but he had no intention of going down with it.

If he could gain just a handful of seconds, he'd have enough time to get back down to the basement and grab a weapon.

He dug deep and quickened his pace. As he reached the halfway point of the third floor, an idea struck him. His cousin's suite was ahead, and Rally had mentioned more than once he kept a pistol in his nightstand both here and at home. Slater might not have time to break down the door before the woman reached him, but there was another way into the apartment. He needed to throw her off his track long enough to use it.

In the stairwell at the far end of the hall were two sets of steps, the main one leading back down to the second floor, and a narrower, steeper set, tucked around the side of the doorway, that led up to the attic. Slater raced up the latter and into the nook where the attic entrance was located. When he opened the door, it emitted a low creak. He slipped inside and left it where

346

it was, to avoid causing more noise.

As he started across the attic, he heard the woman run into the stairwell below.

ANANKE HEARD A groan ahead. Metal or wood, she wasn't sure, as it had been barely audible. It had definitely come from beyond the doorway Slater disappeared through several seconds before.

She slowed when she reached the entryway, and peeked through in case he was waiting for her on the other side. No Slater, just a stairwell leading down.

She rushed inside and started down the steps, but stopped before she went far. She should have heard his footsteps either running down the second-floor corridor or on the stairs heading to the ground level. But there were none.

She was about to continue down when she heard a low whine. She looked back the way she'd come, and spotted the narrow, half hidden staircase leading up to a fourth level.

She smiled.

You're tricky, Dalton Slater. But not that tricky.

SLATER WORKED HIS way around the junk-strewn attic to a dormer window above his cousin's suite. It had been a while since it was last opened, so it stuck a little before finally giving way with a squeak.

He slid it up and poked his head out.

Perfect.

Rally had taken the rooms that had been called the Majestic Suite back in Stanhope Lodge's heyday. Not only did it have two bedrooms and a living room, it also had a spacious balcony that sat ten feet below the window.

He backed through the opening until he was hanging from the frame by his hands, and then dropped the remaining few feet to the wooden deck. The French doors to the suite were locked, but two hard shoves from his shoulder broke them loose.

He rushed inside and ran into the bedroom Rally used. He paused near the foot of the bed, not sure which side his cousin slept on. There was nothing on either nightstand to indicate if one was used more than the other.

Slater went to the left, since that was the side he slept on at home, but the nightstand drawer was empty.

He hurried back around the bed to the right side.

ANANKE CREPT UP the stairs to the fourth floor and pushed open the door. Beyond was an attic littered with boxes and bags and other forgotten items.

She spotted Slater climbing through a window farther down the room. The moment he disappeared, she hurried over and peeked out. A balcony was not far below. Though she didn't see Slater, she did see a door leading back into the building was open.

She climbed through the window and dropped quietly to the balcony.

Slater was not in the main room, but she heard a drawer opening in the room to her right. She moved over to the doorway in time to see him move down the side of the bed. He opened the drawer of the nightstand, and started to pull something out.

ALL RIGHT! SLATER grabbed his cousin's Beretta. Now he could show the bitch who was boss.

He raised it to make sure it was loaded.

One moment it was there in his grasp, the next it was tumbling through the air, accompanied by a geyser of blood erupting from Slater's palm.

"Now see what you made me do."

Slater turned to find the woman standing in the doorway.

SLATER CRADLED HIS injured hand in his arm. Ananke could tell he was in pain, but he didn't yell. Twice his gaze darted from her to where the gun lay.

"Leave it," Ananke said. "My first shot wasn't luck."

"What do you want?"

"At the moment, nothing except you walking in front of me. Now, come on. We're keeping the others waiting."

348

"I'm not going anywhere with *you*."

Ananke walked over until she was just out of his reach. "You are an idiot, aren't you? We either walk out of here together, or I shoot you in the head and drop you over the balcony. What'll it be?"

Slater chose to walk.

They exited the building through the kitchen and approached the van, where Dylan was standing next to the open driver's door. Rally still slumped in the passenger seat, but the driver's seat was empty.

"Any problems?" she asked.

"None. The kid and Yates are tied up in the back of the van. Had to take out his ankles, though."

"The kid's?" she said, surprised.

"What? No. Yates. The kid was more than happy to let me tie him up and administer a little sleeping juice." Dylan looked at Slater. "Evening, Mr. Slater." He switched his gaze back to Ananke. "I see he's still walking."

"He was on the third floor. I wasn't going to carry him down."

"He's not on the third floor now."

"Good point."

Ananke shot the mass murderer in the foot. He dropped to the ground, screaming.

Dylan scoffed. "You could have at least waited until we got him around the back of the van."

Together they put Slater in with Yates and the unconscious driver, and applied their meager first-aid to the man's foot and hand. They then bound him with zip ties and shut the back door.

Ananke moved around to the front passenger door and opened it. The half-conscious Rally started to fall out, but she pushed him back into his seat.

She slapped his cheeks. "Hey, pretty boy. Wake up."

Rally moaned but remained unconscious.

She pinched his nose and put a hand over his mouth.

After a second or two, his eyes flew open. She let go. He sucked in air and then clenched his teeth as he became aware of his pain.

"Hi, Devon," Ananke said.

"You," he whispered, his face hardening.

"Yeah, me. I'm so glad you remembered. Look, I know I should have called before coming over tonight—sorry about that. And I brought a few friends with me, too, which was kind of a dick move, I know. Worse yet, we seemed to have ruined your party. I hope you can forgive us." She snorted. "Just kidding. I don't hope that at all. Taking you down has been our pleasure."

He seemed to struggle with how to respond. She tapped him on the cheek.

"Save your energy. Someone will be by to collect you, but it might be a little while. And you don't want to die before they do, do you?"

She shut the door and turned on her comm. "Liesel, can you read me?"

"Go for Liesel."

"Where are you?"

"About a quarter mile from the lodge."

"Ricky and Rosario?"

"With us. And Tasha and the others also."

"Any injuries?"

"Not one."

Now that's what Ananke called a successful mission. "We're all done. We'll be waiting for you."

THIRTY-SEVEN

WHILE LIESEL AND her group made their way to the lodge, Ananke and Dylan searched it for keys to the cars in the parking area. They came up with three sets, which meant more than enough seats for everyone.

There were hugs and smiles among the team once everyone was back together. Ananke even allowed Ricky a quick embrace. For the most part, the former captives looked both relieved and stunned at the turn of events, while Tasha looked elated as she clutched Morgan.

"The FBI will show up here soon," Ananke said to the freed prisoners. "They're going to want to talk to all of you. If you'd rather not, let me know now and we'll make alternate arrangements."

The young Hispanic guy who'd been introduced as Eduardo raised his hand.

"Okay," she said. "I'll see that they don't get your name and—"

"No," he said. "I'll talk to them. I *want* to talk to them. It's just…there were others who were in the truck with me when I was brought here. A girl named Sonya. I don't know the others' names. What happened to them?"

"You haven't seen them?" Ananke said.

He shook his head.

"There were several people in the barn," Ricky said. "Maybe she's there."

"That's probably it," Ananke said.

"Or they could have sold her."

Everyone looked at Tasha.

"What do you mean?" Ananke said.

"They bring in more people than they need for their…games. The extras, they sell."

Ananke cocked her head. "That's what you learned, isn't it? That's why they took you."

"Part of what I learned."

"Dear God," one of the former captives said.

"There's information somewhere about this?" Ananke asked.

"Yes."

"Do you know how to access it?"

Tasha grinned. "We don't need to access it. I have a copy."

A MEETING WAS arranged. The location: a sedan in the parking lot beside the Cache Bar. The time: 2:45 a.m.

Present were Ananke, Rosario, Special Agent in Charge Lisa Franks, and Special Agent Stuart Taylor. It was agreed beforehand there would be no record of the event.

From the agents, Ananke and Rosario learned the incoming shipment of people had been intercepted, and the parties involved rounded up.

Ananke and Rosario gave the agents a rundown of everything they knew about Rally and his cousins, while providing a light-on-details account of what had happened that night in the woods near Stanhope Lodge.

"Incapacitated how?" Franks asked.

"Let's just say you'll want medical personnel going in with you. And the sooner, the better."

"Any deaths?" Taylor asked.

A beat. "Yes. Three for sure."

Taylor looked at his boss. "A triple homicide? We can't just let them walk away."

"You can, and you will," Ananke said. "We all know that. But if it eases your mind, it would be fair to label anything that happened there tonight as self-defense."

"Self-defense? Are you—"

"Taylor," Franks chided. "You say there are witnesses?"

"Yes. They will be happy to tell you everything they know. I'll text you their location later. There are also others who were taken that are still in Rally's system and are in the process of being shipped out to buyers as we speak. You'll need to move fast to retrieve them."

"How are we supposed to find them?" Taylor asked.

Ananke pulled out the zip drive Tasha had hidden in the leaning dead tree west of the access road to the solar farm. "Everything you need is on here. Plus, enough evidence about everyone who's ever been involved with Rally and his cousins to keep you busy for years."

She started to hand it to Franks but pulled it back.

"Just so you know, this isn't the only copy, so don't sit on it for too long." She and Rosario had made a quick stop at the hotel to pick up their bags before coming to the meeting. On the drive to the Cache Bar, Rosario had backed up the data to her laptop.

Taylor's eyes narrowed. "Are you threatening us?"

"I am." Ananke held his gaze for a moment. "If there's nothing else, we have places to be, and you have people in need of a little medical help before you throw them in jail."

She and Rosario climbed out.

ANANKE AND ROSARIO joined the others at Casa de Artisa.

"Hey, look at that," Ricky said. "They didn't arrest you." He had not been in favor of the meeting.

"Any problems?" Liesel asked.

"No," Ananke said. "But I think it's better if we don't stick around." She walked over to where Tasha and Morgan were standing. "The disk was right where you said it would be. Thank you."

"You gave it to them?"

"Yes."

"They will use it, won't they?"

"I guarantee it."

Tasha stepped forward and pulled Ananke into a hug. "Thank you for coming for me."

"It's what we do."

Once they parted, Ananke held her hand out to Morgan. "I'm sorry I misjudged you at first. We couldn't have done this without your help."

"You weren't the only one who misjudged." Morgan bypassed the hand and hugged Ananke, too.

"You should go home and get some sleep while you can," Ananke said. "I'm sure the FBI will be contacting you in a few hours."

There were good-byes and more hugs, and then the team was alone.

"Everyone packed?" Ananke asked.

The only one who didn't nod was Dylan.

"Problem?" she asked.

"No problem, really. I was just kind of wondering…"

"Yes?"

"Well…any idea how long it will be before our next assignment? I mean, there's no sense in heading home if they're just going to call us right back."

None of them had talked about continuing on, but they all looked at Ananke as if they wanted to know the answer.

So did she.

"I guess we should find out."

She pulled out her phone and called the Administrator.